CW00494034

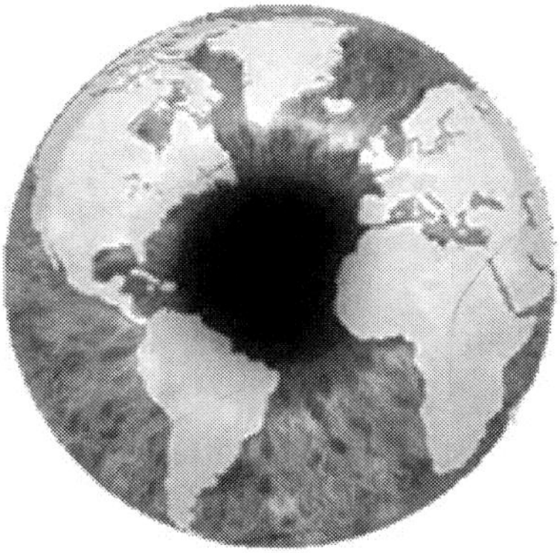

OPTIC FLOCK

NAOMI WICKS

1

When I open my eyes, everything is jet black. It takes half a second for my WOLF lenses to respond and the world is illuminated; a world of sharpened imagery, definition and shades beyond count. I don't tend to think in solid colours anymore, I think in shades. The night is jet black, ebony black, onyx black. I'm sure there was once a time when black was just black to me, but it's long forgotten.

A gunshot woke me. I listen and watch the shades of black morph into the grayscale objects of my bedroom. I'm still alone, but something is different. My gaze is searching. I'm certain I heard something – there's no fragment of a dream lingering in my mind – yet there's no vibration in the air. If there was a receding noise it faded before my conscious could catch up. Now there's no proof I heard anything at all except my pounding heart. My anxiety is in sudden overdrive. I could hide beneath my pillow and seek a darker shade of black to escape to. Instead I force myself upright with my arms tight across my waist. I listen; but the only gunshot I hear now is the one embedded in my memory. One I hear often, even if the action that preluded it was a cupboard slamming or a goat butting the gate. I have to tell myself this is a normal night, an uneventful night. There's no one outside. My father could be asleep in the next room with my mother.

But he isn't.

I count to ten and wait for something else to happen. A dozen shades of dawn stream in through the curtains now my eyes adjust. It'll almost be time to get up anyway. My father could be the one to do it . . . but there are games and there's reality. Someone needs to get jobs done, no matter how many gunshots are fired in the night.

Rubbing my eyes is strongly ill-advised by my doctor, so I blink several times to help my lenses catch up with me. Unlike those issued WOLF 01 and 02, I have to wear my WOLF 03 lenses permanently. Waking up is a tedious process of blinking the ache away and lubricating my eyes with a serum I keep beside my alarm clock. The alarm hasn't sounded, but I don't need it to. I usually have an interior alarm clock inside my head. The sun hasn't yet risen and Hans won't have reached our ranch. The bang I heard wouldn't have been caused by him. I begin to suspect it was merely one of our goats outside.

I step around my books and papers, which I'd put down beside my bed when I decided to sleep. I slot pictures of stars and meteors inside text books and hoist them on to my desk. I had bought them just before summer, still hopeful I may have gone to the university in Fenix with the rest of my friends.

It had been a false hope.

I sort myself out, dressing quietly and brushing my hair. I weave a thin braid into two larger sections of hair to create a single side braid. It's a style my mother did for me when I was younger. If she didn't weave a smaller braid into it, she would use a ribbon of whatever colour I asked for. She used to do it all, cut my hair and style it for me. Not anymore. I slip into woollen tights and gloves and make my way quietly to the door. I don't want to wake my mother yet. The sights within her dreams are too precious to her, second only to her memories.

I breathe in the early morning air and taste frost through my nose and mouth. There's a moment of fear where I look for any disturbance. I look for shadows streaking away in the early sun's light. Trespassers lurking, ready with firearms. I'm nowhere near a weapon myself, not that using one did this family any favours.

But this morning is calm, unlike many others where the wind messes my hair and the grass billows as though caught in a fast current. We rely on the goats to keep it trimmed, or the hem of my skirt would be weighted down with the dampness of morning dew. The sun is creeping up the side of the mountain. My lenses do a motionless dance and adjust to the change in temperature and light. They settle enough for me to look down upon Orbelle with ease. Everything is still and normal and I wonder if I ever heard the noise at all. Perhaps it was just a goat. Perhaps I was only hoping it were more. I'm always hoping for something more.

Spots of cream and chestnut move across the hillside and my lenses focus, sharply defining each goat. I can identify them all at once. These goats are not shy of me. I call them by their names and lead them away from the house, towards the shack. The bells around their necks chime as they give chase. My father kept his weapons in here, including his crook and his rifle. My favourite goat, a young white male named O'Malley, reaches me first and bleats loudly. As I unbolt the door, the goats assemble and cry out for breakfast.

Our ranch is small and isolated on the hill. It's weaved into the web of other roads by the many dirt tracks made by a few trucks and animals, connecting us to the rest of Orbelle, half a mile away and stretched out beneath our hill like a distant neighbour. Hardly anyone visits us; no one ventures this far to see how my mother is doing and how I'm keeping things afloat. If there were any news at all, Hans would tell someone and it's Hans who takes our cheese and milk to sell on Sundays. Those I went to school with have fluttered to the city like birds escaping their nests. People forget all about us here. I look down at the patchwork of rooftops and chimneys and wonder if anyone would be looking back up at the ranch and remembering Linnea Hansen, the herder girl trudging around the ranch with her boots on who said how she would, one day, be an astronomer.

Whilst the goats are occupied with food I look up at what puts Orbelle on postcards and travel websites. They call it Mt Awarnach but we affectionately call it Mt Venus, a thirteen-thousand foot giant that looms over our ranch. The mountain is easily identified by tourists for its bluish colour and crooked back.

The sun's light starts to bear down on the ranch and my lenses are able to adjust rapidly, so the glare doesn't blind me. Without them, I wouldn't be able to see everything in such acute detail. Dew glistens from spider webs stretching across the gate, like a string of translucent pearls and small buds of ivy are sprouting from the gatepost.

O'Malley won't let me forget about him. He knows if he butts me several times I might just share my own breakfast with him. I take a small apple out of my pocket and eat it as I walk, pretending to ignore him. He bleats and pulls at my skirt until I bend down and give him the sticky core. He stays by my side as I head down the hill in the wake of the postman, I've been waiting two days for his visit. I reach the mailbox and withdraw our letters sitting on the stone wall with my knees up, looking for anything addressed to me. There is only one. It bears the WOLF emblem. It doesn't resemble a sharp-toothed canid, as one might expect, but the image of an eye. The iris is like a globe of the earth and the words 'Worldwide Optic Lens Foundation' are printed beneath it. There are two of these envelopes; the other is addressed to my mother.

My lenses use smart technology to bring the letters slightly off the page in a three-dimensional way, making each word I look at leap forward. I wonder what colour my irises are right now. Without a mirror, I can't tell what shade they are at any given time, unless someone else tells me. Right now my eyes could be ocean blue, calming lavender, coal grey, coral pink. I've almost forgotten what my natural hazel ones looked like.

The lenses have sensors to detect a person's pulse and body temperature. The acceleration of either will trigger a response. There is a miniature chip in the lens that will pick up your voice. They say it's not invasive and will merely pick up on your tone to help its readings. Urgent whispering, aggressive shouts and even sarcasm help paint a picture beneath your eyelids. The miniature antenna sends the information back to WOLF HQ via satellite. You're supposed to calibrate the lenses yourself once a month with a program and attend regular appointments.

There appears to be nothing from my father for either of us and I slide off the wall with a sigh. The sun has risen and I spy the first train rolling towards the station. It's far away, but I still watch it from up on the hill. In a couple hours we'll be boarding the train to Fenix ourselves.

O'Malley bleats loudly and I look down to see he's dropped my apple core and is chewing something else. My heart races when I see him stomp down on a piece of red wire, whilst his teeth pull at another black one. He's determined to wrench the wires free from a piece of circuit board. I shove him urgently and pull it from his mouth, noting how chewed and frayed it already is.

“Where did you get this?” I turn the board over in the palm of my hand. It’s grasshopper green and like nothing we’ve ever had up on this ranch. Wherever O’Malley unearthed this, it’s a rare find. I can see a white logo printed on the board. I recognise the logo, but can’t put a name to it. All I know is it came from something electrical and, if O’Malley had a piece, there’s a chance other scrap may be around. People don’t litter in Orbelle but a lot of students have just returned from the city and may have brought new habits with them. Perhaps the ranch is isolated enough up here to be the perfect dumping spot. Perhaps; but unlikely. No one would come up here just to discard a piece of scrap circuit board. I tuck it away in my pocket to stop any other goats eating it.

Unsure what to do next, I decide to meet Hans. I make my way down the hill, following the dirt path. Cows stare as though I’ve interrupted a deep conversation and wait to resume telling secrets once I’ve gone. I meet Hans at the bottom of the footpath. He’s holding his stick in one hand and a bottle of milk in the other.

“Hey!” I call. “Good morning.”

“Mornin’, Linn.”

His tone is flat, but his eyes turn teal when he sees me. Happy is the first primary colour they teach you when you learn WOLF code in school: blue for happy. You only truly learn the colour code through experience.

"I was takin' this to your mother on my way."

"Cow or goat?" I eye the milk greedily.

He hands me the bottle and tells me to guess. I tip the bottle down my throat and taste the creaminess that may be considered common to the city folk.

"Cow," I say. On the hill we rarely drink this unless the milkman brings it specially. We have our own goats to provide what we need, but we can't beat the price or overall preference of cow's milk. Not even I can deny I like the taste of this better.

"You better tell your mother I let you drink that, or she'll think I was gluggin' it." Hans places his stick over his shoulders and stretches his back. He's twenty-seven now, built solid, and as tall as my father.

"She probably won't notice."

"Oh, aye, she will."

This is something I've always liked about Hans. Unlike other people, he won't underestimate my mother's abilities and wouldn't dream of lying to her just because he can. He swore to my father he would look after us both. If it weren't up to him to run the ranch in our absence, I know he would escort us to the city and even help me visit the prison. But I would never ask such a thing. He does enough for us already. Although he's quiet and withdrawn, everyone knows Hans.

"We have our WOLF appointments today." I hand the milk back. "You remember that, right? So you're welcome to stay at the ranch as always. Save you walking up and down the hill."

He salutes nonchalantly and continues his hike along another dirt path. I lick the taste of milk from my lip and wonder where I should go next. It's still early in the morning, although most people are up and working already. But for my friend Anna – who is only back in Orbelle for the holidays – this time in the morning is ghastly unless she has a lecture to attend. If I knock on her door now, I expect she'd create more fuss than all my goats put together. But I do need to see her and make sure she hasn't changed her mind on what we agreed. It might have to wait for now.

I already visited the train station yesterday. The information desk operators know almost everyone by name and I don't mind sharing with them the nature of our excursion. Everyone gets called to the city for WOLF appointments just as they did for dentists and the opticians back in my father's day.

Not many people know I'm type 03. Most people are type 01, the standard lenses that are removed at night but required for full use during the day by law. Although it's difficult to appreciate the changes when you live in such an isolated town. WOLF lenses were initially put in place to reduce the high levels of substance abuse, violence and theft in Fenix. Guilt and truth are easier to identify. Health is easier to monitor. All aspects were encouraged to save Fenix money. I'm not sure how useful the lenses are here. But the law is in place for everyone, rural or urban, and if you're type 01 then your compliance with the law is inexcusable. There are also type 02 lenses, for those who already require vision enhancers. Years ago people wore glasses or clear contacts that gave you standard vision. I have a pair of my father's glasses he wore when he was my age. They're ridiculous to look at and try on. Type 03 breaks the mould by rejecting types 01 and 02. WOLF like to keep an eye on people like me.

There's no point going to the station again. I collected more train times than my mother intended anyway. Tomorrow is another date I'm determined not to miss. A meteor shower is due to grace this side of the equator. From up on the mountain, high above the glow of Orbelle's street lamps or the neighbouring villages, the chance of witnessing the phenomenon is something I'm not prepared to miss. I've already declined my first opportunity to study astronomy to care for my mother. I've had no choice but to practise my hobby through books and star-gazing. Perhaps one day I shall enrol in the city and study it properly, but for now I'm needed on the ranch.

I'm sure my mother will be awake by now and I stroll back up to the ranch. I use my knuckles to rap a large brass bell as I reach the final step of the porch. It was once used to summon milkmaids, so my father told me. They would have been younger than me back then, but I'm the only young maid out on the hill this morning. Those even younger than me will be preparing for school. The bell has rusted over the years, but it still gives a satisfying chime, causing some of the goats to lift their heads and listen. No doubt my mother would have heard it.

She's listening to the radio in her chair. The window is open and she knows to anticipate me. She turns down the volume as I throw myself into another chair.

"Your shoes, Linnea," she says firmly. I kick them off, into the hall. They thump against the wooden floor. I open the letters one by one and read them to her. Her expression doesn't change as I read out bills and reminders. Her face does move however, when I reveal we both have letters from WOLF.

"It's our appointment reminders," I say before reading mine aloud.

It confirms both of our appointments for today, along with a brief overview of what to expect and what to bring with us, including a list of any new medication we're currently taking. The letters have arrived just in time. Our train leaves before midday and, by three o'clock, my appointment should be over. If only post didn't arrive so slowly here. I'm sure everyone else gets their letters a day in advance.

WOLF knew to make our appointments on the same day. I've made some preparations in my head. I wonder if I should even call the prison. I've never done that on my own before.

“Was that everything?” my mother asks. I hesitate and she fills the silence. “You heard it this morning too, didn’t you?”

My breath stills. I was almost past thinking the noise was real. I’d convinced myself otherwise. “You mean the bang?”

“I thought someone slammed the gate, but it sounded so much closer than that. I thought maybe you dropped something in your bedroom.”

I wait for her to reveal her own conclusion, but instead she shakes her head.

“I guess it was one of the goats. They all seem fine this morning?”

“Yeah, fine.” I put my hand in my pocket and touch the wires of the board. Anything to distract myself. “I think you’re probably right. Do you want me to do something else before we go today?”

She begins fussing. I gather papers that have blown on to the floor, brush crumbs from the chairs and draw back a few curtains she missed. The last thing I do is make sure our lunches are made before I go, although she tells me she’s more than capable of making a sandwich for herself.

“I should be making lunch for you,” she grumbles.

I lean in to kiss her goodbye and she pulls me in for a hug. When we part, she's smiling, but her eyes look right through me. There is no colour beneath her long lashes; just the many shades of emptiness.

"I need to see Anna this morning, but I'll be back before eleven." I brush a stray hair away from her face. We have always looked so similar. I inherited her golden hair and slim frame. But I notice a few more greys appearing among the blonde and wonder if there is any point in mentioning it. I promised her I would tell her such things, but it's never been easy. "My bag is already packed and ready."

She insists on going to the front door with me and waves as I head down the path. When I look back, she's still waving as though she will never stop, as if she can really see me. Then she collects the thin white cane in her hand and navigates her way back into the house; her back turned against a world she cannot see.

2

We have to cross an estuary to get to Fenix by bridge, which creates a divide between the country and the city. The beauty of the countryside ends abruptly as fields turn into blocks of houses and industrial warehouses. The water separates the rolling green hills from the man-made colours of grey and copper. They've been left to the devices of age and decay. A first-time visitor wouldn't expect this to be what's known as the most beautiful city in the world, but these are the thorns that surround the rose. I can already see the tall towers of the city centre from the train window.

The changes to the city began before I was born. Despite the reformation, my father always said moving was the best thing he ever did. Whenever the people of Orbelle would gossip about trouble within the town, my father would shake his head and insist none of them knew what crime was. He told me he had seen crime, before the lenses became compulsory. He wouldn't tell me what he'd seen, but I knew he would never move us back to the city. Even after the riots against the authorities and WOLF HQ ended, crime became near obsolete and they began pulling some of the more damaged buildings down, my father had eyes only for his beloved mountain. He said we were safe here.

Now the older version of the city lies, still habited and used, but ignored. The centre of the city embodies all the wealth and effort put in to turn Fenix into something wonderful. But the outside still serves as a gentle reminder of life before the laws changed. Laws they say are meant to improve our lives. Fraud, violence, abuse and deceit are reduced and controlled. Criminals who violate laws are identified immediately. Drug and alcohol abuse is all but unknown. Only prescription pills are altered so as to not affect your lenses. According to the rest of the world, Fenix is a city where good can truly shine. Truth is easily identified, health is better monitored and everyday life is controlled and safe. This city is a most desired idealism. While the older buildings fade, along with memories of the past, the future of Fenix appears golden.

And so we pass the dirty stone walls and washing lines running from wall to wall like spider silk until we roll into Fenix city centre. Advertising boards change from detergent and soaps to celebrity endorsed books and Cornelius Morgan – the face of WOLF – who appears to be promoting yet another WOLF development.

When we pass through a tunnel I notice a handful of young people scrubbing the walls clean of graffiti. They're being surveyed by armed members of city police and I catch some of the words under soap and scrubbing brushes. 'THEY BLINK WITH BLOOD' is one of the comments, and the graffiti artist has depicted the WOLF's globe emblem with a red ocean instead of blue. The red spray paint has seeped into the green used to create the rest of the globe. As such, our land is being swallowed by a bloody sea. Whoever did this will be severely punished. I quickly sit up in my seat and choose to look at my mother instead until we reach the station.

We step on to a clean, shiny platform. It's impressive to look at, but to the ears this station is a living hell. I grip my mother's hand and steady her down from the carriage.

"I'm going to find out where we're going, don't go anywhere." I lead her to the side, out of the way. I don't take my mother into crowds because people don't understand why she stands rigid and unmoving for them. I've seen people shove her in the past, not acknowledging her white cane.

People constantly stare, although she doesn't know it. It's not strictly their fault. Blind people are an exceptionally rare sight since WOLF became known globally. They can cure almost any optic ailment. Except, we've discovered, that which they created themselves. Maybe today they'll tell us there's been a break-through.

She stands patiently, her cane planted squarely between her feet, like a swordsman driving the top of his blade into the earth. I remember some people used sticks to detect motions and sounds from the ground. She looks concentrated, as always, and the rumbling of trains and clatter of footsteps must be deeply unnerving for her.

"Okay." I take her arm again. "Let's go."

We could use the public transportation, but after the train journey we're both glad to stretch our legs. We walk through parks, under bridges that support stand-still traffic and past many monuments before reaching the shops. I find it mind-boggling to watch the other people my age, dressed in city clothing with their headphones in and their hair chopped and coloured. If I'd been born here – as I ought to have been – I suppose I'd be one of them.

Everything always looks fresh here, as though someone's repainted it every time we visit. They probably have. Beauty here is reinforced by how many water features guide your path, how few homeless people walk the streets, and how often businesses alternate their window displays. It wasn't always like this. It took a lot to reform this city after the riots. Fenix isn't completely free of crime, of course, but WOLF lenses eliminate so much potential trouble and make everything so easy to manage. That leaves the authorities with more time and money to focus on appearances.

They've taken WOLF's colour charts to extremes here. WOLF has a shade of colour for every human emotion and the city has done its research to make Fenix an idealistic place. Whether they've succeeded is another matter. After all, you can't take stress out of the everyday. People are still occupied, still impatient and still driven by business deadlines. There's still the everyday bustle; still the endless sound of people chatting down their phones as they hurry; still the need to be somewhere else faster than one can walk. But at least the environment is controlled. Hans would say it's all false and every colour is artificial. But one could argue it's tidy and monitored. The only thing that negatively affects people here is the stress of the working day. I've seen ten black-eyed businessmen already. People are stressed, but they're stressed in a city that knows every shadow of stress and the colours that can be used to combat it. Their favourites are blue, green and brown. The colours most associated with happiness, love and calm. Hans once told me the water in the fountains was dyed blue. I don't know whether to believe him or not, but somehow the water's surface always manages to give the feel of a sunny day, even if the sky is thick with grey cloud.

The trees don't exactly thrive here, like they do in the countryside, but the city has worked hard to keep the ratio of green and brown even and symmetrical on both sides of the streets. The tops of the trees are pruned perfectly. You wouldn't get anything looking so military in Orbelle. In spring the trees will blossom into a beautiful shade of pink. They don't mind such feminine colours in spring, when everything is being reborn. They let the petals fall like confetti, encouraging tourists to take photographs, although they send road sweepers out thrice a day to keep the streets clean.

They present the colour red with a heightened sense of control. You don't have to worry about any of that here. They only use red in reference to something within a contained situation. Some products are permitted to use red to signify things like high sugar content or heightened levels of adrenaline. The only pamphlets and billboards that display red are advertising things like laser tag or glucose drinks.

Nothing dangerous. Nothing the city can't control.

If the city could limit the colour yellow to only one source it would be the natural, glowing sun. But you can't avoid all colours and they use yellow to paint lines to limit parking and on signs warning you away from danger. Yellow puts you on alert, but it keeps you safe and doesn't raise any panic.

"So, what's changed?" My mother holds her face up against the breeze.

I clear my throat and look around. "Well, the butcher's is now a tattoo studio. That coffee shop we once went to is now an internet cafe and there seems to be a new hairdresser above the tanning place. Not much else is different."

"Good grief, there are enough hairdressers in this city to attend each strand on my head," my mother says. "I'm almost glad I don't see some things change. Still, it's all for your generation I suppose. Let me know if you want to stop anywhere, Linn."

I've not visited a hairdresser or bought a new outfit for years. I rely on Anna to grow bored of her old clothes and my own skill with the kitchen scissors. The idea of being able to treat myself is exciting, but I wouldn't know where to begin. I decide we should check in at WOLF HQ and get our main objective out of the way.

I didn't realise WOLF picked a bad day for our appointments.

The streets are filled with military recruits. They're identifiable on sight. These are WOLF X recruits, the city's most renowned military that works in conjunction with HQ. They have the most advanced lenses; unavailable anywhere else in the world. Their uniform is treacle black and tawny brown and their eyes are defaulted the same colours. They don't appear to emotionally respond to anything.

"What's going on?" My mother stops when I do. The street we wanted is roped off.

"I've no idea," I say.

It's clear we'll need to take another route, so I lead her down another street. The path is paved with glass and made to look like running water. When I place a foot down a lily pad will surface to give the impression of supporting me and keeping us afloat. My lenses catch sight of holographic fish beneath the glass. It's mesmerising. But suddenly the fish turn and swim away and I look up to see a group of people marching against the gentle current, carrying boards and wearing shirts with hand painted slogans. I pull my mother out the way and let them pass.

“I think I get it,” I say.

It’s a public demonstration, and these things are usually well scheduled. People are allowed to make statements and share their views on compulsory lenses, but only on WOLF’s terms. They’re a good show, provided the protest doesn’t get too passionate. They help demonstrate why the lenses became compulsory in the first place. There is usually a counterpart to the protest, which will insist upon WOLF’s continued law. Provided no one steps out of line, it helps tell the story to the people. This is part of our modern history, after all. That must be why the WOLF X recruits are on standby. There’s a danger these things may go too far. I think about the words ‘THEY BLINK WITH BLOOD’ and wonder exactly what will happen to the people who went as far as to defile Fenix’s beauty.

I notice none of the marchers are looking up. They keep their eyes on the lily pads beneath their feet and march on. Only when one of them nearly bumps into my mother do I get a glimpse of one of the faces. It fills me with such horror I pull my mother out of the street before she can ask what’s happening. I stop in another street, underneath a holographic rainbow, and collect myself.

“What is it?” My mother listens for me.

“I thought I saw . . .” I shake my head. I couldn’t have seen it. There’s no way I could have seen what I thought I saw. It must have been a reflection in a shop window. I couldn’t have seen red in that man’s eye. Not even during a protest. Red Eye is an appalling crime. I dismiss it and carry on, under the rainbow, and towards HQ. I have a feeling the sooner I’m inside a building the better.

3

HQ itself is easy to find. I spotted it on the train before we reached the station. It's one thousand feet tall and the only building in the world with such a design. It's ugly, I've always maintained that, but no less impressive. Iris – the giant eyeball – is alive and blinking as always. Within the few seconds of me spotting it, it changes to a globe of the earth and everyone in the city knows the next image will be an analogue clock.

This part of the building was officially named The Socket by Cornelius Morgan, who designed and engineered it. It's a giant glass sphere that swells from the neck of the building, encasing a holographic image that alternates between Iris, the globe and the clock. Iris sees almost everything in the city, hence why they constructed a viewing platform just beneath it for tourists. The peak of the building sits atop the Socket like a wizard's hat.

The woman at the reception wears long, false lashes and lenses rimmed with a rainbow. When she blinks, the rainbow rotates around turquoise irises. Lenses that perform tricks unnerve me and I try not to look directly at them.

"Good afternoon," she says brightly. "Are you here for an appointment?"

I'm inclined to retort I'm here for a wedding but sarcasm is something my father would scold and these people will be in control of my eyeballs soon.

"Yes." I root for the letters in my bag. "My name's Linnea Hansen. This is my mother, Eliza Hansen."

The woman smiles at me patiently, fingers poised over her keyboard. I realise she's waiting to enter my identification code in the computer. This isn't Orbelle, where everyone knows one another and addresses you only by your birth name. Without your code in a database somewhere, you might as well cease to exist in the city.

"Sorry. WOLF 0315, Snake F," I say.

"Excellent." She taps away at her keyboard, before lifting a handheld scanner. "May I?"

"Sure." I lean across the desk, accustomed to this procedure.

"Keep them closed." I feel a warm light pass over my eyelids as she speaks. My eyes don't need to be open for the scanner to pick up my lenses. I hear a high beep that tells the computer my identification is confirmed.

"Thank you, Miss Hansen. You'll be with Dr Frost today at two o'clock."

She then has to deal with my mother. She phones through to another department to confirm they are expecting her today at two forty-five. There is no identification code, no scanning with lasers, they have to make do with her name and date of birth to accept her legitimacy. You would think they'd been asked to verify one of my goats. It takes a good five minutes before my mother can sit with me in the waiting area.

I'm sat staring at one of the many holograms that are triggered by sensors. There are circular hollows in the walls at HQ that are lit and adorned with all sorts of holographic ornaments that'll move or glow if you look at them. In the restrooms they have marine seashells that spin slowly. They hang as though in bubbles, suspended in the air. If you swipe a hand through them they disappear. It's all a trick of the lenses. Most pictures are defaulted to appear like paintings until you approach. Then the picture is animated to perform for you.

I'm looking at a plant in the hollow shelf of the waiting room and it blooms into a beautiful flower for me. The building is quick to learn what images you prefer. Most pictures morph into the night sky when I approach. The stars twinkle and the galaxy swirls with cosmic colour. The man sat near me is also looking at the wall. I wonder what he sees. Everyone sees something different.

When my mother joins me I pick up a magazine and read it to her to pass the time. The front cover features an image of Cornelius Morgan with his arms folded, staring into space. Inside is a similar picture, but adjoined to some quote about doing the impossible.

Everyone has heard of Cornelius Morgan. His face is associated with everything about WOLF; being everything from brand ambassador and business executive to its soul celebrity endorser. The man has divided the country between those who want to hug him and those who want to slap him. He has a delicate cupid's bow in his top lip and dark floppy hair streaked with natural strands of silver. Despite seeming to want to grow old gracefully, he's botoxed around his eyes, so his stare seems especially steady and his actual age is almost impossible to guess. In truth, he's early forties, but both young and middle-aged women swoon over him. He constantly addresses himself as a professor of engineering and always wears a necklace beneath an open collar: a tiger's eye pendant on a leather string, to match his trade-mark lenses. Only the rich and famous wear customised lenses. His stare is piercing and calculated. Every shade is tinged with obvious intelligence. He conveys so much knowledge with so few words. He knows how we expect him to look and he's kept this image for years now.

After a while I realise I'm holding the pages forward so my mother can view the pictures. It's a habit I can't break. I only hope today they will give us good news.

My mother was badly affected by WOLF experimentation in her teenage years and the fresh mountain air was recommended to aid her recovery. However, like many born after her generation, those experimented on passed certain defects on to their children. My own eyes were affected enough to reject most WOLF types, and there is a growing concern my vision shall deteriorate rapidly as I age. That understanding haunts me every day. To wake up and not see the mountain or stars anymore would make my existence seem pointless. My mother and I will both be left to sit in darkness, whilst vision technology grows and grows, just out of our reach.

The unit I'm taken to is a specialist area called the XY Unit. Those who reject regular lenses are brought here and I sit in the waiting room, opposite a woman and her young daughter. When the girl looks up, I see she was born with partial heterochromia. Her left iris is two different colours. She stares at me in wonder, probably trying to figure out what is so special about me for me to be here. I've sat in this waiting room with so many rare and interesting cases. The last time I was here, I spied a pair of identical twins. I wondered if they were here simply for research. WOLF love unusual case studies. I give the young girl an encouraging smile. I suspect she's here to be fitted with permanent WOLF 03 lenses for the first time. She seems to relax a little and I guess my own lenses must be teal or lavender. They will have taught her to read colours in her very first year of school. Even without knowing the WOLF colour chart, nothing sooths people more than lavender.

Within a few minutes, I'm called into the doctor's surgery and greeted by a familiar pair of violet eyes.

"Good afternoon, Linnea. It's lovely to see you again."

There is no excusing my reaction to Dr Frost. I've had a crush on him for over five years and, if anyone is trained enough to read lenses flawlessly, it's this man. Even if my lenses could lie for me, I know my cheeks are the colour of raspberries. He addresses me by my name – not as WOLF 0315, Snake F – which I appreciate.

"You found your way all right," he remarks.

The first time I was here, I ventured off down the wrong corridor, got completely lost and found myself outside the building's simulation room and WOLF X unit. I was confused as to where I should be, since WOLF 03 appointments are conducted the other side of the building to 01 and 02. In the end a nurse had to escort me to Dr Frost. It was that nurse who explained to me WOLF X was military. I certainly wasn't where I ought to be.

Mirrors are positioned over my head and white lights force my pupils to shrink. I already underwent the basic eye tests with the nurse before Dr Frost called me in. I read long and short distance fine and my lying skills are nil. When she pricked me with a dull needle on the back of my hand, my eyes turned black. She was perfectly satisfied with me. They ran a very brief cranial nerve exam and checked my body mass index. These sorts of checks are standard. They don't want anything interfering with your readings that could be attributed to poor health. My results are fine, though I'm told I could gain a little weight. I only have one more moment to debrief and reacquaint myself with Dr Frost before he gets to work.

"What we will do today, Linnea, is remove these lenses and send them off for a quick screening. If they pass, we will reinsert them and continue for another twelve weeks. If not, we will take you to the simulation room for optical assessment and you'll be issued temporary lenses until your new ones arrive to be fitted, okay? Either way, you'll be here for a couple of hours. So now our main focus is getting those current lenses out. I'm going to tilt you back and insert just a few drops. Your entire vision will turn blue for a few minutes. We'll do that whilst we give you your shot and I'll tell you when we're about to begin."

With that, our consultation is at its end. Dr Frost and his assistant have placed tinted glasses over their own eyes so the lasers won't affect their lenses. The chair goes back, the lights are adjusted and I'm told to look up whilst the drops are inserted. I blink rapidly, fluttering my lashes, which makes me feel foolish as Dr Frost peers down into my face. I almost giggle in embarrassment before the shot is administered into my arm and I feel it go limp. It's only a couple of seconds before the drug takes hold and I start to enjoy the experience.

Machines whir into life, my hands grip the chair and Dr Frost commentates to me as he goes about applying serum to my eyeballs. I know it's to help dilute the previous solution that helps to stick the lenses in place. I'm allowed to blink a few times so he can wipe away the serum that spills out of my eyes. Then it's back to business and the laser scans both eyes. By now I can't see anything. Each socket feels sticky and overflowing, like tiny cups. All the while Dr Frost asks after my goats to keep me at ease. Finally I feel a slight pressure, a gentle release, and I'm allowed to blink again. My lenses have been removed. I'm given tissues, an eye wash, further drops to prevent irritation and a cup of water to drink and calm my nerves.

"That wasn't so bad," Dr Frost says. "You were very good."

I sit up woozily and take in my surroundings all over again. My lenses usually highlight and define everything, but without them it feels like I'm looking at everything underwater. The sky looks darker outside, as though hours have passed, the marble countertops are suddenly grainy and Dr Frost's skin isn't so deliciously chocolate as before.

My lenses are popped in a sterile container, labelled, and shipped to one of the on-sight laboratories. It feels like they removed an organ and I watch it leave with an odd feeling of detachment.

Dr Frost doesn't seem finished with me yet. He lets me sip my water as he checks my file. Then his tone changes slightly and he avoids making eye contact with me.

"So, Linnea, WOLF 0315. You passed the legal age in January. You can vote, buy alcohol, marry without consent . . ."

If this is his way of saying happy birthday it seems a little unconventional.

"What's more, you are now eligible to be a part of WOLF's program for type 03 candidates. There are seven new additions this quarter, all entered into the same database as you. All WOLF 03. All highly recommendable. You are aware of the program?"

"Yes." My voice is flat.

He knows perfectly well I'm aware of it. We talked about it at length at my last appointment. Or at least, he tried whilst I patiently refused. The program is referred to as Turtle Doves ML. I'm not entirely sure what ML stands for, but Hans and I once tried to guess and we came up with "Mate for Life". It's not a bad guess, even if it's completely wrong. They tried to sign Hans up to it once. It was new and exciting at the time.

The program is a match-making system which pairs candidates according to their WOLF readings. Types 01 and 02 can sign up to the program online and Anna had been talking about signing herself up to see who they would match her with. For her and Hans, it can be seen as harmless fun. But for me, and for Dr Frost, it's a little bit more serious than that. Since I'm WOLF 03, there are fewer of us and we are considered rare. To match us with each other is nothing short of research, something they are eager to look into. It's not enough we're the result of prior testing on an older generation, they're even more curious to see what will happen to future candidates.

"You know I don't like the idea," I say, wishing they would bring my mother in here to fight my corner.

"You might as well weigh up all your options. It won't take much time to enter you into the system and see what happens. That's all we do, enter your WOLF code. No questions and no obligation. In fact it's become something of a craze among young people. Aren't you at all curious?"

Of course I am. Everyone is.

"All right," I sigh. "If it's not going to interfere with my time too much. And if there's no real obligation. Enter me into your system and let me know if you find someone. It can't hurt, I suppose."

"Well, as it happens," Dr Frost says casually, "all eligible candidates are put forward on their eighteenth birthday. We hold any results back until you consent to hear them. In other words, we already found you a match. "

"Of course you did. Fine, who is it?"

"WOLF 0378, OX M." He looks at my file. Good grief, they've even put it in my medical file. This really is serious research to them.

"What's his name?"

I'm not interested in his identification details, although it has already told me his age and his lens type. Of course, he's the same as me: type 03. But now I know he's older than me by four or maybe five years. Thank goodness. To a computer that doesn't know any better, my perfect match could be some eighty-three year old shepherd from the sticks. Except I know that wouldn't be possible. There are no WOLF 03 candidates over the age of twenty-five. This boy would have been one of the first.

"Alec Rouman," Dr Frost says.

"Alec." I play with the name on my tongue.

"He's from Newton Belle. Just a short train ride from you."

I almost snort at the idea.

"I have to go find him?"

"Oh lord, no. You'll be under WOLF surveillance at first."

"How romantic."

"He's looking forward to meeting you," Dr Frost says earnestly. "He asked for you as soon as he came in."

This knocks me back completely. So not only is this boy aware that I exist, he already knows my name and that I'm scheduled to be here. And that surely means only one thing?

"You scheduled his next lens appointment for today, didn't you? He's in the building right now?"

"Ah." Dr Frost looks sheepish.

"Can I back out?"

"You can." He looks crest-fallen. "Like I said, no obligation, but Miss Hansen, he really is keen to meet you."

I wonder how long this Alec has had to think about all this. Much longer than me, it seems. His interest in meeting me feels uneasy. If I don't stick to my guns and keep my wits about me, I'll be selecting wedding themes and colours with the receptionist by the end of the day.

But then I think of the possible benefits. I think of the chances I'll have to meet another boy whilst caring for my mother. Unless I marry Hans one day, I would've probably signed up for Turtle Doves eventually out of curiosity. Where else am I likely to find a suitor, given my circumstances? And with the company so anxious to achieve a successful match for me, putting substantial funding into their research, surely as a WOLF 03 candidate I'm in with the best chance of getting it right? Could this boy actually be perfect for me?

"All right," I say. "I'll meet him. But I have one condition."

"Absolutely."

"No WOLF lenses," I insist. "I want to see him as he is, whilst I'm like this. Pink, swollen eyes and all. If I'm going to meet him, I'll meet him without the mask to hide behind."

Dr Frost would argue our lenses are anything but a mask. More like windows to see perfectly into a person's being. But he doesn't say anything. He scribbles on my medical notes and hands them to his assistant, instructing for Alec Rouman to come to the XY unit.

4

As far as blind-dates go, this could be a lot worse. They have agreed to let us meet in moderate privacy; more than I could've hoped for. I was expecting something like a board meeting, with rainbow-eyed doctors scribbling notes and computers monitoring my pulse, sweat and body language. I'm pleasantly surprised when I'm led to the simulation room and told I can expect no interference.

"He requested this room himself," Dr Frost's assistant tells me as I remove any jewellery and buckles. I pop these in a tray and mentally prepare myself to enter the room.

I've been in the simulation room before. When I was ten they rigged me up in here and showed me images to provoke a response from my lenses. This time I'm lens-free and won't be watched so intimately, although I'm certain there are cameras in here.

The door requires a heavy hand to pull it open and hisses slightly as it swings ajar. I can see the spot lights are on and it feels like I'm about to walk on to a television set or a real-life dating show. In a way, I guess I am. But my audience will be a selection of WOLF doctors conducting research. I'm no less nervous as I step inside and the door closes behind me.

The room resembles a huge, spherical dome. With the lights on you would see it stocked with pipes, cables, power packs, fire extinguishers and surveillance cameras. But with only the spotlights guiding me to the centre, I can only see small dots of light that look like scarlet stars. The lights glow off the skin of a young man and my breath quickens.

He stands up the moment he sees me, his hands rubbing the top of his thighs. The first thing I look for are his lenses, but the abnormally pink whites of his eyes prove he isn't wearing any. I'm assured I'm looking at his true appearance and his eyes are a natural brown. His hair is blond, like mine. That has to be a coincidence. Our lenses don't reflect the colour of our hair, nor would it make us more compatible.

I can tell he doesn't know whether to hug me, shake my hand or pull out a chair for me. He clumsily tries to do all three; moving with both arms, then dropping one for a handshake, before using it to pull forward a chair that was already prepared for me. Without making any physical contact, we both nod and take our seats opposite each other.

Considering he sounded so keen to meet me, he looks nervous and unsure of himself. Or perhaps he just feels alien at having been robbed of his lenses. He blinks a tad too often.

"Hello, Linnea."

"Hello, Alec," I say. "It's nice to finally put a name to the registration number. I've heard a lot about your digits."

He blinks again, unsure if I'm serious or not. We're supposed to be statistically compatible, so I'm anxious to see him work it out. He quickly laughs at my dry joke.

"This is so weird." He shakes his head.

"Tell me about it." This entire situation is bizarre. I glance back around the room at all the various lights on the walls. Alec follows my gaze.

"You didn't want to go anywhere in particular then?"

I'm a bit confused by this. After all, it was him who requested the simulation room. "No. I wanted to meet you in private."

He smiles then, and there's oddness to it, as though I've said something else that was intended to be funny.

"Well then." He sits up straight and looks a great deal more confident than when I first walked in. "You'll have to tell me about yourself. Your no-lenses rule makes you harder to read."

"That's precisely why I wanted it," I say. I hoped he would understand it wasn't an attempt to be difficult, but to really test WOLF's theory. If we're as compatible as they say, then our lenses won't be necessary. Alec offers to be the first to introduce himself properly.

"You already know I'm registered Ox, so I'm a bit older than you. I actually just finished at the university here and returned to Newton Belle about a year ago."

"You don't look like a city boy."

"I'm not really," he admits. "I commuted from my aunt's, who lived just outside the city. I dislike the city really."

He pauses to see if I mind this admission. Most people dream of the city and are stunned when people speak badly of it. But I understand at once.

"Me too. People are ruder here. More impatient. It's a hassle trying to get my mother around. She absolutely hates it here."

"Your mother isn't impressed by its so-called beauty then?"

"She's blind."

"Oh." Alec's eyes widen. "I see. No wonder she hates it. If you can't appreciate they're at least trying to make it look good, then what's the point in visiting?"

He doesn't apologise or offer sympathy. I like that.

"So you went to the university," I say. "What did you study?"

"Engineering. I fancied myself a bit of a Cornelius Morgan when I enrolled. But, to be honest, I prefer the country way of things."

"Me too," I say. "I'm a goat herder."

He stares at me as if I'm joking. Then his mouth breaks into a huge grin.

"You're seriously a goat herder?"

"Yeah, when I'm not caring for my mother. We have a herdsman called Hans. He does a lot of the work. But I tend to the goats as well. They're more like pets than livestock to me. My family own a ranch in Orbelle."

"You mean the ranch on the hill?"

I'm taken aback by this, and he quickly explains. "I see it when we pass through the town by train. Obviously, I've not seen it in any detail."

"That's my ranch," I confirm. "My father took it on when we left the city."

"So you were a city girl originally?"

"Not quite, my mother was pregnant with me when they moved. They . . ." I trail off and glance at all the red lights, wondering which ones are cameras. In the end I decide I don't care. "They advised them to move when my mother started to show the after-effects of the early experiments, you know? Well, of course you must, you're WOLF 03 too. Your mother must have signed up for their experiments. But she didn't go blind?"

"No. I guess she was one of the lucky ones."

"But it affected you, when you were born. For you to be like me, I mean."

"I guess so. Not that it interferes with my life at all. It must be pretty hard for you, though. WOLF issued compensation, I presume? They did for my mother, and all she had were a few mild side-effects that eventually wore off. They must be helping your mother however they can."

A few mild side-effects. What fortune the Roumans had when WOLF first set out to make the lenses permanent. Before they were designed to feed oxygen to the cornea, many of their test subjects experienced irritation and a select few picked up diseases. WOLF categorized these misfortunes, but I only know the disease my mother has: a severe form of something known as keratitis. Since I can remember my mother has suffered ulceration in both eyes, slowly worsening over the years. Compensation can hardly put right the years I've had to watch her eyes deteriorate.

"They did offer compensation," I say warily. "The money she receives helps us keep our ranch. But lately we've started to struggle. My father has argued our case to get her a guide dog. But we can't afford it unless WOLF helps us. We're in the process of trying to work it out for her. A guide dog would make a huge difference for us all, and also company for her."

"Your father sounds like a good man, looking after you, your mother and the ranch," Alec says.

My face changes at once. Alec looks worried, as though he might have offended me. I wonder if I should tell him the truth. Would he be put off? Would it only make him uncomfortable?

"My father's in prison."

He clearly doesn't know how to respond to this.

"Oh. That's . . . I'm sorry to hear that."

"It's all right," I insist. "He accidentally killed someone. But his WOLF lenses helped him, I guess. He was facing murder, but WOLF were able to prove he was acting in self-defence."

Alec looks at me in wonder. "Are you serious? That's amazing."

He's right, it is. For all my family have suffered since they experimented on my mother, WOLF really helped my father out when he shot at a trespasser. Intended to warn the man off, my father was horrified when the trespasser ran at him with Red Eye, intending to kill. My father had no choice but to shoot first and explain himself afterwards. In fact, it really didn't look good for him at all. But with WOLF keeping a solid record of everyone's lens readings it was soon proven my father had no Red Eye in his records, whilst the last reading of his victim certainly did. Although the lenses turn white when people are rendered brain-dead, the man would have died with eyes the colour of blood. My father never denied shooting him, thus we're still waiting for him to serve his time for manslaughter. No one was more distressed by the event than he was.

As I retell this story to Alec, his eyes are wide enough to insert new lenses. He breathes out heavily and, to my relief, he actually smiles.

"So WOLF saved the day there."

"Well. I suppose they did. In their own way."

"You mustn't know how to feel about it all," Alec says gently. He immediately shuts up, glancing at the cameras like I did. I understand what he means however, I often think of it myself. With one parent suffering the negative aspects of WOLF, I have another whose fate was made slightly better by them. My opinion of WOLF goes between bitter resentment and sheer gratitude.

And here I am now, in the midst of one of their experiments, meeting a boy they claim will be my perfect partner. Do I trust them or not? Do I remember my mother sat in another doctor's surgery somewhere, or do I remember my father placing his face in his hands with relief as WOLF officials stepped forward with the evidence needed to reduce his sentence?

My thoughts are interrupted by Alec, who gives a wry smile.

"Your life certainly seems more eventful than mine. My mother works at our local chemist. My father works in Fenix as a banker. I work at Grapha, developing circuit boards. That's about it."

He blushes a little, embarrassed he can't offer a more exciting story. But they sound perfect to me. Grapha is a well-known manufacturer that often does business with WOLF. It's a respectable occupation. Suddenly my mind returns to the piece of circuit board in my pocket. I thought I recognised the logo, and now I'm sure it's a product of Grapha. It would seem weird to produce it now, like I always carry scrap with me, so I don't mention it.

"You live in Newton Belle?"

"Yes. It's one of the detached houses, though not a big ranch like yours. It snows more in Newton Belle, and we have a lake instead of a mountain. It does look lovely this time of year."

"I'd like to see it," I say truthfully.

"You would? All right." He sits forward and I'm left feeling puzzled as he draws a touchpad on to his lap.

His fingers skate over the surface, looking for something, and then he hits a few buttons. I manage to spy a few random digits before the whole room lights up. The white lights dazzle me and I look up, expecting to see light bulbs. But instead my breath is stolen by an incredible sight. Although our seats are still rooted to the platform, we appear to be in the middle of a snow-covered town. I almost stand up in alarm, but I quickly remember what this room is actually designed for.

Each of the red lights is an individual stand-by light to one of a hundred buzzing monitors. They cover the room like large tiles, reaching almost up to the ceiling, and give us a 360 degree view of whatever area Alec just typed into his touchpad. I'm marvelled by the speed it took us to arrive here, and by the sights of this new location. I can see everything Alec described, from the snow-capped rooftops to the frosted fir trees. Lanterns are lit above doors, illuminating the snow.

The closest building is over my right shoulder and I turn in my seat to see it. We're stationed right on its doorstep. This must be Alec's house. The code he entered would've been a part of his address and, in a humbling yet weird way, it's as if he's already inviting me over to visit.

As magical as it initially feels, I realise that it's projected a perfect reconstruction of Alec's hometown for the simulation room. I'm not looking at the real thing, just a captured image. Although small specks of snow continue to fall around us, I can't be sure if this has been digitally added to enhance the experience. In any case, the scene is certainly a romantic one and I turn back to look at Alec. He's already looking at me and, for the first time, I find myself wishing he were wearing his lenses, then I would be able to read him better. I suddenly care a lot about what he makes of me. I've never been on a date before and it now occurs to me I'm impressed by him. I wasn't prepared for this.

"Can you do the same thing with Orbelle?" I ask after complimenting his home.

"Sure. You can do it yourself." He hands me the touchpad. Talking me through the instructions, I find myself able to enter Orbelle's area code and we're immediately transported to our train station.

I suppose I'm curious to see if its beauty translates on to screen and if the simulation room has done it justice. I'm pleased to see it has and I look at Alec to see his reaction. Of course he's already seen Orbelle, but he looks no less impressed by this simulation of it.

"It's lovely. Somehow it makes sense you live here. It looks fresh and invigorating." He rethinks his wording and becomes flustered. "I mean, you look healthy. You look . . . like someone who would spend a lot of time outdoors. Your cheeks glow."

He falls silent, afraid he's overdone his attempt at flattery. To spare any awkwardness I turn my attention to the mountain behind the hills, and try to explain to him exactly where our ranch is located.

"Can you change it to night-time?" I suddenly ask.

"Night-time?" Alec looks curious. "I suppose so. Just a moment."

He plays with the controls a little more and suddenly we're bathed in near darkness. Across the top of the simulation room, stars are dotted like the red sensor lights. I tilt my head all the way back and find myself identifying constellations and my favourite stars.

"This is perfect," I say delightedly. I feel the need to explain myself. "I love astronomy. It's what I wanted to study, if it weren't for, well, circumstances."

"You know there's a meteor shower scheduled soon? You should be able to see it from Orbelle."

"Tell me you're not into all this astronomy stuff too. This is far too strange."

"I'm not," he admits. "But this sort of thing is featured in the science magazines we have in our house. I'm glad you didn't start asking me questions. I can only identify one or two stars. But I could learn. I mean, you could probably teach me."

"Sure," I say. Anna has gotten bored of me talking about stars and moons. It would be refreshing to have someone else to talk to. "Shall we put it back to day-light now?"

Moments later, I'm looking back at the mountain with the goats huddled under the low sun.

"Maybe I can see it one day," he says. "Properly."

I think about it for a moment.

"Sure."

I don't know if we've been running on a timer, or if those watching have decided our meeting is over, because suddenly a buzzer sounds and the spotlights come back on. I suspect the latter, since they would probably like to end things on a positive. To confirm our time is up, both doors to the left and right of the room open slightly to allow us to exit. Alec and I stand, feeling very odd, as though this really was all a show for the cameras. But as soon as the lights go out, Alec uses the opportunity to take my hand and kiss my knuckles gently. We give each other one final glance, understanding that moment was for us; not anyone else. It clarifies our sincerity about meeting again. Then we both turn and head out the doors.

I'm greeted by Dr. Frost's assistant, who was clearly able to watch the whole thing. She's grinning in triumph.

"That went very well, didn't it? He wants to see you again."

"I suppose so." I shrug. "What happens now? Will they give him my contact details?"

"Dr Frost will discuss that with you," she says. "Now, here are your things, you can put them back on here."

"What about my mother? Did her appointment go okay?"

"Your mother is here, waiting. You can go on back and collect your lenses. They've returned from our labs in excellent condition."

I hurry to assemble my belt and earrings and then I'm led back to Dr Frost's surgery. They've given my mother a cup of tea and a biscuit. Her eye examination must be over. Her expression is grim. There must have been no improvement. The last time she was here she could just about identify light from dark. Now they confirm her vision has deteriorated further still. Deep down I already knew this would be the case. I start to think about the near future, about her care and our future on the ranch. Chances are by the time my father returns, we may not be ranch owners anymore.

My depressing thoughts are interrupted by a nurse telling us someone is on the phone for Mrs Hansen.

"I could barely make out what he was saying because of his accent," she tells my mother as she leads her from the room. I wonder what on earth Hans could be calling here for. I know his accent becomes thicker if he's agitated. Since Dr Frost needs to reinsert my lenses, I can't leave myself. I'm all done, and dabbing my eye with a tissue, when my mother returns.

"Hans was wondering when exactly our train home is tomorrow," my mother says. "He insisted everything was fine, but something must be wrong. Why else would he be anxious to know that?"

"Perhaps a goat is injured?" I say. This is unlikely though. Hans is licensed and experienced to shoot a dying animal, plus he knows more about goats than we do. If he can't heal or euthanize the animal, it's very unlikely we can.

"I think we should head back tonight, poor lad is up there on his own."

Maybe he saw a wolf on the hill. It has happened before. Not while I've been awake though. I heard them howling once, but I've never seen one. If a wolf is patrolling the hill for a juicy goat then maybe Hans would feel better for some company.

We collect our stuff and I'm given Alec Rouman's contact details. They're stamped on a card. I never expected to be leaving here with a suitor. I put the card in my bag and shake Dr Frost's hand. It feels like we completed a business deal here today.

The next train home promises a two hour wait at least, since my mother refuses to board a train during rush hour. Once the many uniform wearers have been and gone, we're seated in a less crowded carriage, eating our sandwiches as the train rolls out of Fenix station and towards the bridge. We enter the tunnel and descend into darkness.

We're only five minutes into our journey when suddenly the train stops. I feel the brakes being applied and everyone shifts forward. Luggage bags topple in the overhead storage areas. There's an exclamation of surprise throughout the carriage, but it's mostly just pantomime and no one appears too worried. Everyone turns to the windows although there's nothing to see and strangers start to converse about what the disturbance could be. Before the excitement can make way for concern, the driver's voice sounds over the speakers.

"Sorry about this, ladies and gentlemen, there seems to a small problem with the line and there's a chance we'll need to make our way back to the station. We apologize for the inconvenience. Another service should be made available as soon as possible. Please hang tight while we communicate with the station and find out more information. You can remain seated for the time being. Thank you."

There's a groan of impatience by those who hoped to get home sooner. We realise Hans may be left wondering where we are. My mother offers me another sandwich to help pass the time but I'm distracted by the ticket inspector who hurries through the carriage. He purposefully avoids eye contact with anyone and ignores any questions about refunds. He pauses by the carriage door and speaks over his shoulder, so no one can see his lenses.

"Close all the windows, please. And remain in your seats."

It's not a polite request, it's an instruction. Another member of staff opens the carriage door and speaks with him quietly. They look at the windows and I hear the ticket inspector mumble: "but how will we explain that?"

Within moments, he decides to do as his colleague advises and they both make their way back along the carriage, pulling down the blinds and stealing our view of the tunnel. There's no point denying something's wrong. Once they know the passengers have guessed this they start to request our obedience.

"Blinds down, all blinds down," they instruct, waving their hands. "The lights may go out. Don't be alarmed."

"What on earth is going on?" a man demands.

"There's been some disturbance," the ticket inspector says, hesitating. He doesn't know how to explain it.

"Is it to do with the meteor shower?" I ask. I know sometimes they can affect the power within towns and cities. He looks at my face and I realise how silly that question was.

Why would we close the blinds for an electrical fault? This is all down to something far more close to earth. But no less imminent. There's a crackle over the speakers and the driver tells us all to stay calm. "Don't panic, ladies and gentlemen, we're waiting for permission to send the train back to the station. Please move away from the windows and doors until we arrive. I'll repeat that: can all passengers move away from any window and doors and remain calm."

With these words, the lights go out.

Fear and adrenaline rise in my chest. No one moves away from the windows, instead everyone crams to see what could be happening in the dark. Besides, we're trapped now. The windows are our only way out and no one's willing to distance themselves from them.

The ticket inspector makes a mad dash to close the remaining blinds, but it's too late. The carriage is silently bathed in a dim, fiery glow. A dozen torches appear at the windows. They look like sticks of glowing ember. Normally that would make me feel warm, but my body now feels very cold. They gather around the train. The carriage receives a series of harsh bangs and violent attacks. People finally begin to clamber away from the window seats.

“They’re rioting in the city,” the ticket inspector says. The glow is on his face like a fierce blush but I can almost hear the yellow in his eyes. “It started as a protest but quickly escalated. When they closed the estuary to pedestrians and barred the toll office, they went for the train tracks and entered the tunnel. We were waiting for WOLF X teams to arrive at the station and secure our safe return. But it seems just as unsafe to go back as it does to continue. We don’t know if they’ve done anything to the line ahead. Now we’re stuck in the middle.”

I start to stand up to get a better look but a loud thud to the side of the train startles me into sitting back down and shrinking into my seat.

“They’ll break the glass,” someone cries out in fright.

“They can’t.” The inspector says firmly. “They can’t break the glass.”

What little I can see and hear makes me feel like we’re caught in the belly of a monster. Everything is dark red, the pounding echoes within the tunnel sound like a heartbeat and I begin to feel like I could run out of air. I grip my seat tightly and close my eyes. Behind closed lids my lenses search for light between layers of skin. The tighter I squeeze them shut the more spots of colour pop, but it's just the speckled memory of the last shape my lenses saw. Suddenly my eyelids omit a glow that makes my eyes open. Everyone on the train exhales in relief. The lights are on and the train starts to pull away and head back the way we came. I see dozens of faces outside the window, illuminated by the carriage lights. They're being restrained and beaten by soldiers, but continue to throw things at the side of the train. The window is streaked with blood-like paint.

"Oh thank god," the inspector says. "Excuse me."

As the train picks up speed, so does he; hurrying down the carriage and out of sight. Everyone starts to open the remaining blinds and wait for sunlight. We pierce the air like a bullet, leaving the tunnel like the end of a terrifying ride. The edge of the tracks are lined with WOLF X recruits and they watch us pass with rifles in hand. They keep the tracks clear until we reach the station and, as soon as the doors open, a man in uniform gets on to great us and instruct us on what to do. The station is completely empty.

"The platforms have been cleared and closed due to bomb scares," he tells us. "Everyone please collect your belongings and follow me, we will be taking you to a safe place to wait."

When we're all off the train he slams the door shut and tells everyone to stay together. "Once the disturbance is over, we'll send another train along the Sparkwell route." His eyes glace up and down the train. "Obviously not this one."

We finally see the damage done to the train. The dents that mark the metalwork are glossed over with vibrant paint that spell the words 'SEE FOR YOURSELF'. Someone was halfway through spraying on an eye with red irises but they must've been pulled away mid-spray. I look at the window, where my mother and I sat, and see just how close the vandals were to us. The dent beneath our window was too close for comfort.

"See for yourself," I say aloud as we're away by the recruits. Our footsteps are especially loud against the station floor and I grip my mother's arm so she can keep up.

"That's old," she muses quietly. She doesn't seem surprised or afraid. "They were using that phrase the last time people protested against WOLF. That was many years ago now."

"Did you see any of the riots back then?" I ask. "Did my father?"

"Of course we did. I was in more danger than most, because I signed up as a test subject. I was helping them with their developments. A lot of people didn't take too kindly to that. When one of the riots started I was in the laboratory and we had to seal ourselves inside until it was over. It was frightening."

"Did my father have to do that too?"

"Your father?" My mother starts to smile in spite of herself. "Your father was one of the men outside."

I almost stop walking to ask more questions but we're told to go into one of the station cafés and wait. They've opened up the metal security doors and a young member of staff starts to work the coffee machines to provide refreshment. My mother sips her latte like nothing's happened. Perhaps not being able to see can have its advantages. I decide to probe her memory, since she can clearly see things from the past.

"My father was one of the protesters?" I ask quietly.

"Like I said, it was years ago," my mother replies. "Before he met me. We often spoke about it later, how for all we know I was on the receiving end of one of his group's attacks. He used to get very humble about it. Of course your father wouldn't abuse anyone in any other circumstances. But he had a cause to fight for and your father was a passionate man who believed in change. By the time we met, he was done protesting and I was done being a test subject. My vision was starting to worsen and I had made enough money to move on. Your father never really accepted the law, though. We moved to Orbelle a few years after we married."

"Because of WOLF?"

"Indirectly. Once the lenses were made compulsory, crime plummeted, youths were kept in line – by that I mean kept in school and sober. People had no choice but to improve their work ethics. You couldn't dodge the system. They watched everyone with the lenses in place. And although people didn't like to pay up, WOLF made the government millions in taxes. The publicity Fenix received was overwhelming, the first city in history to introduce compulsory lens wear. People suddenly wanted to visit. They brought business and tourism. With that money the government could transform Fenix into the most beautiful city in the world."

"So why did you leave?"

My mother grins. "We could have nearly bought the ranch out-right for the typical asking price of a Fenix apartment in those days. Besides, we found out we were expecting you and your father didn't want you to grow up in such a city. He wanted somewhere remote enough to live life the old-fashioned way. He wanted you to be virtually free of all that. He didn't want his son or daughter to be kept strictly in line. I think he wanted you to be naughty sometimes. He wanted you to have a personality and be free. He didn't want you to grow up under WOLF's influence."

"It sounds like he wanted her to be one of the youths attacking the train." A man sat on the table next to us turns around with an unfavourable look in his eye. My mother is sat facing away from him and doesn't move. She hasn't kept her voice down whilst speaking and her words have attracted attention from neighbouring tables. The man stares into the back of her head irritably. "Kids today have no idea how good their lives are now," he says, looking at me. "No idea at all. Yet they act like this; it's disgusting."

"You can't expect them to be grateful," my mother says solemnly. "Most of them are too young to appreciate why some of these changes were made."

"Then most of them aren't old enough to be paying WOLF's taxes yet," the man retorts.

"How can they when half of them can't seem to get jobs?" My mother says. "Technology is taking over, computers do everything now. They don't know what to do with their idle hands, and the devil has eyes only second to WOLF. They have no outlet, they can only protest. It gives them the false impression of a purpose. It's not just the young ones either. They don't interview people like they used to. They employ based on the results of non-optional lens screenings. They look for perfection. No one receives the benefit of the doubt anymore."

"Would you employ a man if his lenses said he could spell trouble?"

"Oh, why not," my mother says mildly. "I married one."

He's had enough of her humour and the fact she's not looking directly at him. He stands up and means to come over. I clear my throat loudly, so my mother will turn her head toward me, and reveal her eyes. It does the trick. He stops in his tracks once he realizes he's picking an argument with a blind woman and sits back down, grumbling under his breath. I sigh with relief. No one wins the debate, but that's not surprising. The subject of WOLF lenses will never have a winner.

Someone puts the café's television on to help pass the time and opts for the news. There's nothing about a riot in Fenix. Instead, they're showing a segment recorded earlier today about the expected meteor shower. A female reporter is standing in front of a truck with its windscreen shattered and flanked by goats eager to chew at her microphone.

"Behind me is an example of what many astronomers are hoping to see over the next few nights; a display both dazzling and possibly dangerous. Yes, it's the long anticipated meteor shower due to grace our skies this week. But it seems to have arrived unexpectedly early. The windscreen of this truck behind me is the remarkable result of a meteorite coming into direct contact with us here on earth. Incredible as it seems, the fragment of rock" – she picks up an example, the size of my fist, and holds it up to the camera – "said to be no bigger than this, is capable of such damage. So what do we advise when rocks the size of apples hit our cars? Well, according to the experts, we have nothing to worry about since the chance of this happening is one in two hundred fifty thousand. However, this reporter is taking no chances!" She then proceeds to unfold an umbrella and holds it jokingly above her head, her eyes turning a calm shade of lilac. The report then goes on to explain where best to witness the expected showers.

“They could’ve shown us the actual rock,” someone says, disappointed.

It’s not a rock, it’s a meteorite. But I’m not really thinking about that, or the fact I’ve already missed one display I’ve been counting down the days for. I’m looking at the screen and wondering how on earth I’m going to tell my mother that it was our ranch, that was my father’s damaged truck and those were my hungry goats.

5

The moment we step off the train, I'm somewhat surprised to see the ranch the same as ever on the hill. There are no reporters, no sign a camera crew was ever here. There's just one police car parked halfway up the hill. Out of habit I hit the brass bell on the porch before opening the door and calling out Hans' name. It's a police officer who greets us.

"Are you Linnea?"

"Yes." I lug my bags to the side of the hall before leading my mother in behind me. "Is Hans here?"

"I weren't expectin' you back." Hans steps out from the kitchen, looking surprised. "Sorry if I made things sound urgent on the phone, I just didn't know what to think at the time."

It's odd to see someone else making use of your kitchen whilst you sit. Hans busies about, making tea and passing the mugs around. The police officer talks to my mother, but mostly looks across at me. When my mother listens, she sometimes forgets to speak or move, so she looks like a robot that's stopped functioning. I have to nod and make noises to show we're both listening to him. I don't know where my father's truck is.

"We never sent for a television crew," the officer says, clearly still annoyed about it. "We never told anyone it was a meteorite. We cleared the area, took this young man's statement, and before we knew it WOLF officials were at the door with a warrant to access the truck and that pretty lady with the microphone started her little segment about shooting stars. Honestly, it didn't matter what we said to them, how much evidence we gave to suggest otherwise. As soon as they were done they left again, telling us to report it however we saw fit. So we're still going with our first suspicion."

With that, he reveals my father's truck was, it seems, bombed by vandals.

"Good lord," my mother exclaims. "They could've damaged the house. What happened?"

The police officer waits for Hans to finish making his own tea before joining us and telling his side of the story.

"The goats were goin' crazy. I was expectin' a wolf and was grabbin' my rifle from the hallway. Then the windows lit up and there was this almighty bang. I looked out the window but everythin' outside looked normal. Except the truck.

Smoke everywhere. When I finally stepped outside, I saw whoever it was had blown the windscreen in."

"Obviously, your absence was known to someone in the town," the officer tells us. "We've not encountered any other cases of home-made bombs being used in this area. But it's not an uncommon joke for these youngsters. We can only but think, for now, that your truck became a target because it's not on the road anymore. They might have regarded it as junk and an ideal target to practise their bomb on. I highly imagine they didn't realise how big the blast would be. I doubt their lenses would show any serious signs of intent, since they most likely did this for fun, not out of malice. In any case, they'll be lucky indeed if they didn't harm themselves."

Once he has left and my mother is unpacking her bags, Hans leans in close to my ear. "Disappointed it's not really a meteorite?"

"Extremely," I admit.

"Ah well. Do you want to see the aftermath of a truck bombin'?"

"Okay." However annoyed I am that my father's truck has been vandalised by something earthly, I'm still morbidly curious to see the wreckage.

“We’ve already cleared some of the glass from when WOLF opened the doors and were sniffin’ about. Didn’t want the goats gettin’ hurt. But other than that, it’s left as it was.” Hans strolls across the grass to the back of the house. They’ve moved the truck so it’s not on display and now stands alone in the shadows. The bonnet has been dented and blackened, but the windscreen is completely gone. Fragments of glass still cover the dashboard and seats.

“I’ll clear it all properly tomorrow,” Hans says.

“No need,” I say. “I can do that. Wow, they really shattered it.”

“Aye, like I said, it were a hell of a bang.”

“I wish I’d been here.”

“I wish you’d been here too.” Hans momentarily gazes at the mountain and thinks. “Thing is, Linn, there’s somethin’ else. Somethin’ I’ve not reported but I wonder if I should. I saw someone on the hill.”

“You think he was involved with the truck?”

“No, I don’t think so. He didn’t look the type. I’m no good at guessin’ people’s ages but I’d say he were late thirties.

Dressed well, short hair. He looked more interested in the mountain."

"A tourist?"

"I thought so at first. So I was gonna go over and make conversation. Make sure he knew the land was private. But as I approached him I saw he was armed. I think it was a gun, anyway. My lenses clocked it before he moved. I wouldn't have seen it otherwise. But it were there, under his jacket, I'm sure of it. He had somethin' in his hands too. Some kinda device he was using. Couldn't tell you what, I don't know these things."

"You didn't ask?"

"No, I went and got your father's rifle. Thought I better have it with me, just so he could see it. But when I went to confront him he were gone."

"Do you think he'll come back?"

"Possibly," Hans admits. He pauses for a while, not sure how to broach his next subject. "Did your father actually show you how to use your rifle? I know he bought you one but I don't know if he ever practised with you."

I hesitate. The idea of touching a gun after what happened, the association with eyes red as fresh blood . . .

"We were applying for my licence," I recall. "And I did fire it several times. You think I'll need to?"

"No, no. There's no need to feel panicked. I just thought I'd check. You two are my responsibility now." Hans never blushes, but his irises now look like marmalade, which is no different to me.

"Will you show me how then?" I relish the idea. Shooting practice with Hans sounds like a great way to pass an afternoon.

"Aye. It wouldn't hurt, would it? I've already given your father's rifle a quick fire and it shoots alright. It's old, mind, your father weren't one to get with the times."

"Do you think we should explain to my mother?"

"I can't decide." Hans looks tortured and thinks for a while. "No. Perhaps not. Sometimes it's best not to worry people if you can help it."

I'll remember those words tomorrow when I'm halfway up Mt Venus.

"Okay, I won't say anything," I promise.

"Good, that's settled. So, meteors and bombing aside, did you have a good day? How did your appointments go?"

Is he joking? Have they really not mentioned the riots during the news? I suppose it's not surprising. Fenix wouldn't look so perfect if they did. I decide to keep the conversation simple for now and tell him about our appointments.

"Good and bad. Mine was good. I had my lenses assessed and reinserted before I came home. They work perfectly. My mother is worse though."

"Aye. We already knew that, didn't we?"

"We did," I agree. "And they'll be looking into her care a bit further, as always. Oh but here's something new. I got signed up to Turtle Doves ML."

"Oh heck, are you serious?" Hans laughs.

"They found me a match."

"I'll bet they did." Hans rolls his eyes. "Who? A forty-year old with a hunchback?"

"That wouldn't even be possible. I was only put forward to match other type 03 candidates. Alec is one of the oldest at twenty-four."

"Alec?" Hans looks serious again. "That his name then?"

"He's an Ox, so only a few years older than me. He lives in Newton Belle and studied in the city."

"I bet he'll be a right idiot." Hans looks unimpressed. "Newton Belle boys are generally pompous fools who don't appreciate the countryside."

"He happens to have studied engineering," I say defensively. "And he isn't a pompous idiot, thank you very much. He was actually really lovely and polite."

Hans stands very still for a moment. "You met him?"

"Yeah, they arranged our appointments for the same day."

"Sneaky gits," Hans remarks.

"I know," I sigh. "I don't think I'd have done it if I hadn't been put on the spot. I always thought I'd keep refusing. But it turned out to be good in the end. I liked him, and he feels the same way about the program as I do. In fact, although I hate to admit it, they were right: Alec and I have a lot in common. Except, of course, his mother can see and his father isn't locked up."

Hans takes a long time to reply and, when he does, he draws his gaze away.

"Linn, they won't give your mother a guide dog for doin' whatever Dr Frost asks. She's entitled to compensation. You don't have to enter their stupid programmes."

This silences me for a moment. Still, what does it matter? It was only a dating program and I shrug at Hans without saying a word. I'm prepared to stand by what I said. I did like Alec.

"Well, I hope it works out for you."

"Hans, I can see your lenses."

He lets out a low laugh. "Okay, fine, I think the whole thing is stupid and just a scheme for WOLF to get more government fundin'. Don't be surprised if Alec turns out to be an axe murderer."

"Thanks." I suppress a laugh.

"Don't mention it. All the more incentive to teach you how to fire a weapon. No one takes advantage of Miss Hansen without gettin' shot in the kneecaps."

"Bang." I pretend fire with my fingers and look at my father's truck again. "They never showed the rock. They hyped it all up, making out we'd actually been hit by something from outer space. But never showed the evidence."

“Well, there weren’t any.” Hans shrugs. “No doubt they were trying to score more ratings for their meteor shower coverage. Never let the truth get in the way of a good story, eh?”

“I suppose.”

“Besides, I doubt they’d admit to the public if it were a bomb. The city’s all about terrorists this year. Threats of organised groups wantin’ to hack into WOLF’s system, sever WOLF’s connection to the common people. Stop the lenses from workin’, or at least recordin’ data.”

“Yeah, but bombing an old truck in Orbelle wouldn’t bring them any success,” I say. “They need to aim for WOLF HQ to have any impact at all, surely?”

“Aye. If this opposition exists then they probably will, in time,” Hans says. “And good luck to ‘em. Wolves are hunters and scavengers, I don’t object to takin’ one or two out with my rifle to keep their numbers down.”

I don’t respond to this. I immediately think of my father at Hans’ age. What would he say if I told him about the riots today? Would he be shocked? Would he be glad? I wonder what Hans would say if I told him all about it.

I look up at the moon, which hangs in a cool blue sky. It's waning and hard to see in daylight, but I can still make out the various craters caused by direct hits from meteor showers.

"I'm going to be hiking with Anna tomorrow," I say casually. "I might stay over her house. If my mother needs something, you might get a phone call."

"No problem, you deserve a day off with your friend," Hans says. "We'll start shootin' practice when you get back. By the time your father comes home, we'll have made a proper rancher out of you, I bet. You'll be taking out wolves and leadin' a flock yourself by the end of this summer."

It's a herd, not a flock. It's a herd of goats, and a flock of sheep. But I don't say anything. I expect I've got a long way to go before I'm a match for wolves, whatever shape or form.

6

I'm pleasantly surprised to see Anna on our ranch so early in the morning. She only ventures up here if she breaks up with a boyfriend or has issues with her dissertations. Since she's neither crying, nor holding a wad of paperwork, I'm suitably impressed.

"Hey!" I wave from the truck.

"Hey. What's going on?"

"Someone blew my father's windscreen up with a home-made bomb." This is probably the first time I've had something cooler than her to say. Her eyes widen and she peers down at the glass I'm sweeping.

"A bomb? Since when do people in Orbelle have the brains to bomb anything?"

"Since there is nothing else here to do but feed goats and water plants," I say. "And I wouldn't call it brains. The police will probably catch them soon. They'll be the kids with no eyebrows."

“Serve them right.” Anna leans on the skeleton of my father’s truck, careful not to snag her jacket on broken glass. “That’s a lot of glass to sweep up. Someone clearly thought you needed an occupation this summer that didn’t include goats. A bomb is a bit much though.”

“The news reported that it was a meteorite fragment.”

“A bomb sounds cooler.”

I stare at her. Does she really think a bomb made by delinquents is more impressive than falling fragments from space?

“When do you want to make a move and get the train?” I ask inconspicuously. My mother is nowhere around but unless I reinforce the secrecy to Anna, she will probably forget and tell someone our plan.

“Internet is dead,” she says, by way of answer. “Not just my house, internet is dead for everyone, so is phone signal. Televisions are acting up too. Orbelle is such a dive. Basically I’m happy to leave whenever.”

“I’m just glad you’re still up for it. I thought you would back out.”

Anna picks at her nails and sniffs loudly. "I still reckon we might."

"I won't," I say firmly. "I've waited for this shower for months. I've got all the times written down, put new batteries in my camera and packed my bag. You'll remember everything, won't you? Your sleeping bag, heat packs."

"Am I leaving my common sense?" Anna raises an eyebrow.

"It's just one night."

I promise her all the gossip about Alec Rouman, although I'm not sure a polite kiss on the hand will reward her curiosity. I promise her a perfect camping trip between friends. I choose not to mention the freezing temperatures and consequences if either of our parents got wind of it. A night camping on Mt Venus is enough to give my mother a heart attack.

"Okay, we're on," she says. "But if this all goes terribly wrong then at least we'll be able to laugh and tell the story later."

"It won't go wrong."

Temperatures below zero, wolf sightings, avalanche warnings creeping up as summer temperatures rise. My lenses serve me well today; she doesn't notice my uncertainty.

The chairlift will only take us so far up the mountain; about a quarter of the way. Once at the top a passenger can enjoy a wide view of the surrounding valleys and a bite to eat at a constructed picnic area. When Anna and I would see each other most days, the chairlift was an ideal escape from other people. We would journey up the mountain and talk about our problems, approximately four-hundred meters above the rest of the world. This trip serves to remind me of old times as we fasten our backpacks and set off.

The small team who operate the chairlift wave us off and we thump in our seats, pulling down the safety bar. There is the initial thrill of being transported across trees and houses before the effect wears off and we talk about more personal matters.

I was right to pack for more than just myself. We've only been climbing for ten minutes when Anna begins to complain about the cold. It's only mid-afternoon and I worry about her tolerance when the sun starts to go down. I pull out additional gloves and hats and Anna gladly takes them. I can see only her eyes peeking out from between her scarf and hat by the time we reach the top.

I step off the chairlift with a chill starting to spread under my skin, but it's nothing a brisk pace can't fix. Once we start trekking across the snow I warm up considerably. When we arrive at the picnic area, I feel myself starting to sweat.

I prepare hot chocolate and devise a plan, whilst Anna does nothing but shiver and make discontented noises. I keep my eye on her to ensure she doesn't resort to the provisions she will need later. The heat packs in her pockets, for instance. I relay what I expect us to have achieved by the time the sun goes down. I also try to establish some sort of emergency procedure, in case we get separated, but Anna is too busy cringing at the ginger I put in her hot chocolate.

I hand her my own compass, although I'm not convinced she can use it. She lifts and waves it slowly above her head, the same way she does when her phone is out of signal. She deliberately looks away from me a lot so I can't see her lenses. From here on, it will just be the two of us in the wilderness.

Anna has already lost her momentum and trudges along behind me like a disheartened anchor. I have to hoist her up harsh slopes and keep our two-man party afloat with words of encouragement.

By the third time I've prevented her activating her heat packs and listened to her wail they'll never find our bodies if we die, I realise I can still see the chairlift station across the mountainside. We've made little progress together in an hour compared to what I could've achieved alone. To my dismay, a single star is already starting to appear overhead. I've already lost valuable time. With the station still in sight I make a decision and tell Anna she can turn back.

"What, and leave you out here on your own?" She sounds appalled.

"I'll be all right," I say, although not even I'm entirely convinced. "I'm better equipped for this than you are. Do you really want to continue for another few hours and then wait for the meteor shower overnight?"

"No." She doesn't even bother lying. I can see in her lenses she's irritable and without motivation. Whereas mine are still burning with determination and I'm sure she can see it. She has limited time to make a decision. Once the sun disappears it'll be dangerous to navigate her way back to the station alone. If we're to part ways it's now or never.

"If I go, will you promise you'll head back first thing?"

"Of course. I don't suppose I'll sleep tonight so I'll start walking as soon as it gets light. I'll board the first chairlift down."

This appeals to Anna. If I can fulfil this promise then our mothers don't even need to know we were here and much less that we separated. She opens her backpack and hands me anything that'll help me on my journey alone. The only thing she doesn't surrender is her collection of heat packs, which she activates eagerly.

"You be careful." She offers a hug before picking her way back over the sloping terrain. Once she's a good distance away I turn and continue marching, relieved of the extra burden.

I'm truly on my own now. Whatever horror my mother might have had at the notion before, knowing I'm going solo fills me with further guilt and unease.

But it's too late to turn back. I've climbed high enough to know I've crossed some invisible line. Once you've gotten so far, it feels all the more acceptable to continue. After an hour I tell myself, if I started to head back again, it would be dark before I reached the bottom anyway. I'm better off seeking shelter and staying put once the sun goes down.

I notice a banner cloud has formed at the top of the mountain. Its appearance is similar to a white flag blowing east. I know as I climb the weather conditions will be prone to change. I try not to think the mountain is advising I surrender already. I'm surrounded by jagged rocks frozen deep into the ground. They jut out at parallel angles as if they gave up themselves but froze before they fell. They protrude out from the mountain's face like fungus and make my journey more difficult. My hands are too heavily gloved to grip and feel the surfaces I rely on. It's too cold and too slippery. I could so easily stumble or fall and I worry I'll never be found now Anna's gone. Everything about the world up here signifies loss of life. White is a colour WOLF associate so closely with death I try not to acknowledge the vast spread of snow and wilting colours of grey and brown around me.

Everything is so sapped of colour my lenses start trying to recalibrate and make sense of their surroundings. The only colour comes in the form of lone pine trees. My lenses grab hold of them and bring them into focus. I have to examine a few pine needles and the different textures in the bark before my lenses are satisfied they're working correctly and stop drifting out of focus. If they continue to search for clarity, I'll struggle to watch my step even more. It's impossible to see what lies beneath just a few centimetres of snow. Luckily, if the terrain shifts or crumbles, my lenses will pick it up. I need my lenses to detect shade and sparkles on the surface of the snow if I'm to make sense of this uneven path.

Something suddenly moves and I look up quickly. My lenses are fast to lock onto the movement and follow the shape that takes to the sky. It's a red kite, circling the mountain. My lenses effortlessly capture the sight of something in motion, with more colours to detect and savour. It's striped like an airborne tiger, with piercing eyes of gold set in a smoky white face. I wonder how comparable our vision is now. If I focus hard enough, my lenses will bring images towards me so I can see them clearer. If I wanted to hunt prey, they would be the perfect tool. I stop trying to navigate my way and turn to follow the kite's stare. I can't help but smile to myself and marvel how well I can see. I've spotted the small red squirrel darting about the grass, far down the mountain's slope. I almost hope the kite knows I spotted it too, since I've always thought birds of prey to have a superior look about their faces. I want him to know he's encountered a match up here. I look away now and try to stay focused on more than just my surroundings. I have an objective, and it's not hunting squirrels. But seeing the kite has motivated me. I know I have superiority over most creatures up here on the mountain. I'll spot any oncoming danger before it arrives. I'll be a kite, not a squirrel.

I thump each tree trunk with my knuckles like a high five for getting so far. I chug on water and keep my legs moving, even when I can't feel any of my joints. The closest thing I feel to warmth is the glow of the sun as it starts to set, and even that feels icy.

I've no idea how close I am to my destination. I could've passed that part of mountain already, or I could be hours from it. There are no distinguishing features I could identify. When I turn and squint against the setting sun, I can only barely make out the trees that dot the hill of the ranch. I can't be far from where I wished to be, so as long as I can find a decent look-out spot, I'm happy to call it a day.

There's a ledge overlooking a steep decline ahead of me. It's somewhere I expect people have sat before, because rocks don't form themselves into seats so conveniently. There are five pulled into a circle, so I guess some time ago a handful of hikers made a fire here. There are no remains of their stay, only the frosty rocks that attempt to bite through my clothes when I sit.

I swig soup, lukewarm to taste. The odour is overpowering when I unscrew the bottle cap. I swallow it all quickly so all I can smell is pine and snow again. I reckon I have less than five minutes to get ready before daylight vanishes.

I assemble blankets around my knees and shove on extra hats and gloves. I also get my binoculars and camera ready, although holding and focusing either of them is difficult under such thick gloves. I suppose when the time comes I'll have to remove them and cope with icy hands. I have ten heat packs in total, which I've collected for this occasion, although I'm not sure how affective they'll be. I hope they last as long as the packaging says, but my intention is to only use them after the meteors pass and I want to sleep a while.

A few hours pass. I avoid my torch and sit with my back against a bigger rock, trying to ward off the cold with sheer will-power. I play a game where I pretend I'm in a hot spring, but it fails to warm me. There are many times I wish I'd gone back down the mountain with Anna. Then something happens that completely distracts me.

Each light in Orbelle soundlessly goes out.

Until now I could see the distant street lamps against an ebony carpet. It was reassuring to know, at all times, I could see the town even if no one in town could see me. Now it's gone, swallowed up by a huge black hole. I shiver.

A power-cut would seem the most likely explanation, although terrible timing for me. Suddenly I don't want to be on the mountain anymore. I want to run back down as fast as I can and make sure Orbelle is still there, that it wasn't just wiped off the earth. But I can no longer see unless I use my torch and I know how stupid it is to attempt a descent in the dark. I could fall and hurt myself. Instead I lift my head firmly to the sky and watch the new lights that have replaced the ones below. I snap the metal disks in each heat pack and slide down beneath the blankets so only my nose and eyes can feel the immediate chill. Here I wait, for what seems like an age, staring up at the stars. With nothing else visible around me, I'm caught in a void between these stars and the ones on the other side of the planet.

7

Nothing's happening. I feel disappointed, stupid and frightened all at once. I could've watched the meteor shower from my hill, it wouldn't have been as adventurous but I would've been safe and able to ask why the power has gone out. I wonder if my mother has noticed. Unless she was listening to the radio, it's unlikely.

In the last hour or so of waiting, the power hasn't come back on. Orbelle is still in complete darkness. It must be within the early hours of the morning. My eyes are feeling weary. Anna was the clever one. The most I'll bring away from tonight is frost bite.

Then the mountain roars.

The next thing I know Orbelle is lit up beneath me. Not by its own lamps or windows, but by a white light that arrives so quickly and unannounced I barely have time to grab my camera and stand before I'm rewarded for all my hours of waiting. I can't believe what I'm seeing with my own eyes.

A meteor bigger than anything I could've imagined passes over the mountain so close and fast I hold the camera low, desperate to record the sight in my own memory. All the while my finger repeatedly hits the shutter button.

Its speed and ferocity is like nothing I've ever heard described in articles. As the white light subsides, I realise it's going to hit the earth. I force the camera to follow its flaming tail as it sails out of sight. I picked the wrong side of the mountain to witness the impact, but I hear the sound of something hitting the ground and forming a crater I know I'll be dragging Anna to find tomorrow. I didn't just see a shower; I saw something huge actually make contact with earth. I start to whoop and cheer, regardless if anyone can hear me. What I just witnessed was more incredible than I ever imagined.

I'm so eager to get back and develop the photographs I begin my descent at once. I've not slept and there's only the faintest shred of light as I climb down over rocks and slopes. The power may not be up and running yet, but I'm sure it will be by the time I reach the chairlift. I'm in such a good mood I'm sure I'll share my story with the first person I see.

I don't make it as far as the chairlift. I'm making my way down one of the flatter slopes, my ankles deep in snow, when I think I hear something. A hoot, a cry. I'm not sure. I stand perfectly still and wait to see if it happens again. Instead, a second noise rips through the air. I turn my head. I could swear I just heard a gunshot. But what I see behind me is more terrifying than a gunman.

An ocean made of ice is gushing down the mountainside.

Its foamy breath is hard and a hundred white horses appear to be thundering towards me. They gather speed, crashing into trees and smothering rocks. I suddenly realise exactly what I'm facing. I don't even have time to start running properly before a wall of snow hits the back of my legs and throws me at an odd angle, limbs flailing. My head goes under and I don't resurface. I feel the avalanche swallow, sending me backwards into its icy belly and consuming me whole.

My scream is silenced.

I remain awake the entire time, and now the movement has stopped. But I'm still waiting for the nightmare to end. Everything is dark. I can't move my limbs and I'm panicking. My breathing is far too fast and I know that'll only make the situation worse. The harder I breathe the more oxygen I'll use and I've no idea how much time I have.

The first thing I do is wriggle. My father told me to always make an air pocket if you are submerged in snow. I shift my shoulders and turn my head from side to side. The snow moves a little and my nose carves a groove large enough for me to practise another snippet of old advice.

I suck saliva into the front of my mouth and spit as hard as I can. The warm spit slops back on to my face and trickles down my lips, but I'm pleased. Whilst buried under snow, I can't be sure which way I'm facing, but gravity has enlightened me. I know I'm facing up and can concentrate on determining just how deep I am. To my delight, I find I was able to clutch my stick throughout the ordeal. I use it as an upwards probe, wriggling constantly. To my surprise, it soon wobbles freely and I realise I'm not as far under the snow as I thought.

I keep the stick moving and shunt my body forwards, desperate to taste cold air. All of a sudden it rushes at me and I'm spitting snow away from my mouth.

"Get up," someone says urgently.

I realise I've been pulled out of the snow by someone with a sharp, male voice. I don't move right away, so he takes me by the arm and hoists. I try to use my stick to steady myself, but it's wrenched from my hand and thrown far to the side. I'm left trembling and facing someone I can't even see. When a bright red light suddenly shines, I'm shocked to find it pointing at my chest.

"Put your hands where I can see them and don't move."

I realise I'm in an even more dire situation than before. My earlier thoughts of a gunman seem all too real and, as my eyes adjust, I see I'm staring into the barrel of a rifle.

"Identification and WOLF code," he demands.

Now the cold and exhaustion takes over my entire body. I feel overwhelmed, as though my every muscle has been bruised. I've just enough time to say: "WOLF 035, Snake F . . . Linnea Hansen" before I stumble backwards into the icy coffin I just managed to get out of.

"Hey," a distant voice calls to me. "Hey, you can't pass out. Come on, you've got to get up."

He sits me up against a tree. My arms are being lightly shaken, as though he's trying to get a television to work. This time I can just about see the outline of his body. He's not quite as big as I thought he'd be. What's more, he's placed his rifle over his shoulder and seems more interested in keeping me alive than shooting me.

“Who are you?” My voice comes out as a groan and he scrabbles for his gun as though he considers me the greater threat. This must be the person Hans saw on our hill.

“That’s none of your concern,” he says, as though I have a nerve to ask.

“You just saved me.”

Despite the gun he had pointed at me, I know gratitude is due and perhaps it would do me a favour to show it.

“You fired a warning, didn’t you?” I persist. “When I didn’t see the avalanche coming. Then you helped dig me out. Thank you.”

He pauses, taking in my sincerity.

“Can you stand up?”

“I’ll try.”

I heave myself upright and he steps back, keeping the gun fixed on my chest. It actually starts to annoy me. If he wanted to shoot me then he’s had plenty of time to do it. I note he’s stripped me of my backpack and walking stick, which I could really do with now.

Despite my weariness, I find my eyes have adjusted enough to note several new things about this arrival. For one, he's not much taller than me – although well built in the arms – and for another, he's wearing a uniform that gives him immediate distinction. I can't see his lenses, but I know he is a WOLF X recruit.

"Keep your head still, kid," he instructs.

I predict what's coming next, as a flickering red line appears and passes over my eyes. It almost blinds me, but I don't move as the laser identifies my WOLF code. I have to blink a couple of times to stop seeing a pair of cherry red spots. Then I can look at him again.

I'm not good at identifying any modern weaponry, but the gun he's carrying looks like a scarier version of my father's old rifle. I couldn't even begin to name the various modifications this equipment has gone through. On top of the scope is where the tiny laser was emitted, although it's no longer shining. He's still staring into the scope, which I assume is where he can see its reading.

"What did you say your name was again?"

"Linnea Hansen."

"Linnea." He lowers the gun slightly. "I have one or two questions for you."

Of course his first question is predictable.

"What're you doing up here?"

"Meteor," I say woozily, leaning back against the tree.

"I don't know who that is," he says. "There's no one living this far up here."

"No," I explain. "A meteor shower. It was scheduled to appear tonight. You must have seen it. There's no way you couldn't have."

He stops to think for a moment.

"So you're involved with space and astronomical forecasts for the defence ministry," he concludes. There's a tone in his voice I don't like and I notice the gun is being re-angled, where it'd dropped before. His words almost sound like an accusation.

"What?" I frown. "I've no idea what that is."

"No? Then what are you exactly?"

"I'm a goat herder."

The sudden silence is broken by laughter. He may not believe me, since the gun is still pointed at my heart, but he finds my claim hilarious. He actually has quite a jolly laugh.

"Of course you are."

"It's true," I insist. "Look into my lenses and I'll tell you again."

"We don't follow those rules," he says. "WOLF lenses are more deceitful than insightful."

That's the first time I've ever heard someone say that. It gives me food for thought as he considers what to do with me next.

"So if I look in your backpack, what can I expect to find?"

"You didn't already look?" I'm surprised. Clearly when I fainted his only concern was reviving me again. Otherwise he might've used that time to inspect my belongings.

He doesn't respond and bends down to open my pack. He picks it up from the bottom and its contents spill on to the snow.

"Please don't mess up my charts." I can't bear the thought of snow touching the paper. His torch flies over wads of printed out information and dates about meteor showers, including a drawing I made. I'm confident this'll back up my claim.

“I’ve told you who I am,” I say firmly. “Are you going to tell me who you are now?”

The sun finally breaks over the horizon. He lifts a hand over his eyes, shrouding his face from the glare. All I can see is a military uniform and an Adam’s apple. Slowly he lowers his hand and I step aside so I’m not just a silhouette against a bright backdrop. We look at each other and his irises dilate. He’s clearly just as shocked as I am.

He can’t be any older than me. His hair is golden brown, not blonde like mine, but dark and rich. His eyebrows are darker still. He has a single scar on his bottom lip. Like most WOLF X recruits, his appearance is tidy and poised. He stands tall, especially when he sees my face for the first time. He gives me the once over and I see his mouth twitch into a smile. I’m clearly no threat. I’m wearing more wool than a llama and my hair is falling out of its braid. I start to feel sorry for myself. I’m cold and confused and without any means to defend myself.

He bends down and picks up my stick, handing it out.

“WOLF X23, Dragon M,” he says.

“Who’s that when he’s at home?”

Dragon M. I was right; he may not even be a year older than me. The dragon is the year after the snake.

He grins at me. It's a strange feeling, because I'm not sure what I'm doing to deserve it.

"I'm Joel."

"Thanks for the warning shot, Joel."

He nods and lets me assemble myself. Even when we take just a few steps, we move in a circle, not sure what to make of each other.

This can't be the person Hans saw on our hill. He's too young; and that's not a pistol he's carrying. He's a city boy, I expect. He may be holding a weapon and wearing a uniform, but, apart from the scar on his lip, he has tweaked and altered his appearance the way the rest of the city people do. He holds his rifle with smooth, un-calloused hands. He doesn't look like the sort for hard labour. He has the kind of appearance better suited to negotiating business and charming people. He has the twinkling eyes of someone confident of getting their own way. He pulls this off without even using his lenses, which I notice are a light brown, like two cups of tea.

I know not to trust his lenses entirely. WOLF X can control their lenses at will. According to Hans, they're defaulted to turn red when threatened, even when the wearer is petrified and they ought to be saffron yellow. Perhaps Joel is deliberately manipulating his lenses so I can't read him. Brown is the most neutral colour on the WOLF charts and Joel seems to have perfected the art of not letting his lenses show unnecessary emotion. He lets the muscles in his face talk for him, smiling and lifting eyebrows. I amuse him; that much is perfectly clear.

"So where did you come from?" I ask. "You're overdressed for star-gazing."

"And you're under armed for a night on the mountain," he replies. "You know wolves are spotted around this region?"

"Is that what you're doing? Patrolling the area?"

He contemplates for a moment, although his eyes don't change colour. "I'm patrolling the area, yeah. Lucky for you, I'm the only person this side of the mountain and happened to spot you."

"Then you're here to protect people, not shoot them?"

"Of course."

"So then why-?" I refer back to the gun pointing at me. His lenses do change now; the brown fades slightly. He doesn't seem to like this question.

"Precaution," he says. "It's unusual for someone to be up here on the mountain like this. I'm trained to respond in such circumstances. I wasn't expecting to meet a star-gazing shepherd at this time. Sorry for startling you."

"That's okay."

I'm pleased there will be no more brushing noses with guns. Joel plants the gun down by his side, holding the barrel away from us both. He's still staring at me intensely, as though something just occurred to him.

"Where're you from?" he asks.

"Orbelle," I say. "I'm heading back there now."

"You're heading back to Orbelle," he repeats slowly.

This isn't a parting of ways. I can tell by his face something is wrong.

"The chairlifts aren't operating. The power's out. I'll escort you back."

I guess the chairlift stopped when Orbelle's lights went out. It's a good thing Anna left when she did. I stare at him;

this boy I don't know, and wonder where this sudden gentleman came from. He keeps a moderate distance from me, keeps the gun pointed away and his voice is sincere.

"Oh." I suppose it can't hurt. He's WOLF X, after all. No one's military is better renowned than those associated with WOLF. "Okay. Thank you."

I've never interacted with a WOLF X recruit before. I feel both nervous and exhilarated as he motions for us to walk together. I can't help but want to look across at him, but every time I do I see he's watching me with the same expression.

He asks me about my interest in astronomy and about my WOLF 03 lenses, but he seems particularly interested in my occupation. I wonder if he's mocking me when he asks about my goats and what we do all day; but he does seem to find the answers genuinely interesting.

"So you're WOLF X." I decide to turn the questions back on him. "What does that mean?"

"It means I'm very secretive and the one holding a gun," he says. But he's grinning and I find his mannerisms oddly contagious. When I smile back, it seems to encourage him.

"Is it true you can see in the dark?"

"Our lenses are equipped with night vision technology," he confirms.

"That's how you knew I was there, isn't it? You were watching me?"

He doesn't reply, so I think of a new question I've always wanted answered. "They turn red on command, but never yellow because yellow means fear?"

"That's right."

"You can take photographic images and send them back to base?"

"They're working on it." He cocks his head in amusement. "Who tells you these things?"

"Our herdsman," I say. "I think he secretly fantasised about being a WOLF X recruit. But he hates the city and doesn't take well to people outside of Orbelle. A lot of people struggle to understand his accent anyway. He's of old descent."

"Like you?"

"No, we moved when my mother was pregnant with me, for her health. She took part in WOLF experimentation and it made me type 03."

Why am I telling him this? It's not his business and can't be of any interest. But apparently it is. He turns his face to stare at me.

"That explains why you're accent is muddled. I guess you're special then, being WOLF 03. I'm a typical WOLF 01 when I'm not on duty."

Special. That's the kind of thing Dr Frost would say.

"I don't feel special when they're drowning my eyes with serums and lasers."

He laughs. Once again I acknowledge how jolly it is.

"Aren't we all supposed to bow down in gratitude to WOLF?" he says.

"I don't know, are we? You're the one who works for them."

This silences us both to the point where neither speaks for a while. He's thinking about what I just said and I'm wondering if my mother will have learned of my absence by now. As soon as her radio stops working she will notice a power cut and attempt to contact me or Hans. I can see the chairlift station, we're almost at the place Anna and I parted ways.

“Maybe the chairlifts are working now,” I say.

“No,” he says simply. “They’re not working. I’ll walk you down, it’s not a problem.”

His lenses must include something that lets him focus on things much clearer. I can’t see if the chairlift is operating or not, but apparently he can. In fact, I struggle to see the chairlift clearly at all. It must be the dim light of morning and I’m still shaken by the avalanche. Everything feels hazy.

“Oh.” I hesitate. This will lengthen my journey more than I expected but I suppose I’m glad to have someone armed walk me the whole way back. It’s like having a personal bodyguard. Anna would be kicking herself right now if she knew she’d missed out on a WOLF X recruit escorting her home. He’s not typically handsome by Anna’s standards, but that doesn’t matter. He’s wearing the uniform and holding a gun.

“That’s very kind of you.” I lead the way. Since we won’t need the chair lift, we can bypass it altogether and set off down a different route. When he helps me down from a rock, he lets me jump with both hands on his shoulders. I realise he’s staring at my eyes the whole time. Something about WOLF 03 must really interest him.

"Are you trying to read my thoughts?" I ask.

"Huh? Oh. Yeah." He looks away. "Sorry, force of habit."

His are still a neutral brown, which is annoying but also challenging. I'm learning what makes him laugh, makes him quiet, and what topics he prefers to discuss. Strangely, he prefers talking about me.

"So do you come up the mountain often?" he asks.

"Not really. Only during avalanche season."

"Ah," he says seriously.

Avalanche season; I made that up. Surely if he patrols the mountain then he knows that? I don't say anything, but I'm wishing I could read something other than brown. I look one more time, only to see he's already staring into my eyes again. It starts to unsettle me the further we walk.

There's no informative colour in his lenses, but I can read the look on his face. It's a mixture of concern, angst and intrigue. Like he knows something I don't. And he fears the moment I'll discover whatever that something is.

8

We walk over several small hills and begin our final descent into Orbelle. I can see the hanging baskets, the short fences and the many brick chimneys. Yet something's troubling me.

"Which one is your house?" Joel asks.

"That one." I point up the hill.

"Where are your goats?"

"I don't know."

They're not on the hill. Did Hans take them off somewhere? Perhaps the other side of the ranch? I start to feel anxious. Not simply because my goats aren't to be seen. Something else.

"I don't know where anyone is."

We walk in near silence. I listen to wind-chimes and distant birds. But there's no other sound. No one's outside, and I can't see anyone through their windows. It's as though everyone has vanished. I also realise everything appears to be dull and distant. My lenses don't focus on things and bring objects forward when I look at them. The sun is in the sky now, the grey fog of early dawn is over. Everything should be alive. Everything should be vibrant. But it isn't. Something's wrong and I don't know if it's the town or me. Eventually I break into a run.

"Wait!" Joel holds his rifle in both hands and takes after me, up the hill. I don't stop until I'm on my front porch. I hit the bell to announce my arrival, even though there is no point. I know she's not here.

"She's gone. They're all gone." I place a hand on my forehead and try not to panic. I run between the kitchen and our bedrooms until I'm back in the hall. Joel's silhouetted figure is standing in the doorway.

"No one's here," I say.

He doesn't respond. He just steps into the house properly and has a good look around out of his own curiosity. There are pictures of me at various ages across the wall and they attract his interest.

"Did she take anything with her?"

It's a fair question. I've been too busy fearing she'd been abducted, but now I do a second check in all the rooms. It's only when I enter my own room again I pay close attention to what's on my bed.

Although I'm currently wearing my bag, it's clear what's assembled here was supposed to be packed. A small collection of clothes, tooth and hair brushes and a juice carton. It's all here waiting for me. I just wasn't here to take it.

“Television and radio aren’t working.” Joel steps into my bedroom. “Neither is the phone. Are you all right?”

“She packed for me.” I feel nauseated. “I was supposed to go with them. What do you think happened?”

“We should go,” Joel says. “Do you have a spare change of clothes?”

“Of course I do. If you’ll leave me alone for one minute.”

“I meant for me.”

I’m not sure why he would opt for new clothes over his uniform but I tell him only women live here and request some privacy. When he’s gone, I reorganise my backpack and try my best not to explode with worry and guilt.

I walk to the bathroom and run the cold tap, splashing water over my face and washing away any traces of snow and dirt. I look up to see my hair is a mess and my eyes are welling up. It takes longer to focus than normal. I freeze.

I was expecting to see honeyed yellow or greasy black – the colours of distress – but my own irises stare back at me. Natural flakes of tarnished gold, pecan brown and olive green. It’s like my irises have been caramelised. I hardly recognise them. I blink rapidly, hoping it will somehow wake them up. But they remain inert.

For the first time in my life my WOLF lenses have stopped working.

Joel comes in so quietly I barely notice until he speaks.

"I'm sorry," he says. I'm not sure what he's apologising for exactly. Then I recall he kept looking into my eyes whilst we were walking here. "It's just I've never seen hazel eyes before. They're quite interesting."

No, I don't suppose he would have. I keep looking at objects, waiting for the images to define themselves. To see my reflection in every droplet of water. The individual flakes of dust that hang in the air. Nothing happens. This isn't as nice as I would have hoped. Everything feels dull and different. I feel tears pricking my eyes, but I mustn't cry.

"The television, radio and phone are all dead," Joel repeats calmly. "Whatever's affecting them has obviously affected your lenses. I guess they've all evacuated for some reason, so you should get your things together as quick as you can. Don't worry, you're with me."

I swallow hard. I hardly know Joel well enough for him to be of comfort to me. For a brief moment I feel like telling him I'll be fine and he may leave. I can make my own plan. But my plans haven't been working lately. I gather my things and we assemble by the front door.

I've opted for a white blouse with bright yellow flowers stitched into the collar. It belonged to my mother when she was my age. I've picked one of Anna's long, burgundy skirts and a belt she gave me, in hope it will make me look more up-to-date with city fashion. I'm slimmer than Anna and pull the belt tight, exposing a few worn-out notches I never had to use. I'll keep warm with a knitted scarf, two pairs of woollen tights and a coat. Joel looks me up and down in his uniform. The contrast between us is almost comical.

"I don't want to go wandering to the city like this."

I want to ask why, but instead I hoist my backpack on to my shoulders and walk on.

"We'll stop by Hans' house," I say. "I want to check things out there and he'll have stuff you can wear. He's taller than you, but his stuff is more your age."

Our age. He's only a dragon, that's a matter of months. But he has stepped out from a different time. A technologically advanced time. Now my lenses have stopped, I'm nothing but flesh and fabric.

As we set off back down the hill, I turn to Joel and my questions pour out at once. Where did they all go? Why are we going to the city?

"Seems most likely that's where they'll be," Joel says. "We'll go to WOLF HQ. That's your check-in station. You can have them track your mother's lenses for you."

"No I can't. She's blind."

"What? Since when?"

"Since about two years." Somehow that never managed to come up in conversation and Joel looks astounded.

"Did WOLF do that to her?"

I nod, not wanting to go into the whole story. We have more pressing matters at hand.

"Well." Joel rethinks. "You can track this Hans bloke and he'll probably tell you where she is."

Good idea. Hans is my best option now.

The house is empty, as I expected. The back door is open. We push it forward and let ourselves in. I enter Hans' room for the first time by myself. Without asking, Joel opens the chest of drawers and begins rooting for shirts. I almost scold him but what's the point?

I wander back into the living room and kitchen to see if there is any clue as to where he went. The place is a mess. The dustbin has been knocked over, the tablecloth has been pulled, and the floor is smeared with mud and something that makes me stop in my tracks.

"Did this guy fancy himself as a bit of a biker?" Joel emerges in one of Hans' jackets and shirts. He notices the look on my face and we stare at each other for a moment.

"Where's your rifle?" I ask.

"It's . . . why?"

I point to the floor. There are inauspicious paw prints everywhere.

"I'm guessing this guy doesn't have a dog?"

"No."

We soundlessly edge back into Hans' bedroom and Joel picks up his weapon. I drop on to all fours and retrieve a rifle hidden under the bed. Hans told me he kept it there in case of intruders. Joel closes the bedroom door and we sit on the bed, preparing.

"I wasn't planning on giving anyone a shooting lesson today. You're a ranch girl; you know how to fire one of these, right?"

"I have fired one. But that was . . ."

"Oh, don't tell me. At tin cans. And most of them you missed."

I don't answer. Hans and I were going to start practising when I came back from the mountain. After a quick de-brief, we rise off the bed and discuss what little plan we have.

"We're going to walk to WOLF HQ," Joel says. "We'll follow the train tracks. It's the most direct route and I doubt anything will be running right now. It might take a day or two, so we'll grab whatever this guy has in his cupboards and get going."

“You’re going to come with me?” Somehow I still can’t accept the sudden companionship.

“Yeah. I can’t exactly go back.”

I don’t ask why. I have a feeling Joel was anxious to get out of his uniform for a reason and it had nothing to do with fashion. I’m not going to question him though. He has a military weapon, WOLF X lenses and most importantly a plan. I have an old rifle, redundant lenses and a bag full of astronomy charts and clean underwear. Right now I need him and his military training.

We leave the house and Joel beckons me out on to the porch with him. We stand for a moment, gazing down the street with rifles in hand. He closes the door behind him with his boot and positions himself in front of me.

There are no signs of life, welcome or not. We still stick to each other’s side as we walk down the steps, until Joel throws a hand up so sharply he almost hits me in the nose. His head is poised to listen. Something is making a sound nearby. The more I listen, the more my heart begins to pound. I know that sound.

The noise we hear is a low jingle, like a milk bottle rattling in a crate. I’m about to tell Joel not to worry, when an animal comes out on to the path and Joel pushes me back on to the porch. I could chuckle. What I see is hardly cause for alarm. But closer inspection through the railings makes me anxious.

"It's a goat," Joel says, as if I would never have guessed otherwise.

"It's one of my goats," I say.

It's O'Malley, and he's severely hurt.

"Does he always walk like that?"

O'Malley is limping so badly, I know at once the situation is helpless. One shoulder has all but collapsed and he has to drag himself.

"He's beyond help," I say dismally.

"Don't you need a crook or something?"

"I don't need one for him. He'll come to me if I call him."

"Why don't you do it?" Joel looks amused at the idea, as if I'm going to tip my head back and yodel.

"Quiet."

Thank goodness he can recognise a serious command when he hears one. I add: "Something's not right. He's been attacked."

I pick up Hans' rifle and stand. O'Malley is bleating pitifully and it enters my mind to call out and beckon him over to where I'm hiding. But then he hops around, clumsily, and I get a proper look at one of his hind legs. His injuries would be considered too bad to bother calling a vet out to the ranch. In fact, there's a very simple way we deal with an animal in this much pain. As much as I would rather not involve myself, I don't want this target moving any closer to us.

I lift the rifle, causing Joel to almost cry out in alarm. He clearly thinks I've gone mad as I adjust myself. I pray my aim is better than when I last practised. But Joel stands, places a hand over my arm and pushes it down. I look at him warningly, then realise he's offering to take out the poor creature himself.

This seems to make a lot more sense. At least, this way, I won't have to watch.

"Oh god." Joel ducks down beside me.

I turn my head to watch through the wooden railings. A wolf appears on the footpath and all my childhood fears collect my throat so I can't speak. I've never seen one, I only heard about them through Hans and my father. My mother preferred to make out they didn't live on Mt Venus at all. She hoped I would sleep better if I believed that. But this one is very real and it circles O'Malley and snaps at his legs. It's a young wolf, perhaps not so skilled at hunting. O'Malley bleats in distress as the wolf antagonises him.

"Shoot him," I beg in a whisper.

"He's too busy moving."

"Not the wolf, my goat," I say. "He's taunting my goat."

"I'd rather shoot the wolf, to be honest. Before it knows we're here."

I find the wolf too frightening to think it can be killed as easily as a goat. My father would let me shoot an injured goat, I'm sure, but he always told me to flee from a wolf. Without my father, or Hans, I don't even consider the idea we can kill the wolf ourselves. But I'm sure Joel can. His rifle is far more superior to my father's. I ought to trust him and let him take control.

Finally, the wolf goes for O'Malley's throat. I put my fingers in my ears to drown out the sound. Joel is sympathetic. He doesn't disturb me until the goat is dead and I can turn around. When he does, he puts a hand on my shoulder and squeezes lightly.

The wolf stands over a fresh kill with a glistening snout. We clutch our rifles and nod at each other. It goes without saying this animal needs to be destroyed before it finds us here. But just as Joel starts to move, the wolf tips its head back and howls. I grab Joel's trouser leg to pull him back down.

Joel ignores me and lifts his rifle. He takes aim and fires once, sending an echo between the empty houses. He shoots again and I hear the wolf snarl. Joel has either repeatedly missed or is having little effect.

"Damn." He steps back.

Although he's a WOLF X recruit, I find myself panicking as I realise Joel is our main means of defence. If he fails then we'll both get hurt. My courage hangs by a thread and then as he swears once more under his breath it snaps completely. I can't stay on the porch. I stand and run for the front door of the house. I hold Hans' rifle in my hands as I dart around Joel, but it feels like I might be holding an umbrella for all the harm I think I could do.

The wolf no longer considers Joel a threat, since he has failed to kill it too many times. It looks at him as an equal opponent and bares its teeth. Every puncture wound in its fur is bleeding a vibrant red. The colour we're naturally raised to fear.

Red means aggression.

Red means to attack.

There's red all over the wolf's face and body.

Red spits from his teeth when he snarls. He sprints for the porch.

I almost toss Hans' rifle aside so I can open the door with both hands. I shout at Joel to follow me back into the house.

But he isn't prepared to run and lifts his gun to fire at a closer range. The wolf is meters from him. He'll surely kill it now.

Snap. Joel pulls the trigger and stares at his rifle in exasperation. "Oh god, no."

He's out of ammunition. He attempts to fire two more times. Nothing.

He hasn't given himself enough time to run. He barely lowers the gun before the wolf jumps up and is atop the wooden railings, its back legs pushing itself towards Joel. I open the front door but close it again, since Joel won't be able to follow me and can't fight it off alone. He lifts his rifle in both hands and wedges it beneath the wolf's throat, pushing its snapping jaws away from his body. The mutual effort on both parts locks them in place; Joel forcing the wolf away whilst the wolf keeps its back feet against the railings and stands as firm as it can. It wrestles against the rifle and Joel can't draw his gaze away to look for me.

"Get inside!" he shouts urgently. He won't be able to get out of this unharmed. I dither by the door for too long and Joel starts to shout again.

"Your rifle!" he gasps before using a huge surge of strength to heave the wolf off him. He sacrifices his grip on his rifle to do so, letting go with one hand as the wolf is pushed to his side, away from me. He hits the ground and backs away sharply, kicking the porch with his heels as the wolf repositions himself to attack Joel on all fours.

There's no point holding back now. I raise the rifle up to my face as the wolf lunges and fire once. Joel digs his face into the crook of his elbow to avoid the onslaught of teeth but the wolf drops. The sound of my shot echoes on the porch like a cracking whip as it hits the floor. It doesn't move again.

After catching our breaths, we peer at the entry wound weeping from above one of its eyes. As Joel stares at me I realise I killed it outright. I'm far too shocked to congratulate myself.

"Dear god," Joel says breathlessly. "I meant for you to throw me your rifle. Not fire it yourself. I thought you weren't any good?"

"And I thought you were," I reply.

Perhaps I'm being unfair. If Joel hadn't run out of ammunition I'm sure he would have been able to kill the wolf as it got closer. But that hardly matters now.

"We have to go," I say.

I'm already preparing the rifle as though I'll have to use it again. Joel is now staring at the wolf on the ground. I grab his arm.

"They hunt in packs," I say. "That howl was probably a call to others."

“What do we do if a load of them show up?” Joel asks. I send him a look to remind him of who he is. He’s holding a WOLF X weapon, after all, even if he can’t fire it.

“I haven’t really prepared for large-scale wolf attacks,” he says defensively.

“Neither have I.” I think of all the wolf encounters on the ranch. They’re incredibly rare. My father didn’t prepare me for one, let alone a pack. “We’ll just have to run for the station.”

“Right,” Joel says. “Well then, I guess I’m following you.”

9

He manages to let me lead whilst staying by my side the entire time. We hold our rifles down at parallel angles to each other and keep our gazes moving. Neither of us says a word until we've made it five minutes without any encounters. Then Joel asks a reasonable question.

"Why don't you prepare for them when they come so close to the town?"

"They don't. Not usually. They stick to the mountain and come down occasionally to look for food. I've never seen one so close. They must've quickly realised the town is deserted. With our livestock roaming the place it's easy to see why they dared to investigate. That or something has driven them into the town."

I think of all the conversations I've had with Hans about wolves. He always told me I never needed to worry.

"They'd better not get too comfortable," I mutter. "We'll be coming back."

Joel says nothing and is happy to lower his gun and peer ahead at the train station. We continue up the steps to the fence that separates our town from the rolling countryside.

I'm sure to bolt the gate behind us and we stand for a moment, as though waiting for something to pull up on the platform. As I expected, the information booth is empty.

"Try to buy a ticket from the machine." Joel looks around. "See if it accepts your money."

"Machine? We have a man who sits in the booth," I say. "And he's clearly not here."

"God this is creepy," Joel says. "This place is so outdated."

I know what he means. As unsettling as it is to see an entire town deserted, it's stranger still to be standing on a station platform that's barely changed in fifty years. It's easy to imagine the platform is lined with ghosts and we're the only people left alive.

Convinced no trains will be running, Joel hops down on to the tracks and takes my hand to lift me down. It's surprised us both we're still in each other's company. My mind is far too preoccupied to make conversation. Unfortunately, once Joel starts talking, he rarely stops. He does a circular turn as he walks, checking to see if we're still on our own. Joel does his circular turn so often I start to hum inside my head and imagine him doing a dance. He raises an eyebrow.

"What are you smirking at?"

"You. Do you think your rifle will stop an on-coming train?"

"No trains will be coming through here," Joel says. "As long as the power's out and the town's empty, nothing will be passing through."

"We might have been able to flag down a car though. Perhaps we should have stayed on the road."

"I don't think cars will be coming here either."

"Why? The town's probably been evacuated due to avalanche warnings, but that doesn't mean they won't send surveillance teams out. Someone's sure to be checking in on things."

"Perhaps, but this is the most direct route to the city. I say we continue this way. Off road."

"Sir." I mock-salute. I don't feel capable of arguing with him. The sooner we get to where people are the sooner I can be taken to WOLF HQ.

Joel shrugs heavily under Hans' jacket. I was right; it's too big for him. He catches me watching and strikes up conversation.

"So this Hans bloke is the herdsman and you're the goat girl?"

"Yes."

"And you also care for your mother on your own? How long did you say she's been blind?"

"She's been almost completely blind for about two years now." Why is my life so fascinating to city people? "I care for her as best as I can. I had to withdraw my university application to be with her."

"That's too bad. When did your parents split up?"

"What? They never split up."

"Oh, sorry." Joel scratches his nose. "My father left us when I was three. I just presumed. So when did your father die?"

"What?"

This time I stop walking and stare at him.

"Ah." Joel looks uncomfortable. "You said only women lived in your house. So unless your father sleeps outside with the goats . . ."

"My father's in the city. He's involved with law," I say strategically.

Usually that would be dull enough to change the subject. I realise, however, I've picked the wrong person in Joel. He looks even more interested.

"Really? My mother's a solicitor in the city. How's your father involved in law?"

"He broke it."

"Oh." Joel blinks. "What, he didn't pay the rent in time? Overcharged people for cheese? Got too many ranch . . . penalties?"

His waffling is almost too much to bear. It's actually satisfying to see his face fall.

"He killed someone."

"Oh, wow," he says. "Are you serious? They got him for Red Eye?"

"No, because he didn't do it on purpose. My father would never do that. WOLF proved it."

I dare Joel to say another word to agitate me, but instead he carries on walking as if I just told him something boring. I suppose he's WOLF X after all. A bit of Red Eye is something he's expected to deal with.

"Good old WOLF," he says quietly. I sense insincerity in his voice, but I don't question him. I want this conversation to end.

"So aren't they going to be looking for you?" I ask. "Whoever's in charge of you?"

"Perhaps," Joel says. "But I'm a big boy."

"Yeah, but surely your absence has been noted?"

"No doubt it has." Joel shrugs. "But should I have let you walk to Fenix by yourself? That wouldn't be very honourable of me, would it?"

"There isn't much honour in deserting your post either."

He turns around, his eyes darker than normal. Perhaps I've said too much. He considers his response for a moment and then his eyes turn brown again.

"Who says I've deserted anything? I was patrolling the area and decided to help a civilian."

Yes. Conveniently the night the power went out and the town was evacuated. He said himself he couldn't go back. Which suggests he is, or will be, in trouble. I daresay he regrets telling me that.

"You were patrolling the area during avalanche season?"

"That seems like the most appropriate season to be on patrol, don't you think?"

"Sure," I say slowly. "Except there is no avalanche season, I made that up."

His eyes widen.

"Of course, I knew that." He marches on, determined to change the subject. "So how long is your father locked up for?"

This appears to be a battle of words; our ammunition being touchy subjects. I start to swell, adamant to start questioning his duties again. Joel sighs. "Actually, don't answer that. I'm sure the amazing WOLF will have him out in no time."

He sounds almost sour, as though releasing my father would be a questionable decision. He looks back at me and grins. "Oh, look at you, all furious. Sorry, does your father's story irritate you?"

"No. You're irritating me."

He laughs. It makes his lenses glow pink like a rose. Surely WOLF X would discourage such a feminine colour in their lenses? Somehow Joel wears it well beneath his dark hair.

"Okay, I won't mention your father again. How about, in return, you stop questioning my duties and let me get on with my job?"

"Which is what exactly?"

"To get you back to your mother. And I was hoping to make you look less glum in the meantime. I'm not having much luck, am I? You country folk are more serious than I thought."

I smirk, but it's hard to stay angry when he's grinning like that.

"Don't take that as an insult," Joel says. "I find your outlook interesting. I couldn't do what you do. Don't you ever just want to scream? It's like you just pick up your crook and take your goats to graze and wait for meteor showers. It all sounds very sweet, but I can't say I believe it. I get that you're repressing yourself a little. Even without your lenses I can tell you teeter on the edge of sarcasm, but you hold back. You've trained yourself to be polite, haven't you? Come on, you must want to punch people."

I stare at him in disbelief. If there is anyone in the world I would want to punch right now he's the prime target.

"You think I'm stupid to just get on with everything?"

"Hey, calm down. I didn't say that. I don't think it's stupid. I think it's admirable. You have to care for your mother, wait for your father to get out of prison, keep the ranch going. All right so you have this Hans guy, but all the same, you just get on with it?"

I don't know what to say. I do get the feeling he is complimenting me somehow, but I can't appreciate it. It's like he's talking about someone else, not me.

"I don't do it all without feeling annoyed," I admit. "It's just hard to pinpoint that annoyance in one direction. One minute I hate WOLF for making my mother blind, the next I hate the trespasser who forced my father to shoot at him. But whatever I'm feeling I have to keep it to myself. I can't let my lenses show it. I can't let them get Amber readings from me. Not when we need that compensation money so badly."

I turn my face away from Joel and stare at the floor. When these thoughts are heavy on my mind I struggle to contain them. I even find myself angry my mother put herself forward for the experiments in the first place, although I understand WOLF offered money no struggling citizen could refuse. I feel irritable my father chose a ridiculously difficult career for us to undertake without him. I feel bitter each time I see Anna with her new shoes and mobile phone. A constant reminder I'm stuck in Orbelle, alone save for my goats and Hans.

I feel my cheeks burn.

"I've made you feel worse, haven't I?" Joel says.

"Well you're not making me feel better."

"Sorry."

I know he is. I guess that's why I can't stay angry with him. He's asking me questions no one has ever dared to ask before. I wonder if I should even feel a little flattered.

"That's okay," I say. "I do appreciate you coming with me. You didn't have to. You could've gone back."

"Well, you're not a bad person to have around. You can shoot wolves in the face. You should consider WOLF X when your father comes home. Maybe look into the defence side of things. Astronomical forecasts and so on. I think you'd be great at that. I'd recommend you to any recruitment agency."

Is he joking? I decide he isn't and smile inwardly. It raises my spirits for someone to think I have potential for anything other than Turtle Doves ML.

When the sun begins to set, Joel decides we should stop and get some sleep. He reasons neither of us had slept the night before, and he's right. My muscles ache and my eyes are weary.

Not far from the tracks is an open field used for livestock. We can't see any animals but the grass is trampled and tractor marks spoil the even surface of the land. It seems likely the animals here were recently moved. On the edge of the field is a solitary wooden barn.

"I expect people out here were given a bit more time to evacuate." Joel rests his rifle atop the stone wall, staring out at the field and assessing the barn. "So they'd have moved their livestock to fields further from avalanche warnings. I reckon they won't be back here until the people of Orbelle are allowed to return."

I glance back at the tracks and observe how far we've walked in one day. We're far from Orbelle now, but as the sun lowers I find myself feeling anxious. Wolves won't follow us along the train tracks but my eyesight is much poorer now and I don't want to rely on Joel's lenses when darkness falls over the countryside. I like to have my own wits about me. Things already appear to be darker than normal. I can't pick stars out of the sky or see as far into the gloom as I'm used to.

"So what do you think?" I ask. The answer is obvious; Joel is already bearing the weight of his upper body on the wall and preparing to push himself up. Even the flimsy wooden door of a barn is preferred to no door at all. We'll be shut away from most dangers if we can find a way into the barn and seal ourselves inside. Joel bounces on his toes a few times and then hoists himself up and over the wall. He extends a hand to help me follow.

I hesitate. We're separated now by a wall of stone and the division gives me a sudden need to reassess matters. He's holding his rifle, which is empty, and I hold Hans' to my side, remembering it was me who shot the wolf. Perhaps I'm more capable of caring for myself than I thought and if so, would it be wise to stay with someone I'm already suspicious of? He pulled me from the snow, which I appreciate, but wouldn't anyone else have done the same? What's more, I still don't know why he's here now. Do I really want to shut myself in a barn with him? I don't expect him to harm me at this point, but I do wonder about the people he's avoiding. What if he's being followed?

"What's up?" Joel peers over the wall. "Come on, it's not that high."

I put Hans' rifle on the wall and step back to take a small run-up. The rifle stays there a few moments by itself. Joel's hands reach for it and my breath catches. I suddenly feel panic rising in my chest. He's now holding the only working weapon we have. He only needs to ask for my backpack and he's equipped with food, lenses and ammunition. I don't know how to react. I'm sure I trust him not to hurt me – but am I really wise to do so? He pointed a gun at me before and I wasn't harmed. I don't want to walk to HQ hungry and alone though. Would he really do that to me? Have I given him any reason to do so? He looks up and sees my hesitation.

"Don't scuff your hands," Joel says. He places both rifles on the grass and removes Hans' jacket. He drapes the wall in leather and holds out his hands to help me over, leaving both weapons on the ground behind him. I pause for a moment, then dart at the wall with enough energy to heave myself over and land with his arms guiding me.

"Right." He grins. "Let's hope we can find a way in without damaging someone's property." He picks up his own rifle and leads the way. I clutch Hans' rifle and hide a smile. Now that I think about it, he has never proposed we switch. Even though he's military trained and I'm not, he's let me hold the only working weapon we have between us. If he's afraid of being pursued then surely he'd want to be the one completely in control? I follow him without a word.

10

The barn is tall, with one window high in the wood, just beneath the roof. Through it we can see wooden beams and cobwebs that hang like drapes. Everything else is sealed by the wooden planks used to create walls. The door would be hard to distinguish if it weren't for the metal knob and hinges. It's locked, as I suspected.

"I'm not sure we can reach the window," Joel says. "What're you doing?"

"Never mind the window." I'm foraging around the sides of the barn, rooting around scrap metal and grass. I kick over every stone and peer behind any loose plank of wood that's standing against the wall. I didn't expect to find anything on the ground, but it was worth a look. I straighten myself up and reach under the low rafters with my fingertips. I have to stand on my toes as my fingers brush spiders, dust and splintered pieces of wood. It's unpleasant but I run my hand up and down, searching.

"There's no house nearby," I explain as I go. "So unless the key is always kept in the same tractor . . . Ah!"

My fingers catch on a metal hook and guide me to what I'm looking for. I give a small jump to unhook it and produce the key. Joel makes a noise in his throat and looks impressed. As a small part of my triumph, I open the door and usher him inside like he's my guest. When the door bangs shut behind me, releasing dust and dirt into the air, we both exhale in acceptance. It's hardly the most homely of buildings. The floor is concrete, the walls adorned with farming equipment and the smell is thick with manure and rusting metal. The only clear floor space marks where a truck would have parked and there is a pool of dried oil in the centre. The window near the ceiling lets in a golden ray of light and any illusion of fresh air is contaminated with the dancing particles of dust we disturbed on our way in. My lungs feel thick with it already but at least we'll be safe in here. I lock the door and we both find positions on the floor to sleep. Joel keeps his back straight and his head resting on one of the walls. His gaze watches me as I lie on the concrete, wrapping my blanket around myself.

"Will you be counting?" he asks.

"What?"

"Sheep." Joel moves his finger in a half circle in the air. I realise he's pretending to make his fingertip jump over an invisible fence.

"No, I won't be counting sheep, thank you very much."

"Oh, right," he says. "You're into goats. Sorry."

That's not what I meant, and he knows it. But he's so amused by himself I just close my eyes and block him out.

I struggle to fall asleep. I lie there and listen to Joel breathing. He's a heavy breather and that would normally annoy me. But I'm glad to know he's still there without having to look.

When I open my eyes I see a lot of time has passed. The sky appears brighter through the window and Joel's chin has dropped further down his chest. He's still sat upright, his arms folded and his head down. With his eyes and mouth shut, I can look at him without being distracted. I can't see his WOLF X lenses or expect an off-hand remark. I look at the scar on his lip and wonder how he got it. His chest rises and falls gently. It's relaxing to watch. That's when I realise I've never seen a boy sleep before. I'd wake my father in the morning when I was younger, but that was different. Joel is different.

I shift to feel more comfortable and his eyes open slowly. He's alert, even to the slightest sound. For a moment we stay still. Then I smile, though I'm not sure why. I guess I'm just grateful he's here and can't find the words to say so. And he didn't take Hans' rifle away from me, like he might've done. He smiles back and I worry the first thing he'll say will be a joke. Instead he lifts his head and frowns.

"Are you all right?" I ask.

He nods, but I know he's listening for something. Then I hear a rumble from somewhere I can't pinpoint. It seems to be everywhere.

"Train!" I sit up and stare at the door. From what I can tell the tracks are hissing, as though something will come by in a matter of moments. But Joel isn't convinced and stands.

"That's not a train."

I'm still wrapped in my blanket from the chest down and I move my head from side to side like a periscope, listening for noise. Perhaps a tractor is on its way to the barn? When the sky suddenly lights up, I wrench a hand free and point.

"Joel, look!"

He follows my finger in astonishment as a light passes the window of the barn. It doesn't just light the window. Half the barn is illuminated. Every crack in the wood is filled with a piercing white light, as though we're being engulfed on one side. I grab the key and rush to the door. When I throw it open I cry out in alarm.

"Oh my god!" My voice is weak and feeble against the sight I see from the doorway. I feel like I've opened it to an entirely different countryside. For one thing, there were no sheep in this field before. Now they're running past the barn as fast as they can. A herd of cows squabble over by another section of stone wall, desperate to enter the field. They can't jump the wall but lift their heads and stomp their hooves in panic.

My body is bathed in the glow of white lights that tear through the clouds like claws. Giant meteorites streak over the grey morning sky. They're not far from us and when I feel the ground shake I know the first of them are already making impact with the earth around us.

"Get out." Joel shoves my back hard, so I'm forced out of the doorway. "Linnea, get out now."

He's holding my backpack and blanket and runs with his face upturned to the sky.

"Damn, it's late," he says. "It should've been the night before."

The night before? That was when I saw the first meteorite fall. Except it's different this time. This time I see one of the impacts as it hits, less than a mile away. The explosion is so loud I cover my ears and look down, as though the noise will hurt my face. After a few moments I look back and see the window of the barn has cracked. Another hit like that and the glass will shatter. This isn't nearly as exciting as it had been the night before. This time I'm terrified.

I follow Joel, even though I don't know where he expects us to go. When he suddenly stops running I collide with him and find myself being weighed down by the bag and blankets. He passes everything to me and starts sprinting back to the barn.

"Stay," he instructs.

"Joel?" I call after him. I don't know what to do without his guidance. Does he expect us to seek refuge in the barn again? If so, why would he tell me to stay behind?

"Our rifles are in there," he shouts.

I ignore his instructions, drop the blankets and run after him. I'm desperate for him to come back. I can't hear my own voice but it's as if I've conjured a meteorite and sent it in my scream's place. It sails over my head, towards Joel and misses him by no more than meters before hitting the side of the barn. The building bursts in a shower of wood and fire. From where I stand the wooden planks fall like bits of straw and glow like matches. One half of the roof caves in and the whole barn leans awkwardly over a burning wound. The wooden structure moans as though in pain. Whether he tripped or fell on purpose, Joel's body is on the floor and his hands are over his head, shielding him from the falling wood and flakes of fire caught in the air. He's sure to come back now.

"Joel, get up!" I beg.

He deftly lifts one leg into a kneeling position and rubs his arm. Perhaps the heat from the meteor burned his skin. But I'm wrong, he's not injured but waiting for a chance to enter the barn. Once he seems assured the building won't collapse he picks himself up and runs for the door again and disappears. I groan in dismay. Once his body has vanished I abandon him to his foolishness and decide to fend for myself. I grab my backpack and head for the stone wall. I can't stand to be out in the open and would rather crouch beside something – whether that be the right protocol for a meteor shower or not.

Once my body is pressed against stone I watch the rest of the meteors fall and wait to see if Joel will re-emerge from the barn. I can hardly breathe through my own panting and the adrenaline pumps through my body like fire itself. I'm both terrified and thrilled. I'm relieved when the barn door opens and Joel sprints back out with both rifles in his hands. He looks around for me and then runs for the wall.

This can't really be happening. I must be dreaming.

To the left the barn is burning. The barn we just slept in. I still have the key buried in my hand, piercing my skin and bruising my palm. To my right, high in the sky, I see more meteors descending on the countryside, some close, some miles away. And running straight towards me is a WOLF X recruit clutching the rifle I used yesterday to shoot a wolf dead.

"Why are you laughing?" Joel demands when he reaches me. "Are you hurt?"

"No, I'm fine." I stand up on shaking legs and take Hans' rifle. I can't imagine why Joel would think it was so important to go back for these.

"You're in shock." Joel grabs my waist and lifts me onto the wall. "Quickly. Follow the tracks."

I hop down and wait until he's over the wall. He grabs my wrist. Although we can't outrun the onslaught of meteorites, he pulls me with him. His hands are clammy yet firm. He won't let me go.

Joel spots a meteor headed towards us and stops. I run into his body and he wraps his arms around me tightly. I want to keep running but Joel stands firm. He keeps me in place and the blinding light passes overhead like a flaming bird.

Joel pulls me off the tracks as the meteorite hits. Judging by the noise made by the tracks, I assume it struck the path ahead. It sounds like two trains have collided on the track and the noise rumbles inside my head. I stand rigid, my gaze on the sky.

They look beautiful. Each sports a glowing tail. What I'm seeing doesn't seem real. I feel entranced, yet foolish. I wanted so much to see a meteor shower and now I wish to wake up in my bed at home.

"Hey, you're all right." Joel shakes my shoulder. His eyes are raven black and change between colours like pools of oil. I realise we haven't moved for some time. The rifles are wedged between us and I step back from his body to collect my thoughts.

The shower has subsided and everything seems oddly calm. Smoke trails paint the sky white overhead. My heart is in my mouth. Joel forces me to sit down and rest for a while. Eventually I feel a bit more normal and find my voice.

"That was incredible," I breathe.

"If you say so," Joel says. "But I don't like the thought of what'll happen to the next train they send through here. I think one of the meteors hit the tracks."

"Then we should pass it eventually." I open the palm of my hand and see the barn key is still eating at my flesh. I toss it to one side and feel the skin ache with relief. "Well, no one will need this anymore. Let's move on."

I look over my shoulder as we go and see the disaster we've narrowly escaped. The barn is still on fire and the sound of crackling wood carries over the field. Smoke fills the air and trees are aflame around the countryside. I can't count how many meteors must have struck. I try to forget the one that could've killed us inside the barn and keep my mind focused on the one that hit the tracks ahead.

It takes a while to reach the place of the impact. When we finally spot it we exchange looks and Joel whistles loudly.

The tracks have parted and severed. I pick my way around gingerly, not wanting to step on any metal. For some reason I fear it'll burn my shoes. But there's little sign of heat or smoke. Joel walks over the tracks in his boots and kicks aside splintered pieces of timber.

"Amazing." I look around at everything. "The rock itself couldn't have been as big as I thought."

"Still pretty frightening." Joel observes the twisted metal. He taps it with the toe of his boot and turns around. "Do you want a picture?"

"Oh, yeah." I remember the camera in my bag. I take it out of its case, excited and grateful Joel brought it up. I would've forgotten to capture this moment otherwise. I switch it on and back up, waiting for Joel to pose. Instead he cries out and covers his face.

"No, none of me," he insists, holding out the other hand. "I'll take them. We'll make sure you're in them."

I'm surprised by his reaction but we switch places. I hop on to the tracks and position myself in the middle of the destruction. I've no idea how to pose, so when Joel finds the angle he wants, I let him order me around.

"Come on, you just survived a meteor attack. You're the first person to be photographed here. Look like you're happy about it."

I start laughing. He's right; for all my years of waiting to witness something incredible I'm the first to have my picture taken on the broken track. I'm genuinely ecstatic. When Joel puts down the camera he shares in my excitement.

"Hey, look at this."

I expect more wreckage to photograph. Instead Joel kneels by the side of the tracks and peers at something covered in soil and debris. He doesn't want to touch it, so he uses his heel to dig it out and move it into view. I put my hand over my mouth.

"Joel, do you know what that is?"

I don't need to explain. It's obvious.

"Can I hold it, you think?" I kneel next to him and stare at the meteorite in amazement.

It's no bigger than an ostrich egg and bumpy, like a lump of coal. My hands hover over it, but I'm afraid to pick it up. Joel places the back of his hand as close to it as he dares and concludes it's not hot. He rolls it into his hand and holds it up for me to look at.

"It's beautiful." I reach out and touch its surface.

Perhaps I sound silly. It looks like a dirty mound of stone. I feel the need to explain.

"You know, this was probably part of a bigger asteroid or comet, orbiting the sun for millions, perhaps billions, of years." My fingertips run over its surface. "It's come all this way, broken up and burned through our atmosphere. Now you and I are the first people to hold it. It's the most amazing thing I've ever seen."

Whether I sound daft or not, Joel is smiling. He looks across the meteorite to my face, and his eyes start to glow.

"Oh!" I point. "Your eyes."

It's like electricity. Joel's pupils dilate within two orbs of emerald green. He blinks twice and then drops the meteorite.

“I don’t know what happened.” He looks dazed. His eyes immediately return to their neutral brown.

“Your lenses.” I retrieve the meteorite from the ground. “They reacted weird. You looked up and they were green.”

“Were they?” Joel looks amazed. Green is a rare colour in lenses. I’ve not seen green in real life for many years.

“Perhaps there’s something about this meteorite. We’re the first people to make contact with it.” I stare down in wonder. “Perhaps something about it made your lenses react.”

“Some sort of radioactivity?”

“It’s doubtful, I know. They’ve never been able to prove such a thing before. Maybe your lenses are just malfunctioning.”

“Malfunctioning?” Joel smirks. “WOLF X lenses? That’ll be the day.”

The same week avalanches bury me, my lenses stop working, wolves take over Orbelle and meteors fall from the sky. This week would be the perfect week for WOLF X lenses to malfunction.

I wrap the meteorite up and stuff it into my backpack.

“You’re taking it with you?” Joel asks.

“You bet. I’ve wanted to see one of these since forever. I’m claiming this.”

“Okay,” he says. “If you want the extra weight. I say we continue walking now. Even if they get the trains running, nothing can make it to the city now the line is damaged. Let’s keep going. We should be there tomorrow. Then we can find your mother.”

My mother. How will she react to everything I’ve done? But for now I enjoy the feeling. I’ve had my heart pound more times in the last two days than I ever have in my whole life. I’ve never felt as alive and happy as we walk together now. If my lenses were working, my eyes would be bluer than the morning sky, which is still streaked with fading star dust.

11

When WOLF lenses first initiate after being shut down, the sensation is nauseating. It's like two bees writhing in each socket. I put my face in my hands and make a noise as though I'll throw up.

Joel stops walking and waits until I draw my hands away.

"Ah," he says. "So we've officially crossed into a new area."

I don't know what he means at first, but then I realise my vision has drastically improved. In my backpack is a bag filled with serums and a compact mirror. I find the mirror and see my eyes are no longer hazel. When I look around, the world is restored to the vivacity I'm used to.

"Orbelle's lenses were down. Probably due to a satellite issue. I would bet it's because of the meteor shower," Joel says. "Let's have a look at you."

I stand still and let him position my face towards the sun. He pinches my wrist without warning and I yelp.

"Black. Great, they're working."

Joel doesn't sound pleased. If anything he sounds disappointed. I suppose he admitted he liked my hazel eyes.

Now it'll be harder to pretend his jokes are funny. I relish in being able to see everything clearly again. I can read signs that are far away, observe the different textures of the clouds and pinpoint every golden strand in Joel's otherwise dark hair. In fact, I can look at Joel again like an updated version of himself. I can see every freckle and every pore on his face. His scar is like a vein stretching across his bottom lip, which is otherwise smooth and pulsing with blood, turning them baby pink. My lenses accentuate every detail. He's not displeasing to look at. He suits his features and I enjoy looking at them with renewed vision.

He points ahead and I see the train line curves to the right.

"If we keep going this way, I reckon we'll be there in the morning. Told you everything would work out, didn't I? We've only been attacked by a wolf and giant balls of fire. It's been like school camping, wouldn't you say?"

I guess my eyes show the right shade of amusement, because Joel looks pleased.

"We're almost out of food," I remind him. "We haven't enough for tomorrow. We'll have to find a shop. There should be one nearby."

Orbelle is long behind us now. I'm expecting to hear traffic at any moment. The road isn't far from us and Joel agrees we can venture a little further from the train line to look for a petrol station. We don't have one in Orbelle and I have never needed to buy petrol, so I find them fascinating. My father would never come back from the kiosk without buying me a chocolate bar. It may comfort me to get one along the way.

We stay as adjacent to the road as we can without losing sight of the train tracks. Joel is still wary of traffic. If he thinks he hears something he will keep his head down. When a solitary vehicle pulls out from a distant junction, he ducks behind the hedge and advises I do the same. But instead of ducking, my heart leaps.

It's a camera crew. The first sign of life I've seen since Orbelle and it's heading this way. Joel grabs the cuff of my sleeve and pulls me down beside him.

"They can help us," I say.

"No," Joel says sternly. "No cameras, no television. They can't see us."

I'm crestfallen. The idea of riding in a van seems luxurious compared to what we've had so far. Surely if I announce myself as a missing evacuee they will help?

I stare at Joel resentfully, wishing he would explain himself. It's clear when he says they can't see us, he means they mustn't see him. A difficult prospect, since they pull up alongside the hedge.

The doors roll back and the crew assemble. Joel puts a finger to his lips. We're spectators, his eyes tell me. I feel like abandoning him. Running out with my arms waving and begging them to take me to where the rest of the evacuees are. But I don't. I watch and listen as the reporter stands straight and a man gets out beside her, flicking his floppy hair from his eyes.

"Oh my god." Joel's voice is hollow.

It's Cornelius Morgan.

Although I'm star-struck, I'm completely unprepared for Joel's reaction. He growls in his throat and I turn to see what bothers him.

I almost scream.

Joel's irises are turning a congealed blood colour.

Like he's bleeding from the pupils. I've never seen Red Eye up close in real life. It's too horrible to imagine. I don't know how to react. All I know is those eyes aren't meant for me.

He's staring directly at Cornelius Morgan and bringing his rifle up with both hands.

No! I want to cry out. He can't possibly shoot Cornelius Morgan from a hedge in the middle of a television appearance. Has he lost his mind?

"Joel!" I grab his arm. "They're filming."

"He's right there."

"You'll go to prison," I promise him. "We both will."

But Joel doesn't aim his rifle. He's out of ammunition and hasn't forgotten that – although for a moment I certainly had. I feel like I've been winded. I'm so relieved I put my head in my hands. Joel curses under his breath. I'm beginning to think he's gone mad. His eyes remain red like currants for the remainder of Morgan's television appearance. I can hardly stand to look at them.

The cameraman gets ready and calls out instructions.

"Okay, pink eyes Katherine. Think pink. And Mr Morgan – lilac please, if you would. Hold it there . . ." He adjusts the camera and tells Katherine her eyes are too watermelon. When her eyes are the colour he wants he offers a countdown for her to begin.

"A terrifying meteor shower has left several people injured, homes devastated and mobile networks wiped out when it entered our atmosphere this week. Footage taken by unsuspecting onlookers has been captured and shared with the world. This particular image was captured just outside Newton Belle . . ."

I'm guessing when they air this they will cut to a photograph on screen.

"But the shower was expected, and star-gazing enthusiasts were left disappointed by the delayed phenomenon. It was scheduled to arrive the evening prior. As this footage clearly shows, there was no need for telescopes or binoculars to witness what was to come. In fact, this particular meteor you see now seems quite impossible to miss. And filmed in this exact spot. Many onlookers have said they feared a plane was falling from the sky. All of this has occurred just a day after the town of Orbelle was evacuated."

"Cut to a shot of Orbelle deserted," the cameraman says. "Okay, now blue eyes, Katherine. On my count, look at Mr Morgan and turn blue."

"Of course, the most concerning aspect of this shower is the affect it could potentially have on the ALPHA satellite. With me now is Cornelius Morgan from WOLF HQ. Mr Morgan, I think the question a lot of us will have right now is: will any damage to the satellite be enough to affect WOLF lenses?"

"That's a good question," Morgan says calmly. "And the answer is no. Absolutely no faults or sudden changes can be expected. As you know, all lens information is received at WOLF HQ. Whilst the impact means there will be a slight backlog in our systems, it's nothing we're not prepared for and know how to handle. People can carry on as normal and be perfectly at ease. We've still got our eye on you, don't worry."

"Give me your rifle," Joel says under his breath. "He has to be taken out."

"What is wrong with you?"

Joel and I stare into each other's eyes. Both are hot with determination and I doubt I can overpower his stare. But I stand firm until he slumps to the ground. The television crew eventually board the van and drive off.

My fast-pass ticket to the city goes with them.

12

We stand properly as soon as they're out of sight.

"Linn, listen." Joel begins to speak, but his lips are silenced by my hand. I strike him across the face so hard his lenses turn black.

"You wanted to kill Cornelius Morgan!" I shout.

Why did I stay put? Why didn't I cry out? This boy is clearly mad and I opted to stay with him instead of joining people destined to reach the city in a few hours. What is happening to me?

"Wow," is all Joel can say. His left cheek is crimson. He can't seem to believe I hit him. He actually looks impressed.

"Stay away from me," I insist. "You don't have a working weapon anymore. I do. Stay away."

I break into a march, assembling my rifle in my hands. I still follow the train tracks but I feel more confused than ever before. More alone and frightened. I hear his footsteps following me.

"Are you deaf?" I turn around.

"No, but I'm sorry you had to see me like that."

Red Eye.

He wanted to kill someone.

Not hurt them, not protect himself like my father had. He had seriously intended to assassinate a celebrity.

"Why?" I demand. "Cornelius Morgan, of all people? You wanted to shoot him."

"Plenty of people want to shoot Cornelius Morgan."

"Not literally! People might want him to resign from television and get a haircut. No one actually wants him dead!"

"You're wrong," Joel says simply. "Look, I'm really sorry. Please don't think badly of me. I don't want you to think I'm something I'm not."

"I don't have a clue who you are."

"Come on, don't be like that."

"The system will find you," I say. "They'll pick up Red Eye and investigate."

"Or perhaps that's one of the perks of WOLF X. They're defaulted to turn red if we're scared, remember? They wouldn't waste their time investigating one of their own recruits. Even if they do detect Red Eye, as long as no one's dead they won't have to cover anything up in the media. They won't arrest me. That's one of my privileges at least and a good reason to stick around with me."

Joel attempts to flash one of his grins, but he looks desperate. He doesn't want to leave me yet, it seems. For whatever reason, he still wants to escort me to the city. I'm starting to figure out this isn't a case of wanting to help me move forward. It's a case of him not being able to go back.

"Why did you desert your position?" I ask.

He blinks in surprise. I give him a moment to think about his answer.

"I wanted to get you back to your mother."

"Liar."

Joel shrugs. I suspect there is some truth to what he says. He might not offer me the whole story, but whatever reason he had when he left, it's plausible I'm the reason he didn't change his mind and go back. He's run away from something and I suspect I just gave him an excuse to keep going. Something to help justify himself. If that theory's correct, then he needs me more than I need him.

"We get rid of these." I signal to both rifles. "Yours is useless now, and draws too much attention. No one around here would own something as jacked-up as that. And I'm not having you pinch mine. I don't want to carry it into the city anyway."

"Fine." Joel appears relieved my next plan still involves him. But he hasn't won me over just yet. One more flash of Red Eye and I'll do more than slap him across the face. We both know I'm a better shot than expected.

We light a fire not far from the train tracks. We can see the estuary and city lights ahead. The buildings are dark giants inked against a bronze and indigo backdrop. Dusk is usually my favourite time of day. When sunshine soaks through the leaves and turns them a fiery shade of gold. It's around now the first stars will be coming out. But I struggle to feel at peace after everything that's happened. Joel offers me tinned rice pudding and I take it with the curtest of thanks.

We've thrown our rifles into the water. I feel guilty, knowing it was never mine. I'll have to replace it when I face Hans. Joel has been unquestionably kind this evening, offering me food and drink. There's not been a trace of Red Eye in him since earlier and I find it hard to believe I actually saw it at all. We eat in moderate silence, unsure what to say.

"Linn," Joel says slowly. "I really do wish I could explain everything to you. But I can't. I'm WOLF X, you know. I'm supposed to be top secret. And you . . . you're this goat herder from Orbelle."

"You think I won't understand."

"It's not that. I don't think you *need* to understand. In fact I promise you. You don't need to know. I'd rather just focus on getting you back to your mother and your goats. I'll know then."

"Know what?"

"That I did something good," he says. "Even if it got me in trouble. What's going on right now, it shouldn't affect people like you and your mother. You did nothing wrong. I just want to get you back to her and then that part of my mind is clear."

"And Cornelius Morgan?"

"Again, I can't expect you to understand it."

"I might. You don't know. You said plenty of people wanted to shoot him. But he's a national treasure. Yes, he's a prat, but people love him."

"People don't know him," Joel sighs. "They see only what he wants them to see. All people ever see is what WOLF wants them to see."

They are more deceitful than insightful, I recall him saying. There's a long pause and the only sound is the fire crackling.

"Did you see what they did with their lenses?" Joel asks eventually. "That reporter and Cornelius Morgan."

"What do you mean?"

"*Turn them pink.*" Joel impersonates the cameraman. "*Not that pink, that's too watermelon. Okay, that's it. Perfect. Now hold it.*"

I suddenly realise something that had never occurred to me before.

"They can change the colour of their eyes on demand? Like WOLF X?"

"You bet," Joel says. "Anyone inside WOLF HQ can. That's how they control everything. Subtle, suggestive. It's all a show. Never make an enemy of them, too much Red Eye – or even just Amber – and they can have you shut away. If something was to prove a threat to them, it's too easy for them to put Red Eye on that person's record."

"They can't do that to someone."

"Of course they can. And they're perfectly capable of doing the opposite. Did you ever actually see your father's eyes when he shot that person? Where there actually any witnesses?"

I'm too shocked to speak. No wonder he looked so stern when I told him my father's conviction. If I understand right, he's saying someone might have done my father a favour. Erased the Red Eye from their database to give him a shorter sentence.

"So what you're saying is, even with the lenses you can't trust if you're looking at a person's true colours?"

"Of course you can't. I'm amazed you thought you could. I'm amazed anyone thinks they can. WOLF . . . they control our perception on everyday life. Who we vote into parliament by making people look more trustworthy, making advertisements more appealing by using blue-eyed actors . . . Colours influence us. The lenses manipulate us. We think we're seeing things for what they are, but we're not. It gets worse. Last year, over thirty homeless people were rounded up in Fenix alone and never seen again. WOLF persuaded people to believe they were a threat to society. One too many Amber readings. Heart-rate monitors were switched off prematurely, without giving people a chance to recover. They said their eyes were too far white to save them. Whatever cut-back Fenix wants to make, WOLF has a way of achieving it for them. And a lot of it is done through the mere art of suggestion. Most people don't even know they're being influenced."

I'm too horrified to respond. Although I know his suspicions about my father aren't true, the rest sounds disturbingly plausible.

"But they always told us how Fenix was before. How crime got too high, how as soon as the lenses came in, people couldn't do as many illegal things anymore. How can you support them if you think so badly of them?"

He looks up at me with one eyebrow raised. The fire continues to crackle, filling in what would have otherwise been a very potent silence. I'm not sure if Joel frightens me or enthrals me. Being in the presence of someone capable of killing without a second thought, and yet who is risking a great deal for me . . . it makes my pulse serge a little faster. I don't interrupt the silence. I let it linger whilst I think about everything Joel has told me.

When the sun starts to rise, Joel recommends we add everything we don't need to the fire. My bag's already open and I spy the mounds of paperwork under the meteorite. I pull it out, along with my clothes and camera, and hand it to Joel.

He takes the bag and I assemble my blankets. I only turn my head for a minute and there's a bang, followed by a scream of pain.

I turn around and see him buckling, one hand cupping the back of his leg and the other in a tight fist. I just blink at him. "What did you do?"

He doesn't answer. He's too busy yelling obscenities. I look back to the fire and the contents of my bag he's emptied on to it. Clearly he didn't inspect what he was tipping on to the flames.

"You idiot," I groan.

A few scrunched-up tissues and some old gun cartridges are resting on the fire. The tiny metal pins that serve as a trigger are still nestled in the base of each one.

I duck down in case more start firing.

“Who the heck trained you and said it’s okay to throw cartridges on an open fire?”

I get nothing but abuse thrown back at me. I creep over to where he’s attempting to collect himself. If it had been anywhere else on his body I would offer to be more helpful. Instead it’s all I can do not to start laughing.

“Oh very funny,” Joel growls.

“It’s not.” I try to compose myself. “Would you like me to look at it?”

He tells me to forget it and attempts to stand. He has blood on his hand, but the hole in his trousers is barely noticeable. If he wasn’t limping and swearing you wouldn’t know something had hit him.

“What the hell was it?” he asks through gritted teeth.

“Those were pinfire cartridges.”

“I know that,” Joel says. “I know about pinfire cartridges.”

“Clearly you don’t. Or you wouldn’t have chucked them on the fire. I do believe there’s a tiny metal pin in your leg.”

I can tell by the look of disbelief on his face he thought he’d been hit by something bigger. He sucks air through his teeth and attempts to stand tall.

“You’ll need it removed,” I say. “You know that, right? You need to have it looked at and treated.”

"Yeah," he says. I can tell he's really not looking forward to explaining this to other people.

We don't leave immediately. We let the fire burn out and gather our bags at his chosen speed. I find Joel a stick to walk with. It's initially too long, so I snap it across my knee and now it's too short. He's agitated and in pain, whilst I carry both our bags and try to keep a slow pace with him. He walks so awkwardly I can't help but take pity on him. I suggest we flag down a car.

"No," Joel says. "I'll be fine."

This makes no sense to me. We're near people who can help us; who can take us straight to WOLF HQ and a doctor. But Joel will have none of it.

"You're not wearing your uniform," I point out. "And you don't have your rifle anymore. People won't know you're WOLF X. They won't question you."

"It doesn't even hurt that much," he says. I don't need his lenses to tell me what a lie that is. They're watering enough for me to know he's in agony.

He's surprisingly resilient. He walks the length of the bridge over the estuary and continues on past the industrial outskirts of Fenix. I look back at the bridge and observe how smoky grey the water looks. It's a cloudy day but I can't help wondering if my lenses picked out the blue before and accentuated it. In fact, I'm not sure my lenses are working properly. None of the usual colours are popping out at me. I would ask Joel to look, but he's determined to keep walking forward. The only noise he makes is a hissing between his teeth.

We both know our way to HQ, so we keep our gaze ahead and make little conversation. Only when we have to climb some steps to the main road does Joel let me hoist him under the arm. I feel him tremble with each step.

When we reach the top Joel takes a moment to put a hand back on his leg. He removes it to reveal a fresh smear of blood on his palm. The blood is a sharp reminder of his lenses when faced with Cornelius Morgan.

It chills me to think this blood isn't nearly as red as that look in his eye.

13

I step up to the reception desk with Joel at my side. The sound I make reminds me of one of my goats bleating.

"I'm looking for my mother."

The receptionist wears lenses encircled with cream. She half smiles and proceeds as though I never spoke.

"Identification please."

I lean forward to have my lenses scanned and verified. She frowns and confirms my earlier suspicion.

"Your lenses are faulty. You'll probably need them recalibrated and checked over. We've had issues with lenses from certain areas. You must be from one of them. You'll have to tell me your WOLF identification code."

"WOLF 0315, Snake F. My name is Linnea Hansen."

She asks for my area code and occupation. I tell her I'm a goat herder from Orbelle, but I guess I'm technically unemployed now. And homeless.

She enters my details into the computer and large printing device whirrs into operation beside her. As it starts to print, she turns her attention to Joel.

"Identification?"

"I registered yesterday with one of your colleagues."

"I see."

She looks him up and down with pursed lips and then retrieves something from the printer. It's a white band with my details printed on it and she secures it to my wrist.

"This'll enable you to access our facilities. WOLF welcomes all refugees at this time."

"Where's my mother?" I say it louder.

"Oh, of course. Do you know her identification code?"

"She doesn't have one."

I'm met with a look of disbelief and almost annoyance. It forces me to act defensively. I don't have time for this computer nonsense.

"She's blind. She has no WOLF lenses. I don't know where she is, or who is looking after her."

The woman looks blankly at her screen. The computer is reliant on a WOLF code to proceed. Joel picks up on my distress.

"Just look for her name," he says. "If that doesn't work, surely you know how to use a telephone? Just do what you can."

It's an order and the receptionist knows it. Something about Joel forces her to abandon the senses she entrusted in her computer. She gets up from her chair, makes phone calls, and sifts through paperwork and folders. When she returns she looks disappointed for her efforts.

"I'm afraid we don't have an Eliza Hansen with us. Is there someone else we can search for? Another family member? Your father perhaps?"

"I know exactly where he is," I sigh. "There's no need for that."

Joel pokes my arm. "There is another. Your herdsman."

"Hans!" I say. "Hans Fotland. He's type 01, Tiger. I don't know anything more than that. Can you find him?"

"Is he a relative?" the receptionist asks. She's looking at her computer screen with renewed hope and begins to type in some details.

"No. An employee." I hope our efforts won't be thwarted by any confidentiality regulations. "He works for my father."

The receptionist tuts once and draws her hands away from the keypad. "The good news is: we did have a Hans Fotland check in with us. Unfortunately we don't have any record of where he went next."

"Can you tell us where most of the other refugees have gone?" Joel asks.

"They've all gone to stay with relatives or at refuges, which are all over the county. WOLF HQ serves as a check-in station but they've all moved on since. It's been a little while since Orbelle was evacuated. I'm afraid Mr Fotland hasn't left any information about his next move. No refuge known to us anyway. So I can only presume he's gone to stay with relatives."

So no one from Orbelle remains at HQ and no one knows where Hans has gone. I had been so certain someone would be waiting for me. I step back from the desk and sigh heavily. The receptionist seems to realise Joel and I must have had quite a journey on foot. She's about to start asking questions when Joel takes my arm.

"We'll be back," he says. "This one needs a good meal."

"You'll need a wristband to get food. Didn't you get a wristband yesterday when you registered with us?"

"I did, but I returned it."

"And you just stumbled on this young lady today? Aren't you a lucky girl."

She's clearly worked out we came here together. We're dirty, exhausted and hungry. Perhaps for this reason alone she doesn't question us further.

"Go and eat something," she says. "I'll put a message out to all the refuges we're in contact with and let them know you turned up."

Joel insists we eat somewhere in the city. He limps his way out of HQ whilst I try to evaluate what is going on.

My mother isn't here. Hans isn't here. I'm stuck at HQ with Joel, who I feel compelled to follow everywhere like a lamb. I stare at the back of his head, which bobs as he limps, and wonder if now would be a good time to cut him off. To turn around, go back to HQ. I can have a hot meal in the canteen and get my lenses checked with Dr Frost. I can wait for my mother surrounded by people I know a little better. But I can't seem to detach myself from Joel.

With nothing else to focus on, my mind is free to look around the city again without my lenses. I'm almost taken aback by the change. The city looks like an old painting. Gone are the many vibrant shades my lenses would purposefully pick out. Last time the city looked like a chest full of treasures. But now the greens look like moss, not emeralds. Brown looks like mud, not chocolate. Gold looks dirty and silver looks tarnished. The city used to stand like a proud peacock, with its feathers on bright display, but without my lenses everything is flat and stale. As such, the noises no longer compliment a city full of the colours of life. I can hear the impatience behind horns blaring, the urgency of roaring traffic and the clatter of feet as people push and shove. The streets are more intimidating than I ever imagined. It now crosses my mind whilst the city has changed drastically the countryside never seemed to alter this much without lenses in.

I suppose this only highlights how artificial Fenix really is. I hurry after Joel and try to avoid the many grey eyes we pass.

I let him lead me to a place where he feels comfortable. He chooses a free house that promises good food, televisions and where no one will interfere with us once we occupy a corner table. Over our table is a large, framed photograph of a magnifying glass and compass sat on top of an old map. They've let their outdated décor appear intentional. Most other pictures on the walls feature men wearing monocles and spectacles. There are no holograms or visual displays here. This suits us well. We have to go to the bar to order food and drink. I brush salt from the table and stare at the thousands of rings left by beer glasses. I must look downbeat because suddenly Joel puts a hand on my wrist.

"We'll find her. That woman will put the message out. No doubt your mother's looking for you too. I'll bet she's with that herdsman of yours."

I manage a smile. Joel shifts awkwardly in his seat and I realise it's the first time he's sat down since his injury.

"Please let someone remove that pin."

"I will," he says. "Just not in that place."

"Because if you don't let them take it out -"

"If they scan my eyes to let me on the premises then they'll know who I am. And if I need an X-Ray I'll need to have them taken out or disabled for the laser, therefore scanned." He folds his arms and says no more.

When our food arrives I nibble on garnish whilst Joel's fingers appear and take chips away with them. I'm not up for light conversation, so it's fortunate one of the televisions faces us. Joel is watching the news broadcast with interest. Thankfully it isn't the same segment we watched them film earlier. It's an entirely different reporter speaking.

"Experts now say some of the after-effects of the meteor disaster are being treated as suspicious. Whilst many videos and sightings we've shared on this network are certainly evidence of impressive meteor showers, areas such as Orbelle and Sparkwell are said to be the main focus of a new investigation. The satellite known globally as ALPHA is said to have lost communication with these parts of the country. A coincidence? A direct collision with falling meteor fragments? Or the work of a terrorist group? All these possibilities are currently being looked into whilst Orbelle remains evacuated due to extreme avalanche warnings."

Joel withdraws his hand from the back of the seat and sits straight for a moment. When he notices I'm watching he manages a casual smile.

"Incredible, don't you think? What are the chances of a meteor hitting that?"

"ALPHA is the satellite that controls the WOLF lenses, isn't it?"

"Well, it doesn't exactly control them. That would only be too easy. What I mean is, communication between some of the lens readings and WOLF HQ will be interrupted if not completely severed."

"And it was disrupted three nights ago?"

"According to the news."

"The same night you and I met."

Joel gives me a quizzical look. "You think I shot it down with my rifle?"

"No. I don't know what I'm thinking."

"Chip?" Joel holds one up, as though to feed me. When I refuse it he sighs.

"Don't worry, everything'll be fine."

"The system can't find her," I remind him. "And she may not even be at a refuge."

"No, but you're registered now. You don't think your mother will be phoning HQ every few hours? It's only been an hour since you checked yourself in. I give it another two, tops. WOLF know where you are. They'll confirm with your mother you're safe and in the area. Once we're done here, we'll go back and ask if anyone has enquired about you. You're being looked after now. WOLF gave you your wristband and promised you a bed. You'll be fine until your mother comes for you."

He's right. I'm being protected now. I'm being fed and cared for, with a place to stay. Yet Joel is still here. Despite having escorted me, as he said he would, he's made no sign of leaving me yet.

I'll miss Joel. He's been good company and he's the only person who can confirm I shot a wolf and saved our lives. Hans won't believe that story if I tell him myself. Joel picks himself up and makes to leave. Hans' jacket peels away from the flaking leather seats.

We pass shops and statues until we hear a procession taking place in one of the main streets. It's hardly a carnival or celebration. It's a string of vehicles escorting evacuees across town. Most are walking alongside the coaches. People are gathering to watch. It's morbidly fascinating to see the people who have been forced to leave their homes. My mother would be on one of the coaches if she were here. I seize Joel's arm and tell him we have to scout the vehicles for my mother.

"I don't know what she looks like."

The coaches come to a halt as market stall holders clog the streets. Now is a good time to do a round of the coaches, check each window and hope for an Orbelle civilian.

"She's the one with the white cane. Just ask people," I say. "Everyone knows my mother."

I don't wait to hear his reply. Once the road clears this group will move on. I run to each window, dodging bystanders and WOLF X recruits who are insisting the market holders let them pass.

"Excuse me." I ask anyone who will listen. "I'm looking for Eliza Hansen. She's my mother. We live in Orbelle."

I blurt out Hans' name. Anna's name. The names of people I went to school with. Nothing. I round the coaches, craning for their faces. Eventually the coaches start to move and I'm told to get on to the pavement by an armed officer.

This procession has nothing to do with Orbelle. These must be the poor people whose homes were hit by the meteors yesterday. Only now, as I soak in my disappointment, I realise Joel is gone. I start to worry, but then acknowledge something right in front of me. Military uniforms by the dozen.

I should have known. Just as I'm working desperately hard to find someone, Joel's been trying not to be found.

Before long the streets clear and I know Joel isn't crawling back out from wherever he skulked off to. I'm now on my own. Not that it's too daunting. HQ is only five minutes from here. But this is the first time I've truly been alone since Joel dug me out of the mountain snow.

I round a few corners, following the large WOLF signs. I've journeyed over fields and train tracks to make it to HQ. Only now do I feel unsure of myself. I stop to stare at one sign, which stretches so high I have to tilt my head back. The globe-like iris catches the sunlight and shines above metallic wording.

This is the wolf I'm starting to feel afraid of. The giant corporation, whose intentions and capabilities are beyond my understanding. No one can shoot WOLF in the head. I think of my father and wonder why he ever bothered. Did he really think his cause was so important he would risk arrest just to vandalise and frighten the people who worked for WOLF? Even if someone were to take out the satellites the wolf would only be lame for a little while. If this whole situation in Orbelle is the result of a terrorist group then they're wasting their time. You can't bring down a beast like this one.

They have no new information for me at reception. No one has asked for me and no one called Eliza Hansen has checked in anywhere else in the county. I'm taken to a bed for patients undergoing surgery and given a pair of slippers. They've recalibrated my lenses for free and given me tokens so I can use the internet and television. I swing the screen around so it's above the pillow and lie, fully clothed, waiting for the news.

What would my mother think if she could see what was happening? She won't be able to see the footage. She could only listen to it. I have an idea and my heart leaps. I scan through the channels until I find the one I want. It's a frozen screen, permanently showing the radio station's logo. I turn up the headphones to listen to the live broadcast taking place and imagine my mother sat in her chair at home listening to it.

"That's quite extraordinary, Katie," the broadcaster is saying to a caller. "So what did you do then? Were the meteors falling right at that moment?"

"Yes, Jeff. I was thinking: even if we get this car moving, are we going to be taken off the road like a human pinball, you know? Because they were falling like hail stones at that point."

I turn the volume up and wait.

"Well that was Katie from the Newton Belle area. Thank you Katie. Remember, we want to hear your stories. If you had any encounters with the meteor showers this week. Give us a call on this number . . ."

I leap off the bed and hurry to the reception desk in my slippers. The receptionist looks exasperated to see me again today.

"I need to use the phone," I say at once. "It's important."

It doesn't take much time. Someone connects my call immediately. I can practically hear their excitement when I tell them why I'm on the line.

"Now we have an exceptionally gripping story from one of our callers. We're talking live to Linnea Hansen, an evacuee from Orbelle. Linnea, you told our phone operators you're actually still looking for your family since you were separated during the evacuation?"

"Hi, Jeff," I say self-consciously. "Yes, I want to get a message out to my mother, Eliza Hansen. She's a listener of your show. She listens every day. I want her to know I'm all right."

I'll bet Jeff loves this. He prompts me for details. Where I am and how I'm feeling. More importantly how I came to be on my own in the first place. I explain as best as I can, leaving out details such as shooting a wolf, eating out of battered tin cans and being buried under an avalanche. I tell him all about my encounter with the meteor shower and the first meteor I saw pass over Mt Venus.

"That was around two-thirty in the morning, three nights ago," I say. "And when I returned, back to the town, the place was deserted."

"You must have been so afraid," Jeff says sympathetically. "To go through that all on your own. You sound like a very brave young lady."

"I wasn't on my own," I admit. "I had someone with me. But what's important is my mother knows where I am and how to find me."

"Well, Linnea, we took your details and your whereabouts. If your mother calls the show we can give her all that information. I'm sure you'll be reunited soon. And since you're such keen listeners and such an inspirational young lady, I'm sending you both autographs. How does that sound?"

To a blind woman? I force myself to sound pleased.

"That's great. She'll be delighted."

I return to my bed and close my eyes. I realise now how much they ache, along with everything else. My feet throb, my shoulders are stiff and my fingers are still nicked and tender after bashing open tins of food. I could sleep now. Truly sleep. I know, if my mother has access to the radio, she will have heard my message. I won't be alone for long. Then I'll be back with her and Hans and, eventually, permitted back to our ranch. We'll buy new goats somehow. We'll get by. All of this will be a bad memory and nothing more.

But I stay awake for a long time. When the blankets accidentally cover my face, I resurface with a jolt remembering how it felt to be trapped under the snow. I throw the covers back and consider counting goats. But as sleep takes over my conscious mind, the goats are devoured by hungry wolves until there is no one left on my ranch except me. And no one can hear me crying wolf.

14

I wake to the sound of a vacuum cleaner outside the ward. The cleaner comes in backwards, humming loudly. The door swings shut and she turns around. Her bland eyes turn a buttery shade.

"Good gracious, girl, you frightened me!" She places a plump hand on her heart. "I didn't know anyone was in here."

"You don't know if anyone has called for me then?" I throw back the covers and stand. "I'm Linnea Hansen."

"Sorry, pet, I'm only paid to scrub and dust. Have a word with reception."

I'm not sure my celebrity status from yesterday will hold up today. I approach the desk and stand there.

"Good morning Miss Hansen. Someone came in for you earlier."

"What?" My heart almost stops. "Why did no one wake me? My mother, is she . . . ?"

"Sorry, it wasn't your mother. We've heard nothing from her yet. But he's over there."

It's too early to open the main doors and the cleaners are still working around the tables and chairs. Across five of the chairs is a sleeping figure. Hans' jacket is over his head to block out the morning light and his arms are folded. I stride over and stand beside him. Joel's chest rises and falls slowly. Hans' shirt has lifted up to his navel, exposing his stomach. I don't know if I'm pleased to see him or not. The cleaner turns her back and I seize the nozzle of the vacuum, press it against Joel's bare stomach and switch it on. He scrambles off the seat with the jacket still over his face, though he tenses when he puts weight on his leg. His hands grapple to pull the nozzle off.

He wipes his forehead and blinks slowly. I stare at his flushed face.

"Are you okay?"

"Yeah, I'm fine." He rubs the light mark I've made on his stomach and pulls his shirt down. Then he looks me up and down. "So where'd they put you? These chairs are awful."

"They put me in one of the wards." I put the vacuum to one side. "And I thought you were sleeping on a bench or something last night. Had a change of heart, did you? Abandoning me like that."

"What did you expect me to do? The streets were crawling with . . ." Joel rolls his eyes. "Of course I came back. I don't need to ask if your mother or this Hans bloke came for you, do I?"

"No," I say. "And Hans will want that jacket back. Perhaps it's better you hang around for a bit."

"You didn't recognise anyone yesterday then?"

"No. Did you?"

Joel shoots me questioning look.

"You disappeared before I even noticed," I say. "Was one of those men from your team?"

"I didn't really hang around long enough to find out. Can we talk about you instead?"

"Okay. Did you happen to listen to the radio last night?" I'm not expecting him to say yes, he'd have brought it up himself otherwise. As I expected, he frowns and shakes his head. Before he can ask what I'm talking about, we're told we can shower and eat in the canteen before the building opens to the public. I'm sent to the female shower room, whilst Joel is sent elsewhere. I realise I haven't washed properly in a while. The closest thing my hair has experienced to water was being submerged in snow.

When I strip down, I'm surprised by my naked appearance. My right shoulder is slightly purple, but the bruise is already healing nicely. I remember now. The feeling as the rifle forced itself against the bone as I shot. Oddly, I find myself rather liking it. I almost want to show Hans and prove I shot at something. If the wolf's body is still outside Hans' porch then he'll be able to see it for himself. He'll probably take a photograph with me next to it, as is custom in his family of hunters. The thought excites me.

I rub thick, scentless shampoo into my hair and clean my teeth. They feel sensationally smooth once I'm done and the cracked skin on my lips is already healing. One of the cracks faintly resembles the scar on Joel's lip. I run my tongue over its rough surface and wonder if this is how his scar feels to him.

Once cleaned and dressed, I make my way to the canteen. Joel is sipping water. He looks up with droplets on his lips and a smooth chin.

"You've shaved," I say.

"Well, aren't you observant. Oh, your eyes aren't hazel anymore."

"No. My lenses got checked. As long as they don't malfunction again I won't need to see a doctor. They just needed reinitiating via computer, no need to take them out."

I sit down and take a slice of toast he already buttered from his plate.

"You're one of those annoying people who'll never get their own food, but will always help themselves to others'," Joel says, although he doesn't seem hungry. "I suppose you've always been able to get away with it at home, haven't you? Your mother would never know, would she?"

"Ha! She would. She knows what's on her plate. Or in the sink, or the washing basket. She doesn't miss a thing."

"She sounds pretty cool."

"She is." I smile.

"I look forward to meeting her. I like her already." Joel sounds sincere. My smile catches. I don't know what my mother would possibly make of Joel.

"Miss Hansen," a familiar voice says. I turn and see Dr Frost standing with a mug of coffee.

"Dr Frost." My cheeks suddenly feel hot. "Good morning."

"Good morning to you too. What a pleasure it is to see my favourite patient." His eyes move to Joel, who seems to concern him. "You're not one of my patients though. I don't believe I've seen you before."

"This is Joel," I say. To Joel I explain quickly. "This is my own practitioner, Dr Frost. He specialises in WOLF 03 lenses. He's been my doctor for years."

"Nice to meet you," Joel says flatly.

"Likewise." Dr Frost looks back to me with a pointed expression. At first I don't know what he's trying to communicate. Then it hits me.

"Joel is a family friend," I say. "He came here with me from Orbelle when we were evacuated."

"Ah yes, of course. I did hear your broadcast on the radio," Dr Frost says. "So this is the boy you were referring to. In any case, well done, that was some good initiative. Even if your mother didn't hear the broadcast, someone she knows would have. I expect you'll be in better places by this evening. Well, it was lovely to see you again, Miss Hansen. Excuse me."

I watch him walk away and then look back at Joel. I'm taken aback by his expression. His eyebrows are knotted together and he's staring at me like I stand accused of something awful.

"What?"

"The radio? You were on the radio?"

"Yeah. Last night, when you left me. I phoned the station my mother always listens to and put a message out for her."

"And you mentioned me?"

"Not you specifically. I just said I wasn't alone. It was so she wouldn't worry too much. I never said who you were."

"There's only one person missing from Orbelle, as far as anyone knows, and that's Linnea Hansen. You don't think people are going to ask who this boy is? If his family are looking for him?"

"Dr Frost didn't look too bothered if your family was looking for you."

"Just as well. Because there is no family looking for me." Joel stands up from the table. It takes some effort and I'm sure he urges a little. "But other people are."

"What're you doing?"

"I have to go," Joel says. "Before anyone I don't want to puts two and two together. You told them you were here right?"

"No one has to know who you are," I say.

"You just told that doctor my name. The moment someone asks who escorted Linnea from Orbelle, the name Joel is going to come up and I'm in deep shit. So thank you."

"You should thank me. I've been your meal ticket for the past few days. You'd still be eating out of tin cans if it weren't for me." I'm only arguing to stall him whilst I think of something that will keep him here. "Look, I know you're worried, but stay and let a doctor look at you. You're not well. Don't pretend you are."

"You don't know anything and I'm fine. I don't have to explain myself."

"Maybe not to her," another male voice says. "But that'll be my favourite jacket you're wearin'."

I turn in my seat so fast my drink almost spills. His hands are in his pockets and his lenses softly change between dark shades. It's never been so wonderful to see him.

"Hans!" I could hug him, but Hans isn't usually the hugging type. He'd rather shake my hand. But it's not me he's looking at. It's Joel. There will be no hand shaking between these two, judging by the look on his face.

"So you're Hans?" Joel says.

"Aye, that's right."

They stare at each other a moment longer, then Hans turns his attention to me. He finally gives the slightest of smiles. "Clever girl, using the radio. My mother was the one who heard it. I got straight in the car to come get you."

"Is she in the car?" I ask at once.

"My mother?"

"No, mine."

"Ah, no. Don't worry, she knows you're all right. I'm takin' you there now. We just need to discharge you from HQ. Sooner the better. I hate this place."

"Great," I say. But now I look back at Joel. He looks deflated and I feel a pang of uncertainty.

"You were leaving now anyway, right?"

"Yes." He doesn't sound as firm as before. "Yes I need to leave."

"You're not goin' anywhere," Hans cuts in. "I have one or two questions for you first."

He doesn't interrogate Joel right away. He lets me inform reception I'm leaving and I hand back my wristband. He tells me to wait whilst he uses the telephone to tell my mother we're coming. I would like to speak with her myself, but I don't want to argue with Hans right now. I go and sit next to Joel, who keeps looking at the main doors. His forehead looks glossier than usual and he keeps wiping it with his sleeve and breathing heavily.

"You can go if you like," I say. "I can tell it's what you want to do."

"I do," he admits. Something is holding him back. Perhaps he's deciding he should see a doctor after all. I hope so. He's looking worse by the minute.

Hans strides over with some paperwork for me to sign.

"Just need your signature to confirm," he says. "It's your mother's idea. I'm havin' myself put down as your next of kin."

"Next of kin?" I don't argue, he's more like a brother to me and much more useful in an emergency. I sign the form and he takes it back to reception. There's nothing Hans wants now, besides an explanation.

"Look, mate, I don't want to get you into too much trouble," Hans says to Joel. "You had to get here, you stopped by my place. I get that. Did you take any money?"

"There was a twenty in the jacket pocket."

"I hope he fed you with it," Hans says to me.

"He did."

"Well then. I won't interrogate you further. I appreciate you stayin' with Linn. That were good of you."

Joel just stares at Hans. Without the uniform and rifle, he's a boy standing in front of a man. Hans turns to me. "Got your bag?"

"Where are we going? Can we return to Orbelle now?"

"Orbelle?" Hans shakes his head. "Whole area is off limits. Supposedly due to avalanche warnings. But I never heard such warnings. My father stopped askin' questions a day ago. No point arguin' with the authorities. We're up country in Doverhaven but I'm takin' you to your mother. She's in Newton Belle."

"What?" I blink. "Newton Belle?"

What on earth is in Newton Belle for my mother? We've no connections there.

But I'm wrong.

"Your Turtle Dove stepped in," Hans says. "I've got to hand it to the boy. He's dedicated. He were here lookin' for you within an hour of us showin' up."

My mouth drops open. I haven't thought of Alec for days. My Turtle Dove, the boy I'm compatible with. I'd forgotten about him. Yet it seems he didn't forget me.

"He's taken my mother in?"

"The both of you. His parents agreed you can stay with them until Orbelle is habitable again. He's been frantically trying to find you, phonin' every refuge. We've been terrified, Linn. He's been just as worried as the rest of us. In fact, I don't want to admit this, but he's been a pillar of strength for your mother. Not quite the prat I thought he'd be."

Joel finally finds his voice. He looks far more alert behind those weary eyes. "You signed up to Turtle Doves ML? They found you a match?"

"It's not quite as serious as that," I say. "I only met him the once. Literally a few days ago. There's nothing to say about it."

"He's searched the county for you," Hans reminds me. "I think he finds it a lot more serious than that."

What exactly is happening? I look between Hans and Joel, unable to speak. I can see exactly what Joel is thinking: Turtle Doves ML. Another WOLF ploy to achieve funding. He thinks I'm a fool. He's appalled with me. So much so he zips up the jacket and turns to leave.

"I'm glad you found them," he says.

"Joel, wait."

I attempt to grab his arm. I have to explain. But his arm isn't there anymore. His whole body has suddenly dropped. Joel falls on to one knee, his hands raised like taut claws. Then one hand grapples the back of his leg and I understand at once. When I touch his shoulder he's shaking furiously.

"He needs help," I speak so loudly the receptionists are drawn over. "He's got a cartridge pin in his leg. It needs to be removed before it gets infected."

Joel looks horrified and attempts to stand. When he realises he can't he reaches out for me.

"I'm sorry." I put a hand on top of his head and realise how hot his brow is. "But you really do need treatment."

He doesn't argue any further. They're fetching him a wheelchair. WOLF X lenses can't portray fear, so there is no hint of yellow. But I know.

"Don't leave me," he whispers. "You can't. When they scan my lenses . . . Just don't leave me alone with them. Promise me."

His palm is sweating when I take his hand and the receptionists let me help him into the wheelchair. I walk alongside as they wheel him down the corridor.

"Linn?" Hans has no idea what's going on and doesn't seem willing to stay. I don't look at his face because I don't want to be reminded of everyone else waiting for me. They can wait a little longer. They'll have to.

15

Joel is in so much pain he doesn't attempt to get away. He just hisses between his teeth and his grip is like a vice. We come to a stop outside one of the doctor's surgeries.

"You may wait out here," one of the nurses says. Joel squeezes my hand so hard I feel the blood swell in my fingers.

"It's okay. I'll stay with him," I say. "You're only going to remove it from his leg, right? It's just a little pin."

"We might have difficulty locating it and require an X-Ray," the nurse says.

"You can't," Joel says at once.

"He can't take his lenses out," I say. "Not without a proper doctor. He's WOLF X."

"Is he now?"

The interest in Joel intensifies as they back into the doctor's surgery. It all proves too much for Joel and he makes one last attempt to escape. He lets go of my hand and leaps up from the chair. They try to grab his shoulders but he's up and trying to decide which way to run.

"Joel!" I watch in anguish as he falls again. He lands in the middle of the corridor, cursing loudly.

"Good heavens. This one's nervous," one of the nurses says. "No need to be scared of a silly needle and an X-Ray. Whoever made him WOLF X?"

"I did."

A man in military uniform rounds the corner, flanked by a group of other men in uniform identical to Joel's.

"Although I must admit I often wonder why." He stops a meter short of Joel. "Get up, Edgecombe."

I attempt to help but Joel bats me away. He ignores his leg and stands tall. Tears of pain spill from his eyes. He doesn't wipe them away. It seems you can wear the uniform on your face, etched in every taut muscle. He's not Joel in this moment. He's WOLF X23, Dragon M. I back away and let the inevitable unfold. The game is up. Clearly he's just been discovered by his superior. Slowly he starts to buckle under the pain of his leg but his face remains still.

"Major Lance Ouren, WOLF X." The man introduces himself to the nurses. "This boy is one of mine. Joel Edgecombe, we finally located you. Took a while and a lot of needless effort. I would have you stand on your feet properly when you face me, but I fear that may not be possible. Ladies, have that wheelchair brought forward. The cold floor is no place for a WOLF X recruit. Certainly not a member of my team."

Major Ouren. His left eye is completely unmoving. I wonder if it's a trick before realising it's made of glass. I mustn't stare, but it's fascinating. He's opted for a dull brown colour. I would have assumed if one could choose a permanent colour for their glass eye, they'd opt for something more impressive. I've seen glass eyes perform spectacular tricks in the display cabinets here at HQ. I've seen irises swirl like water going down a plug hole. Irises that wax and wane, like the moon. I've seen irises pretend to crack open and hatch a new iris of a different colour. Ouren, however, has chosen something far more natural and bland.

The uniform wearers step around him and hoist Joel into the chair. He no longer struggles and they wheel him into the surgery. Ouren stops one of the nurses and speaks in a low tone. "What is the nature of his injury?"

"He has the pin of a pinfire cartridge in his leg," I speak up. "Right at the top, around the back. It's been there since yesterday evening."

Ouren's eyes study me for a moment and he turns back to the nurse as if I never spoke.

"If this can be carried out without anaesthetic, then by all means. A lesson needs to be learned here. Any more issues with him and you ask for me. He's my responsibility and I'll not have him disgrace me again."

I don't know what to say or do. Joel wanted me to stay with him, so I guess I should follow the nurses.

"Just a moment, young lady." Ouren holds me on the spot with a single raised hand. "These nurses have a job to do and I have a few questions. We've been looking for this boy for three days."

He turns to one of the men at his side. "Have her taken to the X unit."

"This one has already been discharged," the nurse says.

"Oh." Ouren sniffs and fixes his good eye on me. "Then you can kindly check her back in until we're finished here."

Am I being arrested or something? I step back and speak loudly. "I want Hans with me. He's in the foyer, waiting to take me home. He's my next of kin. I won't go anywhere without him."

Ouren nods and walks into the surgery. The men who accompanied Ouren look me up and down, clearly amused. I don't like their stares. A young man with dark skin and soft, teal eyes steps forward.

"You're the radio girl? You're Linnea?"

"Yes," I say.

"Thanks for watching out for our boy," he says. "Did he only shoot himself in the leg? We were expecting much worse from him."

There is a ripple of laughter, which I sense is unkind.

"Joel's always been entertaining," the boy explains. "Always one to watch out for, whether it's firing arms, using hot water . . ."

"And now he's shot himself in the arse," one of the other boys hoots, forcing the laughter to resurface. An older member of the group rolls his eyes and looks at him unfavourably. This older man stands rigid and waits for Ouren without a word.

"He saved my life," I say so loudly the laughter stops. I won't have Joel mocked by his team whilst he suffers. "He pulled me out when I was buried by snow. Then he risked punishment from your major to save my life and make sure I got back to my family."

"We don't mean to make fun," the boy assures me. "But Joel will be laughing himself within a few days. A bullet in the backside is nothing to feel sorry about for too long. If it were anywhere else on his body he would be showing off the wound."

I hate to admit it, but he's probably right. I decide I don't dislike him. Instead I shake the hand he offers me.

"I'm Theo," he says. "Seriously, thanks for not letting him get into too much trouble. However clumsy he is, we need him."

"Do we heck," the older man mutters, but Theo argues this.

"Ouren wanted him back for a reason, Johannes. You know that." He turns back to me and smiles. "It was nice to meet you, Linnea. I'm sure Joel will tell us all about you."

I'm sure he'll have to. Some of the other men seem very interested to know about our time together. Some of the younger ones even nudge and pull suggestive faces at each other. It's fascinating to see the people Joel left behind. This was the team he was determined to hide from? I can't help but wonder why. All noise stops when Major Ouren steps back out from the surgery.

"He has a puncture wound in his semitendinosus," Ouren tells his team.

"Is that his arse, Sir?"

"Shut up, Warren," Johannes says irritably.

"Enough." Ouren silences them both. "You can both be quiet. If I want an opinion from you, Warren, I'll read your lenses. Edgecombe's been given pain killers and they'll be removing the pin as soon as they can."

"Can I see him?" I dare to ask.

This time Ouren acknowledges me properly. "So you're Linnea Hansen; the cause of all our troubles." He takes a good look at the woollen tights, the old blouse and the messy braid.

Like everyone else I've met lately, he seems surprised I could be of any disturbance. I can tell I'm nothing but a huge inconvenience.

Finally, Hans is brought into the corridor. His expression is one of utter disbelief.

"What's going on? You're not takin' her anywhere, you hear? She's comin' with me. Her mother's waited long enough."

"Then we had best get this over with quickly," Ouren says simply. "Who are you?"

"Hans Fotland, WOLF 0167, Tiger M. She's done nothin' wrong." Hans looks so agitated I worry he'll start shouting. "You can't keep her here against her will."

"Hans Fotland?"

There is a glance between Ouren and Johannes. Hans' face suddenly falls and he stares at Johannes intently for a moment. He then looks at me urgently and I think I understand. He's seen Johannes before. Most likely on our ranch, staring up at the mountain. But neither of us gets a chance to mention this. Ouren looks back to me and his tone changes.

"Tell me, young lady. If you discovered a WOLF X weapon in your back garden, what would you do?"

This question throws me off. I hesitate before answering. "I would report it."

"Edgecombe had a rifle when I last saw him. Do you know where it is now?"

"He discarded it to draw less attention to himself," I say. "He didn't want to concern people or arouse any questions. He threw it out into the estuary as we crossed into Fenix."

"Not far enough, it seems. Two rifles washed up on the bank of a civilian's property. Edgecombe's and another weapon we have investigated and identified."

Oh god. I try to send a few warning glances to Hans, but they go unnoticed. He tries to take my arm.

"This is ridiculous. We've stayed here long enough," he says. "This is no concern of ours. You can punish your men how you like, but this one's coming with me."

"I'm afraid neither of you are going anywhere just yet, WOLF 0167, Tiger M."

Hans is about to argue, when a rifle is passed into Ouren's hands. He holds it up for us to look at. Hans simply stares at it.

"Hans Fotland, this weapon is registered to your name and was improperly disposed of. What's more you have knowingly harboured a WOLF X deserter. You'll both be staying at HQ for the time being. Warren, Johannes, escort these two to the X unit for questioning. Neither of them will be leaving here for a while."

16

It's not long before our stories are verified. Their database confirms Hans checked into HQ and registered as an evacuee three days ago then accompanied his family to Doverhaven.

I explain I took his rifle for protection and threw it into the estuary when we entered the city. The same time Joel discarded his. There isn't much else they can keep Hans here for. Except he almost broke Warren's nose when his shoulder was seized. Hans is free to leave, but will need to produce his weapon's license and complete some paperwork within a fortnight.

It seems there's still plenty they wish to know about me. I haven't seen Hans for over an hour, although they finished talking with him ages ago. I know he'll be waiting impatiently for me, but there is little I can do about it. I sit in the X unit, drumming my fingers against a table and waiting for human interaction.

It's entirely my fault for calling the radio. If I had waited, of course Hans or my mother would have called HQ to see if I'd checked in. They would have come for me. I just had to sit tight. Instead I've landed everyone in trouble and I wonder what they're doing to Joel. I have no idea how they punish their deserters.

The WOLF X unit is initially much like the other units. It has the same marble countertops in its surgeries, the same royal blue seats in the waiting areas. But we're taken beyond that, into areas inaccessible to the public. It requires lens recognition to allow us through certain doors. From there the unit resembles a laboratory. It's stocked with machines and staff wearing different colour coats. Doors are marked with codes instead of a single doctor's name. I suddenly feel like I'm in one of their billboard advertisements, except it's not anywhere near as colourful as portrayed on the screens. I suppose they don't need to make the effort. This area isn't meant for patients. There are no holograms, sculptures or paintings. Performances are for the public. This area is solely for production.

Prior to them placing me in this office, we were interrupted mid-corridor by a man who seemed to anticipate Ouren's arrival. Whether he'd heard the sound of military boots approach or spied us on a surveillance camera a door opened and he strode out, in step with Ouren, hands in his pockets and a knowing look on his face.

"Ouren," he said in mock surprise. "You're back. Everything under control I gather?"

"Far from it, Rusten. I'm afraid our suspicions about ALPHA were correct. The meteors did more damage than we feared. Minor damage, albeit, but enough to have an effect. Orbelle's lenses are out of action. But by coincidence the place was evacuated due to severe avalanche warnings. We should have things restored before the surveillance teams see fit to return the people to their homes."

"Excellent. I expect you were first on the scene, weren't you?"

"I appointed my team to Orbelle as soon as the meteors began their show. We had reason to believe it had begun early thanks to a damaged truck within the town. Blew the windshield in. Lucky no one was hurt. Our men were stationed to monitor signals from ALPHA within hours. They're an efficient team, Rusten. I take pride in my lads."

"So you should," Rusten said. He glanced over at Theo and smirked. "How Cornelius Morgan must cherish you. I heard you lost one of your efficient lads in Orbelle."

"Incorrect. Edgecombe took it upon himself to help a lost evacuee. No one need question my recruits. They're a damn sight more honourable than previous men I have worked with. Well, if you would excuse us, Lieutenant. I'm sure Morgan has you working on something very important."

Must everything involve me lately? It was my father's truck they'd referred to. My suspicions were confirmed. It wasn't a bomb that destroyed the windshield. Whatever hit it was cleared away by the authorities before the media could intervene.

I've been left alone in an office I assume belongs to Ouren himself. The door bears only a frosted window, and no name. But there's a picture on the wall of Ouren with both eyes intact. In fact he looks very different. His hair is shaved much shorter and he's wearing a wedding band and different uniform. A lieutenant's uniform. Another picture shows him in a group with Rusten a few paces aside from him and shaking Cornelius Morgan's hand. I note the look on Ouren's face. Both eyes are fixed on the hands of Rusten and Cornelius Morgan. The picture is dated two years ago.

Ouren walks in accompanied by Theo and the boy called Warren, who I've taken an instant dislike to. Warren doesn't offer talk or smiles. He just stares with unblinking eyes. I ignore his stare and look at Theo if in doubt of what to say. I assume Johannes is with Hans. He had the right air of authority about him and is probably the next in command. At least he seems more respectable on sight. Warren fondles the weapon at his side like it's a toy and looks at me like I'm game.

Ouren's questions are short and simple. What's more he doesn't interrupt when I answer. For all the time I've spent waiting in the X unit, my questioning has been surprisingly brief.

I understand why I had to wait so long when Ouren produces my medical file and places it down on the desk.

"Linnea Marie Hansen. WOLF 0315, Snake F." He reads the label aloud. I have an inkling he's already read my file and has good reason to bring it here for reference. "I've had an interesting chat with Joel and verified a few details with your own practitioner, Dr Frost. Your file tells me your mother is permanently blind. Correct?"

What does this have to do with anything? Ouren is staring at me expectantly.

"Yes, she's blind."

"A result of experimentation, I understand. It happened to many people. She suffered severe keratitis I presume? Yes, it was terribly unfortunate. Frustratingly avoidable too if you ask me . . . Your file also tells me you're registered to Turtle Doves ML. Can you confirm that for me too?"

"I'm sorry but what's this got to do with anything?" I'm aware Warren is smirking at me. I'm determined not to look at anyone in the eye.

"Registered to Turtle Doves ML," Ouren continues, "and successfully matched?"

"Well, supposedly," I say.

"Another WOLF 03 candidate?"

"Yes."

"I see," Ouren says. "And – forgive me – how would you describe the arrangement, young lady?"

"Excuse me?"

"Beg your pardon. What stage in this relationship would you say you're at?"

I look at Theo for help. He's the only one not judging me. All he can do is nod.

"We met once, six days ago I think. That's it. We met in the simulation room and exchanged contact details. I've not spoken to him since."

"Can we check these details?" Ouren turns to Theo.

"We can run it through the system, certainly."

"Do that," Ouren says. "In the meantime keep her under surveillance. By that I mean keep the young lady comfortable. With a cup of tea. Right then, Alec Rouman, let's see if you are who they say you are. Warren, come with me."

In the time it takes for him to confirm Alec's legitimacy, I'm brought a cup of tea and two biscuits coated in chocolate. I hope this means I'm in no real trouble. I'm sure the X unit doesn't offer chocolate coated biscuits to those under suspicion.

"You can relax," Theo says when he returns alone. "Alec is no different from yourself."

"Why would he be different?"

"WOLF might have had someone pose as a perfect match for you. Conceived a partner designed to appeal to a young WOLF 03 female."

"But why would they do that?"

He hesitates, looking at my baffled face. "That's really a question for Johannes, not me."

He swiftly starts a new topic. Theo likes talking. I quickly worked that out. Not being able to answer a question really troubles him. After a moment he points to his bottom lip and tells me I have chocolate on my mouth. It's the same evasive response I would expect from Joel. He seems keen to keep our conversation going. I think up another question.

"Does this mean I can see Joel now? Ouren said he'd spoken to him. Is the pin out of his leg?"

"It is, but I doubt they'll let you near him just yet. Ouren was angry for days at losing contact with Joel. But I think you've helped his situation. I can't guarantee he'll get off lightly. The matter will be taken to someone above Ouren. Joel may have to restart his probation, lose some privileges.

Ouren will defend him, but with Ouren's status already what it is . . . it's difficult."

"Why? What's wrong with him?"

"Well, some people have concerns with Ouren lately. Some think he's losing focus." Theo smiles at his own light joke.

"What happened to his eye? Did someone injure him?"

"You mustn't ask him about that," Theo says. "It happened some time ago."

"Back when he was a lieutenant?" I gesture to the pictures on the wall. "Did his injury force him to step down a rank? Or did he resign?"

"You're sharper than you look," Theo says. "Joel was right to stick with you."

"So what happened?"

Theo looks back at the frosted window. There are no figures moving beyond. He lowers his voice and steps closer.

"Ouren stepped down. Before that he was on compulsory leave for six months. They said he was mentally unstable. Many people think he shouldn't have returned at all."

"Somebody injured him?"

"You mean his eye? No. He stabbed it out himself with his lieutenant's badge. No one really knows why. His team had only just returned from a mission and were receiving honours.

Several of his team were able to stop him taking out the other eye and he was forced to take leave. When he returned, he was appointed major and set up a new division, made up with his own selected recruits."

"Including you and Joel?"

"Including me and Joel."

"He really did look after me," I insist. "Everything I said was true. He's not the joke that Warren seems to think he is."

"I know. He's the reason I didn't crack under Ouren's training and beg to go home. He's part of the reason I stayed."

"He encouraged you?" I smile to think Joel can be genuinely kind at times.

"That. And he's a bit gorgeous," Theo says whimsically. "Not that he feels the same about me, I'm sure."

I don't think Theo minds I find this surprising. My lenses must have shown it. He grins before opening the door for me.

"Ouren would say goodbye himself, but he's been waylaid by some other officials. Our return from Orbelle has been anticipated, as you may have gathered. In any case, you're free to leave. Your friend is waiting for you in the reception foyer."

Hans doesn't look the slightest bit pleased to see me now. His eyes are like thunder.

I feel extremely guilty as I walk over to him. I'll go now, without attempting to stall a moment longer. What he has been through feels most unfair. He's lost an outfit and weapon, as well as being detained and questioned by WOLF X.

"Let's go," he says gruffly.

I pull my backpack on to my shoulders and make to follow him.

"Don't you want this back?"

I turn around with a lump in my throat.

Joel is back in WOLF X uniform, holding a pile of folded clothes. Hans doesn't look too bothered about taking his stuff back, but I unzip my backpack and allow Joel to slot the shirt and jacket inside. His fingers touch the meteor nestled at the bottom and he looks up at me.

"I need to talk to you," he says. "Alone."

"I know," I say. "But I think this is where we part ways, Joel."

I know what he's thinking. This isn't the right way to say goodbye. We weren't supposed to stand in the foyer of HQ, under Hans' watchful eye and with hours of interrogation still fresh on our minds. There are things we need to say. Things we've yet to discuss. I don't know how I'll ever contact him again.

"So you were being looked for," I say. My voice is neither triumphant or disappointed. "I knew it. You almost convinced me otherwise when you let me keep Hans' rifle, but then you had to go back for your own when the barn was unsafe. You didn't want someone else to find it and report it, did you? You ought to have left it there. The barn was on fire. Your rifle might have burned."

"Exactly," Joel sighs. "Our rifles are like our lenses. They're individually linked to us by our WOLF codes. If they receive severe damage or the identification chip gets destroyed they automatically alert HQ. I wanted to bury it, but you were with me. Water seemed like my best option."

"Well, you almost managed to fool me," I say grimly.

"But I didn't." Joel suddenly looks into my eyes. "I realise now I was wrong. About you not needing to understand everything. I want you to know why I've done everything I have and caused all this trouble. I don't want you to leave thinking something terrible of me. Especially after what happened with Morgan. I need you to understand."

"Listen," I say. "I think I do understand a little of what you're doing. I can't be sure, but I think I do. What I do know is I can't involve myself. I have to look after my family. My mother . . . I'm all she has."

I start to look away from him.

"Thank you for helping me get back to her. It's a shame you won't meet each other."

A door opens and Ouren appears. There is nothing more we can do but stand opposing each other. Hans over my shoulder and Ouren over his. We act as a pair of ventriloquist dolls. Each saying what our onlookers wish us to say. He's biting his bottom lip so his scar is hidden. I wish he wouldn't. I want to see it before I go.

"Bye Linnea."

"Bye Joel."

The memory of Alec politely kissing my hand passes through my mind, but I can't imagine anything less appropriate for Joel to do. He's not quite the gentleman Alec was.

So there is nothing else. No smiles and no hug. Hans places one hand on my shoulder, as if to stop me backtracking, and we leave HQ.

17

When we're outside Hans inhales so deeply you'd think he'd forgotten the taste of fresh air. I suppose, for him, that was an extremely long time to be indoors. I rarely hear Hans swear, but he curses loudly as we walk down the steps. He's still in shock. I can see it in his face.

"Let's get out of this place before they change their minds," he says.

I follow him down the steps and suddenly my gaze is captured by a butterfly near one of WOLF's flowerbeds. My lenses grabbed the motion of its wings and I'm drawn to the colours of orange and gold, framed by a jet black outline. It makes me immediately aware of the change. I look up at the city and it's like someone has switched all the lights back on. The peacock has found his beautiful plumage again and the city has returned to what it was. Yellow looks like sunshine, blue looks like the ocean and green looks like the mountainside. I'm both unsettled and relieved. If this is deception, then I'm oddly comforted by it. I didn't like the reality of what I saw without my lenses.

Hans walks me to a truck parked on yellow lines. He curses once more to see the parking ticket on the windshield.

"WOLF can pay that, the buggers. I'm writin' them a letter." He wrenches the door open and leans across to unlock the passenger's side.

Everything feels unnaturally quiet when I pull the door shut. This truck belongs to Hills, Hans' father. The floor is caked in mud and straw. No more chemical smell of floor cleaner and latex gloves. I bathe in the scent of home. It's now so quiet I can practically hear the questions ringing through Hans' mind. Then he laughs.

"You okay?" I ask nervously.

"Dear god, Linn. There I was expectin' to find you sat in the foyer lookin' like a lost lamb. But look at you! You all but got me arrested – I weren't expectin' that. What happened to you overnight? You sneak up Mt Venus, take my rifle, camp across the countryside with a WOLF X recruit . . . how am I tellin' your mother all this?"

"Does she need to know?"

Hans swallows the remainder of his laughter. "That's somethin' I need to consider. Enough has come back to bite me today. I don't need further problems. But she's gonna ask questions. You're her little radio star. What exactly did you plan on telling her?"

"Can't we just go with your expectations of finding me in the foyer, ready to go?"

"I'll think about it," Hans says.

There is a long pause. His fingers are holding the keys in the ignition and he's unsure of himself.

"That was definitely him."

"You mean the man you saw on our hill?"

"Aye. I had to really look at him. But I'm sure. I should've said somethin'."

"He was probably to do with the avalanche warnings," I say. "He may have been the one who issued it. He's WOLF X, after all. He was probably surveying the mountainside."

"Probably," Hans says doubtfully. "Because you need a gun for that . . ."

He starts the engine and pulls into city traffic. I sigh, knowing he isn't taking me home. Then I sit with my eyes very wide. I'm on my way to Newton Belle, where Alec Rouman is expected to greet me.

"He weren't so bad actually," Hans says.

"Who? Johannes?"

I look at him questionably so he clears his throat and tries to polish his accent.

"No. That Joel kid. He was all right. I mean, I'm glad you weren't entirely on your own."

Me too. I tilt my head and rest it on the side of the car. I can see my reflection in the window and how exhausted I look. I'm finally going to be with my mother. The person I've been trying to find. I'm safe and everything feels a little more familiar. I'll be staying with people who care about me. Tomorrow this'll be a memory.

It occurs to me now I'll never see Joel Edgecombe again. Since the moment I discovered Orbelle deserted I haven't let a single tear fall. Now my eyes swell and the tears feel hot. I let them fall, one by one, hoping Hans won't notice. We eventually drive into Newton Belle, and the tears practically freeze to my face. I catch an icy breath when the engine stops.

"Ready?" Hans asks.

I wipe my face with the back of my sleeve and peer out the window. I recognise this place. I've been here before. I've seen this house, the little street lamps and frosted trees. Their porch is painted like a duck-egg. I was here less than a week ago.

The simulation room did it justice. It's as pretty as a postcard and I see figures moving behind a netted curtain. My mother would've heard the car pull up in the driveway. They're all waiting for me.

I step down on to crunchy grass and feel snowflakes tickle my nose. I slam the door behind me, leaving the memory of Joel inside the truck, and prepare to meet Alec Rouman again.

18

When I see my mother I stop rigid in the doorway. She's standing against a backdrop of beige wallpaper and cream furniture. Hans stops abruptly and bumps the back of my legs. It spurs me on and I step into the room.

"Linnea!"

She extends her arms, but I don't go to her right away. I look around at the unfamiliar faces that must be the Roumans. I don't know this house, or these people. I keep my eyes on my mother and edge forward to hug her. Over her shoulder I finally spy Alec. I keep my gaze down and inhale my mother's collar, hoping for a trace of goat. I can't seem to speak.

"She were waitin' in the canteen," Hans tells everyone. "Tuckin' into toast, like nothin' were wrong. After all that worry."

I nod in silent thanks and my mother releases me.

"Let me look at you," she says.

She runs a hand through my hair and touches my face. The Roumans exchange glances. Her choice of words must seem odd to them. After all, my mother can only get a sense of me;

with my wavy hair and cool cheek. She rubs it lightly with her thumb.

"I'm so pleased you're all right."

"She's been worried sick. We all have," Mr Rouman says. He's a small man, Alec has his blond hair but little of his features. "It's a pleasure to finally meet you, Linnea. Such a shame it's under these circumstances."

"Still, you're here now. That's what matters," Alec says.

I try to recall my first impression of Alec, but it feels like a distant memory. In truth it was only a week ago, but it feels like I only saw a painting of him last time. Now he's free to move and behave how he likes. It's as though he's jumped out of a frame. Out of the simulation room I can properly acknowledge his smile and blond hair. I try to feel familiar with him, but I also notice things I hadn't noticed before. He's taller than I remember. Almost as tall as Hans. And he has a subtle dimple on his face when he smiles. I guess the simulation room made that harder for me to notice.

I realise he'll also be picking out features he couldn't see before. He'll be able to see the faint freckles on my cheeks and the cuts I've recently added to my lips.

And this time we're both wearing WOLF lenses. His arctic blue irises are melting into an earthy green. My heart swells. I know what Green Eye means. Everyone does. I've not seen it properly since my mother went blind.

Last time Alec was clumsy with his greeting, but this time he's confident and takes my hand. I expect him to kiss it again, but he uses it to pull me forward and kiss my cheek. He's not so presumptuous as to go for my lips, but it feels like an electric shock all the same. A week ago I had never had a boy kiss my hand. Now I feel his breath on my face and the smoothness of his nose. I blink at him several times before smiling. I'm safe with Alec. He's my Turtle Dove. My perfect match. I squeeze his hand.

"Thank you," I say. "You didn't have to do this. You didn't have to take us in."

"Don't be daft. Of course I did," Alec says brightly. "We've had a good time. Except worrying frantically over you, of course."

My mother is nodding earnestly but I catch sight of Mrs Rouman and her face tells me a different opinion. I suspect she rather agrees with me. They didn't have to take us in and it may not have been convenient at all. She's staring at me with an unfavourable colour in her eye. My mother doesn't notice, of course, her own eyes are as pale as the pearls Mrs Rouman fondles around her neck. She's comparing me to her expectations. The real Linnea to the girl she heard on the radio. Her lenses tell me I've a lot to prove over the next few days. Turtle Doves ML may pair you with your perfect partner, but I realise now they promise you nothing of your in-laws. Hans says farewell and I have to stop myself pleading with him to stay.

I could smell supper cooking as I walked in. The air is thick with starch and mint. My hopes rise. I've arrived in time for a meal. But first I'm expected to wash and familiarise myself with their house, which couldn't be more different than the ranch. Mrs Rouman leads me upstairs. She explains where the bathroom is and fetches me a towel. She starts the tour with a story of how they redecorated the stairs, and follows with how the towels and soap came back from a country I've never heard of. The Roumans live a much more luxurious life than I'm used to.

It doesn't matter I showered at HQ. I'm expected to wash the dishevelment from my face and hair. I'm sure Mrs Rouman senses it all.

"Oh dear," she tuts.

She moves my braid from my shoulder and spies the blouse underneath my cardigan. I want to tell her these aren't clothes from a donation box at HQ. These are my own clothes. I re-stitched some of the flowers myself. But I'm too embarrassed and let her leave in silence. Before she goes, however, she focuses her lenses on the shower unit. Water bursts from the shower head, as though it's afraid of her heavy glare. She notices my face and smiles proudly.

"I always hated having to reach in to turn it on. Always gets your arm wet with freezing cold water, don't you find? No matter how fast you do it. Right, I'll leave you to it."

As she goes to leave, the light turns off. She laughs and apologises. She says they never have to use the switch and turns it back on manually so I'm no longer in the dark.

"We'll get you put on the system as a Guest tomorrow," she says. "My husband will do that."

I realise this is a lens-controlled house. I've heard of houses like this. Appliances come with sensors instead of knobs and respond to a person's stare. To those who aren't registered to the system, it's unbelievably difficult to feel at home or in control. For one thing, there's no temperature control on the shower unit. Your lens readings will tell the shower which temperature you prefer and adjust accordingly. There's no such response from my lenses. I've never known a shower so hot and aggressive in my life. Within seconds the bathroom is a sauna thick with steam and I feel the water chiselling my skin. I scrub myself with lotion and I worry about how I'll turn the shower off. Fortunately it times-out after five minutes.

I don't look much better for taking a shower. I look swollen and sorry for myself. When I brush my hair I'm dismayed to see several blonde strands have fallen into the sink. WOLF lenses must be both a gift and a curse to someone who seeks to eliminate dust and dirt. Mrs Rouman's lenses are sure to make minuscule things hard to miss against such a white backdrop.

I tidy up after myself and try to compose. I don't want Alec to see me looking so disheartened after everything he's done.

Mrs Rouman's laid out a hairdryer and clothes on their bed so I can prepare myself properly before heading downstairs. I never dry my hair this way. I always braid it damp. Now it dries rapidly in a soft river and appears longer than usual. I don't bother tying it up and let it fall over my shoulders. Finally, I pull on a cashmere sweatshirt and jeans. Mrs Rouman claps her hands in delight when I emerge for supper.

"Oh, there now. Much better! Doesn't she look lovely?" She turns to my mother and realises who she's talking to. Her face falls and my mother just smiles. She must have had days of hearing about interior design she can't even see.

Every question at the table is aimed at me, of course. What I have been up to, what it was like to be on the radio, and how I felt when I realised everyone else had been evacuated without me. I answer as pleasantly as I can, avoiding as many details as possible. Throughout the meal I notice Mr and Mrs Rouman looking back and forth between my plate and Alec's. I eventually realise why. We both seem to enjoy large helpings of chicken and only eat carrots with a mouthful of meat to disguise the flavour. We both opt for spring water over juice. What's more, our glasses are both three-quarters full. Alec drinks when I drink. He puts down his fork when I do. Neither of us are deliberately doing this. But suddenly I feel like I'm back at WOLF HQ, being observed by a team of doctors.

One huge relief in all of this is my mother has already filled them in on our situation at home. They talk back and forth about work without needing my input.

"Of course this'll all be taken into account when you return home." Mr Rouman talks of our potential losses since the evacuation. "Your insurance will cover any loss of livestock, I'm sure."

"Of course," my mother says, but a bean catches in my throat and seems to swell to the size of a lemon. Insurance? They don't know everything, it seems. I don't say a word.

"They can't expect you to just walk back in and resume business. There'll be loss of earnings to claim for. I'm sure Orbelle's entire agricultural community will come together over the situation. This is where community works best: during setbacks such as this. Land and livestock isn't easy work. One month setback and you'll reap all year."

"Quite right." Mrs Rouman sips her cordial.

Alec notices my mother and I have little to say and clears his throat.

"I'm sure WOLF HQ will continue in their charity and help those in need. They'll be glad of the publicity. Cornelius Morgan may even put in a guest appearance. You know how he is."

Do I? He's speaking of the same people who wouldn't grant my mother a guide dog. But I daresay he's right. If the publicity's there, perhaps we can milk what we can out of WOLF. Especially if I'm able to introduce myself as the young evacuee on the radio.

"You'll be allowed home any day now," Mrs Rouman says. "No avalanches have been featured on the news. I expect it'll all pass soon. They won't want to keep Orbelle empty for long."

"That's right," my mother says. "You'll be back feeding O'Malley by the end of the week, Linnea."

I put down my glass. "O'Malley's dead, mother."

"What?" She turns her head, but looks towards Alec, not me. "How do you know?"

"A lot of them are dead." I decide not to mention the fact Joel and I attempted to shoot him. Not in front of Mrs Rouman. "Wolves came down from the mountain. O'Malley was attacked. There was nothing I could do. I saw him die."

A hush covers the table. Most of us use this moment to take a drink. The sound of swallowing and clinking of glasses fills the silence.

"I'm sorry, Linnea," Alec says sincerely.

We finish supper and Mrs Rouman makes everyone tea. Alec uses this opportunity to steal me away.

"Shall we take a walk?" he asks before fetching my coat.

I worry about leaving my mother, but she's spent days without me here already. We slip out the door whilst the rest of them busy with the tea.

Around the back of the house is a stretch of garden buried deep in snow. I follow close behind Alec until we come to what I originally thought to be a garden shed. But I'm pleasantly surprised. It's actually a gondola lift.

Unlike in Orbelle where our transport up the mountain is a chairlift, other places upgraded to cable cars. This one sits in a bed of snow with net curtains in its huge windows. It's deep colour, resembling a giant cherry. They've lined the front of it with potted plants and placed a wooden owl on the roof.

“There’s this metal scrap yard on the industrial estate where I work,” Alec explains. “You might have heard it mentioned on the news. It got hit with a bit of meteorite fragment. Anyway, they brought this gondola in and my father bought it. He planned to convert it into a sauna for my mother, but it didn’t quite work. Rather than sell it on again for scrap we tried to make a summer house out of it.”

He pulls open the door and offers me to climb inside.

The twin padded seats face each other and have been covered with patchwork blankets. On the wall is a shelving unit and a small heater sits by our feet. Alec switches the heater on before producing cans of cream soda from one of the seats. They’re hollow and used for storage. I didn’t think I could stomach any more vanilla today, but it mingles with the scent of snow and smells fresh.

“This is lovely.” I admire what they’ve managed to accomplish. It’s cosier than any of the rooms indoors.

“This is where I escape.” Alec smiles. “Sorry about my mother, she fusses because she cares.”

Yes, about her house and her belongings being touched. Not about me. Alec is still smiling at me warmly. The sun has almost set and soon I won’t be able to see his face properly.

“Is there a light?” I ask.

"There was, but the bulb went and we've been meaning to order a replacement. This is all I have." Alec reaches down to where the heater is plugged in and hits another plug. The gondola lights up. I hadn't noticed before, but the back of the seats have been rigged with fairy lights in the shape of stars. They let off a milky glow and bath us in faux moon light. I can't help but smile.

"I hoped you would approve; being the astronomer," he says. "The girl who goes to look at stars and gets left behind during an evacuation."

I snigger and sip my cream soda. The last time I saw Alec bathed in a soft light was in the simulation room. Being watched by an audience of researchers. This time we're completely alone and my hands start to tremble. Alec doesn't seem to notice.

"I'm sorry this has all worked out the way it has," he says. "When I got home from the city I wondered if I would ever hear from you again. I didn't want to be presumptuous. My parents never knew I signed up for Turtle Doves, so I didn't get any questions from them. I just kept wondering to myself: should I call you the next day? That was until I saw the news."

Alec pauses and sips his drink. I can see the memory still troubles him.

"I didn't think about what I was doing. I didn't even explain to my parents. I just got on the train and waited for you to arrive at HQ. I had to make sure you were okay but you never checked in. Instead I found your mother with her white cane and somehow I found the courage to introduce myself to her and your herdsman. She was inconsolable, wondering why you hadn't been in your bed that night. Wondering where you had gone. The next thing I knew I had invited her to stay with us until you showed up safe and sound. You can imagine my mother's face."

I shudder. Hearing about everything that went on whilst I was walking around the countryside with Joel makes me feel incredibly guilty. But I was okay, and she was okay. There's nothing to worry about now I'm here. There's no need to talk about it anymore.

"So, then." I hold my can steady because I don't know what else to do with my hands. I'm more nervous than I expected to be. "Forgive me. I wanted to ask you last time: when did you first hear about me?"

"Let me think." Alec tilts his head back as he remembers. "It was during my first WOLF appointment this year. They told me a few new girls had been brought into the database. They asked if I would be interested and I supposed it wouldn't have hurt to have a look."

"A few?" I can't help but wonder if the prospect of Alec meeting another girl before me would make me jealous.

"They had all your information. I was given a quick overview of three. Two city girls and one . . . I mean you."

"You chose me because I was from the countryside?"

"You were considered the most compatible. The system matched us almost perfectly. Higher than any other potential candidates. They said you were new to the system, so I guessed you would be eighteen. You obviously hadn't enrolled to the university. They said you worked full-time. I asked for a little more detail and they said you were a carer."

"So from two potential university students and me, you chose the most statistically compatible, yet the most boring?"

"In a way." Alec's cheeks start to burn red. "I couldn't really argue with the statistics. They told me we were ninety-five percent compatible. I agreed to let them pair us because you certainly sounded like you would be the most like me."

"Like you?"

"The most lonely."

I blink in surprise and remain quiet. Alec panics.

"What I mean is you might have appreciated the company more. A city girl . . . she would be free to anything and anyone. You sounded like you might be glad of a new friend, if nothing else. I've offended you haven't I?"

"No." To be honest, I'm not sure what to think. It sounds like I would be the most unappealing person in their database. The idea someone would choose me out of pity makes me bite my bottom lip.

Alec is so worried he's upset me he moves from his seat to mine and looks into my face. His eyes are speckled grey, like granite. None of this is out of pity, I realise. If I had been made the same offer I would have done the same. I would have chosen him.

"I'm glad you picked me," I say.

I don't know why I said it. And although I mean it, I also know exactly what to expect next. Perhaps if I didn't feel so haunted by the last couple of days, I would look away quickly. But I don't. I crave stability. I crave friendship.

We embrace in the middle of the gondola. Our lips gently pressing. His touch is feather light. I've never been kissed before. I don't know if I'm being clumsy. All I know is I want to forget everything that happened this week. I want to forget my poor goats, the nights on the ground, the interrogations, and the fact I'll never see Joel again. Turtle Doves ML would have never paired me and Joel together. I must remember that. I just want to forget everything. I keep my eyes shut and will Alec to take it all away.

We remain holding each other until his mother calls us inside. Alec checks his reflection in the window, although he looks just as smart as before. Why would he be any different? Then I realise he's looking at his lenses for any obvious signs of arousal before he faces his family. His eyes are like jade and shining like tinsel.

I look at my own reflection and see my eyes are blue. The shade is undeterminable but I suppose blue is better than nothing. It would be mortifying to have brown eyes after a first kiss. I can't deny I would have wished for green. In the films, a woman's eyes are always green after a kiss.

But Alec doesn't seem to notice. He's too busy drifting around in his own emerald ocean. I'm unsure whether I'll sink or swim before I'm able to go home.

19

There's nothing to do in Newton Belle. It's beautiful, but I find myself staring at the peak of Mt Venus and wishing I could see what's happening at home. I miss the ranch horribly and would like to go back before I become too reliant on the technology here. Without it will be like returning to the dark ages. Perish the thought I'll have to use my hands to operate things again.

I've been added to their home system now and I have access to all of these lens-controlled features. I can have a shower without being scalded and walk in and out of the house as I please, without a physical key. It took some getting used to. You have to use the right stare with the sensors. I can't deny how convenient things become. Getting my arm wet by turning on the shower never used to bother me. Annoyingly, I know it will now.

A lens-controlled house is supposedly the future of modern living. Focusing on a switch with intent will trigger the system into doing what they want. Be that turning the television on and off, opening and closing the window blinds or unlocking a door. Individual lamps brighten or darken depending on someone's need of light. The Roumans walk around their home as if they're telekinetic.

If only it were as easy for my mother. She exists in this household as more of a ghost than a guest. She's an entity with so little control I pity her. I never pitied her before. She never gave me any reason to. How awful it must have been for her to realise the toilet doesn't have a manual flush. At least Mr Rouman was able to find an old radio for her.

"Off limits". That's what we continue to hear over the next week. Each day enquiries are made about Orbelle, and each day we receive a phone call from Hans to say we're not permitted to return.

"Avalanche warnings at an all-time high," Hans says. "But it's not too dangerous to send an entire team of WOLF X recruits out there and set up station. They're monitoring the disturbance with the ALPHA satellite or somethin'. Apparently Orbelle is an ideal location to do that. Which means they've got the government go-ahead to do whatever they want there."

I can't get hold of Anna. Her mobile phone won't connect and I wonder if she left her phone charger behind in her haste to leave. She doesn't know where I am, so she can't possibly get hold of me either. I've no idea who to voice my concerns to. None of them are the person I really want to talk to. Unfortunately, neither is Alec.

I meet him from work every day. I take a detour to the metal scrap yard he mentioned. I've walked out to it three times now to see the minor damage the meteor did. It's a small reminder of what Joel and I narrowly avoided on our way out of Orbelle. There was no serious panic here. Hardly anyone took notice as this meteor sailed over the countryside and hit the concrete. You wouldn't know something was amiss with the floor littered with metal, oil stains and soot. But I get a feeling of excitement and fear again as I press my nose to the fence and look at the yard. They filmed a segment here for the news and people have already walked all the way out to have a look in curiosity. But I'm the only person here now.

I look back up at the mountain and remember the meteor I saw falling. Its tail had been alive and burning, and it had worn a bright starry helmet that lit up the sky as it fell. I imagine it hitting the scrap yard and imagine the damage would have been far greater. But no news' footage has documented that meteor.

No footage from phones or surveillance cameras manages to capture what I saw that night. I watch the same grainy footage over and over, but fail to see the same spectacle I saw.

I can only assume it's because these were filmed in daylight whereas what I witnessed lit up the entire mountain against the black of night. In a way I feel privileged, as though the entire thing had been a display just for me. A reward for climbing the mountain to see it.

But Joel must have seen it. Like so many other things lately, only Joel experienced that with me. He was on the mountain too. Yet he's one of the many people I can't communicate with. The only person who knows what I know deep down.

It wasn't a meteor I saw.

I step away from the scrap yard and rub black dust from my nose. Joel knew that, didn't he? He knew I saw something up there that had nothing to do with the meteor shower. That's why he stuck with me and insisted we avoided people. That's why Johannes was on our land. That's why Ouren was so interested in finding out who I was. Joel was looking out for me because . . .

Because I saw something I shouldn't have.

Each day I'm unable to contact Joel makes me more certain. I try to pin-point where that object would have landed and devise various routes that would lead me around the mountain to investigate. But then I sit at the dinner table with Alec eating homemade pie and sipping elderflower cordial and I start to feel normal. Or as normal as I can considering this isn't my home and our welcome is gradually running out.

On the one hand I think I'm best getting on with things. I should bond with Alec and his family and wait for news like everyone else. But, on the other hand, I yearn to know if the reason we're being kept out of our homes is because of something only I witnessed. They evacuated everyone hours before that object fell from the sky. The more I dwell and stare at the mountain the more I have the same thoughts over and over, until it's the only thing I can think about. I didn't witness a natural phenomenon that night. I witnessed a man-made operation that has cost me and my family everything. And only Joel can tell me why.

Joel.

I would give anything to speak to him. I could ask him questions. If he fails to answer them I could at least tell him how much I don't enjoy being in a lens-controlled house. I could tell him about Mrs Rouman. I know Joel would detect my sarcasm and make some joke about things to cheer me up.

It's not that I dislike Mrs Rouman. She's a very respectable woman who hasn't failed to feed me or change my bed sheets, which she does annoyingly often. But what annoys me most of all is how much time I'm expected to devote to my mother. I'm expected to hold her hand whenever she stands, talk to her constantly and never leave her in a room alone. I appreciate she needs someone to operate the sensors for her, but they even hand her a different mug and plate to the usual china in case she drops it. When she goes to the toilet they look at me as if I must go with her. I don't want the chore of flushing a toilet after her, and she wouldn't want me to. She's only inept because their house is built to be used by lenses, not people. But I daren't risk losing their hospitality. We have nowhere else to go.

Joel asked me how I do what I do without wanting to scream. Now I see why he asked. One more ignorant comment from Mrs Rouman and I may smash one of her precious plates. One more afternoon chained to my mother's side and I may shout at her too, and that's a horrible thought.

As a result, I deliberately find myself sneaking away from them all and avoiding contact with anyone other than Alec.

I've been here twelve whole days and no green eyes have looked back at me in the mirror. People may argue these things take time, but clearly time accelerated for Alec and I'm envious. I know mine will surely turn green in time. After all, we're a near-perfect match. But the time it's taking frustrates me. I don't care what shade – pear, lime, mint – but I need something. I've started to feel as though green eyes will be the only thing to bide us more time and stay in the Rouman household.

On the twelfth night I rediscover my backpack, which Mrs Rouman had tucked away in a cupboard. I'm washed and wearing a pair of Alec's pyjamas when I decide it's time to find my camera. I need to see those photos and determine what I saw. I fish it out the bottom of my bag and my knuckles graze something else. Something hard and rough.

I sit cross-legged on the floor and roll it from one hand to the other. Its surface is as black as coal but reflects silver as it turns. It's beautiful. I'd almost forgotten there was a meteorite in my backpack. The only thing I have left of Joel. I know there are no photographs of him on my camera – he made sure of that – but this meteorite feels like a connection to him somehow. We were the first people ever to hold it. I recall that memory with my eyes closed and try to remember how happy I'd been in that moment.

I remember something else. Alec's are not the first green eyes I've seen since my mother went blind. Joel's went green too. Not like grass or grapes. Not the same earthy colour Alec's turn. His eyes had come alive and burned like plasma. The most electric green I've ever seen. Why had they done that? Was it because of this meteorite? The ALPHA satellite disturbing his lenses? Or was it because he was just as entranced in that moment as I was? His lenses only turned green when he looked at my face. Was it a technical error or the deepest of emotions?

I hug the meteorite to my chest. I've not shown it to anybody else, nor will I. It belongs to us and only us. I wrap it in my old blouse and then again in one of my cardigans. It had travelled so far and now it sits at the bottom of my backpack. The most dormant it has ever been in its lifetime. I try to seal the thought of Joel away with it. I pick up my camera and find Alec.

"Can I get these pictures developed somewhere in Newton Belle?" I ask.

"Sure," Alec says. "I can do that somewhere on the industrial estate."

"Great. It has photographs I took during the meteor shower," I say. "I'd love to see them properly."

"I'll make sure you do." Alec kisses me. He'd do anything for me, I've learned.

Two days later I make the long walk from their house along the various paths to where I always meet Alec. Except today he surprises me by turning up on the path much sooner than he usually does. He's holding a large folder and his eyes look like dying sunflowers. My heart beats faster.

"What is it?" I ask at once.

"I was using the contact printer to create reverse images for an important company," he says. "We then transfer it to a projection screen to check for faults. But today I decided to use it to make an enlargement of another image. I enlarged your meteor picture."

"You did what?"

"I wanted to do something nice," Alec explains. "It was an impressive photograph. I thought if I blew it up for you and developed it, you could hang it on your wall. I was going to surprise you, maybe frame it, but . . ."

"But what? I mean, it's a lovely idea Alec, thank you. I don't understand why you're so worried."

"It could be nothing. I'm just an operator." Alec rubs the back of his neck. "But there's this thing. Part of the reason we've all been doing overtime is to work on a new order by WOLF. I shouldn't even be telling you this. I signed a contract and everything. It's just that the order is one of the most expensive ones we've ever had. It's a repeat of another order we received six years ago, the first job I remember us working on. We had WOLF officials inspect our work, conduct regular audits, and monitor everything. The boards we were designing were to go into the ALPHA satellite."

I stare at him for a moment. I feel something significant has just been said, but I can't quite work out what it is.

"I tried to erase the image from the computer, but I'm not sure if each artwork we scan is automatically stored on the system. Even if it is, it might be no one ever looks at it and no one will ever ask. But I think I need to consider the option of presenting my line manager with those images."

"No, you can't do that," I say quickly. "Why'd you feel you'd need to do that?"

"Think about it. Why are we working to replace ALPHA? Why are we remaking a previous order? The satellite is way more damaged than the news is telling us. There is fear that ALPHA was targeted by a terrorist group opposing WOLF," Alec says. "Your image was taken the same night the satellite started showing problems, and I accidentally scanned the date and time of the image with the rest of it. They now have a copy somewhere on their system. Face it, Linn, that's not a meteor you captured. The enlargement shows it plain as day. That's a part of ALPHA."

"I know." I back away and clutch the folder to my chest. In truth, I've known for days. "I mean, I suspected it was. But you can't show anyone. You'll have to delete the system file on your computer."

"Not without reporting it I can't," Alec says. "If they discover images of ALPHA like this and find out I developed them, the boy who started working there the same time we received the first ALPHA order in the first place . . . it's unbelievably suspicious, wouldn't you say? I won't just lose my job, Linn, I'll probably be arrested."

"Let me look at the images," I say desperately. "We can figure out what to do and tomorrow you can take them to your boss. I'll come with you, if you like. Prove I took the images and not you."

What else can I do? How can I keep this a secret and let Alec face a troubling situation? Joel's no longer my concern. Besides, only now am I absolutely certain what I saw up on the mountain was a man-made spectacle. Someone brought a part of ALPHA down from the sky and I'll bet Joel knew all about it. I can't send Alec, a mere sheep, into the lions' den to save the hyena. How do I know I can even trust Joel? He never actually told me anything.

Well, that's not strictly true. He told me a lot. More than I wish I knew. I see it everywhere now, especially in the media. Every commercial on the television aggravates me now. Artificial colour after colour. Concealed lie after lie . . .

Blue for happy. Purple for calm.

Blue to lure us in. Purple to keep us there.

Joel has undoubtedly made me cynical, but I see it everywhere now. I look back at the folder full of my photographs. Someone, somewhere, mustered a team of people to oppose WOLF and temporarily stop them manipulating us. What are they trying to protect us from?

Joel's a part of this. He has to be. There's no other explanation. What will happen to him when I take these images to the officials and face inevitable questioning? I can't tell them his name. They'll be after him like the pack of wolves they are. But I have to protect Alec. He's my Turtle Dove. He's the one I'm expected to be with.

So why does my heart feel torn in two?

20

I didn't think it was possible to feel guiltier than I already do. But that evening I discover I'm wrong. I'm so terribly wrong. I hate watching television with everyone else so I wait until ten o'clock, when everyone has gone about their own business and readying for bed. I take the remote and sit by myself, ready to learn what's happening in Orbelle. What I'm not prepared for is how close to home their first story will be. It's like a punch in the gut when I hear the news-anchor's opening words.

"Our top story tonight: the discovery of a missing girl from Orbelle has left local people both in shock and relief. Days after the evacuations, many believed the young girl to be dead. But, finally, she has been reunited with her family . . ."

I stare at the television, open mouthed. At first I feel sick. I dread the mention of my own name and feel mortified my disappearance has made the news. I didn't think anyone knew about it until I phoned the radio station. But confusion takes over and I shake my head. This is all wrong. I was reunited with my mother ages ago. No fuss was ever made and no one had put an appeal out to find me. It can't possibly be me.

They finally state the girl's name and a picture appears on the screen. My breath escapes me. I'm right. It's not me.

It's Anna.

The story that accompanies my best friend's picture is so dreadful I'm left shaking. Anna never made it back down the mountain. Whilst I was off watching the skies and meeting Joel, Anna had been suspended on the chairlift. High above the snowy ground she waited for over seventy-two hours. I can hardly contemplate this as the news' story reveals all the horrid details.

"Young Anna Harris told her parents she was off for a walk that fateful day. What no one knew was that she would be boarding the chairlift and be left at thirty-seven feet above the ground when Orbelle's power went out. There she sat, alone and in freezing conditions, whilst her parents were forced to evacuate without her; wondering frantically for their daughter's wellbeing."

It cuts to a shot of a chairlift swinging, empty and frosted with cold – though not one of the ones in Orbelle. They clearly weren't allowed near those.

"Anna's condition had drastically worsened as the night went on and during the long day and night that followed. Her memory of the ordeal has gone and her suffering can only be traced by her lens readings. By the time she was found, her need for medical attention was at a critical stage. Doctors have been working to save some of Anna's fingers and toes but along with hypothermia and dehydration, Anna Harris has a long and steady battle ahead of her."

I close my eyes and breathe slowly. This has to be a bad dream.

My name wasn't mentioned once. No one knew to look for me or that Anna was supposed to be with me that night. If only someone had asked for me I could've told them where Anna was and sent help for her sooner. But I was missing myself at that time. It only occurs to me now Anna hadn't done the same in return. She hadn't raised the alarm when Orbelle was evacuated and told my mother where I was. I hadn't considered that before. I'd forgotten all about Anna. I would've thought it odd she hadn't explained to people I was still up the mountain. But now I know she couldn't have because she was still up there herself, slowly losing her fingers and toes and her hope of being found. She must have prayed I would walk back the same way and pass beneath her so she could call out for me. We were supposed to stay together and should never have separated. Now the realisation hits me. For all my troubles, choosing to do the reckless thing and stay up the mountain overnight, it was Anna who suffered greater, for making the smart choice. She had opted to go back and chose safety. And here I sit now, with all my toes intact and five of my ten fingers gripping the remote. It's infuriately unfair. No matter what I've been through, things continue to peck at my conscious and my passiveness is cracking. Joel would be amused if he could see my face. I finally want to start screaming.

21

The following evening Hans calls for me. No matter how unenthused he sounds, I revel hearing his voice. It's familiar and homely.

"Evenin'." His thick accent is like putting a plaster over a minor wound. It temporarily sooths me and makes me feel a little better. "How's the HOLE?"

HOLE is a term Hans coined. It stands for House Of Lazy Eyes. Or it could stand for House Of Little Excitement. He said I could pick one. The idea is so the Roumans won't know we're discussing their home

"It's not so bad," I say. "The HOLE has learned what music I prefer to listen to. Yesterday I was annoyed at something and it started to play classical harp music to calm me. But my mother still needs my lenses to flush the toilet."

"Oh good lord. Can they wipe themselves or have they found a way around that too?"

"Hans, that's gross."

He snorts. "So it's not convinced you to upgrade the ranch when you get back?"

"No point," I say. "Not unless they introduce lenses for guide dogs."

"I wouldn't put it past them. In fact, you should pitch that idea to WOLF. You could make a bit of money."

"I thought we didn't like WOLF?"

"We don't. We just like being able to buy bread. Or some new goats. Lord knows how many we'll have left. Anyway, as you might have guessed, there's a reason I'm calling."

As my newly registered next of kin, WOLF have informed him of my recall to HQ.

"Your lenses were out of action for a few days and they're worried it'll have affected them somehow. Especially since they already malfunctioned once and weren't actually sent off for screenin'. Your name has flagged up on their data base and they've asked you to come in immediately. No appointment necessary. I'll come get you tomorrow mornin'."

"No need," I say. "Alec will take me. You stay with your family."

"If you like. I must say, you did a good job findin' a Turtle Dove with money. I know they pair you with your ideal match but I didn't know your taste was so expensive."

Normally I would find that funny. But my laugh comes out more like a sigh. There's a pause and I hear Hans inhale deeply.

"You heard about Anna, didn't you?"

"Yeah." I lower my mouth even more to the phone and speak quietly. "Yeah I did."

"It's not your fault, Linn."

I blink away tears. I've spent an entire day and night telling myself it wasn't my fault. Hearing someone else try to convince me makes me feel like it was all along.

"I know," I say thickly. "When did you hear she was missing?"

"I didn't hear anythin' for days. No one thought to tell me she was missin', why would they? If I'd heard anythin', I'd have told them she were with you. Then again, how would I have known that were true? You said you would be with her that day, but perhaps you were lying? I figured that were a lie when we found you alone and no mention of Anna's name."

"She was with me," I say guiltily. "She changed her mind and went back. She thought it was too dangerous. Hans, if it wasn't for me . . . We were supposed to stay together. I let her down."

"You did not." His voice becomes hard as stone. He pronounces each word so bluntly he loses his accent. "She let you down, Linn, not the other way."

"Yes but . . ."

"No, listen. Who was lookin' for you? None of her lot. No one in her family mentioned that Linnea Hansen was missin' too. You know why? Anna never told them she would be with you that night. She never mentioned stayin' anywhere overnight, with anyone. A walk. That's all she said. She fully intended to be back home that evenin'."

"Oh. Then she never meant for us to see the meteor shower at all," I say heavily. "She thought I would change my mind and go back with her."

"And when you didn't, she should've tried harder to persuade you. Heck, she should've stayed with you. The fact she turned around and went back, leavin' you there . . ." Hans' anger rises like boiling water beneath ice. When I eventually put down the phone, Alec asks what the conversation was about.

"Same old tale," I say. "We aren't returning to Orbelle yet."

The subject of Anna aside, I realise I have another journey ahead of me. Back to HQ for my recall. My intention is to go alone and leave a note. I write it when everyone else has gone to bed and put it on the table. My mother walks by without giving the table any notice. No one will read this message until daylight.

My bag is packed with a bonded folder containing the photographs Alec developed. The folder's marked with the date the images were captured. The night I was on the mountain.

I time my exit with the arrival of the postman. I'm able to ghost his footsteps with my own so none of them hear me leave. I catch the first train leaving Newton Belle. Since Orbelle is inaccessible it arrives early to allow for the detour it will take through Horval. I filter on to the train and stand with my hand on one of the ceiling rings, and observe just how disorderly transport has become since Orbelle was closed off.

Initially we journey in the opposite direction to the city, loop around the countryside and end up re-joining the original route, forty-five minutes behind what would otherwise be just a two hour train ride. Shortly before we arrive we pass through the same tunnel I was trapped in. My heart pounds to remember. When we exit I see the graffiti is gone but my mind recalls the words 'THEY BLINK WITH BLOOD' and how bleak the city looked without my lenses in. I feel my heartbeat quicken as I step into daylight and the smell of oil and coffee. I make it into Fenix before nine o'clock and set off for the city centre.

Iris appears to have anticipated my arrival. I know part of the illusion is she seems to watch people wherever they go, but from the minute I walk out of the station I feel she has been waiting for me. Her gaze is locked and I feel it burn. Eventually it proves too foreboding and in an attempt to lose her heavy stare I take a sharp turn in my path and find myself outside the prison.

This wasn't part of my plan.

I've never been here alone before. I'm not sure whether I'm even allowed inside without giving prior notice. I stay rooted to the spot until someone in uniform takes note of me and comes out to see if I'm all right.

"Sorry love, you can't visit just yet. Is there someone you want to see?"

I look at him appreciatively but don't know what I want to do next. There's so much to explain to my father. We're homeless, our goats are gone, my mother can no longer see light and dark, and we're living with a boy who WOLF considers my perfect match. There's so much to say to my father who can't possibly do anything. He's safe in his brick bubble. If I enter I'd intrude like a thorn. I back away.

"No, thank you. It's not important."

I turn around, defeated, and follow the path guided by Iris. The sight of her only goes away when I pass under the arch of HQ's entrance.

I check myself in by explaining their need to evaluate my lenses and don't mention my other reason for being here. At some point today I'll present my photographs to Dr Frost and no doubt he'll contact the relevant people. Whether it be Lieutenant Rusten or even Cornelius Morgan himself. From there it'll be over for me and I can return to Newton Belle with the situation washed from my hands. I don't know whether that's the right thing to do or not. Joel never gave me any instruction or hint as to what these pictures mean. But we have barely anything to return home to. We need our goats and our ranch. We need that compensation. So I must appear loyal to WOLF, whether my actions bring me joy or not.

Dr Frost greets me just before midday. "Linnea Hansen, you're becoming quite the regular here. They'll have to issue you your own room soon. Come, let's have a look at you."

I take off my backpack and place it next to the chair. Nurses put on latex gloves, the chair is reclined and suddenly I'm no longer anxious. This is all routine and I just focus on getting out my lenses.

"We've done a quick computer check and your name flagged up as one of the many lenses affected by the satellite misfortune. With Orbelle evacuated and your poor self out in the wilderness for a day or two we have a back-log in data for your readings. Furthermore we can't be sure if the lenses have properly recovered from their sudden shut-down and re-boot. Have you experienced any abnormalities with your vision?"

I tell him I haven't since they were reinitiated, but that doesn't deter Dr Frost. He wants my lenses out.

"We'll get these screened and reinserted by the end of the day. Do get yourself comfortable. We'll give you your drops and then you know the rest. This is all a precaution, don't worry. Best to get these things checked over."

We're only five minutes into the procedure when the power fails.

My eyes are full of serum but even I see the lasers go out and then restart. Dr Frost wrenches the apparatus away from my face.

"Susan, what was that?"

"Power shortage," his assistant says. She steps into the corridor a moment. I can hear staff walking about and murmuring.

"Is it safe to continue?" Dr Frost's other assistant asks, whilst holding a tissue to my damp face. Susan reappears without concern.

"It happens all the time at my house," she says. "Every time a train goes past the window."

"Then let's continue," Dr Frost says loudly, directing the lasers back at my face. I don't have a chance to voice my own concerns. Nothing else falters though, and soon I'm sat back up, waiting for my eyes to stop swimming.

"We've never had that before," the assistant says, handing me more tissue paper. Susan has taken my lenses to be tested. When she returns, she pulls Dr Frost to the side of the room.

"Possible meteor interference," I hear her mutter. "They're expecting it to happen again. You've been called upstairs. Seems urgent."

"Of course. Miss Hansen you'll have to excuse me," Dr Frost says as he removes his gloves. "Feel free to have a walk around, but don't leave this area. Blink those eyes better. Don't rub them. Apply more serum if needed. I'll be back with you shortly."

When he leaves, the assistant makes to clean up after our procedure.

"What's the date today?" I ask.

"Beg your pardon? It's the 28th isn't it?" she says.

This is wrong. There is no scheduled meteor shower today. Not so soon after the one I photographed. I should know. My bedroom's covered in charts and calendars. I waited months for that shower. I would know if another was due so soon after. Unless I'm mistaken the next one isn't for another five months.

I swing my legs off the chair and stand unsteadily.

"I can go anywhere in this area?"

"Yes, go for a stroll," she says. "Get your bearings. Take care though, you may feel a little funny for a while. I can come with you if you like."

"No, thank you. I'll be all right." I walk gingerly to the door and pause only to retrieve my backpack. There couldn't be a better time to bring up the subject than during suspected meteor interference. It's almost too perfect.

I comply with Dr Frost's request and don't venture out of the area. But I do find myself wandering to the edge of the XY unit. I'm standing next to the simulation room – directly opposite the X unit.

Joel isn't here. His team would have moved on. Besides, this isn't the actual WOLF X military base, only the research and medical centre for their lenses. There's nothing for me behind those doors. Still I prepare to confront anyone who leaves that unit and offer them my photographs. In fact, I'm prepared to hit the buzzer and summon someone so this whole thing will be over. It doesn't frighten me to go beyond the WOLF X doors. I've been there before. I remember the corridors and rooms where I was held for questioning. I vaguely remember the faces and smell of chemicals. Perhaps once I would have been too afraid to go any further, but now I hit the buzzer and wait.

My backpack hangs off one shoulder and I hit the buzzer again. There's no sound and no vibration. I expected there to be something. A beep, a whirr, a crackle of electricity. Something to show there's life in this door. But whatever caused the power surge has left the intercom inert, so I knock. The door moves slightly. It swings open enough for me to catch a glimpse of the empty corridor beyond.

I'm not brave enough to walk into the X unit without permission. I pull the door closed again and decide there's only one thing left to do: hope someone spots me if I wave at the surveillance camera on the ceiling. I hold my bag in place and thrust the other hand up, signalling for attention.

"Hello? Your buzzer isn't working," I call. "Can I speak with someone?"

The camera points at me but there's no response. Clearly everyone's preoccupied with the power surge and making sure any technical problems are resolved. I would've thought they'd focus on security first. I'm not even sure the camera is operating. I could be anyone about to enter the X unit. That thought alone sees me back away from the unit and consider returning to Dr Frost's surgery. If the cameras are experiencing problems then it's unlikely the intercom system will work. If they call me back I might not hear them.

But I don't return.

My eyes fall on the door to my right and to the huge sign jutting from the wall. I'm outside the simulation room. The place I met Alec for the first time. The chairs that line the off-side corridor are empty. The magazines are piled up on the side table. The lockers destined for people's belt buckles and jewellery are lined up with their doors open, waiting to be used. The area is unmanned. Clearly no one is using the facility right now.

Dr Frost said I could go anywhere in this area. I take my bag with me, ignoring the lockers, along with my shoes which I would normally remove.

I don't want to actually operate the simulation room. I just want somewhere I can sit and think about everything. Somewhere familiar where I can consider what to do next. As I expected the security on the door has momentarily lapsed and I pull it open with a heave. The emergency spotlights lights are on. I pull the door shut behind me and hear it clunk into place. For my own reassurance I open it again and am relieved to know it won't lock behind me. Anyone can come and kick me out if they wish. For now, I take a seat.

The room hums, even though the power has been supposedly shut down in this room. Only a few features seem to be operating and I fail to resist temptation when I find one of the touch pads. I hit the power button out of curiosity and suddenly regret my decision. The spotlights go out and the stand-by lights replace them, dotted about the now black walls like red stars. Worst of all I hear the two main doors lock on either side of the room, sealing me inside. I have no idea how to let myself out. I'll have some explaining to do when they find me.

There are worse places to find myself trapped. I familiarise myself with the red lights. There must be over two hundred of them. I might as well make use of my time in here. My heart pounds as I tap in an area code and watch the screens light up.

I'm finally home.

Although it's only an image, my heart wriggles its way into my throat and sticks there like a boiled sweet. I can see my goats on the hill and all the flowers that line the station flowerbeds. It's like stepping off the train after the longest journey of my life. The ranch is exactly how it has painted itself in my mind, unspoiled and unaffected by any sudden evacuation. The goats graze, the tracks leading up the hillside are fresh and earthy and I know my mother and I are safely stored away in that house. No one can touch us as long as this image isn't altered. We are frozen in time.

If someone walks in now, they'll be shocked to see me crying. Perhaps they'll understand and not scold me for sneaking in here to see my home again. I don't know when I'll next see it. Surely they'd understand that?

Suddenly the lights go out and there's a shift in the ground. Like when an elevator stops. Every hair on the back of my neck stands up and the screens flicker back to life, one by one. An image of a wolf appears on each individual screen. Two sets of eyes and a snout, multiplied a hundred times. There's no sound to begin with, and I realise this is WOLF's default screen when the power starts back up. I start to relax, thinking the simulator will start working again any second. Then the words sound.

"THEY ARE WATCHING US."

It comes out of each speaker as a hollow crackle. Each screen appears to have its own, so the words ring out from dozens of monitors. The wolves on the screen don't blink or move. But the screen changes. A greyscale image of the earth appears, filling the whole screen. Little tiny white dots cluster in each country, filling the space like ants in a jar.

It's us. Each flickering dot is a set of lenses.

"THEY ARE WATCHING US."

I've had enough now and run for the doors. I attempt to pull open the first door but it's locked tight. I hammer with my fist and call out for attention, but something tells me this message isn't just for me. This is being broadcast all over HQ, perhaps all over the city. No one is going to be watching me in the simulation room. I'm stuck here until it's over, until the people hacking into WOLF's system are done with their message. This is the follow up to the ALHPA disturbance, that much seems clear to me. They disrupted the satellite and now HQ has been targeted. What I can't foretell is if this is a warning or an impending assault.

The next image is a shot of HQ from outside. I walk back into the middle of the room to look at it. At first I think it's just a frozen image. Then the holographic image of the globe changes into the clock and I realise it's a live streaming of events outside. The time on the clock is suddenly incorrect. It should be approaching one o'clock but the clock rewinds itself until the image shows it at only a few seconds to twelve. As the final seconds tick, the voice sounds.

"THEY ARE WATCHING US. WE ARE HERE TO STOP THEM."

The clock morphs back into the eye just before the explosion. I hear it from deep within the simulation room. There's a tremble like thunder across the ground and I listen for screams. Iris just blew up like a microwaved egg. Smoke is billowing into the sky so the screens show nothing but thick smog. They've manage to manipulate WOLF's projection into their own message. The clock, the eye, the earth's globe . . .

Time is up, WOLF is momentarily blind, and I'm guessing the whole country just watched it happen.

22

When the door finally opens I flee from the simulation room as if from the jaws of a rabid animal. Unbelievably, everything looks normal in the corridor. I wonder if I'm safe. If the building collapses will they know to look for me under the rubble? It seems clear to me the rest of building will have been evacuated and I have to find my own way out. So it comes as a huge surprise when a team of security guards round the corner and start shouting my name.

"WOLF 0315?"

They block the corridor like a wall with their bodies and demand I announce myself. I come to a halt and wonder what the protocol will be. Dr Frost steps around the corner and spies me.

"That's her!"

It takes a moment for me to realise what's happening. I'm suddenly grabbed from behind and forced on to the floor. I'm pinned in place by the weight of the security guards.

"She came in earlier this month with one of Ouren's men. They have some kind of correspondence. I should have seen it coming. Her lenses were sent for screening. The opportunity was right there."

I wriggle in protest and shout I don't know what is going on. I tell them I was in the simulation room the entire time. Surely we need to get out before the whole place collapses. I tell them to call Hans Fotland. I tell them to call Alec Rouman. But the only interruption comes from the nurse who usually operates the simulation room.

"Doctor." She hands a folder to Dr Frost for his consideration. I'm still restrained whilst he glances at its content. It takes me a moment to see the woman is holding my backpack and the folder is mine. The date of the ALPHA interference is written boldly on the front. I don't even attempt to explain. I know there's no helping myself now.

"Call the authorities," Dr Frost says. "And when Cornelius Morgan gets here be sure to send him straight to the X unit. This young lady is sure to be under arrest."

He reels off a list of accusations and I struggle to recollect if I'm guilty of any of them. He says I deliberately attempted to break into the X unit after sabotaging the buildings' power supply. He says I tried to operate machinery I had no right to, for purposes they suspect are damaging to WOLF. And I carry incriminating evidence of ALPHA that surely makes me a part of the satellite disturbance.

I just stare at him, open mouthed. When I try to protest he insists I remain quiet. I try to process everything he's accusing me of. I snuck into the simulation room – yes. Those are my photographs – yes. But when I hear the word 'terrorism' my entire body seems to fold itself inside out and I buckle. They pick me up and force me to the X unit whilst the lights above my head continue to flicker.

23

I don't need to be led, since I know where the X unit is. But they do need to drag me, since I stall as much as possible and scream so they will listen to me. I want Dr Frost to believe me now, not after yet another interrogation. I make sure they know how I feel. I dig my heels into the corridor floor. I grapple at door handles to stall us. When that fails, I shout he's crazy and try to pull my arms free. I realise, once we enter the X unit, I may have made myself look guilty. When the doors seal behind us, I give up and try to regain my composure. I know there's no point now the door's locked. They hold my shoulders continually in case I try to bolt anyway.

It becomes clear within a few minutes there's no fear of the building collapsing or catching fire. During our walk to the X unit I hear snippets of information as it passes between staff. The building has been closed and the upper levels have been sealed whilst The Socket is ventilated and cleared of smoke. I hear the words "hologram" and "illusion", which is what I thought Iris was anyway. I also hear the word "bomb" several times, which frightens me. But there's no hurry to clear the building. Cornelius Morgan will be with us shortly.

"Don't I have the right to someone? Like a lawyer?" I ask. "My mother at least? You don't really think I'm behind all this?"

They don't respond, although there's a murmur between them at the mention of me requesting a lawyer. If they have a strong enough case against me then the police will take me away and I can begin proving my innocence from there. They can't keep me here forever.

So what are they waiting for?

I'm not led to one of the offices. Everyone congregates in one of the larger waiting areas and I'm seated opposite a table of science magazines. The magazine on the top of the pile features Cornelius Morgan on its cover. He's not smiling. His eyes always smile for him in photographs.

It's a matter of minutes before a face I recognise appears from one of the offices.

"Lieutenant Rusten," Dr Frost says. "This is Linnea Hansen – WOLF 0315, Snake F. She's from Orbelle. You'll probably want to conduct some sort of background check. We have her medical files but Morgan will expect more."

"This?" Rusten looks me up and down. He had the same hungry look about him when he spied Major Ouren a few weeks ago. "This is our criminal?"

"Our suspect for now," Dr Frost confirms. "At any rate, we certainly won't be letting go of her until Morgan's happy."

"That could take time. I just spoke to him on the phone. He'll have someone sent down by the end of the day. One of Ouren's would suit me greatly."

I want to tell them this is all a mistake. But what would be the point? No one cares for what I have to say. Since I'm assured none of us will be blown up in the next hour or so I'm resolved to sit in silence and watch the news broadcast on television.

All we see is smoke. Thick, white smoke billowing into the sky outside HQ. There are helicopters and reporters everywhere, although none dare to get too close for fear of being engulfed. There's panic in the street. The area is being roped off and the fire-engines are on standby. It's hard to believe this is all going on whilst we're sealed away in the X unit.

"Clever." I hear Rusten comment as he watches. "Although not too difficult to achieve. If I had done it myself I would've dyed the smoke black at least. Make it look as though the building were actually on fire."

There's a patronising tone as he glances in my direction. No offence is taken. I have nothing to do with this.

"Any danger?" Dr Frost says. "To someone up in that area?"

"I would think so," Rusten says. "No more than breathing in ordinary wood smoke, however potassium nitrate isn't something I would want to inhale for long. If any more of those fools are up there then I'm sure the police would have us smoke them out. We quickly sealed off all other levels. Who would've thought their smoke bomb could be so affective? Let's hope if anyone lingered up there they'll cook in their own creation."

A smoke bomb? I stare hard at the television screen. I observe the soft white colour of the smoke pouring out of The Socket, like a smoker with its throat cut mid-exhale. It's a grim image, but I note there are no flames. The smoke is clean, not mingled with ash and heat of burning. So we're safe. The building isn't on fire. It was a trick.

My heart almost stops when I see Cornelius Morgan enter the unit. There's a flurry of anticipation as his footsteps approach. I hear his name announced as a prior warning to everyone and then he's here. He opens the double doors with both hands and his Tiger's Eye irises sweep the room for the fastest explanation someone can offer. His patience appears to hang by a thread.

"What was that?"

His voice silences everyone. Someone in the far corner was using the water fountain but now even the trickle of water halts. The reluctant drip of the machine fills the silence.

"Mr Morgan, if you would come to the office," a senior member of staff speaks before being shot down by his golden glare.

"Professor," Morgan corrects him sharply. "And that, everyone, was a direct attack on WOLF and a blatant attempt at spurring global protest."

"Professor Morgan," Lieutenant Rusten speaks up as he steps forward. His chin is higher than the crown of Morgan's own head. "If it was such an attempt, then it is a failed one. The public are waiting for your statement – no, your reassurance – that these trouble makers will be caught and dealt with. And despite the fumes, which have been contained within The Socket, no damage has been done to the building save for the shattered glass. The whole thing was a clever, holographic illusion."

"Trouble makers," Morgan repeats.

His gaze moves until it settles on me. Does he know who I am? The girl on the radio? Certainly he doesn't know I was standing right beside his potential assassin. If Joel had been holding a loaded weapon Morgan would be dead right now.

"This one." Morgan points at me. "What is she doing in here? If there's no threat to patients then why is she in here? Take her back to her ward."

"Professor." Rusten takes delight in muttering in Morgan's ear. "She's one of Ouren's. She came to HQ three days after the Orbelle evacuation, and in the company of one of Ouren's men. We've found images in her possession. Images of ALPHA debris during its descent. I told you, Professor, it's Ouren."

"You've said many times, Lance," Morgan says irritably.

"Professor, I was there that day. I was one of the men who rushed in and wrenched the badge from Ouren's hand. The badge WOLF honoured him with. I tried to prevent him going completely blind and he attacked both me and Johannes Steyn. You didn't hear what he said in that moment. Then he re-emerges, accepts a demotion and assembles his own team as though nothing ever happened? It's suspicious, you can't deny it's suspicious. He wanted his own recruits for a reason. He's going beyond WOLF to recruit them. Taking on people who aren't officially WOLF X. And this girl is another one, I swear it. Just like the other girl we found. This one'll deny it too."

Morgan's eyes widen. I shake my head desperately but Morgan won't hear what I have to say.

"Who was the boy she came with? Which of Ouren's team?"

I won't answer. They can accuse me of what they want. I won't tell them.

"Joel," someone says.

My heart sinks. I forgot I'd introduced him to Dr Frost.

"Joel," Morgan repeats. "What is his last name? What is his WOLF number?"

"I didn't learn that," Frost says regretfully. It's enough for Rusten to step in again.

"Ouren had reported a deserter from his team. A Joel Edgecombe. Stated he had gone missing during the evacuations. He backtracked a little when I asked him about it. Made out Edgecombe never went missing at all."

"A decoy?" Morgan supposes.

"It's certainly possible. Throw him off our radar whilst he secretly plotted with this one," Rusten says, looking at me.

I can't take anymore. I throw my hands down on the table as I rise up. The magazine showing Morgan's face slides off the pile and onto the floor. My shoulders are immediately seized.

“None of that is true. I have an explanation for everything,” I say. “I’m a victim in all of this. I’ve lost everything, you hear me? Everything! Why would I throw it all away to help blow up that eyeball? I just want to go home.”

“And where is that?” Morgan asks, although he’s ignoring me and looking at Rusten.

“Orbelle. She and her family own a ranch there. Or did. We ran a background check whilst waiting for you. Her mother was blinded by WOLF testing during the earlier years of the company. There’s understanding with Dr Frost the girl herself may suffer blindness in due course.”

I feel numb as I realise what’s happening. Rusten thinks he’s uncovered a motive. That this may be some outrageous revenge plot for the way my mother and I have been affected. Morgan stares at me until a realisation dawns on him.

“She isn’t wearing lenses.”

“No, Professor. They were taken out for screening. No more than twenty minutes before Iris was destroyed,” Frost says.

“Convenient,” Morgan says. “So we’re unable to read any activity during that time.”

“They’re being screened right now. If she has any incriminating information at all then we’ll find it.”

My hopes dare to rise. So they're waiting for evidence? Once my lenses are cleared I'll be able to demand they let me go?

"Of course it won't be fully reliable, since her readings stopped once ALPHA was affected. We have at least two days without readings from her," Dr Frost says regretfully.

I look at my doctor, wounded. Does he really think this of me? I've always been a good patient. I let him sign me up to Turtle Doves ML.

Oh lord. Alec. What will they do to him when they learn these images were developed at Grapha? When they learn Alec was a member of the team responsible for manufacturing parts of the satellite? Will they suspect he's a part of this attack too?

"Well keep her under close surveillance until those lenses return." With one jerk of his head Morgan signals for me to be removed from his sight whilst he and Rusten talk.

I barely seem to have sat for five minutes in one of the offices before the door opens again and I'm told to come with Rusten. Expressions are stern, yet something seems to have excited everyone. They've all lined the corridor in anticipation. The double doors are opened manually and a hospital bed is wheeled into the corridor, sporting someone concealed by a blanket. Morgan is the first to inspect the newcomer, drawing the bed to a halt and craning over the patient. Rusten uses this moment to take my forearm and mutter in my ear.

"A WOLF X recruit, wouldn't you know it? You'll be pleased to know he isn't dead yet, but his condition is hard to determine. They found him once the worst of the smoke had cleared. Smoke inhalation. A nasty way to die. Mechanical ventilation is advised – no, critical I would say. He may not have burned his respiratory system, what with the lack of actual heat. But that's nothing Morgan can't fabricate with the media. What do you say, Miss Hansen? Care to have a look at him yourself? Tell us what you make of his condition. You know him better than any of us."

A lump swells in my throat and I can't reply. I allow him to shove me in the direction of the hospital bed and I prepare myself for what I'm about to see. Morgan steps aside so I can see the WOLF X uniform peeking above the sheet. One of the casualty's arms slides off the bed and the nurse picks it up and drapes it across his chest. His hand is dark. I quicken my pace and draw myself up alongside him, staring at his closed eyelids.

"This isn't Joel," I say loudly. "I only know Joel Edgecombe, and only by chance meeting. This one I've never seen before."

Perhaps Morgan knows it's a lie. Perhaps he suspects I'm trying to hide Theo's identity. He turns back to the nurse and asks if this boy is wearing lenses.

"Professor, if you will observe." She leans forward and prises open one of Theo's eyelids. His WOLF X lenses are swimming with colour, even as he lies unconscious. His eyes are bloodshot; raw from smoke and persistent rubbing. You're not supposed to rub when lenses irritate. Everyone knows that.

"He needs help." I look at the line of doctors. "You will help him, won't you?"

He means more to them alive, surely? They can prosecute him so long as he recovers.

Morgan nods once and the bed continues to be wheeled down the corridor, flanked by Dr. Frost and his team of nurses.

"Certainly, he will be taken to the correct care unit and given the hospitality he has earned himself. Single-handedly destroying my Iris . . . I look forward to discussing it with him. As for you, young lady, thank you for everything you have told us. Might I ask who expects you to be here today? You mentioned your mother. Is she nearby?"

"She's in Newton Belle," I say. "But she'll know I'm here. She'll have seen the news and be worried. She and my next of kin will be here shortly."

"Of course they will."

Morgan summons a female staff member and sends her to reception. "All threat within the main building has diminished. Return to front desk. Answer the phone to no one. But do call the family of Linnea Hansen and tell them she's here undergoing treatment."

"Thank you," I say curtly, surprised by his sudden kindness. Only when he stares at me do I acknowledge what he said. "Wait. Undergoing treatment?"

"It's unfortunate," Morgan remarks. "Two cases of severe smoke inhalation and, what with the power out, not the sufficient equipment to treat them. Their families will want them well. They'll be patient and wait whilst their loved ones are in recovery. They'll wait all night, no doubt. Shame the building is unsafe for the public right now. Perhaps they could've sat by your bedside. As it is . . ."

"You can't do that!" I think of my poor mother and can't believe they would be so cruel as to worry her. "You can't let them think I'm hurt! Why would you do that? Why?"

Morgan turns away and Rusten resumes his place by my side, one hand firmly holding my forearm and the other signalling to let him pass. These are the people I consider animals, yet they remain composed as I scream and lash out. Rusten pulls me further into the X unit like a feral creature requiring termination, my shouts echoing down the corridor.

24

They place me in the same care unit as Theo. My bed is directly opposite his. They force me to strip from my clothes and into nothing but a backless hospital gown. They place a wristband on me. They hand me slippers and a bed pan. Then they take my clothes, my dignity and my answers and lock themselves the other side of the door with no window.

I rattle the handle a few times before backing away. I'm being held here against my will and what's more, there's nothing Hans or Alec can do whilst they think I'm being treated for burns. Morgan's right, they'll leave me under the care of professionals. There's nothing I can do but wait to see what happens next.

"Why are you doing this?" I shout when I hear footsteps pass the door. "You have nothing against me. Nothing."

There's no television and no interruptions. I sit on my bed with my knees up to my chin.

The machine they've rigged Theo to hums gently. I choose to think of it as a sign of life, since his body remains unmoving. They've secured him in place with an oxygen mask and catheters that snake from his arms. It all makes me feel uneasy. Blood seeps from the puncture wounds in the back of his hands and is now stuck beneath the adhesives that secure the catheters. I don't enjoy seeing blood outside a person's body. I observe how red it is. Just like the colour of Joel's eyes when Morgan was in range of shooting. I wonder now what would've happened if Joel had succeeded and Morgan had been killed that day. It would've made him a murderer. He would be in prison with my father now. But would Theo have endangered his life like this if the head of WOLF had been removed?

They seem to believe Theo acted alone in this. I believe so too. If more of the team had shown up then it might have aroused suspicion whereas Theo got into HQ undetected. Whatever the truth may be, Ouren can claim Theo acted entirely alone and not on his orders. In fact, I wouldn't be surprised if Theo's reported as missing within the next few hours. If Ouren doesn't hear from his recruit soon then surely he'll know they caught him. What will Joel think, knowing Theo is in the hands of these people?

They won't harm him. That much I can hope for. He's rigged to a machine that breathes for him because they'll want to question him. They'll demand to know who gave him the means to destroy Iris. I may not be a technical person, but from what I heard it sounds like Theo managed to create his own hologram and animate it to look like Iris was exploding. Complete with a smoke bomb and message to the public, it was an impressive and realistic stunt. The Socket was shattered but I'm sure their main concern right now is how

Theo even managed to get through security.

I lower my knees and stare at him. Now it makes a little sense. Theo would have needed an accomplice to get in. Someone from within WOLF HQ. I may not have any knowledge of locks and computers, but my folder full of Grapha-developed pictures says otherwise. I may dress the common country girl, but the evidence suggests it's all a charade. For all they know, I'm smarter than I appear and somehow disabled the locks whilst Dr Frost was out of the surgery. Improbable – absurd even – yet what else can they suppose? I'll have to sit and wait whilst they think it over.

They're monitoring his cardiac rhythm with a device strapped to his wrist and pads stuck to his chest. The heart-rate monitor on his wrist covers half his hand and secures around his thumb with Velcro. The screen resembles a large watch face and rests on the dorsal side of his hand. His fingers are curled slightly and the skin stretches beneath the device, which displays the current colour beneath his eyelids. Two full circles, both the colour of charcoal, flicker ever so slightly as the device constantly reads for any change. Underneath is a digital reading of Theo's heart beats-per-minute and the current lens colour. It's written in a numerical code so they can refer to their charts.

I suppose, by looking at the screen, number 605 is a shade of black. The computer next to his bed must be keeping track of all readings. Each time the screen flickers I expect it to have made a new recording.

The flicker is my only indication of time. Each one is another ten seconds of my experience locked away in this room. By now the screen has flickered well over a hundred times. The room darkens enough for the sensor lights to come on and then off again after thirty seconds. Each time they do I wave a hand for the sensors and bring them back on. It's the only thing I have to occupy myself. I wonder if it'll annoy Theo if he can detect any trace of light and dark. He's shown no sign of movement in hours. By the time the light has come on for the nine-hundredth time, I stop waving at the sensor and settle back on my hospital bed. No one has brought me any news and I hear nothing from the corridor. I put the pillow comfortably under my head and stare into the darkness.

I didn't know I'd fallen asleep until I'm woken up by the weight of someone sitting down on the end of my bed. Someone with lilac eyes.

"I didn't mean to wake you," Cornelius Morgan says gently. I start to sit up but his voice is so kind I settle where I am, my head slightly raised off the pillow. His face is bathed in a soft light from the corner of the room.

"What's going on?" I ask in quiet voice to mimic him. I'm aware of other nurses around Theo's bed, but they're mere shadows and only Morgan and I speak to one another.

"It's okay, Linnea, everything is sorting itself out." He calls me by my name, not my WOLF code, and any earlier scepticism has gone from his voice. Whilst he may have squawked like a silver heron earlier, he's as gentle as a lamb now and puts a hand on my knee. I feel the weight on the blankets and remember he's a celebrity. His very touch is rare and valuable. "I apologise deeply for the events of today. Your lenses have returned from our labs. You must understand our earlier concern. With their readings and some other background checks you are free to go. But please, rest first. We wouldn't send you on your way without a good night's sleep. And you are so very tired."

I spot the watch on his wrist. 2 am. No point going anywhere now. Besides, his gaze is making my head so heavy. His eyes deepen in colour. I can practically smell the lavender that oozes from them. Deep pools of mauve that glow, even in the dark. Feel relieved. Happy. Even the urge to reach out and hug him. But instead I return his wary smile and rest my head back on the pillow. So very tired. Once my head is down I don't have the energy to lift it again. Morgan reaches out and brushes a few hairs from my forehead. His touch is so soft it's like a breeze against my skin.

"Tomorrow is a new day," he whispers. "All of this will be over and you will go back to your Turtle Dove, back to your mother. Rest now."

"Okay," I murmur, watching the shadows move behind him and arrange Theo's bed. I hear them whisper faintly. I hear them tell Morgan it's time to leave now. He stands and draws a curtain around my bed.

"Goodnight Linnea."

I settle back peacefully, as though the hard day has been replaced by a hot bath and a fluffy towel. Too comfortable to move, even though sleep doesn't come for me yet. I stay awake, breathing in the scent of the sheets. I'm sure Morgan left traces of lavender on them. I lie still, absorbed in the silence except for a door creaking far away. But gradually the feeling of calm fades into a light sleep. As dawn approaches I wake alert.

That's when I realise the room is now quiet.

Too quiet.

Save for that low noise that sounds like a door creaking elsewhere. It takes a moment for me to realise the noise is Theo. His breath is ragged. I force myself upright, on to my elbows and listen for the soft purr of machinery.

Nothing.

I should go to sleep. Morgan said everything would be all right. His lilac eyes sang their lullaby and tomorrow everything will be fine again. But all of that feels like the fragments of a dream, and is slowly ebbing away. I shake my head free of his gentle stare and force myself to sit up.

Something's wrong.

I feel it under my skin with every breath Theo takes. When I stand up to look closer at his bed I see the plugs have been pulled. He's no longer connected to the machine that breathes for him. I suppose this is good and he mustn't need it anymore. But still I go to him.

"Theo?" I don't want to trigger the light in case someone sees. "It's me, Linnea Hansen. Do you remember me? I'm here too. They think I have something to do with all this."

Theo doesn't stir but I see his eyelids move. Perhaps he's dreaming, or perhaps his irises are searching for me behind closed lids. I edge closer, putting my hand on his arm and bending down to whisper.

"You did a good job, you know. Even I thought it had truly been destroyed. Everyone saw it. It was incredible. Major Ouren will be pleased with you, and Joel . . . I bet Joel will laugh when he sees the news, don't you?"

It's only the slightest of movements, but I spot it nonetheless. Theo stirs enough to bite down on his bottom lip. He breaths out heavily and I back away, not knowing what to add. I suppose there's nothing more I can do. Tomorrow I'll go home and Theo will have to recover on his own without me. But he would've known the risks when he came here.

But I can't seem to move. There's something too disturbing about the noise Theo makes. It sounds strangled. Painful. I wonder just how much damage the smoke did to him.

Then I slowly recall the nurses that filled the room whilst Cornelius Morgan spoke to me. I remember the attention given to Theo. I remember the hushed voices and the assurance this would all be over tomorrow. Suddenly I find myself replaying the whole thing in my head. But instead of watching those enchanting eyes I listen to the sound of Morgan's voice. It's like I'm hearing it for the first time. I stand rigid for a while as I absorb everything again. The room goes dark. I feel sick. I back away from Theo and the sensor lights come on again. I find myself staring at the clipboard attached to the front of his hospital bed.

I remember the sound of a nurse scribbling. The pen scratching on paper. I remember the machine being switched off. The mask being removed. But only now as I read what is marked quite clearly on Theo's notes do I fully understand what they have done.

Theodore Lobbett, WOLF X37, Rabbit M: WHITE EYE

The sound that comes out of my mouth is like nothing I've ever heard before. I didn't cry out like this when meteors chased us across the countryside. Nor when the avalanche buried me. As this scream leaves my body I feel as alive and real as I must have done the day I was born. I scream as though it's the only thing in the world that will save him.

"Turn it back on!" I let my voice find every corner of the room. I hope they hear me out on the streets. I hope they hear me in Newton Belle. I hope that somewhere on Mt Venus itself my voice can shift even the smallest flake of snow. If it doesn't I'll somehow scream louder.

A team of doctors enter the room without a sound and pull me back on to my own bed. They inject me with something that makes the scream fade to a whisper. I taste metal in my mouth and my tongue finds the angry split in my lip that continues to throb to the sound of Theo's dying heartbeat.

When they leave the room they're assured I'll not create a fuss again. They're right. I can't. My voice won't sound and my arms don't flail. I'm too weak and too delusional to fight back. The drug that consumes me only allows me to pick myself up and stagger to Theo's bed again. I flop down and land alongside him. I hook one arm over his chest to make sure I don't fall and lean into his ear.

"Theo?" A whisper is all I can manage, my throat is too hoarse. I put my fingers over his eyelids and lift them open. He has to look at me. If he does then surely he'll see someone who doesn't want him to give up. Then he'll fight. "Theo, don't let yourself go."

His eyes are raw and unmoving. His irises don't even wobble as I shake his body with my other hand. My arms barely do as I will. He doesn't respond at all.

"Please," I beg. "Please wake up."

He doesn't understand. Wherever he is, he doesn't hear me anymore. My voice breaks and I shake his shoulder as desperately as the drug will allow.

"Wake up. You have to wake up. You can't let them do this to you."

Now Theo makes a noise inside his throat and his chest movement lowers. It lowers so drastically, I grab him and raise him up with my arms.

“Don’t be afraid. It’s all right.”

I don’t open his eyes a second time. Instead I clutch him to me and feel him slip away. When I look up at the screen, my own eyes soaked with tears, all I see is white. I don’t want to look, but I have to understand he’s gone. I prize his lids open and see toadstools: white circles on a blooded canvas. I don’t know why I keep hold of him, but I do. It could’ve been Joel, after all. I cry and cry even though no one can hear me anymore. When I finally fall asleep, I’m curled up in the crook of his arm and holding his hand to my face. Feeling for a pulse that will never sound again.

25

The nurse isn't at all surprised when she walks in and sees Theo's monitor reading white. She does seem vaguely put out, however, that I'm on his bed.

"Up, up, up," she chirps, clapping her hands.

It's only now I realise I'm lying over a corpse. Theo's body is cold and still. I jump off the bed, lost and frightened. The floor is freezing under my bare feet. The nurse taps away at the computer and then looks down over Theo's face and tuts.

"Look what you did to him," she remarks, straightening his body and lifting his shirt back over his shoulder. She takes the bandage away from his head. Bits of white fabric are stuck to his face and the bandage is speckled with skin and blood. Am I supposed to feel like I did something wrong?

"You killed him," I say flatly. "You let him die."

She observes me mildly, as if I'm telling her about a dream. She certainly doesn't seem disturbed by the accusation. Her silence chills me further.

"Are you going to do the same to me? Will you hook me up to a machine and stop me breathing? Tell my mother I was White Eyed and you had no choice but to switch me off?"

The nurse lifts the sheet up and over Theo's face. When she speaks I hear Cornelius Morgan's words. "No, sweet girl. You won't be rigged up to anything. Your lenses have come back and you'll be allowed to go home today."

"I will?" I can hardly believe it. So my lens screening was some sort of test and I passed?

"Get dressed," she says. Another couple of WOLF workers arrive and wheel Theo away. The door locks automatically behind them and I'm left alone and bare foot. I can feel the draft tickle my legs under my hospital gown.

I can go home. Where is that exactly? The ranch in Orbelle? Alec's house, surrounded by people who'd rather I weren't there? I don't know where I belong now. Another nurse comes in to give me my clothes.

"Do you want some tea?" she asks.

No. I want to see Joel. I watched his team mate die. I need him here to share in my grief and tell me what to do.

I'm finally led from the room and to one of the surgeries where my lenses are reinserted. It's a horrible task. The procedure is carried out by faces I don't recognise and there's no small talk to put me at ease. Once the lenses are in I'm ushered from the room without a cup of water or further instruction. But the same nurse is waiting for me outside.

"You ought to eat," she says. "You look dreadful. We need to put a comb through your hair and put some colour in your face. As for those eyes . . ."

She grips my chin and pushes my face up. Even though she looks deep into my irises she doesn't seem to see another person before her. I'm just an object.

"We have a term for these eyes. Obsidian eyes. This won't do. They won't let you walk out those doors looking like a stormy day. Less black, more blue. I'll get right on that. You pop your shoes on, there's a good girl."

I have no idea what she's talking about but I don't argue. I put on my shoes, brush the tangles from my hair and look at my face in the mirror. There are creases on my cheek and they stand out like veins. It makes me shudder to know they're from lying across Theo's clothes.

"Professor Morgan will be ready to meet you in reception. Now then. Look here." She clicks her fingers above my head so I look up. She holds a device that emits a small laser and she directs the beam into each lens with precision.

"It won't affect you. No damage will be done. We use these often for calibrations. It will instruct your lenses to perform under their neutral state. Neutral being what?"

It's a prompt. I find the correct word.

"Brown," I say. "Brown is the neutral lens colour."

"Good girl," she says. "This won't last long, ten minutes tops. Keep your chin up, attempt to smile and your lenses will do the rest for you."

I'm told to leave the ward as if this were a regular appointment. They permit me to leave the X unit. The nurse escorts me back through XY and to reception.

I knew to expect Cornelius Morgan, but I wasn't expecting how I would feel. Thankfully my eyes are in a neutral state. Otherwise my expression would've been not unlike Joel's. Everything suddenly feels as though it's burning.

His eyes have returned to their Tiger's Eye state. He glances at me with shades of gold and mahogany. It makes me sick to remember them lavender. They had shone with false trust, and when I was most vulnerable. I can scarcely look at him now. His gaze is poison.

"Miss Hansen," he says steadily. "Everything is in order I see. Let me look at you."

He cocks his head and checks my lens colour.

"Russet," he muses. "I would have preferred something more chocolate. But no matter. Brown is brown and will serve its purpose. Time is ticking against us. Now, a few things to clear up before this happens . . ."

He motions for me to step to one side. I glance at the doors but he puts out an arm to prevent me running. He holds a clip board in his hand and uses it as a barrier. Besides, there are security guards positioned either side of the revolving doors. Clearly they've stepped up their security. They don't take their eyes off us.

"What happened last night was unfortunate, Miss Hansen. Most regrettable of all is the fact you were there to witness it. However, you understand we have incriminating evidence confiscated from your person. Things we can't quite pretend we haven't seen. You may very well continue to turn up in the wrong place at the wrong time, but the fact remains that you are of great suspicion to many here at WOLF. There are those who would like to see you detained further."

My mind turns to Rusten and the ill look he gave Ouren. He must truly believe I'm linked to Ouren's team. The fact I cried over Theo's dying body can only support such a belief. Morgan clears his throat.

"Now I for one would like to overlook these things. Your mother . . . you're her soul carer, are you not? And Dr Frost says you're a cooperative candidate in our Turtle Doves program. I shouldn't want there to be any further controversy in the media concerning WOLF and how we care for our patients. Therefore I'll speak with you frankly. No more disturbances from you, or those you are suspected of associating yourself with, and I shall personally see to it you are rewarded."

I look into his eyes and wonder if he can see the mistrust behind the russet. He certainly can't mistake my frown and sudden grind of my teeth. Still he continues. He extends the clip board and lets me hold it.

"You requested a guide dog for your mother, several times. That's understandable and most certainly something I can help with, and more besides. If you agree, I'll sign this form right now and have one requested within the day. You may not be surprised to know how fast my signature can move a form along. Keep yourself in line, Miss Hansen, and when you eventually return to your little ranch in Orbelle, there will be plenty of compensation and reward for you. We can even look at installing lens-controlled features in your home to benefit you. If you cooperate."

I don't speak and he takes this as an agreement.

"Excellent. I'm sure you'll see this is the right thing to do. And if you should hesitate or have any doubt . . . well, I'm confident you'll change your mind right back again. You are free to leave, but you'll understand how crucial your cooperation is. Stay in line and there will be no issues. There's just one more thing left for us to see to and you'll be allowed to leave the premises. Do we have an understanding?"

I look at the paperwork. It outlines the need for a guide dog to be issued to one Eliza Hansen of Orbelle. It states we're to be prioritised. The box for his signature is dated and just needs to be signed. I don't know what to say. I just want to leave. Besides, what do I have to lose now? For the first time in a long time I may actually gain something for us. A shred of good news after everything else we've been through.

"Okay," I say.

"Marvellous." Morgan takes back the form and scrawls his signature with flamboyant movement. He dots the 'I' in 'Cornelius' with gusto and uses the clip board to point me to the doors. "Now, if you please. I'll see you out. Are we ready?"

He's speaking to his bodyguards now. They consult their ear-pieces and motion for us to stand before the doors.

"They know you're on your way out," one of them says.

"Who knows we're on our way out?" I ask, but Morgan doesn't answer me.

"Eyes open, Miss Hansen, chin up. Choose your best side and follow my lead."

We step out from the revolving doors to the sound of applause.

Light bulbs flash and I have to shield my face so much I look down and stare at Morgan's shoes. There are people everywhere. I feel like a fly caught in the presence of a spider. I can't move.

"Cornelius! Cornelius!"

"Cornelius – over here! Smile for us!"

His hand rests on my shoulder and I feel his lilac eyes bearing down on me, instructing me to do what he says. Over the heads of the press I can see the city laid out like a vibrant candy shop. The sights are too sickly sweet now. I can't digest the colours as I used to.

"Smile, sweet girl."

He speaks through his teeth and is no longer looking at me. He's holding up the other hand to silence the reporters gathered around HQ.

"What a display, eh?" he chortles. "Impressive and no doubt very time consuming. What a shame, their efforts did so little."

"Mr Morgan," a voice cries out. "Who are 'they'?"

"Fanatic trouble makers," Morgan says. "Fans of mine, it seems. Thought they would try their hand at manipulating the hologram. As I said, it's impressive. The ringleader wasn't much older than my young friend here. He's being dealt with accordingly. Ladies and gentlemen, this is Linnea Hansen from Orbelle. Her bravery is unspeakable. She was undergoing treatment when the smoke bomb went off. Gave us all a shock, didn't it, little lamb?"

I'm not a lamb. I'm a goat herder. I attempt to shrug off his hand but he continues to hold me in place.

"I'm happy to tell you none of the recent events have affected the treatment and ongoing research here at HQ," Morgan insists. "In fact, the so-called damage you see above our heads is nothing more than a mere blip. A technical error. Although I'm sure there are many still sceptical about my word and will require some proof all is well. If I could ask you all to congregate a few paces back. Thank you very much. Linnea, step with me."

I'm led to the front of the doors. Does he plan to publicly execute me to show I'm not a threat to society? Does he mean to brand me some sort of terrorist and shame me in front of all these cameras?

There's no such humiliation. I'm given a large remote with a single button.

"And so we resume our watch over the city," Morgan declares. He squeezes my shoulder so hard I take this as some sort of cue and hit the button. I hear gasps and people start to clap. I don't need to look to know what's happened. The button is removed from my hands and I'm shoved once towards the steps. I won't be needed again. As I stumble off the premises, I look back and see Iris is back and seemingly more glorious than ever. I just unveiled her. It makes me feel ill. I did it for the promise of a guide dog, whilst Theo's body still lies cold somewhere in the building.

"Look this way, girl!" someone yells. I have to endure a few more photographs before I'm able to walk off and leave that horrible building behind me. Iris watches me go and stares into the back of my neck.

26

I don't recall anything else as I walk away from HQ. I don't acknowledge the people or the signs. Rain taps against my forehead and the wind forces my hair about my face. I'm walking back the way I came yesterday and suppose I'll arrive at the station as long as my feet keep moving. I just hope I have enough money in my pocket to buy a ticket. I try not to look up, but when I do my heart throbs inside my throat.

Something inexplicable has happened to me. Or perhaps it's not so inexplicable at all. Perhaps it was inevitable now I've seen Fenix beyond the charade. Whilst the world they created still looks the same through my lenses, somehow I can see beyond it. I can now look behind the make up and see the flesh of the city as they don't want us to. Behind the carnival-like colours and shining features, I can see the details we're supposed to miss. Everything appears cartoon-like until I concentrate. I can see the dust and dirt caused by exhaust fumes, thus I can taste and feel them in my lungs in a way I never could before. Although my lenses pick out green, I see some of these are the weeds seeping from the cracks in the pavement. They too are caked with the dirt of pollution. The trees are tired, and although they are tidy and pruned they look miserable, like they've been chained and imprisoned here. The flowers don't flourish like they do in the countryside. They've been bred to look richer and more glamorous than they truly are. But they're not meant for the city air. I only really saw their colours before. I didn't acknowledge the wilting leaves and drooping heads. It's as if the flowers themselves feel shame for tricking us all into thinking this city is perfect. The only colours that truly shine with vigour are the ones powered by electricity and fixed with paint. This city is a manmade paradise – if you're happy to let yourself be fooled and never look beyond the vail of colours. Now I can see the shadows and they haunt my steps as I prepare to flee this nightmare place.

I'm only a few paces past the prison when someone seizes my shoulders.

"Well there's some timing," Hans says. "My next stop was to collect you from HQ."

"They sent you to fetch me," I presume. "My mother must've been frantic. I'm not surprised. I am surprised Alec didn't insist on coming with you though."

Hans hasn't started the engine yet. He's resting his wrists against the wheel and peering across at me. He takes a deep breath. "Linn, do you know where we're goin' now? Why I was here, at the prison? Do you have any idea at all?"

"We're going back to Newton Belle."

"No," he says slowly. "Not this time. She tried to organise a hostel. They have several in Horvel. They put up a bunch of refugees across the country. But your mother was paranoid about going anywhere unless she had contacted me first and arranged for someone to find you. I won't lie to you, Linn, it's a mess. It really is a mess. I had no choice but to come here and tell your father. I'm in over my head. I said I would take care of you and I'm doin' all I can. But this . . . I didn't even know what to say to him. I didn't know where to start."

It shocks me how calm I am about my sudden realisation. "We've been kicked out. Mrs Rouman's finally turned us away."

I'm surprised, I can't deny it. I didn't think she would do this now. Certainly not whilst I was being kept at HQ after a supposed attack. How could she do this to my mother? I wait for the anger to boil inside my body but, surprisingly, it doesn't. I'm calm as I listen to Hans.

"I suppose this were the straw that broke the camel's back," he sighs. "In a way you can't blame the woman. Right now you appear to be more trouble than you're worth."

"So she's sent my mother to a hostel?"

"It's not a bad hostel. Not what you'd think. It's nearby my aunt's place in Doverhaven. My aunt would take you in but she's already got my family stayin'. But we'll be close to each other. Which is good for me, I swear, the money you lot cost me in petrol. I could rebuild the ranch."

My head finds the cold window. The rain thuds against my temple and I close my eyes wearily. "It's fine. Just take me there. The people there, their job is to look after people like us. People with nowhere to go. They won't turn us away. They won't have an opinion or judgement. Just take me there, Hans."

Perhaps he knows I'm broken. He doesn't speak as he starts the engine, although he sits for a few moments and contemplates what to say. There's a lot to ask, and I've so much to tell him it all crams in my throat and lodges there, clawing at my breath and sealing my lips. Eventually I ask only one question.

"Why didn't Alec come? He didn't insist on joining you?"

"He doesn't know I'm here. You're right, he would've insisted on comin' if he did. But he's got too much to deal with right now; it didn't seem fair on him. No matter how much time he'll have on his hands now." Hans looks truly sorry for what he has to say. "As of last night he's servin' his suspension. He won't know if he's lost his job for good until the information's been looked into properly. Somethin' about photographs he developed at work. Grapha will be investigatin' those for a while. I wouldn't want to be in his shoes. His manager I'm sure I could handle; but his mother . . . I'd rather be White Eyed."

A joke. I know it's a joke. He's trying to lighten the mood, since this is terrible news for me to take. But his choice of words make my head turn so sharply he looks across to see me staring.

"Hey, you'll be all right," he says. "I'll take you to my aunts' and if you want to stay at the hostel you can. You know Alec's phone number and can call him, although heaven help you if his mother picks up. It can't be long until we can return home and then we'll work on restorin' the ranch. Your father's aware of everythin' now. Linn? I'm sorry. Your eyes were brown earlier and now they're . . ."

He can't find the correct shade in his mind. I suggest it for him.

"Obsidian. These are Obsidian Eyes. Cornelius Morgan coined the phrase."

I turn away from his concerned expression and stare at my reflection in the window. I ignore the scenery that passes by and stare at the dark, hallow pits in my face that would once gleam like sapphires and convey feeling. My only consolation is that they let me go. I still can't believe it. I don't know how Morgan could possibly trust me enough to let me leave with his secret.

We arrive in Horvel and Hans ushers me inside the hostel under the fractured glow of a faulty streetlamp. He announces himself to the security camera and they allow us to come in. The wooden door has swollen with the rain and needs his shoulder to shove it open. There is no WOLF technology here. That would have comforted me, had I not felt so downhearted.

"We're lookin' for Eliza Hansen," Hans says to the receptionist.

"She's not here."

I look at Hans and he frowns. "She is here. I spoke to her this mornin'."

"She's not here now. They came and got her a few hours ago."

I don't panic initially. Hans' family are nearby, perhaps they found room to accommodate us. But the look on Hans' face fills me with dread. He asks the question. "Who came and got her?"

"WOLF did. They sent a car for her, posh one. They said her daughter was being praised for her bravery and was spending time with Cornelius Morgan himself. Apparently she was going to be part of some unveiling and they wanted her mother to witness it."

What sense was left in my head is now scrambled. This is all horribly wrong.

"What time did they take her?" I ask frantically.

"Oh, I don't know. Two hours ago? Could have been less."

"We left around two hours ago." Hans is clearly confused. "We've been on the road all that time, and the unveilin' already happened. Damn. We probably passed their car going the other way."

Suddenly my anger explodes.

"Why did you let them?" I demand. "Why did you let them take her away?"

The receptionist is shocked and glances around for another member of staff to help her. "Well, why wouldn't we? They were WOLF officials. The man we spoke to was a military man. Besides, your mother was happy to go. They said she and her daughter would receive accommodation and we checked her out of our system."

I'm too horrified to speak. Hans is craning to see the clock behind the desk. He shoots me an apologetic look and sighs.

"Linn, I'm not driving back to HQ now. Can we go tomorrow?"

He doesn't understand.

I should have explained everything in the car. He has no idea how much danger my mother is in. I'll have to tell him now. I'll have to insist we drive back and tell him everything on the way. He won't believe it, but he will have to.

But Cornelius Morgan's words play on my mind. He was so confident I would agree to his terms and not cause any trouble. He said there would be no issue as long as I stayed in line. He's put me in an impossible situation. I realise I can't make a scene. The idea of telling Hans what happened feels like I'm securing a bad fate for my mother. I have to be good. At least, until I can think about it properly. My hands are trembling and my throat feels tight.

"I need Joel."

Hans barely hears me and peers into my face to check I'm all right. It's clear I'm not. But if I can't have Joel talk with me, then I need to think on my own. I can't have Hans' aunt force polite conversation from my mouth and shove unwanted food in. I can't be a guest in this state. I can't have voices all around me. I'll go mad.

I speak a little louder. "I need to sleep. Can I just stay here tonight? I don't want another car ride."

My mother thought she'd be meeting me the other end. She took all my clothes with her. I have nothing.

My dislike for Mrs Rouman intensifies. If she'd let my mother stay, they would've taken longer to find her. But since she had to be registered to a hostel, she was just sat waiting for WOLF without knowing it.

Hans says he'll call the hostel in the morning and I can see the weariness in his lenses. I find I don't care. If the most he has to endure is another car ride then he can get over it. If he shows any sign of resentment I'd rather not see his face. For the first time I wish Hans gone from my sight. When he leaves he gives me a concerned glance and tries to smile. I stare blankly at his face. I want him to stand there and let me shout at him. I want him to rush forward and give me a hug. I want to tell him everything. I want to tell him nothing.

I've never felt so alone.

27

The staff here must be concerned. My lenses have been jet black since I arrived and my mood is even darker.

I started rubbing my eyes in the truck. I wasn't aware I was doing it until Hans offered to stop by a chemist and pick up some WOLF serum. I assured him I was fine and it was just a speck of dust. But by then I'd already realised the thrill of doing something I was told not to do by WOLF.

I haven't stopped rubbing them since. My eyes are bloodshot and my lashes have stuck together so my eyes look like black-bellied spiders.

I've not spoken to Alec. I don't know what to say. I inserted money into one of the hostel's pay phones and listened to the dialling tone. My fingers eventually began to dial, but I lost all courage and spent the rest of the evening on my bed, facing the ceiling with the television on to distract me from the anger and dread I feel.

The news has caught my interest. As coverage over the HQ attack subsides (I've seen myself unveil Iris twice now), a new headline appears: Sparkwell is pending evacuation due to avalanche concerns and problems since the meteor phenomenon.

Sparkwell never used to be of much interest to me. It's the other side of Mt Venus but with the gigantic landform between us. I've only visited once as a child, but now I find myself watching the television for updates. Perhaps because I'm bored and perhaps it's because it reminds me of my own situation

At least Sparkwell will receive the correct help. Orbelle remains uninhabited and its livestock unattended. Sparkwell are taking their time with their evacuations. Many people have started to make their own way out through the various country lanes. Others stand by their businesses until the authorities insist they abandon them.

So far no one has required this hostel. Why would they? Most will have a plan in mind, relatives who will take them in. I don't suppose they'll even need to use HQ as a check-in station. I look around this small room and wonder if I would have been happier back with the Roumans.

True to his word, Hans calls me in the morning. He says no one at WOLF HQ knows where my mother is. They've sent an enquiry to Cornelius Morgan and will call Hans as soon as they know. I don't pin any hope on them calling Hans. The message is perfectly clear: I won't find out where she is until this satellite issue is resolved. If I want her back sooner, I'll have to volunteer information. This makes me feel physically sick. I know so little, yet I could lose so much more than I already have. My only hope stems from the small belief they won't kill her. Theo was different; he was directly involved with the Socket.

I can't process this fear into something I can work with and use to make decisions. I feel as though I'm the one suffocating now.

I do nothing. I can't see how I can do the wrong thing if I do nothing at all. I remain quiet on the phone and agree to wait for that phone call from HQ. The call I know won't come. Not for a while, anyway. Not until they've found someone else to pin the blame on.

"Hans," I say flatly. "Do you think my father would have enjoyed everything that's happening with WOLF? Do you think he would be supporting the people against them?"

"How would I know?" he says. "We never discuss that. When I visited him yesterday he were too preoccupied with you guys. He's annoyed with me, obviously. Says I should've come sooner. But how were we to know how bad things would become? When they evacuated us they said it were only a precaution and we'd be back in a few days."

“Why should he be annoyed?” I shove my knuckles into my tear ducts and twist. “He’s the one who got himself locked up, away from us.”

Hans says nothing and I wonder for a moment if he can sense me rubbing my eyes.

“Linn, is everythin’ all right with you?”

“I told you. Everything’s fine.”

“You’ve spoken to Alec?”

“Yes.”

He swallows hard. He wants to understand me so badly and to know what is going on in my head.

“Linn, he called my aunt’s house. You didn’t think I’d forget to give them the contact details of where you were? He called to talk to you. He doesn’t know what’s going on, or if you even want to talk to him. What the heck was I supposed to say? I was going to give him the hostel’s number but I worried you might actually be avoidin’ him and wouldn’t want that. I said you’d call him. Are you gonna call him? You need to do somethin’, Linn. You need to make a decision.”

I say nothing. In fact I put the phone down. I slam it so hard the hand piece ricochets off and hangs by the cord. I can still hear the dialling tone as I make my way down the corridor. I suppress my guilt by gritting my teeth and squeezing my eyes shut so tight my head trembles.

I'm no longer myself.

I feel the old me slipping away with each day that passes. When I open my eyes I'm faced with the hostel and the waking reminder of our hopelessness. When I close them all I see is Theo. In my memory he's lying with his eyes open, pale and orb-like. He didn't look so haunting at the time and yet the more I remember the more the vision intensifies. It cries out to me.

Why didn't I do something?

The only thing that banishes Theo from my mind, during my darkest hours, is Joel. In all my other memories I see the events happening as though through someone else's eyes. I see myself lying over Theo's body, I see myself over Alec's shoulder so he can't see my eyes and I see myself standing beside Cornelius Morgan. I see these things as though it happened on television to someone else. But when I think of Joel I remember looking up over that meteor fragment and seeing his eyes shine. I remember his weight resting on me as I helped him walk to HQ. I remember the last look he gave me as we separated, though I can scarcely remember the words he used.

I do a brief calculation in my head and realise I spent five times as many days with Alec than I ever did with Joel. In fact I could work out my time with Joel down to the hour. For some reason that thought unsettles me enough to resume rubbing my eyes.

He won't be thinking of me anymore. I'm stupid to still think of him. I must stop remembering his face and that scar on his lip.

The image of Theo returns and I start aggravating my tear ducts until they feel sticky when I blink. I'm perfectly aware of my foolishness, but as soon as the pain fades I resume rubbing them. Eventually I can't bear it any longer and retrieve the serum from my bag.

Since this is a new bottle fresh from WOLF's laboratories it's still sealed in its box with the information leaflet. I retreat to the toilets and trust no one will disturb me. Even if they do, I'm sure they'll be pleased to see me facing one of the mirrors and holding WOLF serum.

I spread the leaflet out across the sink. The pages latch on to droplets of water, soaking and stretching the hundreds of words. My lenses define even the blurriest of letters so I can still read them. I search for the section in my own language. It's a bullet-pointed list of precautions. It recommends I use a separate towel for my face and to not operate heavy machinery if I encounter any of the known side effects. It's all very standard and familiar. Still I study these precautions and make note of which ones I have yet to abuse.

There's little in the leaflet to help me quench this wretched feeling inside; the same feeling that makes me want to force my nails between my lids and prise the lenses out.

I decide to leave the hostel altogether and walk around Horvel. Unlike Newton Belle, this is a city with attractions and activity. I've heard the fights take place in the street at night and the constant thump of music. None of these things remind me of home so I head for the park.

There's little here besides broken bottles and the occasional dog walker, but it's green all the same. Not the rich green of our hill, but it will do. My lenses will force what little colour there is to brighten for my pleasure. The trees don't look quite so dismal here and there are a few flowers yet to be trampled. I spy a bank that will raise me above the trees and grant me a moderate view. I climb until I can see the horizon and take the binoculars from my pocket. I was fortunate not to have these confiscated with my backpack. They're small enough to slot inside my jacket and I was relieved to find them with my other belongings at the hostel.

This is my last chance to salvage some sanity. If I can at least glimpse Mt Venus and remember how it was to see it from my bedroom window then perhaps I'm not so lost.

I put the binoculars to my face and focus. All I see are chimney tops and a heron-coloured sky.

There's nothing there to hold me together.

I can't seem to cry. Perhaps if I did this would hurt less. The mountain is too far away and I've rubbed my eyes too savagely to squint harder. Even holding the binoculars to them feels sore. The rim of each eye piece is moist with fluid.

It feels like I'll never see the mountain again. We'll never go back, and if by some miracle we do we'll have next to nothing except the small hope of a guide dog. I catch a bitter laugh inside my mouth. I'm the one who needs guidance. Not my mother. I wish I could summon the swelling from my throat and spit the anger on to the grass. I can't stand to live like this anymore. It's not enough I rub my eyes and no longer dare to hope. The idea they're still watching me, sharing in my movements and feelings, makes me furious. When I close my eyes and attempt to blot them out, I see Theo's face. I see the whiteness of his eyes like clouds over an empty world. When I open them, all I see is a false painting. Someone has taken the real world and streaked it with fake greens and blues and browns. Ironically, to make us all just that little bit happier. Just that little bit easier to control.

There are no clouds over Horvel; just clear sky. The sun is shining overhead and I feel the beginning of sunburn on my neck. I'm not accustomed to the sun like this.

I swallow the lump in my throat.

My fair skin is sensitive, but not nearly as sensitive as the human eye. I won't let them control me anymore. These eyes are mine and I'll smoke them out if I must.

"Burn."

I say it as though they'll hear me back at HQ. I lift my face, bringing the binoculars up and pointing them into the sun's light.

My lenses don't know what's hit them.

They buzz like insects have flown directly into them. I blink once or twice, but hold my head steady. It's hurting in a way I've never felt before. But I can't look away now I've started. I hold my stare. The binoculars rattle in my hands until I can't fight it anymore. I drop them and let out a noise that makes it clear I've done something extreme. I bury my face in my hands and keep them there, not knowing whether to laugh or cry. When I attempt to peek between my fingers, I discover the consequence for my action is dire.

I can no longer see.

28

I refused to go to hospital. They'd only refer me on to WOLF HQ and I'd rather suffer a thousand days of this pain than go back there.

I was found sitting in the same spot, binoculars by my side and face still cupped in my hands. I'd been attempting to rock away the pain. People were reluctant to approach me at first. Eventually someone came to my aid, took one look at my face and insisted they call an ambulance. I couldn't see this person – I couldn't see anything at all – so all I could do was yell and protest until they brought me back to the hostel. There I lay, on my bed. There are no more phone calls from Hans. I mumble and drift back and forth in sleep, trying to ignore the headaches and the throbbing.

What have I done to myself? For what good reason? I'd stared at the sun for almost half a minute. Too long to have been an accident.

The only time I stir is to refuse a doctor, but that was never going to be heeded for long. Eventually they find a male first aider and I permit him near me once I'm assured he's nothing to do with WOLF.

"Linnea, can you open your eyes at all?" he asks.

It's been almost twelve hours. I groan and try my best. My lashes are stuck together and crusted with puss. It takes some doing, but I prize my lids apart. I see nothing. No, wait. There's a light. It moves across my face. I follow it, but it's difficult. My left eye is completely uncooperative.

"She's following the torch," the first aider announces. "That's good. Although I don't like the look of that left eye. We need to patch that up."

The following afternoon I sit upright in bed and find I'm able to still see out of my right eye. The left is impossible to tell, it's under wads of cotton and bandaging. They cleaned my eyes with serum and, over the course of a few hours, I'd improved. When Hans walks into my room, unexpectedly, I'm able to see his horrified expression. He's had no luck tracing my mother. He's had no luck comforting me. He's failed us both.

"Oh Linn," he sighs. "Why'd you do this to yourself?"

"I don't know," I whisper. It all seems unreal.

Now I've come to my senses I'm embarrassed to see my reflection. I don't want to be faced with this desperate girl who would hurt herself in such an unnecessary way. One who has spent years fearing blindness, yet would do something so dangerous.

Hans insists on staying with me. He doesn't trust me to stay here on my own. He brings me fresh clothes, a new toothbrush and a sandwich his aunt made me. He promises to stay with me until I'm better. What a burden I have proven myself to be.

That night I listen to the television the same way my mother does. My head is resting to one side and I keep my hands on the arms of the chair. I can't see the news anchor, but I recognise his voice and take in what I can about Sparkwell's situation. My interest deepens when he mentions Orbelle.

"Progress regarding the ALPHA satellite is gradually being fed back to WOLF HQ from the military's position in Orbelle. A team of recruits volunteered themselves into the heart of the hazardous town to take up station and monitor the disturbance. Major Lance Ouren leads the team of brave soldiers willing to put their safety at risk to resolve the problems that may affect up to two-thousand lenses in the area. We received this brief statement from him before his departure . . ."

I turn my head the moment I hear Ouren's voice in the room. The wind is beating against the microphone but his words are plain as day.

"Our concern, as always, is the wellbeing of the civilians here. I suppose you may call it a small blessing the satellite went down during their evacuation, whatever consolation that may be. People don't like to be without their WOLF lenses for any lengthy period of time. We understand that. That's why our soul objective here is to resolve these issues as swiftly as possible and restore normality to this area in time for these avalanche fears to pass. Hopefully that will all be in the very near future."

The anchor man's voice returns briefly to announce the next statement comes direct from WOLF HQ itself. The voice is harder to recognise but I soon identify it. Nausea rises in my throat.

"We believe communication is paramount during any crisis such as this. Who knows what complications there will be if suddenly Sparkwell is cut off too," Lieutenant Rusten drawls to the camera. "We're determined it won't come to that. We're happy to keep our men out there to ensure the matter is closely monitored. Should Sparkwell be fortunate enough to avoid evacuation, we will want to have all WOLF matters operating properly."

There is a change in audio and it makes my head turn completely. I recognise this audio anywhere. I hear the flash of bulbs and the cry of a single name. I don't need to see to know they're replaying the footage of me unveiling Iris. Sure enough, a voice soon cuts in over the repeated footage and introduces the man himself.

"Professor Morgan, many people are still concerned and worried about the recent attack on the HQ building itself. Are there any possible connections between the ALPHA satellite and those behind the attack?"

There's a delay in his response, so I presume they're streaming this live. When he speaks, it's with the same calm tone he used when assuring me. I believed I was safe with him. Everyone believes they're safe with him. His voice is like poisoned honey and it sends a chill down my spine when he laughs. I've never heard Cornelius Morgan laugh.

"Forgive me, no, there's no suspected connection between either events. You see, the culprit behind that impressive display was arrested some time ago. I'm afraid, due to the individual's age, we can't reveal who that person was. Although he shall be dealt with accordingly and, let me tell you, it's a far cry from his known talents to actually interfere with our satellite. That would require an extremely rare talent indeed."

"Or an extremely rare meteor shower in this case?"

"Well, exactly. What we struggle to identify at this time is whether the satellite was physically struck by a fragment of meteorite or simply confused by the change in atmosphere. We're relying on our team in Orbelle to enlighten us in due course and we apologise this has taken so long. We weren't expecting such a prolonged disturbance that would require military intervention. We're sending our thanks out to them this day and hope to have that area restored to normal as soon as possible."

"One last thing, before we let you go, Professor. You said earlier today in the event Sparkwell should evade an evacuation you will be sending out supplies to the residents there?"

"Ah." Morgan has the grace to sound humble. "Yes, I did. I want people to know that, just as HQ was willing to help Orbelle where it could, we will be extending our help to Sparkwell and flying out resources. We feel partly responsible you see. If the satellite stops monitoring their area and we miss important distress readings – well it would be a dreadful thing for yellow and amber readings to go unnoticed. We want them to know our military is here to serve and protect, even with the interference. They can expect a visit from our men in the next few days."

"Thank you, Professor. We'll be updating you all again, as news of this story develops."

The television continues to sound, but I'm no longer listening. I would get up and leave the room, had I the senses to navigate my way. Instead I sit still and digest everything I just heard.

Half of it was a lie. I didn't need to see their lenses to know that. Morgan would be able to manipulate his anyway. Rusten too. Even Ouren was deliberately trying to mask his true intentions, whatever they are.

His team did go to Orbelle just as I thought. Joel will be there now, reunited with his fellow X recruits and slowly accepting Theo isn't returning. Perhaps they know he'd been arrested and are denying any involvement in his hologram attack. Perhaps Ouren expressed sheer disgust at his recruit and told Morgan he can punish Theo how he likes. I doubt very much they know of his death. No one will be allowed to know that beyond those who were there to witness it.

But I witnessed it, and that's enough for me to know Joel is in grave danger. I heard how they spoke of Ouren and his team. Especially Rusten. I knew he distrusted Ouren the moment they crossed paths in the corridor at HQ. He was accusing Ouren then of having some alternative purpose for being near Orbelle when the disturbance began. He suspected Joel and his fellow recruits had more to do with the satellite than they let on. The timing was too perfect.

Whatever they were doing that night, I believe Joel was sent to patrol the mountainside, just as he said. But he wasn't doing it for any civilians' benefit. He was doing it to ensure no one came across the rest of his team and disturbed their work. He was their look-out. I just happened to be in the wrong place at the wrong time.

Perhaps, whilst trudging through snow and clutching his rifle, Joel truly got cold feet. After all, he must've known to get caught would result in a similar fate as Theo. He must have felt their objective was a difficult and risky one. Perhaps he used me as an excuse to break away and abandon his involvement. No wonder he was always so secretive and nervous. Whether he would be faced with Ouren or Rusten, both would have seemed formidable in the scheme of things.

If only I'd known. I could've done more to help him.

Rusten said they were happy to keep those recruits out in Orbelle. That confuses me. If he suspects they're behind ALPHA's disturbance then why not recall them to HQ immediately and detain them all? They have enough reason. Theo was part of their team. I was an associate of Joel's and carrying photographic evidence. Rusten was suspicious even before all that came to light. He must have been itching for this opportunity to accuse Ouren.

What's more, Morgan denies any connection between the attack on HQ and ALPHA. He knows that isn't true and so do I. Then why continue to play up to the cameras? The televisions aren't working in Orbelle so Ouren's team probably won't hear his statements.

But that doesn't matter. I heard them.

I feel my bad eye flicker beneath the bandages. My good eye gazes around freely, picking up on objects and colours. I will it to get stronger and focus on each shade and shape. My motivation soars. I'll be able to use this eye again properly. I'll force myself. And if I can get this other eye to open too then all the better. I'm ready to leave my depression sat in this chair as I stand. The chains of sadness that shackled me no longer resist and I stride to the bathroom.

I'm ready to experience colours again and to go back to living my life as a pallet of emotions. I'm sure my lenses will stay black for a while as I recover. Then perhaps they'll subside into a sickly grey. But eventually they'll relax back into the ordinary and I'll be unremarkable once more. The simple goat herder who lost her flock. I take a deep breath and look into the mirror.

The same breath escapes my lips. My iris is hazel.

It may be encased within a womb of red as my eye's still bloodshot and blistered but it doesn't fade between the soft hues of a forest and gold. Furthermore the tawny ring around my pupil doesn't go away. These are my natural eyes. My true eyes. The eyes Joel spent so many moments trying to gaze at.

Nothing could be clearer to me now. All thoughts of returning to my everyday life escape me like feathers caught by the wind. I know exactly what I need to do. I hope Hans will forgive me for this.

I'm going back to Orbelle.

29

The outskirts of Orbelle are a patchwork of fields stitched together with rivers and roads. I left the train lines hours ago and navigate my way with ease. I can't help but attract attention from livestock. I dodge the advances of hungry cows and sheep and stay as far from the main road as I can. My shoes are caked with muck and water. The mud is thick and dyes the puddles a dirty shade of umber. As I walked through the lanes at dusk it was like walking across blood.

I wonder if Hans has notified people of my disappearance yet. I won't be surprised if he never helps me again. They may find me on surveillance footage, stepping off a train in Newton Belle, but they won't know where I went next. I know once I'm reported missing Cornelius Morgan will be anxious to find me. I wonder if they'll realise my intentions. I'm racing against the clock. Each step I take exhilarates me further and I make tracks across one field to the next. I'm not far from Orbelle now.

As I climb over a gate I spy a faint glow to my right. I land on my feet and crouch, looking up. On a tree nearby is a light that goes out after a moment. When I stand up it comes on again. I can't see what it is, since I'm missing an eye and my lenses aren't working. All I know is whatever it is responds to movement. It must be a sensor. I walk around the tree and peer up. Someone has secured a device to its trunk similar to a small camera. I pass a hand over its face and the small light comes on again. Nothing else happens. I realise why. This device is here to emit a hologram, just like the ones at HQ. Only this time I'm not wearing lenses, so I can't see the image being projected.

My guess would be this is supposed to be a deterrent. The image would probably enforce some sort of security. It could be a pack of dogs, an armed officer or perhaps even a military vehicle. I put my hands either side of the trunk and crane up into the lens of the projector. I want to see the image they've installed. Nothing happens.

Although I'm not wearing lenses – so they can't scan my eyes and identify me – I can't rule out this is actually just a camera. Here I am, potentially thrusting my face right into Cornelius Morgan's vision. I need to keep moving and be aware of other deterrents set up around Orbelle. No doubt each time the hologram is activated someone is alerted at HQ. I might have just cut my time even shorter.

I continue over the next field as quickly as I can, keeping an eye out for more lights. That's when I spot my first obstacle. Or rather, I hear it.

A helicopter hums as it rounds the far side of the mountain, which I can just about see from my position on the flat of a field. A flock of sheep have congregated behind me, stomping their hooves and twitching their ears. They form something of a woollen wall behind me, so I can't turn back easily. It spurs me on and I keep my eye on the helicopter. Clearly Rusten has taken action to pinpoint the first recruit that chooses to leave Orbelle. Anyone who ventures out will be captured. This can't be the only security he's put in place. There must be more than one helicopter watching Orbelle.

It's far away for now, but I notice it moving in a circular pattern and curving over the fields to my left. Perhaps it won't fly over me. Perhaps I'm too far away.

Hans' family farm is on the very edge of Orbelle, where the limit is put into effect. It can't be forbidden to take a walk in fields twenty minutes out. No avalanche would reach me here. This can't be off-limits just yet.

I make the farm my target, since it's the closest thing to me. The sheep bray as I climb the next gate and land in another field. It's like moving across a chess board, from square to square, working out where my opponent will move next.

It's fortunate I know this land. The sun starts to set behind darkening clouds and I have to make my way across grayscale terrain. Eventually I see the lights shine beneath the black dot in the sky. The helicopter hums like a hornet against the clouds. Keeping track of it has never been easier. Unfortunately keeping myself hidden is going to be a lot harder as I spot the farm: a big silhouette against the sky. I officially pass into Orbelle and forbidden territory. I'll now be on their radar if they pass over me.

I run.

I keep to the side of the bank, staying so close to the hedge I feel thorned fingers grabbing at my side. By the time I'm in full view of the cows, I'm sure they're already aware of my presence.

I know Hans would whistle and sing to them to keep them calm. They're familiar with him. I'm hardly going to pass for their regular visitor, but I start to sing softly. It's a song I remember Hans sang as he walked with our goats. The cows still groan and shift their weight with uncertainty, but they don't seem to want to run away. The ones at the back probably can't even hear me.

I edge forward and see tails and ears flicking in the moonlight. I hear the thud of hooves on mud. My eye adjusts enough to see the white patterns on each cow. They're all up on their feet now.

I realise there's probably some level of expectation. Hills would generally only come here to move them on to be milked. Each hungry cow sports a set of udders, and they have only one job to do when the boss appears.

Instinctively they seem to be organising themselves to move. It's at that moment the helicopter appears again, heading directly towards me. Unless it turns, it'll fly directly over the field I'm in. I know it'll use infrared to detect my body and locate me. I have to move now, although it's highly unlikely I'll go unspotted.

I could dive behind the hedge and hide myself from view. But they'll still pick up on my body heat. One of the cows starts lowing and the sound grabs my attention. I dart forwards and throw myself into the herd.

"Whoa," I call briskly, stroking cows on their sides and remembering the phrases used to motivate them. They low and stand rigid as I praise them and smooth their coats. I'm hunched over as I go, and keep my head lower than their backs. My heart hammers as I duck between two cows and the helicopter soars over my head. I'm looking up at its underbelly of flashing lights. It's flying low and I feel blood pounding in my ears as it passes over.

If they suspect anything, they'll turn around and go full-circle over the field. The helicopter tilts and starts to circle the adjoining fields. It doesn't seem to want to hover anywhere in particular and I let out a hard sigh. I got away with it this time, but now I have a journey to make. I have to get into Orbelle itself. I remain still for a couple of minutes until several cows slump down on to the mud. Clearly they don't think they're going to the milking parlour anymore.

A plan forms. I hop back on to my feet and prepare myself. This may not work, but I certainly wouldn't be able to make the dash to town on my own. I'll have to go slowly and use my heat shields to escort me. They already know the way.

"Gee' up!" I call, patting cows on the back and starting to sing again. "Milking time. Gee' up, gee' up."

The cows groan and heave themselves up. They know the route, even in such little light. I know the words "gee" and "haw" encourages them left and right, although I worry I'll confuse the two.

Slowly but surely the procession starts and the cows carry me along in their party. There is no dog running at their heels, no farmer and truck, but these aren't questionable animals and the helicopter will see nothing more than a moving herd of cattle.

I'm sandwiched uncomfortably between two cows. My body is crouched so my head doesn't stick out like a periscope. Often the cows squash me and I fear if I fall then I'll be trampled. But they know I'm here and seem happy enough to walk with me. I dare to think my plan is working. But each time the helicopter comes back I hold my breath and keep my head down.

There are no gates between fields, only gaps in hedges wide enough to let us through. We make our way steadily over two fields and then reach the only gate in our path – the gate that separates the fields from the stretch of concrete up to the milking parlour. The cows congregate around this gate and wait for me to open it. No one has tended to these cows properly for days, I can imagine their udders ache to be emptied. If I open the gate, will anyone spot me? Will they know gate had previously been closed? I only have one stretch of road left until I'm essentially in the town and can pass for one of Joel's team. I can either jump the fence and sprint, or open it and let all the cows through and hope no one realises they've done this with human help. The helicopter's flying the other side of the fields and over the river. So close now . . .

I jump the fence.

I leave a herd of confused cows behind me and run the length of the road. I imagine myself on an infrared screen, white limbs flailing. I remember how a rabbit's tail flashes white as it runs. I feel like a frantic rabbit now as I run hard and fast across smooth concrete. The farm smells of waste and hay and I welcome the smell like a hug from an old friend. The trouble is I don't know where to turn next. The smell of something else draws my attention.

Silage. The smell is unmistakable. They must be storing it in one of the barns.

Many years ago a fire broke out on one of the farms. Hans and my father went to help them deal with it. None of the children were allowed anywhere near it, and so we sat on the hill and watched the smoke rise into the sky. My father explained to me later that sometimes silage can overheat in storage and catch fire. He thrust my hand into a tight mound of silage that made me shriek in disgust. The soft mound of cow food was moist and warm inside. It freaked me out then but now, like so many other things my father told me, it resurfaces like an instruction. I know where to hide until I figure out my next move.

I've taken refuge under the silage bails. It's warm under here and I stink of my surroundings. My body heat is shielded and no one has been in to unearth me. But I'll have to make a move soon, before the sun comes up. Tiredness is setting in. I could easily put my head down and sleep but I must move on. I must think of a plan. Instead my head presses against a bail and despite the earthy scent I close my eyes.

I didn't think I'd fallen asleep, but I must've done because I don't know when the noise started.

At first it sounds like a lot of machinery working at once. I hear high pitched shrieks, mingled with guttural barks and snorts. I'm no stranger to the sound of squealing pigs. They squeal for food. They squeal in fear. Perhaps it's both.

I sit up in my hiding place. Since this is the first time I've heard them, I can only assume they've spotted something. I'm not alone anymore.

Sure enough, I hear the sound of an engine approaching. It draws up nearby. I hear a door open and close. The pigs continue to make their racket. Whether I've been discovered or not, I can't sit here a moment longer. The uncertainty is driving me mad. I wriggle out of the bails and press my back to the wall of the barn. I can hear footsteps, but they don't approach the doors. I may be able to get by, unnoticed, provided they're distracted by the pigs long enough.

I put my right eye to the door and see no one out on the courtyard; but I can see the truck used to get here. If only I'd learned how to drive, I could've stolen it and driven up to the ranch.

Then I catch sight of the driver and think not. There's little I can do against the rifle I see him carrying. He could shoot the window out as I drive away. Probably put a bullet in my head before I turn the key. Fortunately he seems to have no idea I'm here. He's heading for the pig pen.

The groan of the gate tells me he's around the corner and letting himself into the pen. I have time to run around the barn and on to the road. Perhaps he'll find me on his drive back up to town, but I have little choice. I step out the doors to the sound of a gunshot. The pigs continue to shriek, but I suspect their number is down by one. I suppose WOLF X recruits need to eat.

If only I hadn't been so surprised I wouldn't have let the barn door slam behind me. I've no doubt at all he will have heard it. My common sense fails me and I sprint for the truck. I ignore its doors and crouch around the side of it. When he steps into the open courtyard I see him looking around for the intruder. There was a large part of me that hoped it would be Joel, but I'm not that lucky. This person walks to the barn doors, hits every button inside the control panel and lets the lights illuminate the silage bails. After a couple of minutes inside, he re-emerges and skirts the outside of the barn. He heads towards the slurry pit. He inspects every corner with the barrel of his rifle.

Now's the time to run, but I don't. I keep my eyes on him as he walks around the slurry pit. The control panel inside the barn not only operated the lights, but also switched on the automatic scrapers that revolve at the bottom of the pit. It makes a noise as it starts and he wanders near; despite there being no chance of anyone hiding in there. He cranes far over to see the slurry move in a clockwork motion. If he doesn't step away sharply he'll fall into the tank.

And he does.

It happens so quickly. He made the same mistake as me and left the barn door ajar. The wind catches it and it slams shut with such a sound he spins around and loses his footing. There's a yell before he hits the surface of the pit and disappears.

I caught a shout in my mouth as he toppled and now it aches inside my throat. I stand without thinking. If there was anyone nearby they'd go to his aid. But no one does, and he doesn't immediately resurface.

If he hadn't been wearing the same uniform as Joel I would've used this opportunity to move on as fast as I could. Instead I linger, desperate to see his head come back up for air; but I know the chances of that are slim. The current carves thick brown ripples across the top of the waste. It'll drag him down and he'll either be crushed by the scrapers or he'll drown beneath the slurry.

I sprint to where the controls are inside the barn and hit the emergency stop button. No matter what, I can't let Hills and Hans pull a decaying body from the pit when they return. I can't let him die knowing I could have helped.

I run back to the edge of the pit and grab the longest thing I can find from the floor. I already fear the worst until an unrecognisable face bursts from the slurry. He splutters large gloops of waste from his mouth and tosses his body to stay afloat.

"Over here!" I extend the object I picked up. "Grab this."

Whether I can be fully trusted or not is irrelevant. He flings his body from side to side as he swims to the edge. Shock and disgust is still etched on his face. He grabs the end of the object and I heave him up so he can grasp the railings. Once his feet are firmly back on the ground he uses a sludgy hand to wipe slurry from his face. Clear streaks from his fingers allow me to look at him properly. Then we both step back in acknowledgement.

"Goat girl," he says.

"You." I hold the object close to protect my chest. This was the one who stared at me at HQ. The one Theo told me to pay no attention to. The one Johannes told to shut up. His name is Warren, who mocked Joel and almost had his nose broken by Hans. I remember at once why I disliked him. I should've let him stay in the pit after I turned the power off. He may well deserve the extra swim.

"Are you a complete idiot? You would have died in there."

"I thought I was going to," he admits. "What did you do?"

"Emergency stop button," I say. "I know where most things are on this farm. I know more than just goats, as it happens. A friend of mine was raised on this farm. You're lucky I was here."

"How the hell did you get here at all? What happened to your eye?"

"Never mind," I say. "You should be more interested as to what I'm going to do now."

"You can't do anything" Warren's words trail off when he sees what I'm holding. The object I picked up to pull him from the tank is none other than his own rifle. I aim it at his chest.

"Stop blinking," I say at once.

"I have crap in my eye."

"WOLF lenses are full of that anyway, according to your team. And I know how WOLF X lenses work. One more blink and I'll take out one of your kneecaps and shove you back in the slurry. You can drown in the stuff for all I care. I didn't get this far for you to give away where I am."

I'm expecting a snide retort. I expect him to dare me to go ahead and shoot him. But he doesn't. He stares at me and then uses his sleeve to rub his eyes firmly. Joel must've told them about my wolf encounter.

"Why are you here? You didn't have to come here."

"I know I didn't. But there are things your lenses don't tell you. In fact, they've been lying to you. To everyone. Theo died, by the way. I was there. That's when I realised what was going on."

Warren seems unmoved by Theo's name but no less confused. "I don't understand."

"They put it down to White Eye," I say bitterly. "They switched off his oxygen and let his heart fail because according to Cornelius Morgan his brain was dead and his eyes were white. But he was alive. He would have fought if they'd let him."

"So they're corrupt," Warren says flatly. "Surely Joel told you that? You didn't really think this sort of thing didn't happen? That's WOLF. That's our government letting WOLF take dominance over everything in Fenix. They don't care about us, goat girl. The world will turn a blind eye whilst WOLF controls everything. Our trust is based on what we see.

And WOLF controls that the same way you control a flock of goats."

"It's a herd of goats, not a flock. You don't get a flock of goats." We stand in silence for a moment until Warren takes a whiff of the air around him.

"I stink."

"Good god, you're the most pampered bunch of military men I've ever heard of," I snap. I'm trying to goad him into further argument. I have to hear him confirm my suspicions. I need him to tell me what I already know. But Warren won't reveal their intentions to me willingly. "You'll do whatever WOLF tells you, won't you? Take over our town, destroy our livelihoods, switch off life-support machines. They howl and you gather, right?"

"You don't know anything. Wolves eat goats and you're just one surrounded by our mob."

"Pack," I hesitate. "Surrounded by your pack. Although, in your case, I would call you a litter. You're all pathetic."

"We don't work for WOLF!" Warren finally snarls. "Have you learned nothing?"

"So then what are you doing here? Tell me."

"Put down the gun."

"Who says I can trust you?"

"Who says I can trust *you*?"

There's a moment of silence before I turn and throw the rifle into the slurry pit. It sinks like a stone. If he wants it he can dive in and get it. I know where the controls are to start the automatic scrapers again if he does.

"I'm here for Joel. To get him out from under your major's stupid orders."

"And we're here to see our orders through, no matter what," Warren says. "You think we're here on WOLF's orders? So do they. But we're not on their leash. We won't come to heel once this is done. By the time we're finished we'll have put them down for good."

I knew it. I would pat myself on the back, but the situation feels too grim to congratulate myself. I knew all along Joel was part of this. Theo hadn't been acting alone.

"So you're biting the hand that feeds you?"

"The hand that feeds everyone," Warren says. "We're not here to repair ALPHA. Oh sure, we're working on it. To restore it and improve it, but not for their purposes. ALPHA is one of many satellites controlling WOLF lenses. There are more across our atmosphere. But ALPHA is what its name suggests: the first and most significant. That was our mission. To bring this one down and modify it. We had it all planned. We shut down the main communicator and blamed it on the meteor showers heading for this side of the equator. Then we planned to bring it down completely as part of a scheduled collision."

"Hang on." I try to make sense of what I'm hearing. "You planned to bring it down the same time the meteors fell, so you could blame it on a direct hit with a meteorite?"

"Correct," Warren says. "It would all be the fault of a natural phenomenon. Then, once we were given the go-ahead to investigate we would begin work on restoring ALPHA. We could do what was necessary to control the rest of the satellites. Without them circulating the country, WOLF can't monitor the lenses. They'll have no flock to control. We're not going to bite the hand that feeds us. We're going to rip it apart finger by finger."

I'm so surprised I just blink at him with my one eye. When I swallow my mouth feels dry.

"Is Joel here?"

"Yeah, of course. He's part of Communications now. Ouren didn't seem to trust him with patrols since his little adventure with you. He's based solely on that ranch now."

I must have misheard him.

"Wait . . . he's based where?"

30

"Oh god." It's all I manage to say.

Our ranch has been converted into a base. The shutters have been sealed and boarded at every window, and there are vehicles parked outside with tyre tracks snaking up the hill. There isn't a single goat in sight, or hardly any indication we ever lived here at all. Except our belongings are stacked up in one huge truck. I can see my own pillow and headboard nestled among other things.

"Here we are: Communications Central." Warren stops in the gateway and points. I gape in horror.

"This is my house."

"Really?"

"That's my bed."

"We relocated a lot of the beds for our sleeping quarters."

"Dare I ask where that is?"

"Town hall," Warren says. "First time that place has been used properly, I should think. What on earth do people do in this town?"

"We used the town hall to rehearse for school plays and to host harvest festival," I say. "That's the only time I've been in there. You all sleep there now?"

"The majority of us. We managed to make a dormitory out of it. Glad it can finally be put to something useful."

I still haven't taken my eyes off my front porch. I don't want to imagine what lies beyond. "And you said this is now?"

"Communications centre."

"Telecommunication?"

"Yeah. Our window to the outside world; monitoring the behaviour of weather and HQ's broadcasts. Also keeps us in tune with the other satellites. We've completely renovated the place."

"I can imagine. We didn't even own a computer."

"I know. We all had a good laugh about it. Not a problem now though. We've given you top-of-the range equipment. No need to thank us."

He nods towards the huge satellite dish that has been placed on the roof. I'm too crestfallen to respond.

He takes me up the steps and thrusts out a hand before I reach for the doorknob. I can't believe I need to be granted access to my own home, but sure enough there's a security system in place. A shiny metal plaque is secured to the wall with an eyepiece. Warren asks me to stand aside and swiftly passes his eyes over the plaque. There's a flash of red light and the door unlocks.

Warren turns the door handle and steps inside. I go to follow him but stop momentarily to see the brass bell has been taken down from the porch. I can't rap my knuckles against it to let my mother know I've arrived. I sigh heavily and step into what used to be my home.

There are footprints all over the floor. The lights are off and yet I see the dirt everywhere. The rest of the place is bathed in nothing more than the glow of monitor screens. Little lights shine everywhere. When I walk into the living room it's like stepping into the simulation room again. The sofa is gone, the radio we had is replaced with a dozen monitors situated at two different heights for those standing and those sitting. Our dining room and kitchen chairs are in here. As is my father's writing desk, which had never moved my entire life. To think this is just one room. The astronomical charts I had in my bedroom are strung up along the walls, including all the notes I made for impending meteor showers.

"Pretty impressive, isn't it?" Warren says.

"I'll kill Joel," I say shakily. "And every last one of you that touched my stuff."

"It's all for the cause." Warren shrugs. "Are you ready to see your beloved? He's usually stationed upstairs. He complained about having to climb them, but as punishment for deserting his post, we honestly don't give a damn about his comfort."

I was already pre-warned about the shepherd's crook on the way up here. It started as a bad joke between the team. They found my father's crook in the house and continually swapped it for whatever stick Joel used to ease his leg, in honour of his goat girl. As soon as he would sit down, someone would snatch his stick away and put the crook in its place. Eventually Joel decided to adopt the crook and take it literally in his stride, choosing to be proud of it.

"We joked that a part of you was with him whilst he had the crook," Warren explained. "But the joke's almost turned. I think he'd be more annoyed if someone took it away now. Anyway, after you. I guess you know where you're going."

I open the door to my mother's bedroom and remain still once I see him. At first he doesn't notice me and Warren doesn't announce my arrival. Joel's attention remains fixed on the screen in front of him. Although they've set him up in my mother's room, he's surrounded himself with my possessions. My ornaments, my calendar, my books. My father's crook is propped up on the desk. He looks like a badly cast shepherd in a play. Surely his team didn't need to humiliate him further after he shot himself in the backside?

I notice they've taken all the photographs my mother had of me on the walls to make way for a large cork board pinned with notes and charts. The photographs are still in their frames and assembled around Joel's desk.

"Perhaps, if my mother had better vision, she'd have chosen more interesting photos to put up."

He turns his head and freezes.

"Wh . . ?"

Warren attempts to answer all questions at once with an incredulous choice of words.

"She snuck into Orbelle under a cow to see you, mate."

I roll my good eye. Joel looks back and forth between us both. "What?"

"I had to come see you. To warn you," I say. "You're in greater danger than you think."

Joel stands up and I'm pleased to see he's not as heavily reliant on the crook as I feared. He makes his way to me with only the slightest of limps.

"You managed to get here without being caught?"

"I caught her," Warren objects.

"Actually, I caught you," I say. "Feel free to use the shower anytime – second door on the left, unless you changed that too."

Joel looks between us both. "You got all the way here without WOLF sending you?"

"WOLF don't know I'm here. Not yet anyway," I say. "I'm sure Hans will notify them soon that I'm gone. I saw what they did to Theo."

"Theo? He died under intensive care. That's what we were told. But we suspected . . ."

"Yes," I say. "They told everyone he was White Eyed, but I saw what really happened . . ."

I don't need to explain any further.

Joel turns to Warren and orders him to notify my arrival to Ouren. It takes some persuasion to make him leave, and by this time other recruits have started to fill the doorway to get a glimpse of me. I feel like an exhibition in my own house and it starts to make me angry.

"By the way, I love what you've done with the place," I say.

"I did everything I could to save your stuff," Joel insists. "So I could return it to you."

"He wanted everything as a keepsake!" someone yells into the room. Joel barks at them all to leave.

Now we're alone. My heart beats so hard I fold my arms across my chest to stifle any sound. He looks just the same as I remember. His hair is slightly longer, but the same golden brown. His scar is no different, still jagged across his bottom lip. Still I stare at him. He's doing the same to me. Only there are a few substantial differences for him to question.

"Your eye . . ."

"An accident," I say evasively. "We don't know how bad it is yet. Not until the dressing comes off."

He smiles and I realise he's looking deeply into my right eye, not the left. "Not that. They're hazel."

"Oh."

I smile back and, for a moment, I'm sure he starts to lean forward. Perhaps it's only to pick up his crook but my heart lurches so suddenly my body responds and moves towards him. That's when the door opens and Ouren appears with Warren by his side.

"Linnea Hansen. WOLF 0315, Snake F," he says. "What a pleasure it is. I very much enjoyed your appearance on television. Tell me, have you come to stop us all by yourself or can we be expecting Lieutenant Rusten to arrest us at any moment? Don't think we haven't noticed his helicopter. It takes three blinks to alert him, if I'm not mistaken, or do I need to disable your other eye? What happened to the left, a precautionary 'accident'?"

"You could say that." My voice is flat as I stare at his glass eye. "In fact, you would know best. My way seemed better than stabbing myself with a badge at the time. Perhaps less ironic and noble, but it did the job."

Joel looks between us both with no idea what I'm talking about. Ouren, however, takes a breath in, straightens his shoulders and orders Warren to fetch a clean shirt and trousers. They have a guest with them.

31

Ouren steps into my mother's room and looks me up and down. Although he understands I pose no threat, he asks certain questions. "You didn't just materialise inside Orbelle without help. Has she been searched?"

"No, sir," Warren says eagerly. He moves towards me and Joel blocks his path. If looks could kill, Warren's eyes would turn white.

"Lads, enough," Ouren says. "She can explain her story to me first. If I'm not satisfied then she can be screened."

"You still think WOLF sent me here?" I ask.

"Warren says WOLF is responsible for Theo's death. That I don't doubt. Cornelius Morgan didn't include his death during his public appearance. I'm sure this will all make a very interesting story. Warren, send for Charlie. Joel, stay."

"You don't think it's a good idea if I stay too, sir?" Warren seems to enjoy the idea I'm some kind of WOLF spy.

"No, that won't be necessary. And, frankly, you stink like a cow's rear end. I want you to find Charlie and then remove those clothes and wash. Now."

Warren leaves without question. I'm led across the landing to my father's office. Before I step inside, I can't resist turning my head and calling after Warren.

"You'll need to hit the power switch outside the bathroom. My father hid it when I was a toddler because I kept switching the hot water on and off whilst people were in there. It's behind the phone table."

Ouren stares at me in disbelief. "This is your house?"

"This is my father's office, sir." I step inside and see they've rearranged the entire design. I don't know where my sudden brazen attitude comes from, but I take the best seat before Ouren can and fold my arms. "Please, do come in."

Joel is grinning and waiting for Ouren's reaction. His glass eye doesn't move but the functional one is astonished.

"Close the door, Edgecombe."

Joel obeys and I wonder if anyone will be able to hear us on the landing. I'm told to explain everything and suddenly I don't know where to begin. My voice catches in my throat. Once I start, I keep going. I don't stop talking and no one interrupts. I tell them about Theo, about the ALPHA photographs, about Alec working for Grapha. I tell them they took my mother away to keep me quiet and I'm afraid of what they'll do to her once they know I'm here. I tell them everything. I tell them Cornelius Morgan is aware Theo was working under Ouren's orders and there will be a counter attack for what they did to Iris. I tell them if they don't abandon everything they're doing they will all be punished.

"I'm not here to make threats or persuade you to stop under WOLF's orders," I insist. "I'm not. I'm here for him."

I look at Joel. He smiles at me and I find all my previous emotions have built to this. I feel a tear run down my cheek and cover my good eye with one hand.

"That'll do," Ouren says. He looks up at Joel and nods. It's permission for Joel to comfort me. Once I feel his hand on my shoulder I stop crying and there's a knock on the office door. Ouren opens it and stands aside.

"Ah, Charlie. Come in."

I'm pleasantly surprised to learn Charlie is a girl. She isn't much taller than me, although much leaner. Her WOLF X lenses amplify her big, pretty eyes and they shine violet.

"Charlie, this is Linnea Hansen. This is her ranch and we're being most imposing on her property. Joel is about to get her something to eat from her kitchen. Please help to relocate the clothes we removed from the bedrooms whilst she showers. Charlie is our medic. She'll see to that eye of yours. Don't pretend it's seen proper medical attention, I remember how they treat eyes. You needn't tell me what happened, but I do insist you have Charlie look at it."

"Yes, sir," I say.

Before I shower I use the shower-head to wash away any hairs left in the bathtub by Warren. When I'm satisfied there's no trace of him I start removing my shirt. There's a gentle knock on the door. Charlie comes in with two towels folded in her arms. I'm impressed she actually managed to pick my own towel from the airing cupboard. I go to take them and neither of us says anything for a moment.

"What exactly did you do to your eye?" she asks quietly.

"I stared at the sun too long," I say.

"On purpose?"

"I was holding binoculars. Most stupid thing I've ever done. I might never see out of it again.

Charlie raises an eyebrow but smiles. She leaves so I may shower in peace. It feels sensational to use my own bathroom. This room has undergone the least renovation. My razor is on the rim of the tub. They've used all my shampoo, but the block of soap my mother always gets for her birthday is still there. My flannel, my toothbrush, my towels. I could cry with joy. I'm home. It may look different and be full of people I've never met – but it's still mine.

Once I'm dressed and wearing a similar outfit to Charlie she examines my eye and redresses it. When she starts to peel the bandage off I wince in pain. The fabric sticks to my face.

But eventually it comes off and I blink, only to discover I can't see out of it.

"That may change. You'll have to give it time." Charlie produces a black, shiny eye patch. "This is actually one of the patches we keep for Ouren when his eye plays up. It's nothing fancy. It'll just blot out the light and help your eye rest. Sorry, I'm no WOLF expert on eyes. This is the best I can do."

"Thank you," I say and she slides the patch over my face. I already feel better than before. My skin is clean, these clothes are newly ironed and my wounds are treated. Anything could happen now and I wouldn't care. Not whilst I get to stay within these familiar walls.

Joel is ready to greet me when I step outside with Charlie.

"Hey, Linn," he says. "Huh, you look menacing. It's hard to recognize you."

I look down at my outfit and can't help but agree. I'm usually in a blouse and woollen tights. Now I'm in combat boots, a sandy shirt under a large jacket and trousers held up by a belt. When I look up again Joel is more serious.

"Why did you come here?" he asks. "It's not safe."

Oh, don't I know it.

I know more than he does.

"I came here for you." I lower my voice and step forward. "You left Ouren's team once, Joel. I understand why. And I know why you tried to shoot Morgan. You can't stay here. When I explain to Ouren he might not believe me . . . But before I do I need you to promise me you'll get out of Orbelle first thing tomorrow."

"With the helicopter circulating?" Joel raises an eyebrow. "Don't think we haven't figured HQ is watching us. Rusten's distrusted Ouren from the moment he got demoted. "

It's more serious than that, I fear.

"Joel, what are you doing?" I take hold of his shoulders and hold him steady. "What is this about, really? I understand some; Warren filled me in. But what was the plan exactly? Did you think blowing up Iris would really help your cause?"

"No, of course not. And we didn't blow it up, it was a hologram," Joel says. "I said it was too much. I said people would panic and Cornelius Morgan would brand us as terrorists. This is why I originally walked away. We're not here to frighten people."

"What are you doing then?"

"Getting people's attention. I mean, I knew some people would panic and that couldn't be helped. But we needed awareness. We needed people to take note something was going on and understand a reformation was underway. Then when the lenses stopped working we knew people would panic even further .Until they learned."

“Learned what?”

“That they could live without them. Or at least until they understood this stupid compulsory law is unnecessary, absurd and invasive. We wanted people to acknowledge their lack of choice in the matter and to want the option again. We want them to turn and revolt if possible. Supposing the law went to a vote . . . who knows what would happen. That’s exactly what we want to find out.”

“I see. People won’t vote for a change in the law against WOLF lenses until they’re reminded they can live quite comfortably without them.”

“That’s right. They call us terrorists, they say we want to abolish WOLF entirely. Well, we’re not that unrealistic. We want people to see WOLF how we see them. We want them to hate WOLF as we do. But we could only ever enforce a change in the law, given the right support. We want freedom. Is that so impossible?”

“No,” I sigh. “I suppose this was always going to happen sometime in the future. WOLF couldn’t control us all forever before someone took a stand.”

“That’s exactly what Theo said,” Joel says and I release his shoulders.

"Joel, Theo is dead. I'm sorry to keep saying it, but you have to understand why I need you to leave with me. I saw what they did to him."

"I know. Believe me, I know what they did was awful," Joel says. "You don't know how saddened I was to learn of Theo's death. He was braver than anyone I know and he hated WOLF with a passion. He would've been glad to die for this cause."

"But what for? This is what I don't understand. Why are you all so happy to keep going, even now? What is there worth dying for?"

"Our freedom." Even Joel smirks at how abnormally noble he sounds. "Our right to live our lives how we choose. Make our own choices and decisions without WOLF interfering with everything. Look, you didn't get to know Theo so you probably didn't know that Theo was gay."

I did know that.

"He told me," I say. "You're right, it wasn't obvious. I'm sure he was good at concealing it."

Joel raises his head and looks at me. "You would think, wouldn't you? But this is why he joined Ouren's team."

"Because he was gay?"

Joel laughs sadly. "No. There's more to it than that. I knew a lot about him. We all knew each other's reasons for joining Ouren's team, and I knew Theo's inside out."

I'm intrigued to learn more about the boy I cradled as he died.

"Theo was a happy kid," Joel recalls. "He was doing well at school. Then WOLF arrived and gave him his first set of lenses. At first nothing changed. Then puberty hit Theo like a punch in the face."

He pauses, his expression is bitter.

"Theo said he knew he was different. Not on the outside, but inside. He said initially he felt wrong, like he wasn't normal. He didn't know how to handle it. He knew pretty much what it was, but didn't know if it was a phase or something. But before he could make sense of his own sexuality, his WOLF lenses picked it up and it all became too apparent."

I'm starting to think I know where this is going.

"The one who changed it all was a boy called Luke. Theo adored him. He said Luke was all he could think about, although he kept his admiration to himself. But one too many glances at him and it was impossible to hide. Boys don't usually look at each other with green eyes. Soon everyone knew. The names started. Teasing. Bullying. He couldn't shower publicly without boys running away from him, shouting his eyes had turned green and he was in love with them, which was, of course, nonsense. He felt so ashamed and confused. He should've been coming to terms with who he was and dealing with it in his own time. His lenses stole that from him. Theo never forgave them."

I never considered the idea WOLF might unexpectedly force gay people to come out before they were ready. I can only imagine the confusion Theo had suffered. This shouldn't happen. The lenses shouldn't deny people some secrets. It could ruin lives.

For an entire team to assemble and plot to bring WOLF down there must be a thousand cases even more sad and infuriating. Perhaps Joel thinks I may cry because he puts his arm around me.

"Theo was the bravest recruit I ever knew," Joel says. "Far braver than me. I'm glad you were with him in the end."

"So am I." I have to suddenly look away.

"What is it?" Joel asks.

"There's something that's been bothering me," I confess. "I don't want to think about it but it's been playing on my mind since they let me go."

"Let you go?"

"From HQ. They kept me there after Theo was taken away. I didn't see or speak to anyone for a while. I presumed they wanted to keep me out of sight whilst they decided what to do with me. I was beginning to think that was in order to make it easier for when they killed me too."

I pull the cuffs of my sleeves over my knuckles and squeeze the material in the palm of my hands. I haven't been able to speak about this to anyone else. But Joel will understand.

"Why would they kill you?"

"To keep me quiet. I saw what they did. I was convinced of it, Joel. I was certain they would silence me somehow. When they let me leave the building I was sure someone would follow me and attack me once I was alone. If Hans hadn't found me by chance I wonder if I'd have made it to the station. You think I'm stupid, don't you?"

Joel clears his throat. "Better to harm you inside HQ than out in the street."

"But they might have done. They could've killed me right there with Theo. Why didn't they? Why was I allowed to leave? I saw what they did." Inside my sleeves my knuckles tighten and tremble. "Why take my mother away, unless they plan on doing something awful to her."

"They wouldn't have killed you, Linn. And they won't kill her."

"But why not? They killed Theo."

"That was different. They knew who Theo was and what he was trying to do."

"But Rusten suspected me too. That's why they kept me there. They had all my photographs and they know I'm connected to you somehow."

"That's true." Joel considers for a moment. "But, no. You could hardly have been involved. Rusten is smart enough to suspect you, but smarter still to know you couldn't have caused all of this. You're barely eighteen years old. You're no recruit. An associate of Ouren's maybe, but no recruit. How would it look on WOLF X if someone like Ouren could take on an underage female without them knowing? Could take on anyone without them having a full background check done on them? A terror attack on WOLF performed by an eighteen year old goat herder who doesn't even own a computer. I hardly think anyone would have believed you were behind the attack. I'm surprised they dared to take your mother away."

I listen and feel my fear slipping away. I loosen my grip on my sleeves and let my shoulders relax. I don't know why I'm so scared in the first place. I'm alive, despite my uncertainty. They did let me go. But hearing Joel explain why releases me from a spell that has crippled me since that night. Perhaps if I'd been with Joel all along, I wouldn't have been driven to blind my own eye. I start to believe his words and drink in the comfort they bring.

"But they could still murder a young man like Theo," I say with remorse.

"Theo was easy to dispose of. He *was* involved for certain. If they couldn't prove his death was an accident they certainly could've proven his guilt. Perhaps some reporters would've tried to find a way of twisting the whole thing against WOLF, but they'd have been wringing out a dry towel and got nothing. He was comatose and suffering from smoke inhalation. That could all be proved, if necessary. But you? They would've had to think very carefully before handing you the same fate. Whilst you're alive you're unremarkable, unimportant. But the dead rouse so many questions. WOLF don't want people making up their own answers."

He's right. Besides, Theo was very easily killed by switching off the life-support machine. How did I expect them to get rid of me? Strangle me? Poison me? The fact no one was hurt except the culprit made the whole thing easier to brush aside. Perhaps Joel's right: I would've created a story.

I was safe then. But I'm not anymore.

When Morgan finds out I'm here, warning Ouren and speaking out about Theo what will he do to me and my mother? And as for Theo being ten times the recruit Joel was, I think we all possess the ability to find weakness within ourselves. I have underestimated myself my whole life. But here I am, having come all this way to be with Joel and help enforce the change I now believe is necessary. I could leave. I could try and make it back out, just as I managed to sneak in. But I feel the heat within my body; and instead of repressing a smoking ember I let the fire come alive. I have something to fight for now, and there's no point crediting Joel for my inner flame. WOLF have been fuelling it for weeks. I'm doing this for myself.

I put my head on his shoulder and close my eyes, knowing if he decides to stay here and see his job done, then I'm staying too.

32

I become accustomed to their team, although I don't interact with all of them. There are nine in total. Joel joined with Theo, into a pre-established team consisting of Warren, Johannes and two other men named Noak and Jacques. Jacques is their astronomical forecaster and can just about understand English. Noak is part of the original team who established WOLF and oversaw the ALPHA project, so I expect he's had more dealings with Cornelius Morgan than the rest of them. He's the only person Johannes will laugh with, so I assume they're very old acquaintances.

Charlie is one of the latest members to join their cause, having shadowed Theo for weeks and helped hack into WOLF HQ's computer system. It was Charlie who animated the explosion and found the means to perform their smoke bomb. There is one more female, who has only just joined them from Doverhaven. Her name is Adelheid and she spends her time conferring with Ouren and conducting maintenance on all machines, weapons and vehicles. She's also been keeping an eye on the helicopter, which circles the countryside at set times. So far there is only one. Adelheid is convinced it's there to unnerve us, not to actually intervene. She's even suggested it's there to deter us from leaving, not to put us off enlisting more recruits into Orbelle. I'm not sure why that would be.

I don't ask who the other female recruit was; the one Rusten mentioned at HQ. He said they caught one of Ouren's team on the mountain and interrogated her. I wonder if her fate was similar to Theo's. If she were here now the total would have been ten. It appears I've taken her place.

But I knew this team couldn't simply consist of the nine here in Orbelle. They refer to people outside the group and talk of things happening beyond the isolation of the mountain. I even hear the mention of Grapha, who are helping to develop the latest satellite to take over from ALPHA. Something about 'delays' and 'excessive scrap material costing the company'. I can only imagine someone on the inside is deliberately sabotaging the work to waste expensive materials and lengthen the time needed to complete the project. No wonder Alec was suspended for having my images.

In charge of everything, of course, is Major Ouren. Before I viewed Ouren as the hunter out to snare Joel and bring nothing but suffering to him. I now see I was wrong. He's no wolf like Rusten or Morgan, just an old bear. One fuelled with determination and unwilling to risk the safety of his team for one display of cowardice. He takes a moment of our time to think of Theo and what he did for the cause, insisting we pay our respects silently and remember him.

Ouren seems to respect me. He admires my determination and my cleverness at having evaded Morgan's helicopter. He also knows I can shoot accurately, and he knows I have recognised their cause. No other member of his team has been through what I have.

None of them witnessed Theo die.

Ouren sees me as a beacon of light, one that may ignite others. If he can win me to his cause then perhaps he can inspire folk of the countryside. When we stand facing one another our faces mirror each other. My patch and his fake eye conceal our self-mutilation, whilst the other eyes are weary with what we have seen. He looks at my patch as though he recognises a part of himself in me. A part of his past. I recognise what may be my future in him.

The night on the hillside is calm. We sit around a fire made by Joel and Warren on the hill before heading to the town hall. I feel like I'm part of some strange camp. Joel leans against me and places a finger in the air. He points to a light shining brighter than all the stars in the sky. I can't see half as many stars as I could with my lenses. Before I could see galaxies, depth and use colours to try and read the mood of the universe. Now I only see black and white.

"That's it there."

"The ALPHA satellite?" My voice is pensively.

"Tomorrow we'll force it off course and stop all communication with HQ."

"Won't they see it wasn't hit by a meteorite when they retrieve the wreckage?"

"They're already pretty hot on the idea it wasn't a meteorite," Joel says honestly. "You've met Rusten. You saw how sceptical he was about us being here. The whole thing almost went haywire when members of our team began interfering with ALPHA ages ago. A part of the satellite containing vital information was protected in a way we weren't expecting. Despite our hacker's skills, ALPHA detected a potential hack in their system and detonated a part of itself. It was better to have that information destroyed than fall into enemy hands, it seems. Anyway, that action alone was enough to send our team out to monitor what was happening. A fragment of the satellite fell into Orbelle, as we expected, and there was a rush to get to the wreckage before someone else claimed it."

"Wreckage?" I ask at once. "What wreckage?"

"It hit a truck," Joel explains. "So we were told. The person who reported it was instructed not to interfere with the vehicle at all until officials had checked it out. Fragments of the satellite fell in pieces. It must have been a big piece to damage the truck. Once it was removed, Morgan had the media on the scene in a flash to report it as part of the meteor shower. Heaven forbid those who tried to hack the satellite should know they'd caused a stir, eh?"

Joel grins but then notices my face and looks concerned. "Are you okay?"

"Fine," I say weakly. I would show him the piece of circuit board I found on the ranch, but it's still in my cardigan pocket with my mother. Wherever she is. "So they know someone is trying to tamper with the satellite. Won't they piece it all together once they have the rest of the satellite to look at?"

"What they can make out from its burned and battered corpse is up to them," Warren pipes up. He doesn't like being quiet for long and my conversation with Joel seems too intimate for his liking. "I'm looking forward to standing in court without lenses. Just think, we'll be the first people arrested without a WOLF-reliant justice system! No evidence can be given and no testimony can be used. Our statements will go down on paper, like it did years ago."

"Do you actually think you can get away with this?" I have to ask.

"Since Theo's death . . . no," Joel says quietly. "I think Morgan's far too ready to see us all sentenced to let a jury have their own opinion. He only needs to blink twice and we'll be convicted. Still, like Warren says, any trial will be delayed with ALPHA down. No lens reading means no evidence."

"Time enough for people to re-think their opinion of WOLF," Charlie adds. "Once the people have gone cold-turkey for a few weeks, it'll be interesting to see how they receive our statements."

"And you're happy to let people panic?" I ask.

"What do you mean?" Warren looks at me sharply.

"I was there when Iris exploded," I remind him. "And I was also there on a day people attacked our train during a riot. You're potentially starting them all again. They did what they could to make the city perfect afterwards. I just wonder how you'd feel if you undid all that work."

"You think the city's perfect?" Warren sits forward so suddenly I think he's about to stand up.

"No. I don't," I admit. "But it's got to be better than it was. They put too much effort in for it to be the same place as before."

"You're right," Warren says. "It's not the same. It was a real place before. It was imperfect and normal. It had faults. They didn't employ people like us to do what we do. WOLF X have been degrading themselves in that city since Ouren's day."

"It's only degrading depending on your outlook, Warren," Charlie says. "We're not WOLF X just so we can fire weapons and look scary."

"What's degrading?" I turn to look at Joel but he just raises an eyebrow.

"Don't bother asking him," Warren says. "He's too new to how it all works. And thank you, Charlie, I know that. But at least when we were given an assignment we were doing what we signed up for. Gave us a sense of purpose. I hated being granted leave of my military duties. Do you know what that means?"

"You got to go home?" I say.

"Ha. Yeah, I got to go home. And then I was awake early the next morning to go collect my new assignment for the day. They don't let us sit and play video games or watch films. Suddenly it's like working for a theme park. Degrading stuff. From balloon merchants to merchandise vendors, they'll find you something to keep Fenix bright and cheerful. You don't sign up to it; they just tell you what you have to do. One of my assignments was to transport laboratory equipment and they sent me off in a black cab decorated with a big white bow on the bonnet and confetti all over the wiper blades. But you should have seen how many people smiled at me as I drove by. There was no bride, just me in a chauffer's cap and a load of machinery, latex gloves and safety goggles. They had several of those cabs sent out after some protesting. Romantic moments produce hormones which shuts the fear system down. No one ever notices things like that."

I turn to look at Joel, who appears subdued by the conversation. "What about you? Did you have to do any of this?"

"No. But I do remember getting a free balloon when I was a kid," Joel says.

Warren smirks triumphantly. "There you have it. We've all been a victim to it."

Joel shrugs. "I think there are worse things to be fooled by than wedding cabs and free balloons."

"You think that's the worst they do?" Warren challenges him. "That's just for the tourists and citizens. That's just for the day-to-day people. God, if you'd seen what I've seen. Done what I've had to do."

"I didn't say it was right."

"No, but I wonder how happy you are to go along with it. I wonder if this is why you deserted us in the first place. You have no idea what it's really like."

"Shut up, Warren. You're twenty-four," Johannes finally snaps. "What the hell have you seen? What have they made you do?"

"I've shot people."

"You poor child." Johannes tuts.

"It's not a competition," Warren grumbles.

"Oh, it seems to be a competition when you chide Edgecombe. But don't you bother acting so tough with me, boy. Don't you dare. Shooting people who deserve it – that's an order you follow from your Major. You don't choose to do that, you do what you're told. I've seen WOLF members who go beyond that. I've seen people suffer slowly until the end. People wiped out unnecessarily. People who simply got in WOLF's way. I've seen the life and colour drain from their eyes like someone pissing in the snow. Oh, people may start with that red rag waving in their eye – that defiant anger – but it's always a mere piss-stain when WOLF's done with them. As for the women who oppose WOLF . . . there are plenty of men out there who enjoy seeing fear in a woman's eye. It's not just the screaming they enjoy, it's the colour. They make you look at them. They want to see that shade as they erase you of all dignity and courage. Strip you to nothing, until you beg for white. It's exciting when people die in fury but it's just as good when they die in fear. Red, yellow, orange. Doesn't matter how you go. In the end, autumn shades give way to winter. I've helped dispose of many bodies with just one colour left. Some WOLF members don't want you to close the eyes; they want their victims to lie there with that white, empty stare. I always closed their eyes. I always looked away as women were forced. I held back when men were so scared they leaked yellow . . .

'But I saw everything. Every bead of sweat, every tear that ran and every smear of blood. That's one of the curses of these lenses. It's impossible to pretend you don't see it. You can't turn a blind eye, you see more than you could ever possibly want. Go on, Warren, mock me. Tell me I wasn't brave enough. Tell me you're the bigger man here.

Edgecombe doesn't like to see yellow in a girl's eye, but you . . . I've never been so sure about you."

Warren says nothing. He suddenly looks ill.

I pick myself up and sit beside Joel.

"I've never been given a proper helium balloon," I say casually.

"You don't have to humour me." But Joel smiles and I know by exchanging just one small childhood story each we've lifted each other's spirits, despite everything Johannes just said. My thoughts turn to my father, however, and I imagine what might have happened to him, had he been captured during one of his riots. I realise now he had a lucky escape. I think about the people who graffiti the words 'THEY BLINK WITH BLOOD' and wonder if they're alive now for their actions.

"When they take me in, I'll tell the world about Theo and what the city is really like," Johannes says. "I'll shout it into every camera I see."

"You don't have long," I say. "Grapha is already remaking the parts needed to restore ALPHA. Morgan will have it running as soon as he possibly can."

"Perhaps," Joel says. "But he'll have to start from scratch once we hack into the system properly and wipe their records of every Fenix civilian. He's going to have one hell of a job when we're done with his precious." He gazes up at ALPHA and I fear he's placing all of his hope into that one spec of light.

The moon reflects off his eyes and turns them white. Without thinking I grab his hand and feel his pulse beneath my fingers. He looks surprised but pleased. He doesn't let my hand go and we sit looking up at the stars. Tomorrow everything they've been working towards will be put into action and I'll be a part of it. It doesn't matter if all this time I've been looking through tampered lenses and seeing only what WOLF wanted me to see. As I hold Joel's hand and look back at my ranch, life has never felt more real.

33

The following morning puts everyone into their proactive modes and I suddenly realise I don't have a place among the work. I can't involve myself with things I have yet to understand fully. I'm a bit disappointed with myself. I hoped to be more useful. But they all occupy computers and use software I've never seen before. My role can't be to just stand and watch. I burn to be involved.

In the end I occupy myself as a runner. This puts me in a lot of situations with Warren I'd rather avoid. He forgets all too often this is my house and I scold him for opening cupboards and handling things that don't belong to him. I don't trust him to have already pocketed a few of our valuables. At one point I see him stirring a mug for Ouren using a tiny silver spoon. He notices me staring at him.

"We ran out of clean spoons so I found this silly thing in a drawer."

"That was a christening present," I say. "If you look, you'll see it has my name engraved on the handle."

Warren shrugs. I make a mental note to check all of the various places my mother hid her treasures. It's clear they've turned over almost every stone in my house. Johannes appears and tells Warren he needs my permission to use anything from now on. Warren snorts and tosses the spoon back at me. When he leaves, I thank Johannes but can't resist questioning him.

"So you respect my property, is that why you were on my land a few weeks ago, sniffing around?"

"Ah. Your herdsman saw me, didn't he?"

"He did."

I ask something else that has suddenly resurfaced in my mind.

"Theo said something to me when I first met him," I say. "It was about me being signed up to Turtle Doves. He said WOLF might have made Alec Rouman pose as my ideal match, but wouldn't tell me why."

"So you're asking me instead?"

"Well." I look away, feeling unsure. "He said you were the person to ask, not him."

Johannes sighs. "Fair enough. I suppose I am."

"Why?"

"Because I was part of the team that created the program. We pitched the idea to WOLF, but I regretted it. When Turtle Doves ML started to show the same signs as all the other WOLF projects I tried to disassociate myself with it."

"What signs?"

“Oh, the usual signs of WOLF’s corruption,” he says. “First of all, I object to the idea you can find your perfect partner due to lens readings. WOLF can’t really tell you what qualities you need, only what qualities you already demonstrate in yourself. They match you with someone similar to yourself. But being similar doesn’t make you compatible.”

I think of my parents and how different they are to one another. I think of Alec Rouman and realise much of what Johannes says may be true of us. I certainly saw a lot of myself in Alec. But that was an observation I made with WOLF’s influence. I felt an obligation to Alec. Not a genuine attraction.

“So I objected to the idea,” Johannes says. “I told them Turtle Doves could be pitched as a harmless dating scheme, but not as legitimate coupling. It couldn’t promise and it shouldn’t influence. But I was overruled, for reasons that soon came to light. WOLF had a new agenda. They hoped that controlled pairing may bring about controlled breeding. Genetic disorders could be narrowed down, if they paired two candidates correctly. For one thing, if they were at all successful, they could attempt to water down type 03 wearers – types who resist normal lenses – by preventing the gene from tainting potential type 01 or 02 wearers. Type 03 is harder to monitor and the lenses are more expensive to manufacture. People like you cost money. They want your type diminished, where possible."

"Do you think someone would really fall for another candidate just because WOLF say they're compatible?"

"I trust some people won't. I trust there will remain some love out there that's still authentic. You've given me some hope."

"I have?"

"Absolutely." He gives me a wry smile. "You and Edgecombe are nothing alike. No one would have ever paired you two."

I don't know what to say. I'm glad my lenses aren't working. It's bad enough I can feel my cheeks burn.

At midday we're notified there's to be a development involving the satellite.

"What will happen?" I ask.

"Potentially nothing," Joel says. "But our goal is to try to disturb one of the lesser satellites. We've targeted one. Its orbit has been getting closer to ALPHA and we think now would be a good time to try interfering with it. If this is successful we can hope to start a domino effect and target all the others. We can't shut them all down for long but we can attempt to stop communication for a few hours."

"It'll be a black out," Warren enthuses. "No WOLF lenses for a few hours. Just think of the panic."

"We're not trying to frighten people," Ouren says firmly. "We want people to understand they can live without them. A few hours should be enough. The shock will wear off, the fear will subside and people will soon relish the freedom."

"We hope," I mutter.

"Since you say Morgan is aware of our intentions here, we'd better seize the moment while we can," Ouren says. "There may've been a better time to do this. We could've gained more control over ALPHA and paced ourselves. But there's reason to be hasty. I don't like the fact Morgan isn't interfering. I half expected him to send out another WOLF X team to watch what we're doing. The fact he hasn't is concerning."

My thoughts exactly. There's still only one helicopter that periodically flies across the countryside. I chew my bottom lip and look at the sky. I could see ALPHA so clearly last night. It's hard to believe it's still so close and hovering over the mountain. Joel stands near me, even when the rest disperse to continue their work.

“When this is all over and the various other satellites have been hacked, our aim will be to force ALPHA into de-orbiting this area and into a graveyard orbit,” Joel says to me quietly. “They’ll send up another model as soon as they can, but once we pull the plug they won’t get this one back.”

Ouren instructs me to assist Charlie in monitoring the nearest satellite. I enjoy watching, even if I don’t understand what I’m looking at. But eventually I crave fresh air and walk out of my home – or Communication Central –on to the hillside. I keep my legs moving until I’m through the gate and heading down the footpath. It doesn’t cross my mind I could break into a run and leave Joel’s team altogether. It doesn’t even enter my mind I may be better off completely away from them all. Instead I let my feet march until I’m in a familiar street, facing Hans’s house.

I take a sharp inhale and walk across the yard to what remains of an animal. I know my beloved goat would’ve been torn to pieces long ago. Perhaps if I dared to look there may be bone, a hoof or a tiny adolescent horn left of him. But I don’t want to observe the area O’Malley died. I keep my eyes ahead and climb onto the porch. I stand over the matted, decaying remains of the wolf and breathe slowly. Perhaps my shot is still lodged in its brain, the entry wound is too far rotten to distinguish. I feel slightly repulsed, yet I kneel and marvel this is something I faced and conquered on my own. How had that happened? When did I become the person able to save us? I imagine facing the same danger with Alec Rouman by my side and not Joel and I envision him grabbing my wrist and forcing me to run. He would have been practical; he would have fled. Of course he would have. We were perfectly matched. His emotions were mine, his fears and strategies were mine also. But I have changed, and that much seems absolutely clear.

Everything has changed.

I straighten up and look away from the wolf, back up to the ranch. How has my life become so alien? I lift the patch off my face and straighten up so the sun can bear down on my closed lid. It feels good to let air get at it. The breeze tickles and I wonder if can open it. But nothing happens. All the same, I observe the coolness of a clear day and how fresh the leaves and grass look. Even though Orbelle has been evacuated and left for weeks, I can't help but notice how little the town has changed despite losing my lenses. Unlike Fenix, there is nothing artificial here. The colours are the same. Everything looks, smells and feels as it always did. I find that comforting but I can't help but feel this is all too calm. I rushed to get here. I snuck out the moment Hans fell asleep. I boarded the first train I could and ran across fields. Now I'm standing alone with only a carcass for company. Something isn't right. I came to warn them all Morgan knew of their scheme, but nothing has come of my warning. No threats, no ambush, no raid. Rusten hasn't arrived with a team of his own recruits to force us out. There are moments I get caught in the excitement of Ouren's plan and forget the danger we're in. I begin to feel nothing is going to happen to us prior to ALPHA going down.

I'm wrong. I have to be wrong.

We're happy to keep our men out there . . . We're relying on our team in Orbelle to enlighten us. We're sending our thanks out to them.

These words replay inside my head and I sense some kind of foreshadowing. There's a tragedy planned here . . . something for Morgan to lament later. Ouren didn't hear the news broadcast, but I did. I know there is a pre-meditated plot at work. They won't let on the team in Orbelle are opposing WOLF because . . .

Because they won't want to be deemed responsible when something awful happens to them.

There will be no arrests. No scandal and no court case. I don't think they're painting Ouren's men as heroes right before tearing them through the media with tar and feathers.

They're building them up for the ultimate fall: the tragic heroes who sacrificed their lives to help those in need.

But how?

The fear is gradual and builds. I remember the last time I felt this fear was when I was trapped under the snow, just before Joel pulled me out. I thought I'd never resurface. For a moment I thought I'd die. If I had died up there then no one would have known until Anna said something. Except she never made it back either. I would have been buried under the snow and left for dead.

My right eye widens. Suddenly it's as if the carcass on the ground is running at me again and I realise the danger I'm in. A mountain lies between us and Sparkwell. A mountain that stands dominant over a town empty of civilians. Empty due to a constant warning. A threat the whole county has been hearing about for weeks. A threat that could be staged, should someone hold enough power and might to pull it off. No one would suspect a thing.

I break into a run. I move as though the impending avalanche is right behind me and only I can outrun it. I've faced a wolf before and shot it dead, I can defeat this one too.

Only Cornelius Morgan is no wolf. I see that now. He's not like Rusten. He's not so obvious with his intentions. He's too cunning and sly to be a wolf. He's a nasty grey fox. One that sends you gifts and pretends to be your friend. Morgan may be aware of Ouren's plan, but he wasn't anticipating one thing. I faced a real wolf before and now its body lies sodden and in scraps on Han's porch. That wolf wasn't prepared for me.

Cornelius Morgan isn't prepared for me.

34

"How long do we have?"

The question is finally put forward by Charlie. Prior to that there was silence as my words sank in. Half the team look at me and the rest turn to Ouren. He casts his gaze down but his glass eye stays on my face. I clear my throat.

"We've no way of telling. Morgan will send supplies to Sparkwell but will pass over Orbelle on the way, with an alternative purpose. He'll bomb the mountain. He'll be hailed for his generosity whilst the newspapers will go on to report the avalanches. Once he sends his helicopters out we'll be sat waiting for the assault. I think Adelheid was right, I don't think the helicopter was supposed to intervene. Only to monitor how many people were here. I thought it was strange there was only one, but now I think they wanted their security to be considered unremarkable. They may well have seen me enter Orbelle after all. I suspect the idea was to encourage us to congregate. There's a good chance they wanted us all in one place so that they can kill us all at once without having to arrest us. We could have hours. We could have minutes."

Joel has been staring silently out the window this whole time. He now turns and faces Ouren.

"You have contacts at HQ."

"Yes," Ouren says. "But Rusten will be in charge of dispatching the supplies, no doubt. He won't allow anyone to know of their departure."

"Not unless Morgan makes a show of things and televises it," Johannes says. "He may broadcast it live and make a spectacle of his good deed."

"It's possible," Ouren says. "But unlikely, given the true nature behind it." He turns to Adelheid, who has already read his thoughts and is nodding. "If Rusten gets wind we're expecting an attack, he may speed up the proceedings. You're our best hope now."

"Yes sir."

"What will Adelheid do?" I ask Joel.

"She and Charlie can hack into WOLF's computer system and find any hint of more helicopters being sent out. She can hack into Rusten's own personal computer. There may be no evidence on any of WOLF's systems, but if it's there then she'll find it."

"And what will the rest of us do?"

"Target those satellites with not a minute to lose," Ouren orders loudly. "No more delays. No more waiting for the right moment. The moment is now. I want ALPHA disabled and left for dead in space within the hour."

"But you have to get out," I protest. "You can't stay in Orbelle. Don't you understand what's going to happen?"

"They're using our own tactic against us. They're using a natural occurrence to bring us down and appear innocent to the people," Ouren sighs. "But if we can get ALPHA down before that happens then we will. I won't be beaten at my own game. All that remains is for us to take a vote. Those who wish to leave Orbelle and face inevitable arrest, raise your hand."

Everyone remains still. No one wishes to die at HQ like Theo. At least here we're all together.

"Very well. I want everyone here to take turns with the video camera. Say goodbye to your loved ones with nobility. Perhaps you'll see them again; perhaps not. Short and sweet, lads. Focus on why we were here and why we did this."

They were prepared for this. I look at every solemn face in the room. They knew if they were taken out then all that mattered was that their message was heard.

Joel's fingers close around mine. We squeeze each other's hands tightly. I feel the adrenaline pumping through his veins.

"This is it," Ouren says. "When I let you leave now, you will work for your very lives. I want each –everyone to record their message in alphabetical order. Once that's done, resume your stations and make sure our mission is completed. Make me proud to call you my team. Now go, all of you. Except you, Edgecombe, you come with me." Ouren pauses. "Both of you come with me."

The room clears without a word. Joel and I stay rooted to the spot until Ouren beckons us to speak with him outside the house. We follow him out, on to the hill. Ouren stops and inhales the mountain air. Everything seems unusually calm.

"It seemed like such a good idea at the time." Ouren's voice drifts over his shoulder and is delivered to us by the breeze. Whether Joel and I are meant to hear him is unclear. His gaze is fixed on Mt Venus and when he speaks again his voice is louder, as if to address the mountain. I think I understand this a little. The mountain has always stood like a guardian. Clearly Ouren has things on his conscience and the mountain is a silent confidant. "Things were getting out of hand. Crime was escalating, people were abusing more substances than we could control . . . It seemed like such an effective way to monitor the city. To separate the criminals from the civilized. To protect the innocent whilst catching and discouraging the guilty. To understand human behaviour and analyse what makes a community likes ours so quick to turn on itself. We had to make it compulsory. It had to be enforced if it was to truly pay off. Once we were able to prove its effectiveness and its ability to make the country money, the government could hardly refuse. The law was put into place and Fenix was reborn. It's the richest city in the world, and we made it happen."

Ouren turns around and looks at us with a defeated expression.

"How did it come to this?

"I don't know, Sir," Joel says. It's as though he has asked himself this a hundred times over before. I remain silent. WOLF achieved what it initially set out to do. Perhaps it was inevitable that once their goal was complete someone would begin using the lenses for more than originally planned. How does the most beautiful city in the world know when to stop striving for perfection? How many people suffer now, thanks to one company's need for absolute control?

"I noticed you didn't raise your hand," Ouren says.

"Sir, I'm staying with Joel. There are two ways I can reunite with my mother again. One is to leave Joel here and do everything Morgan asks, knowing the danger you're all in. The other is to stay and help you achieve what you need to do and hope they haven't harmed her."

"I understand," Ouren says. "It would be my duty to appoint an escort to take you out of Orbelle safely. Of course there would be only one obvious recruit for that job, wouldn't there?"

"I'm not leaving," Joel says at once. "I can't let you all stay and wait for Morgan's helicopters. Besides, I'm the face they'll recognise first. That doctor will know me immediately. I'm not running into the arms of the authorities."

I agree with Joel and nod firmly. Ouren sighs.

"So our innocent goat herder needs to be kept safe, and my WOLF X recruit needs to see this mission through.

Ouren turns around and our good eyes meet.

"Miss Hansen, should I choose to have Warren or some other recruit force you away and evade this attack, what will you do upon your return to HQ? Will you keep quiet? Or will you attempt to tell the world what you witnessed the night Theo died? Will you tell everyone what happened here when we're dead and cold?"

"I will." I have never been so sure of anything.

"Then I'm decided. Film everyone's segment for the camera and then get yourselves equipped and ready to leave. You have one final mission from me. You are both going up the mountain again."

35

Thirty feet above ground level. That's how high we're expected to climb before the power goes out. It's unclear how big the avalanche will be, but I'm sure the mountain has never experienced such impact. Charlie has got the power running and will give us approximately fifteen minutes before it goes out again. Fifteen minutes until we're stranded with our feet dangling over a mountainside that may soon be swept away. There's no going back once the chairlift picks us up. If the power goes out before we've reached thirty feet then we'll be sat in the direct path of the avalanche with nowhere to go.

The chairlift is operating when we arrive. Ouren sent Noak ahead of us to make sure. We act in haste to dress ourselves accordingly. There's still a chance we'll be hit and forced under the snow or that we'll be suspended in the air for hours on end. We equip ourselves with warmer layers but when I see Joel strapping his jacket to his waist I automatically start to discourage him. I remember being told that extra weight should be discarded if you have a chance to run out of an avalanche's path. But we won't be able to run anywhere and the risk of hypothermia is great. I say nothing except to force a hat on to Joel's head.

"Fifty percent of body heat is lost through your head," I tell him.

We're currently on the flat of the terrain. The chairs rattle on the wire as they come and go. As soon as we've assembled ourselves I feel panic rising with every chair that sails through the station. Joel has the camera secure in his hand and strapped down over his glove.

"Fifteen minutes." He steps up to the platform. "Ready?"

I think of Anna, alone and terrified, wondering if the power would ever come back on and if she would ever be saved. I think of her long after she lost her voice, when only the sound of her teeth chattering and shallow breathing could be heard on the empty air. I think of her fingers and toes turning blue. I suddenly remember she gave me her spare gloves. She said I would need them more. I think of how close she came to death on this very chairlift and I exhale slowly.

I'm not ready. I'll never be ready.

A chair passes through the station doors. The bar is already up and waiting for passengers. Joel grabs my arm and we leap into the seat before I can change my mind. I wrench the bar down until it clunks into place. I press my feet firmly against the foot rest because the idea of not being on solid ground during such a dangerous time is unbearable. There is absolutely no going back now.

I remember our instructions over and over. *Make sure the world sees. Make sure everyone knows what happened here. If you're to do that, then you must survive.*

The chairlift tilts back as it inclines. We're facing the mountain's slope and I look over my shoulder to watch Orbelle slowly pass behind the trees. Joel is playing with the camera.

"Everything will be bloody white," he sighs before snapping the lens shut. He turns it off to conserve battery power and snuggles next to me for warmth. "What do you reckon we're at? Ten feet?"

We only have seven minutes left.

We need to triple our height in half our time. I try to remember the many trips I've had on this chairlift. I was too busy looking at my surroundings to notice how high I was getting.

"If we don't make thirty feet," I start nervously, "then we have to know what to do. When the power goes out, the bar will go up. If we can't hang on and we're forced out, we'll go under the snow. Then you need to swim against it."

"Swim?"

"Like you're working against a current," I say. "The more snow you can get past you then less will be able to bury you. Grab a tree if you can, especially if we have to jump. Then put your hand over your mouth to make an air pocket. You can breathe for a while but if you start to pass out then just let yourself go. You'll use less oxygen if you faint."

"Do you actually think we'll be able to avoid being hit as we are?"

I remember the photographs of one of the worst avalanches Orbelle ever had. My father showed me the best photograph taken. Snow was gushing down the mountainside, spraying either side of trees like waves against rocks. Trees completely disappeared. I look to the side and watch branches pass us at eye level. I don't want to answer so I bite my lip. Joel's eyes are closed and his hand is clamped over his nose and mouth. I wonder if he's practising how to make an air pocket, or if he's gently hyperventilating. He can't panic. Panicking on a chairlift is absolutely no good at all. Besides I need him.

Five minutes.

My watch ticks too quickly and the chairlift moves too slowly. In my impatience, I lean backwards and forward trying to force the chairlift to move quicker but it doesn't work that way. We're nowhere near thirty feet; hardly even twenty. Joel takes a clear, sealable bag out of his pocket and I realise he means to put the camera inside. If we go under then so will the camera, and that must survive even if we don't.

Four minutes.

I can see Orbelle to my right, with all its little houses, once full of people I knew. I can see Anna's house with its twin chimneys. I see can Hills' farm, still dotted with cows. I can see my ranch, where my bedroom ought to be before Ouren turned it into Communications Central. I spend so much time staring at it I can't contemplate the idea it will possibly be buried.

Three minutes.

Joel grabs my hand and we both look down at the ground. We're twenty-two feet, perhaps. Maybe not even that. The treetops are level with the carriage. I could jump into a tree from here. This isn't enough. Our grip tightens on each other's hands. We simply aren't high enough.

Suddenly our carriage comes to an abrupt stop and we're thrown forward.

"It can't be," Joel says. Our carriage bounces on the wire.

"Close enough to fifteen minutes." My voice is weak.

"But this isn't high enough."

"We're on a steep incline." I observe the area. Looking ahead, the carriages in front have climbed over a hump in the terrain and appear to be higher, around twenty-seven feet.

"Only two minutes more," Joel exclaims. "Then we would have been . . ."

"Don't." I can't bear the thought so short a time could have spared our lives. There's no point. We're stuck here now and the wait that lies before us is even more uncertain.

I look at the hump ahead of us. When the snow cascades down the hill, will it part around the hump and spare us the worst of it? Or will it shoot over the top of it and cover us?

"How long do you think we'll be here?" I know he can't answer, but I need to hear someone talk so my mind doesn't focus on how cold it is.

"Minutes? Hours?" Joel shakes his head. He takes the camera out again and turns around so he can see the town and surrounding countryside. His eyes are scanning the horizon for anything headed this way.

Almost two hours pass and we're both sat in silence. The cold has eaten its way through our clothing and nestled under our skin. The clouds shade us in a grey gloom and we can't see the sun. Joel still looks around periodically, but we're mostly just listening. There are no lights on in the town. It's around this time the street lamps would be blinking into life.

It looks as deserted as it did the first time Joel and I made our way down from the mountain.

"If we make it back," he says slowly. "What will you do?"

"I don't know," I say. "It seems unlikely my mother and I will be returning to our goats."

"Will you go back to him? The boy from Newton Belle. Your Turtle Dove?"

He's already shivering. I don't look at his eyes.

"No," I say. "I won't go back to him."

I look up and it's his smile I notice first. He doesn't even bother hiding it.

Then there's a loud, echoing crack followed by a whoosh of air. We turn quickly to see a flare sailing into the sky. But behind that, the horizon is still and unmoving.

That was for us – but why?

Then we hear it. It's a low hum; unmistakable. It has a pulse which beats inside my ear, *dum dum dum dum dum*. The sound of propellers.

"There!" Joel points directly above us.

The helicopters have arrived in a pair. They fly around either side of the mountain; like two people stepping out on a stage. We didn't expect them to arrive like this.

"They came from the other side," I say. "We couldn't see them coming."

Joel is pointing the camera at the underbellies of each helicopter. He zooms so the lens extends as far as it'll go. They circle the mountain once and we see something fall from the belly of one of the helicopters. It's certainly not supplies intended for Sparkwell.

"Here we go." Joel catches his breath and pulls the camera lens back to catch it all on film. He watches the missile hit on a miniature screen inside the camera, but I see it all with my own eyes. Birds frantically leave their trees and rise into the sky. It's more of a sound than a visual display. A deep boom that penetrates the mountain and vibrates across its very surface. There's a shift in the terrain. A chunk of snow the size of a field starts to fall. It seems to happen slowly, but no sooner has the first helicopter retreated, the other circles back around and repeats the performance. This time there's an explosion, although not as big as I expected. The sound, however, hits my ear drums and birds all around me start crying out. By now, the first ton of snow is gathering speed and a huge cloud of white has formed at the front. The mountain has woken up and we're directly in the path of a charging, furious beast. When it becomes apparent not even thirty feet would have avoided it, Joel starts to make a noise in his throat.

"Oh, sure," he splutters. "Swim against *that!*"

I realise he's laughing. It's either that or lose his mind and start screaming. We're going to die and can only wait. Joel draws a deep breath and swallows his laughter. His last words spill out as though he had been holding them in his mouth like a gulp of water.

"What colour are my eyes?"

"What?" I almost shout at the absurdity of the situation, then stop when I actually look at them. "They . . . they're turning red."

Joel smiles, a sad and tortured smile beneath eyes of blood. The roar of snow makes his voice hard to hear. "This is one of the reasons I joined WOLF X. So they'd never turn yellow again. I had a lifetime of them turning yellow. Everyone always saw. I swore to myself never again . . ."

He stares ahead and his eyes invite the oncoming avalanche like someone frozen in a photograph, blinded by the flash. A red stare boring into a world of pure white.

The snow bursts over the hump in the mountain like a tsunami. I grab Joel with both arms, holding him as tight as I can. He doesn't put down the camera, but he places his chin against my forehead and kisses me once on my hairline. It's a stab in the heart to think it's a goodbye. There's a crack – the chairlift rocks so harsh we almost fall – and then it hits us.

My body smashes through a sheet of ice. The cold is as sharp and aggressive as razors. My ears feel like they're being cut from my head, my nose bitten by vicious teeth, my body pounded by a hundred fists. Joel manages to wrap another arm around me.

Are we falling? Are we suspended still by the wire? Are we upside down? Have we been buried ten feet under?

Air pocket. I must make an air pocket.

I force my arm against the snow and press a hand over my face, moving constantly. I wriggle and pat against my own nose, determined to create a space between my mouth and the snow.

Only when the sound of a dozen trains seems to have faded, I realise it must have stopped. Joel is still holding me with both hands. He didn't make an air pocket, he couldn't have. But it doesn't matter, because there's a hard shift and I feel myself sliding. Snow crumbles and I hear the groan of the wire under strain.

We're still in the carriage. I can feel the seat under me. It seems too miraculous to accept. And if the wire is straining, then we must still be suspended somehow.

"Linnea!" A hand bursts through my air pocket and rubs at my face. Joel is swiping chunks of snow away from my hair and neck. We're above the worst of it. The carriage still groans, although it's toppled over and the wire is resting on the top of a tree.

"We made it," I gasp. I kick my feet free and push snow from my lap.

"And at less than thirty feet, who would have thought it?" Joel says in astonishment.

I don't answer. I'm too busy looking down at what used to be my home.

Where Orbelle could previously be seen now looks like a newly iced cake, a smooth white surface atop a crumbly structure. I realise now, whilst the rest of Joel's team is buried under the snow, we faced the bigger threat. This doesn't appear to have been much of a rescue; more like a suicide mission.

Make sure the world sees. Make sure everyone knows what happened here. If you're to do that you must survive.

I can now hear the afterthought that was never said aloud: *survive long enough to record the footage*. Survive the missile attack. From there, it was irrelevant whether we lived or not. Clearly Ouren didn't think we would survive the avalanche. I'm about to voice this realisation, but I find I'm unable to. My eyes are fixed on the town where my goats once trotted around the hillside, people walked casually down the streets and trains rolled into the station. I'm unable to consider my survival as a reason to celebrate. We may still be here, but nothing else is.

36

The walk back is aimless and quiet. There's no direction, no landmarks to follow. Only snow.

Joel and I manage to jump down from the chairlift, but the fall sends pain into his leg. He spends ten minutes hissing before walking. I don't say a word when I fall. I don't even care it sprains my ankle. I just stare at the sheet of snow before me. The shock consumes me and seals my mouth shut.

We take each other's hands again and start our return to Orbelle. At times we sink into pools of soft snow and hoist each other free. Other times we stop and look around, unable to believe what we survived.

"Maybe they're holed up somewhere, in one of the buildings." Joel's voice is distant. "Maybe they prepared themselves with tools and got a fire going. They may survive."

"They may."

The air is unexpectedly filled with sudden gunfire.

It's far away but rapid and pierces the silence. Confrontation. That much is clear. But who fired the shots? Everything falls silent again.

"They're here," Joel says eventually.

"But they don't know we are." I sound braver than I feel.

What do we face now? Do we wait and attempt to find Ouren's team? Do we continue on? And, when we do eventually leave this place, do we hope to evade WOLF for the rest of our lives? Or do we march back and let them take us into custody? We walk until I feel the need to pause and look around once more.

"I think we're in the town," I say. "Well, not in it. Above it. I think this is where the buildings would be."

I spy a small tree to the left and walk up to it. If I'm not mistaken, this is the tip of a much larger tree. I'm not certain, but when I brush the snow from its leaves I think I can identify it.

"This may be the fir tree next to the old phone box." I dig around and find the wooden power-line pole jutting from the snow like a mast. "Yes, this is it. We're in the town centre."

It's impossible to remember what direction the power lines ran. They snaked across Orbelle like spider silk. But I do faintly remember the cable from this post ran directly to the town hall. I hold it between gloved hands and pull on it. The snow springs off the line and I use it to pull myself in the direction of the hall.

"Come on, Joel," I call. "When we find where the hall is I can pin point the direction of the ranch. I can remember the way."

I could run. I'm so sure of my direction now. The various poles stick out from the snow like stepping stones. There may be little of a hill left, but I know it's up ahead of me. I'll find my ranch.

"Come on!" I shout over my shoulder. "We can make it there and call out to them. We can . . ."

"Stop!"

We both turn around and our frozen breath cascades in the direction of a man in WOLF X uniform. Behind him, several meters away, is an electric snowmobile we never even heard coming.

Although I'm frightened, I knew this was going to happen eventually. I just hope they think we're more valuable alive. We've come too far to be shot now; the fear that grips me seems almost unfair after what we just survived.

"I've got another two here," he says into his radio. His mouth twists into a sorrowful smile, but it's only a mock apology. He won't regret his actions one bit.

“I’m expected to shoot you on sight,” he says. “We already got a bunch of you in that house on the hill. We knew Ouren was conspiring against us.”

“Did you?” Joel dares to goad him. “Did you really know? You gave us enough time to get our plan together.”

“Your plan failed.”

“Did it?” Joel raises an eyebrow. “I’m not so sure.”

His apparent lack of fear provokes the man’s anger. “We caught one of you. She denied everything, but we knew she was there for a reason. Why else would she be on the mountain that night? Do you want to know what we did to her? Do you know how it feels to lose your toes one by one?”

I can’t breathe. My lungs forget how. I hope I haven’t got this right.

“Do you know how much ice can actually burn?” he continues. “If Morgan hadn’t stopped us, she’d have lost her nose too. He said it had to look like an accident, no matter how much she refused to talk.” He’s grinning at Joel, who looks utterly perplexed. He has no idea who this man is talking about. But I do.

“You bastards!”

My outburst is sudden and hot with rage. The heat pulses in my cheeks and neck. Joel looks at me in surprise but he can't understand. It would seem they really can harm innocent people. I can no longer trust my mother is even alive. The man grins.

"Ah, so you did know her. She wasn't the only one we got either. The one who blew up Iris; we got him too. You should hear what we did to him."

"I know what you did to him," I say at once. "I was there. Your people murdered him while he was unconscious. And that girl you found, she was innocent. She's my friend. You tortured an innocent girl."

I would shoot him. There's no doubt in my mind. If the rifle were in my hands I would end this by killing him and wiping the smirk off his face. My hands close around nothing – where there ought to be a weapon – and my fists clench tightly. He sees my expression and angles his gun properly. I made his mind up for him. He'll kill me first, before Joel.

"Don't shoot her." Joel steps in front of me and attempts to shield me from view. There's a shift beneath my feet but I wonder if I imagined it. I'm too overwhelmed by anger.

There's a grinding sound as our combined weight sinks into the snow.

"Stand aside so I can see you both," the man says. He strides forward, bringing the gun closer. He intimidates Joel into stepping away from me, but as they both move so does the snow beneath us. I realise what's happening and attempt to cry out.

But my words are swallowed up. As is the rest of me. My body is replaced with the echo of a scream where I previously stood. The ground parts and I don't even realise what's happening until I'm gone.

I hear Joel's voice shouting my name as we plummet. It takes many hard bumps and cracking of wood until I eventually hit solid ground. My head hits stone and the last thing I see is a speck of light overhead before that too is swallowed up by snow and I drift into unconsciousness.

37

I don't know where I am or how long I've been out. The answers to my questions are hidden in darkness.

My head feels as though it's been split open and I genuinely fear it has. My hand sooths the wet bump at the back of my skull and I force myself to sit. I taste dust and grit on my lips. Pieces of debris slide from my body as I move. Nothing feels too heavy and nothing feels broken, but I still wiggle each finger and toe to make sure.

My instinct is to panic. Everything is pitch black. Not coal black, not onyx black. Just empty. I can smell the cold air. I smell the bricks and sweat that has soaked into my shirt. I can also hear better than I think I could before. I hear my own heartbeat although my breath is oddly still.

"Joel?" I can't see what's around me, let alone if Joel is all right. There's someone lying on the floor. "Joel?"

I spread my hands out and feel across his chest and up to his neck. His throat is warm but the angle of his neck is all wrong. He doesn't move.

"I'm alright."

I wrench my hand away, feeling sick. Joel's voice is behind me and certainly not coming from the body on the floor. I didn't realise the man had fallen through the roof with us.

"I think he broke his neck," I say in a low voice. I feel oddly satisfied. Although I didn't want to have touched his warm skin, I'm pleased to know one of Anna's torturers lies at my feet. I'm sorry I can't look into his eyes. I hope they remain as white as his bones when the rest of him rots away. I step backwards and my heel kicks something that clatters against the stone floor. It's the rifle that was supposed to kill us. I pick it up, feeling much more assured now it's in my own hands. Like I'm taking my own life back.

Joel's voice comes as a grunt. He's alive, but I can hear pain in his throat and I know he's perhaps in worse shape than I am. I back away from the body and try to pretend it's not there. But I suddenly feel like I'm in a cold tomb.

I didn't think I was afraid of the dark. Black doesn't usually concern me. I'm familiar with the tone of every shadow. I look around for some clarity, for something I can identify.

I stay still for a while, not knowing what to do. We're both injured, we don't know where we are and we don't know if anyone is going to be able to help us. It's clear I'm the more able of the two of us. This places a lot of responsibility on me. I try to find Joel with my fingers. I have to control this situation. I have to establish where we are.

I wish Hans were with me. He would be strong enough to lift Joel and carry him to safety without breaking a sweat. I wish my father were here to remind me of the recovery position, which I've quite forgotten. My father would know where to check Joel for injury and how to stop any bleeding.

Most of all I want my mother. I remember her eyes used to look at me and turn every shade of green. I remember how she used to plait my hair and sooth me to sleep. I remember the games she invented and all her efforts, even after she went blind. For some reason I wish – more than anyone else in the world – my mother were here to tell me what to do.

She was the only person who ever prepared me for this.

This room has a pulse.

I can feel it in the air. There are sensations to be felt; I just need to focus on them. I stand perfectly still and listen. Every sound is amplified. I push my hair behind my ear and the sound is like a sword being unsheathed. Joel's breath sounds like the wind across an empty field.

This is how my mother experiences the world. I can almost feel her brushing my hair back and I feel the light squeeze on my shoulder as she tells me "go". My challenge is set. I can do this. I can get us out of here.

I kneel and touch the floor. It's cold. Not carpeted. The floor is made of stone. Who owns a stone floor? I stretch out my hands and feel how large the slabs are. They vary in size. They're smooth; worn flat by hundreds of pairs of shoes. This is an old building. The chance of this being someone's house is slim.

I move forward and my shins bump something. It doesn't hurt, but the sudden contact makes me catch my breath. The noise is loud, although the object moves easily. I reach out and feel thin, bumpy plastic. I let my breath go. This is no one's house, I'm sure. Who owns plastic chairs? I give the chair a slight rattle and one leg wobbles freely. I remember sitting on chairs like this. If there's a chair then there's likely to be a table.

I'm correct. My hands feel the smooth surface. There's no wood and no tablecloth. I practically lie and sweep my arms over it. No vases and no placemats. This isn't a table for dining. This is a table for work. The kind of table with hard gum stuck to its underbelly; and no one I know sticks gum to their own table. This is a public building. A public building with a dodgy roof and plastic chairs.

I hear the clock ticking on the wall and the creak of debris in an old dusty room. I can almost hear the echo of hundreds of school children, long ago. I used to be one of them.

"Joel?" I make my way back to him and touch his face. His cheek is wet. Surely he hasn't been crying, I'd have heard him. He winces when I move my fingers to his hairline. I know cuts to the head can bleed more than anywhere else on the body, but I can also feel the swelling and the indent of his injury. Too large to ignore. It needs to be examined properly. Time is everything and I have to get Joel out of here.

"I know where we are," I tell him. "Stay here a moment. I'll find the door."

The layout of tables is unfamiliar to me, so I bump and stagger over uneven stones. When my hands find the wooden door I locate the handle. It's cold and made of iron. I lift it and the door swings open. There's no breeze, just the smell of snow.

I retrieve Joel and explain to him what I know.

"This is the school. They've had issues with the roof. Hans volunteered to help repair it this summer. This room is where they held art lessons. It's the oldest room in the building. I'm not as familiar with the layout anymore. They've rearranged a few things since I was a student here. But I know vaguely where I am. I'll get us out. Can you use night vision to help us? Your lenses were always better than mine."

He murmurs something and lets me pull him up. After a couple of seconds he lets out a discouraged sound and tells me he can't see a thing. At first he panics, afraid of the darkness WOLF X recruits aren't expected to deal with. But then he grips my wrist and his tone changes.

"My lenses aren't working," he says in a whisper, then louder, more triumphant. "My lenses aren't working! They did it!"

He still has the shepherds crook and uses it the same way my mother uses her cane. It helps us avoid tables and I escort him through the door.

I should've remembered the step. Thankfully I make my way out first, so I'm the one who falls and not Joel. I'm only a single step from the ground but it might as well be a cliff edge. There's nothing to grab except Joel, but I release him immediately and brace myself. I just have time to put my hands out and stop my chin hitting the concrete. The skin on my palms tears and bleeds, but I can only be grateful this was a step and not a flight of stairs. I need to be more careful.

"Are you all right?" Joel asks.

"Fine." I push myself up. "Mind yourself, there's a step there. Take my hand."

Each step he takes is followed by a grunt of pain. His footsteps are slow and one foot sounds louder on the stone. He's limping horribly. I need a smooth plan I can carry out with what little memory I have of the school.

"There's another part of the roof," I recollect. "It houses the school bell. I guess you could call it a small tower. Anna and I climbed it once. It might be the best chance we have at digging ourselves out. I don't know how far underground we'll be, but it won't be as far as we are now. It means climbing a flight of stairs and opening the hatch, but it can be done."

"You have a bell tower?" Joel can hardly get the words out, yet he sounds perplexed.

"All the schools and churches had them," I say. "You don't have such things in the city, but we uphold some traditions. We don't ring them anymore, but they're still here."

I intend to keep Joel talking as much as possible. I ramble on about Orbelle's history, or what I know of it. I lead him down another corridor and keep my hand on the wall at all times, even though the rough brick snags the skin of my grazed palms. Halfway down the corridor I hear a crash of debris in the room behind us and realise the roof must have caved further.

I imagine myself as a small girl. I remember the wall where I used to sit and eat my apple at break times. I remember the hopscotch we chalked on the slabs outside. I remember the tree I always chose to hide behind when we played hide and seek. Somehow playtime sticks out in my mind a lot better than work time. I can barely remember the corridors, let alone the path leading back from the art room.

When we reach another door I let go of Joel and tell him to sit whilst I open it. This door is locked, but I run my hands over the wood and find it's fixed with frosted glass.

"Stand back." I reach for my left shoe. He can't see what I'm about to do, so it must shock him when I smash my way through the glass and feel for the lock the other side. My arm catches broken glass, but by now I don't care for cuts and scrapes. The keys hang on a hook beside the door and I fumble for the lock. It takes several attempts to get the correct key and another couple of minutes to locate the lock again each time, but eventually I get us inside.

"This is the main corridor that connects the classrooms," I say. "We switched classrooms with each year, so I was taught in pretty much all of them."

"Linn." Joel grabs my arm and I manage to turn and catch him before he falls. I can't see where he might land and I fear his head injury is bad enough.

“I’ve got you.” I hoist him back up and place my hand back on his head. It’s still bleeding. I tell him to keep it compressed. “It’s not much further. Down here and through another few doors. There’s the assembly room and the stairs are behind another door. Then it’s up to the tower. We can make it.”

“Thank god you’re here with me.” Joel mumbles. “It could be hours before anyone comes near Orbelle.”

“I’m doing the best I can.” I retrieve my shoe and look around. “If only there was some other way to raise an alarm.”

I stop in my tracks. Like thousands of other schools, this school is rigged with a fire alarm. An alarm that made everyone congregate outside. If someone comes looking for survivors and hears the alarm then surely they’ll know someone’s trapped inside the school? I sit Joel down and leave him so I can inspect the classrooms.

There was an alarm trigger within close proximity of each room; around chest-height and just out of reach of children. But I can’t remember where any of them were. I never had to use one. I find plenty of fire extinguishers in the corners of each room, but as for the actual triggers, they might as well be embedded in the walls themselves for all I can find. I dread the idea of my fingertips missing it by centimetres. The idea of Joel dying here, whilst my fingers drift within inches of the alarm, is unbearable.

Finally I find one of the triggers. My shoe is being put to good use today. I lift the heel and shatter the glass with it.

I didn't entirely think this through.

The ear-splitting sound of the alarm penetrates my skull so deeply I scream. I didn't imagine how loud and shrill it would be. My headache intensifies so much my hands grab my head and I pull at my hair, desperate to silence it. I think I understand why they call this a drill. It's piercing my brain like nails. I grit my teeth, I growl in my throat, I burst into angry tears but it's no good. It's like a thousand eagles screaming in both ears and I can't take it much longer. Although it's not possible, I feel the wound on my head open even more; my senses and tolerance spilling out with all the blood and hair. I vomit nothing but bile and stumble once, losing my footing and crashing down on to the floor. Pain explodes in my leg.

"Joel?" I shout, knowing however badly this hurts me it will be intolerable for him. I can't hear him reply so I get to my feet and rush back to the corridor, hitting the doorframe as I go and tripping on a loose bit of carpet. Eventually I find him keeled over and holding his head as though it will burst open.

"Come on." I pull him down the corridor and through the next door, remembering to check for a step this time. I step down, deftly, on to carpet.

"All right." I collect my bearings. "One more flight of stairs to go and we're there. Joel, do you still have the crook? Good. We'll need it to pull the hatch."

"God, make it stop," Joel groans.

"It will," I promise him. "It will stop. Just a little further to go and we'll be out."

We can't see a single step, so we go on all fours and feel for the top. I'm desperate not to lose a single footing because to fall would be like cascading down into a black abyss. When there are no more steps, I hoist Joel up beside me and congratulate his efforts.

"Above us now is another tiny set of steps that come down when you open the hatch. They didn't let children just wander up to the tower, so the caretaker had a hook to pull the hatch down. I expect snow will come down on us. I'm going to need the crook to find the handle."

He hands it over and I hold it by its very end, standing on my toes and swinging the crook like swatting a bee hive. I don't feel anything at first but suddenly it latches and I'm sure I've found the handle.

"Got it," I say. "Brace yourself."

I don't ask for Joel's help but he steps up and grabs the crook too, helping me pull the hatch loose. Our teeth grind, our hands contract, and the crook swings free and snow pours on top of our heads. The steps come down and I scramble to climb into the tower.

Joel stays close behind me and we ascend as far as we can go, before our path is blocked by snow which has wedged in the hatch. I push my way through and my hand brushes something hard and smooth: the bell of the tower. It hangs like a congratulatory post at the end of a dark maze. I could hug it as though it were my mother.

38

"Listen," Joel says.

There are voices. Aggressive voices, followed by gunfire. I hesitate before punching my way through the snow. I emerge like a pale mole. I pause, shoulder deep, and shake my head. Daylight has never looked or tasted so good. I forget myself for a moment and inhale, relishing how it feels to breathe sun-soaked air. Then I plant my hands down flat and attempt to hoist myself out of the ground.

"Stay down!" someone screams.

The command makes me jump and I almost fall back into the tower. Ouren is leading a small number of recruits across the snow with their rifles raised. Johannes, Adelheid and Warren are with him. Adelheid shoots before she reaches me. I try to follow her bullet as it sails over my head and pierces the chest of another WOLF recruit. The blow knocks him off balance and something bites my arm. I cry out and clasp my bicep. The pain is sharp and I realise I've been shot at. It missed my flesh but has grazed the skin enough to bleed and throb like an acid burn. Adelheid races past me and places another bullet in the man's head. Ouren and Johannes stoop down to hoist me free by my good arm. I spot more snowmobiles closing in on us and tell Joel to stay in the ground.

“Is Edgecombe with you?” Ouren asks urgently.

“Yes. He’s injured but he’s right behind me.”

“Did you film the attack?”

“Yes. We got everything.”

“Then get out of here, as soon as this is over,” he says. We look down and see Joel trying to climb out of the snow. He extends the crook and I use my uninjured arm to pull him free. He stays on the ground and I tremble at the sight of his head. The snow sticks to the blood and packs into the open wound in his skull. His lips are pale and his body shakes from head to toe. I didn’t have time to warn him.

“Quick,” Ouren orders. “You’ve got to get that footage shown. Don’t let them destroy it.”

He spurs us towards the place we originally fell through. Not far from the school is the snowmobile that silently pursued us. Joel climbs on behind me, instructing me on how to start it. It comes alive beneath my hands and purrs lightly. The vibration makes every injury I’ve obtained ache all the more. My arm judders and makes me wince. But I don’t have time to drive away. The other snowmobiles surround us and I know if I attempt to leave I’ll be their first target. There are too many of them. I take my hands off the handlebars and clutch my rifle instead.

One of the riders removes his helmet. I identify him at once. Rusten allows his men to surround us with weapons before climbing from his seat. “What a pleasant surprise.”

He sounds unashamedly pompous. He takes a pistol in his hand and strides over, but he doesn’t raise it. He doesn’t feel the need to. His men have got us outnumbered and we stand-off in the snow. Our weapons are there to comfort us a little now, not to partake in a fair fight. We have little control.

“It’s no surprise, Rusten,” Ouren says irritably. “You knew the situation.”

“Of course I did,” he says. “And I’ll be happy to tell Morgan I was right and receive a higher promotion. He’ll reward me for having removed you. Such a shame this is how it ends for us, Lance.”

“You’ve wanted this for a long time,” Johannes snarls. “You always thought WOLF had the right idea. No matter who suffered or died, you always thought it was for the greater good.”

“And I daresay I’ll continue to do so,” Rusten says dismissively. “With you gone it’ll be easier to help WOLF progress. Morgan is easily manipulated. He’s mostly about the money and showmanship.”

"Yet for you it was always about control," Ouren says. "You were prepared to do anything to get it."

"Remove anyone to get it," Johannes clarifies.

Rusten looks at Johannes with interest. "You I'm a little surprised at, Steyn. You always said Ouren was insane."

"Perhaps," Johannes says. "But I happen to think he's got the right idea about you. These lenses weren't supposed to control people, they were supposed to protect them and better their lives. It could still be that way. But not with people like you and Cornelius Morgan behind it. I sided with Ouren because I could never assist you again. I picked the right side."

"And yet here we are, and I'm the one who wins." Rusten shrugs. His gaze falls on my face. "I must say I'm surprised at you even more, Miss Hansen. If that is, indeed, you under there. Been taking tips from Ouren, have you? I certainly didn't think you would be causing trouble again. Not after we took your lovely mother to one of our units. Oh, don't you worry, she's being looked after. Good thing we checked her records and found she was a willing test subject before. We'll happily do a whole range of previously untested procedures on her now we know where her daughter's loyalties lie. Apple really doesn't fall far from the tree, does it? We've looked into your father's background too. Manslaughter, was it?

We'll see if we can tell the system otherwise. Keep him in his current accommodation longer."

"Don't you dare," I say furiously. "Don't you dare touch a hair on my mother's head!"

"This is how you get off, is it Rusten?" Ouren says bitterly. "Same as ever, relishing the power WOLF gives you. You take such joy out of ruining people's lives. Tearing families apart. Destroying relationships."

Rusten's eyes widen before he starts to laugh.

"Ah. So, you're still blaming WOLF for that? Lance you torture yourself. You can't hold us accountable for what happened with Klara."

Ouren looks enraged to hear Rusten speak this name. He clenches his left hand and I suddenly find my eyes trying to find the wedding band he had in the photographs. There is no ring. Just a faint groove in his finger where it must have been worn for many years. What did they do to Ouren's wife?

"We would still be together," Ouren says darkly, "if the lenses hadn't been made compulsory. Make no mistake, helping WOLF achieve that was the greatest mistake of my life. It cost me everything."

"Oh come now. You wouldn't. Your wife stopped loving you and your only gripe with WOLF was that the lenses stopped her living a charade that suited you. You would have tolerated her indifference to you as long as you could both pretend and carry on as before. Women everywhere fake their satisfaction, Lance. You couldn't handle knowing for certain your wife received none from you. Your failure to excite her ended your marriage. Not WOLF. But if it brought you comfort to secretly wage war against us then I suppose you may have my pity as well as my disdain . . . Bring him to me."

His men seize Ouren by the shoulders. He tells us if anyone raises their weapon he'll put a bullet in the back of Ouren's skull. We all remain still as Ouren is forced to kneel in the snow, facing us. We look at him for an instruction, but his expression doesn't move.

My heart beats furiously for the man whose instruction I began to follow like a real recruit. His was a cause I found myself willing to serve. He embodies everything my father stood for and everything I've come to realise about the lenses I wore. I'm glad I found a team able to show me the true colours of WOLF and its puppets. It makes me feel sick to think Rusten has got his way. He wanted Ouren to die at his feet. For me, that makes his death all the more unbearable to witness. It shouldn't be like this. Buried under the snow, shot during combat and holding his own weapon, death by his own hand . . . anything but this.

Rusten raises his own pistol. "The only thing that disappoints me is the fact I won't see your eyes turn white. I would have liked that a lot. You can take that triumph with you to the grave."

Ouren looks up at us all and I notice his expression is far from defeated. There's a faint curl in the corner of his mouth. I can't understand how he can look so sad yet oddly happy about it. He almost appears satisfied. In fact, I think he appears more solemn than sad. That's a good thing, I suppose. I wouldn't have wanted to see him die in fear.

"You'll never be the one to kill me, Rusten," Ouren says firmly. "I would never allow that."

His gaze sweeps across our faces, pausing only to wink at us in turn. First, he winks at Adelheid and Warren. Then he glances at the snowmobile and gives Joel and me a similar flutter with his good eye. It seems strange at first, but I get the feeling the gesture is communicating something. A signal. A joke. A warning. I don't know what it is. I start to panic in case there's a secret message here and I'm the only one missing it. His final look goes to Johannes, who nods once and accepts Ouren's wink as both a farewell and a cue. As soon as his lid opens again, his false eye begins to blink on its own. But the blink comes from within the pupil. A flashing glow of red that quickens until suddenly I understand.

Three winks. Three repetitions. And I have about three seconds to react.

“Now!” Johannes shouts.

39

His voice is almost lost over the sound of Ouren's false eye exploding.

I gave myself enough time to look away, so only the side of my face is splashed with blood. My body shudders as it drips off my ear; whilst the sound of the explosion continues to ring. When I look back, I realise I can't confidently claim the blood was Ouren's. The explosion has opened a hole in Rusten's abdomen and thrown him off his feet. Before he can fully absorb what's happened, we turn in unison and fill his chest with bullets. Death and cold air rush into his open wounds and draw his life away. His heart appears to freeze in the snow, next to Ouren's faceless torso.

Immediately the situation becomes a free-for-all. Rusten's men are too momentarily distracted by his sudden death to realise Johannes is now turning his weapon towards them. He opens fire and Adelheid, Warren and I follow his lead. Each shot sends pain through my arm and shakes me so furiously I can feel the graze in my flesh. Five of Rusten's men hit the ground within seconds. The area is soaked with their blood and littered with the flesh, bone and plastic of both our leaders.

"Go!" Johannes chokes at me. I realise he's been shot. He grips his neck as though trying to stop his life from pouring out from a wound in his trapezius. I seize the handlebars of the snowmobile and accelerate before any of the remaining recruits can stop me.

There's a sound of heavy sweeping as the snowmobile forces its way through the snow, but we move and Joel secures us together by holding the crook across my lap. As we skim over the snow I keep him talking so he doesn't pass out.

"Did you know Ouren's eye was set to detonate with three blinks?"

"No," Joel murmurs. "I knew he and Charlie once discussed the idea of suicide, should they be caught. They said WOLF would accuse us of Red Eye if caught. Like they used to plant guns on unarmed people after they'd shot them. But he never told us how he would do it. He must have told Johannes though. I should have guessed his eye was an ideal place to conceal an explosive. It was a product of WOLF. It's exactly what he would have wanted to blow up."

I ask where we should go now. We could head for Sparkwell. From there we can pose as refugees, for as long as possible, until we find someone to give our footage to. The camera is still in his jacket and digs into my back. It's hard to steer the snowmobile with my arm in constant pain, but I keep going until we pass the boarder of the town and head for grass. We'll soon have to revert back to walking.

I spy another snowmobile heading into Orbelle. It seems to ignore us and I realise the rider probably doesn't realise we hijacked this one. I veer towards him, attempting to cut off his path. Joel shouts at me. I release the handlebars and instruct him to drive us directly towards the oncoming arrival. I have to lean forward so he can seize control of the vehicle as I lift my rifle. The other driver realizes what's happening too late, as we skim past like a fierce jousting opponent. I shoot him before he can lift his own weapon and he falls from his snowmobile.

Unfortunately, so does Joel.

He grabs both ends of the crook again to steady himself and this pulls at my waist so I almost topple. I bring the snowmobile to a desperate stop. I look back and realise my shot didn't kill the other rider. He's running at Joel with a much smaller weapon in his right hand. With his left hand, he's yelling instructions into a radio secured to his shoulder.

"I said don't let Morgan land!" He's yelling. "There are still some of them out here. Keep Morgan and the crew away."

I fire before the people on the radio respond. We'll never know what they have to say. He screams so loud I worry he'll cause another avalanche. I silence him with a second shot to the head. The snow turns crimson with no noise at all.

"Morgan's coming," Joel says as I lift him to his feet once again. The pain in my arm intensifies and I can only imagine the agony I inflicted before killing. "They must think we're all dead. They're flying him over."

"With a crew," I add. "Knowing Morgan he'll want the avalanche televised. He's on his way over to film the aftermath."

"We need to go," Joel says hurriedly. He pauses to observe the body more closely. "I think you got his heart. You really are good."

"Who says we need to go?" I check how much ammunition is left and prepare the idea of using it again. "We know Morgan's coming. He doesn't know we're waiting."

It's easy to spot the helicopter when it comes into view. Once again, it pays little attention to us as we drive across the snow. It carries on across the town and lands no more than fifteen minutes away. I knew they would land there. They've chosen the top of the hill, where my ranch lies buried nearby. They'll get a good establishing shot from up there. They'll be able to film the entire town with one sweep of the camera.

I have little interest in fleeing. They've chosen my land and I'll defend it. I turn the snowmobile around and ignore Joel's shouts of protest. I need to do this.

This has nothing to do with my mother, who I've always tried to protect. This isn't about Joel, who needs medical attention and who I've risked everything for. This isn't for Theo, who is still lying on a slab somewhere. I'm not thinking about Anna, who's recovering from Rusten's torture.

This is for me.

We abandon the snowmobile halfway up the hill to ensure we are perfectly quiet. The incline makes it tougher for Joel to keep up, so he keeps the crook with him and follows me as steadily as he can. I'm not exactly fast. This will require stealth and little haste as we approach. We spot the propellers of the helicopter, now stationary, and hear the sound of Morgan's monologue. They're either filming now, or he's practising. We duck down and hope no one spots us as we advance over the hill.

My ranch is half-submerged in snow. The roof sticks out like a bad attempt at hiding. The avalanche hit the front and half buried it, but around the back of the ranch, the snow is much shallower. With enough perseverance I could probably dig my way to one of the windows and let myself in. We crouch behind the wall and peer out at the camera crew. They're filming Morgan as he gestures to the snowy plain that was Orbelle this morning.

I look at the rifle in my hands and suddenly feel uncertain. This was my plan; to emerge from the side of the building and confront Morgan in full view of his cameras. I planned this the moment I saw the helicopter on its way. But now I feel anxious. Like I shouldn't be here.

"Linn?" Joel whispers. "What do we do?"

"We make ourselves known," I whisper back.

But my voice is shaking and I fear I've made a misjudgement. What if I don't have the stomach to do this after all?

I go to back away from the wall and my foot nudges something under the snow. I catch my breath and look down. Something is just beneath my foot. This is where Ouren's team stacked our belongings. I'm curious to know what possession of mine I've found. I reach down with one hand and brush the snow aside.

My own reflection stares back at me. It's the brass bell that hung on our porch. I lift it up and shake the snow from its hollow body and smooth surface. I see my own eyes: one covered with a patch and the other weary with everything I've seen and done. My jacket is torn and sodden where the bullet caught my arm. There's blood on my cheek and I don't even know whose it is. I see who I've become; what they've forced me to be. I've almost lost sight of who I originally was. But I know this will remind me.

I lift the bell in one hand and rap it with my knuckles. The chime rings out across the snow and I round the corner of the wall so I'm in full view of the camera crew. I hit the bell again so they know I'm home. By the time the sound hits their ears, I've dropped the bell and collected my rifle in both hands.

Morgan doesn't know what to say. I interrupted his speech about bravery and sacrifice as he pays tribute to Ouren's team. Those words fall flat as he stares at me.

"Miss Hansen," he stammers. He glances once at the camera and signals for them to stop filming immediately.

I walk forward, with the shepherds crook in hand, and clear my throat.

"Whatever he offers to pay you, I promise this is worth more. My name's Linnea Hansen and I've got something to say to everyone about Theodore Lobbett and my friend, Anna Harris."

"Cut," Morgan hisses at both cameras. "She's just a goat herder from Orbelle. She's not worth filming."

One camera is pointing at my face and the other is zooming in on Joel. Morgan's eyes begin to waver from their Tiger's Eye state. They're changing colour like someone is buttering them and it spurs me on. I may not be much of a match for him, but Cornelius Morgan suddenly fears me.

I lift the rifle and aim it at his chest.

"Tell them what you did," I insist. "Tell them or I'll pull the trigger. I promise you."

Morgan looks terrified, but in a moment he collects himself and looks defiant. "Theodore Lobbett was a tragic case of smoke inhalation. My people did what they could to save him, but when someone becomes White Eyed . . ."

"And Anna Harris?"

"Again, another tragic case . . ."

"You let Rusten torture Anna!" I shout. "You let them abduct her and when she had no idea what she was being accused of you let them freeze her, piece by piece. Then you had them return her to the chairlift and left her to die. You wanted it to look like an accident. Admit it!"

He won't. Although he's looking at my rifle he knows, while his cameras roll, the public will see nothing but an assassination without cause. He's confident I won't shoot.

He's wrong.

I knew Rusten had to die. In fact, I'd relished it. I enjoyed the sound of my shots piercing his chest. The thud of bullets bursting through his clothes and skin. The spurts of blood that showered the snow like rubies. It had brought the adrenaline back into my veins like a mad rush, after the shock of Ouren's explosion. I wonder if the same satisfaction would come from killing Morgan in front of an audience.

I pull the trigger.

"Alright! I admit it!"

Morgan's scream fills the empty valley. But there's nothing else. No bang fills the air, no thud hits the floor. I lower the rifle and smile. The look on his face is satisfying enough for me. I knew the rifle had run out of ammunition; but he didn't.

Rusten had been an animal let loose. He'd been a driving force; allowed to defile and harm people. Everyday people like Anna. Like me. Morgan, on the other hand, he was the man who was supposed to be in control. We trusted him to protect us. We hailed him above everyone else for steering us into a field of fool's gold. I realise there were three of us all along: the shepherd, the wolves and the sheep. We were Morgan's flock, and he lets the wolves loose on us for the price of fame and money.

For that, he needs to confess.

I drop the rifle on the floor and look at Joel in triumph. To my horror, he's fallen onto his side and is finally drifting into unconsciousness. I seize the crook to hoist him up and it comes free from his grasp. I don't know what to do. As soon as Morgan realizes I have tricked him, he shouts for his men to shoot me. But I move faster. I may have no home, no money, or even that great a knowledge of WOLF technology. He's right: I'm merely a goat herder from Orbelle. Another shepherd.

My father's crook is around his neck before he runs two paces. He gags loudly and falls backwards. I move my hands up the length of the crook and twist, forcing him into the snow. I put one foot on his shoulder and pin him by the throat. His men hesitate. They're looking at the cameramen, not at Morgan. They could shoot me, but I've dropped my weapon and made it clear I just wanted a confession. And I got one. Shooting me now, in full view of the cameras, may not be the best idea.

"So you wanted them to kill us all like animals?" I say. "I wouldn't have thought you, Professor – with an emotion for every colour known to man – could possibly be so black and white."

The cameras move in like hounds to prey on the sight of him writhing. Regardless how insignificant I am, I reckon the world will want to hear what Linnea Hansen has to say now.

40

They taser me so I let go of Morgan. When shooting me seemed no longer an option, they had to step in somehow. The shock of the taser goes straight to my head and I collapse in a heap on the snow, but not before the footage is broadcast live and everyone sees Cornelius Morgan restrained like a goat.

It's the beeping that rouses me. It sends a signal to my brain and I panic. I know that sound. I remember it and it terrifies me. I don't remember why until I open my eyes. I'm rigged to a lens and heart monitor. I try to turn my head and see the lights on the screen, but my left eye doesn't work and it's the eye closest to the monitor. It could be reading anything on the screen. My heart may be pumping but my lenses could read anything.

"I'm not White Eyed!" I need people to hear me. I feel the wires and tubes pull as I force myself upright. Pain rips through me but I don't care. "I don't have White Eye!"

A nurse appears at once and tries to calm me.

"Don't let them," I scream. "Don't let them turn it off!"

She shouts loudly as I start pulling tubes and needles out of my hands. If I can get to the window perhaps I can escape or at least shout out to passers-by. I won't die like Theo.

Instead I'm wrestled back on to the bed by a team of nurses and a male doctor. He starts to speak but I silence him with a punch to the mouth. His bottom lip splits against my knuckles. When he recoils I see the person standing behind him. My hand reaches out and my fingers are encased by the only person who can possibly comfort me.

"Everything's all right," Joel sooths. "You're okay. Nothing bad is going to happen to you."

I try to read his lenses and know if he's telling me the truth. But he isn't wearing any. His sclera is sore and pink. He sits on the bed beside me propping his injured leg up and starts to smooth my hair out of my face. They soon learn moving the monitor so I can see it calms me further. I lie transfixed and watch the colours on the screen. As long as I can see the pallet of my emotions change I'm much less aggressive. They keep me under close surveillance for a few days, treating my injuries and examining my eye. They mend my sprained wrist and sooth the headaches I suffer. Eventually I'm considered well enough to handle the news that followed the bombings. They let Joel tell me everything

I've missed, everything that's currently happening and everything that'll shortly begin.

Joel tells me he was more than dismissed for his actions. He was, in fact, highly praised for them. While Adelheid has made no statement since her survival, Johannes has said plenty from his hospital bed, despite the swelling around his fractured collarbone and throat. Joel's story, told in a certain way, excuses him from any formal trial or punishment. This, Joel says, is the beauty of perspective.

Joel Edgecombe; WOLF X23, Dragon M, disappeared from his post under Major Lance Ouren, the night of the ALPHA disturbance. Although his desertion wasn't officially reported for a few days; it was made known to WOLF prior to the attack on The Socket. His absence was not considered a priority at the time. But now, in retrospect, WOLF understand he did all he could to subtly warn them of the impending attack. Furthermore, escorting a young woman out of Orbelle was a brave and noble move. It put him at high risk with his major. But saving this girl and having her appear on the radio and describe what she saw was a very clever move. In any case, it prevented another story like Anna Harris. WOLF have a lot to thank him for.

As for me, fortune's wheel continues to turn in our favour. I'm soon visited by WOLF officials.

"I hope you understand WOLF shall take your loss into consideration and you will be compensated accordingly," they say.

"My loss?" I say. "We won't receive any pay out. We haven't been able to renew our insurance for years. Certainly not since my father was arrested. Our ranch is gone."

"Beg your pardon, young lady. I'm not referring to your ranch. You shall be compensated for your own personal loss."

"What have I lost?" I ask, but already I think I know the answer. My left eye suddenly throbs behind the fresh bandages. I hadn't even noticed they'd been changed from Ouren's patch.

"Your lenses are guaranteed under WOLF warranty and each patient is given absolute assurance, should there be any fault at all, WOLF will pay for any damages. Whether it be to the lenses or to the patient."

"How bad is it?"

"We can't be sure," he admits. "But bear in mind WOLF will be anxious to smooth over any incident such as this. They're already in enough trouble. Consider this when you make your claim."

He's not joking when he says WOLF is in trouble. Any pay-out will take a long time with the way things currently are. It's the biggest scandal to have hit the news internationally for decades. Thanks to my testament, Theo's parents are launching an official enquiry into his death and Anna Harris is opening her own case against them. Although she was recently fitted with artificial toes and fingers she could control with her lenses, Anna has also reclaimed her original WOLF readings and therefore a shred of the memory they tried to erase. Abduction, torture and unauthorised experimentation are all on her list of accusations. They offered her money to keep quiet, but she's standing her ground and will be giving evidence immediately.

As will I.

"Your amazing act with the shepherds crook has become something of an internet sensation," Joel tells me. "Morgan hasn't shown his face in public for days and, when he did, he was wearing huge shades to cover his eyes. He doesn't want his lenses read. People will want to listen to you. Like it or not, you're almost as famous as he is now."

This makes me feel sick to my stomach.

What I say now is just as important as anything else Ouren's team did to oppose Morgan. If I don't say the correct thing, in the correct way, then the dead will all be turning in their icy graves. However amusing the video clips are; this situation is no fun and games. It won't do to simply humiliate Morgan. Theo's death needs to be explained, as does Anna's suffering. Ouren's actions need to be justified. Half the world is waiting to hear my version. Everything is up to me now.

They brought forward all my lens readings from the past six months. I have a newly calibrated WOLF lens in my right eye. It passes all their prior testing and responds exactly how it should. Once they're satisfied, I'm taken to record my statement and answer all their questions. I try not to blink as I recall everything that happened the night Theo died. I don't want there to be a single fault in their results. As I expected, everything comes back fine.

"Then I won't have to go to court, will I?" I ask when everything is over. "That's my side of things done and recorded. Besides, Morgan admitted it before I caught him with the crook."

I can sense my own naivety, even before I'm given a look of scepticism. This is unlikely to be the end of my role. I have to wait until that evening to watch Cornelius Morgan's own statement on the television. If anything, I fear I may be the one made to look bad. Morgan claims he only admitted to his crimes because I was threatening his life. He says he was prepared to say anything while at gun-point and he lied in self-defence. I should have known he'd say that.

He's also released my mother, though I've yet to see her. He's putting that situation down to miscommunication. The whole thing was a bluff. My mother is fine and has been staying in a Fenix hotel under Morgan's watchful eye. They were merely holding her there to get to me. I have no idea what my mother thinks of everything. I can only wonder what tale Morgan was whispering in her ear.

Now he will have to tell the truth.

He's groomed himself to look dashing and intelligent. He's straightened his hair so it nestles neatly around his neck. He flicks his fringe casually out of his enchanting eyes. He has gone all out, opting for lenses that swirl and swoon, twinkling like a distant milky-way. He's gracious enough to choose a dark tint, for the seriousness of the occasion. But there's enough of a tanzanite-hue to reinforce his mild temperament. When he's called forward, he's in the middle of fondling the Tiger's Eye pendant around his neck. He steps up and faces the inquest the same way he presents one of his documentaries.

There's a lot of talk about what happened the night Theo died. I barely listen to any of that. Half of it is true and the other half is a lie. His lenses never waver. Only when they ask him about my statement do I sit forward and wait for him to respond. They tell him my lens showed no fault whatsoever during my questioning and how he might care to explain that.

"What you have to understand about WOLF lenses being used in evidence by such an eye-witness as Miss Hansen," Morgan says lightly, "there is still too much range for interpretation."

He clears his throat and goes into full-blown Professor Cornelius Morgan mode. He uses his hands to talk and treats the courtroom as a class of students, educating them about the creation that made him a rich and powerful man.

"The lenses don't have a light that goes on when a person tells a truth or lie. The data read from WOLF lenses is taken from a person's emotions alone. This produces a graph measuring changes in several different body functions while being asked a number of questions. It's still up to a WOLF expert to interpret this data and give an opinion as to whether or not the person is lying. Bottom line: there is no standard for reading lens results. So as long as the information is based on interpretation, it can't be admitted as fact. What our eye-witness has told us here today is a figment of her imagination, induced by trauma and medication. Even a typical lens reading without such distress isn't one-hundred percent accurate. I ask you: is this really enough, gentlemen?"

Enough to condemn him for murder? To bring Theo justice? To avenge Anna?

No. I knew all along. It isn't enough.

Cornelius Morgan gives the courtroom his trademark smile and steps away from the cameras. He knows when to signal the end of the show. He knows he has already won.

41

I haven't been told I can leave HQ yet. Joel comes to visit me, which surprises me a little. I thought he'd been told to stay away while the trial continues. He's grinning broadly, however, and seems to have dismissed these terms.

"What're you so happy about?"

"What am I happy about?" Joel grabs me. "Haven't you heard about Morgan?"

"I watched the footage," I sigh. "He's right. My lenses can't be used against him because it's not viable when giving evidence. Apparently WOLF lenses are open to interpretation or something. Not fully reliable when it comes to medicine and court evidence . . . what are you laughing at?"

I'm beginning to think we were watching two entirely different inquests on screen.

"What is it?" I can't stand not knowing what's going on.

"Everything we said about WOLF was true," Joel says. "The way they corrupt things, sweep things under the carpet. Everything I told you about them wiping the homeless off the streets, manipulating, abusing. Everything has been ignored and overlooked, until last night."

"What happened last night?"

"Linn, did you not hear his own words?"

It takes a moment or two to register, but finally it hits me. I can hardly dare to believe my own hope until Joel explains.

"According to the current law in Fenix," Joel says breathlessly, "death is induced in the event an individual has – oh, how did they say it? – 'sustained irreversible cessation of circulatory and respiratory functions'. In other words: an end of all functions of the brain. A determination of death must be made in accordance with accepted medical standards."

"Accepted medical standards? That would include White Eye readings, wouldn't it?"

"Yes. And if Cornelius Morgan was overviewing the patient then who would argue with the man?"

"So if Professor Cornelius Morgan declares someone to be White Eyed, then it's perfectly acceptable to turn off the life support."

"It might have been," Joel says. "Had he not gone to such lengths to dismiss the lens readings of a certain Linnea Hansen. In his own words, he said WOLF lenses can't be admitted as fact. Since Morgan himself has deemed WOLF lens readings to be unreliable, it's necessary for him to provide evidence Theo's death was just. Evidence that isn't dependent on WOLF readings."

"There is none," I realise. "Theo was all right. He was injured and unconscious, but there was no need to turn off the machine. None that I saw."

"Right you are," Joel says. "No other medical records to prove Theo was brain-dead. Morgan has no other proof Theo's death was necessary except by his own interpretation of WOLF lens' readings. And since he himself abolished the idea of such interpretations to be used in court . . ."

My eye widens. "He can't prove he didn't murder Theo without letting all other evidence work against him. Including his actions against Orbelle."

"No he can't. I can't tell you what will become of him, but I can tell you the law of compulsory lens wear is being reviewed right this very moment."

Joel is so delighted by the expression on my face he pulls me forward and kisses me. The scar on his lip catches my tongue and I hold him there for a long time. When he pulls away he lifts me up with both arms and beams into my ordinary, hazel eye.

42

I stare up at our ranch with my one good eye. It's as beautiful as I remember. Goats dot the hill and birds are in the sky above. The mountain is strong and white capped, looking like our guardian again.

I take in sights I never paid attention to before, like little flowers in the hanging baskets and individual knockers on people's doors. Each goat looks relaxed as it grazes and each cloud hovers overhead like a lazy passer-by. I want to stay looking at it forever, because I never thought I would see it again.

"Miss Hansen," a voice says over the speaker system. "Your time's up, I'm afraid. Your results are ready."

They shut the lights off, one by one. Each monitor turns black without a sound. When there's nothing but the red lights to guide me to the door, I pick up my belongings and leave the simulation room.

When they asked me what I wanted to do whilst I waited for my test results, I only had two requests. One was to see Alec and the other was to revisit the simulation room. We say our final goodbyes in the same room we first met. There wasn't much to say and without lenses in our eyes it was hard to know what the other was thinking. Interestingly, I much preferred it that way. After all, this was how we met.

He didn't even protest as I terminated our Turtle Doves experiment. I'm not ignorant; I know it was always more to him than that. I know I've broken his heart and that will never be easy to live with. But when he walks away I breathe a sigh of relief. For as long as we lived, I would never have known anything other than what WOLF set up for me.

They told me Alec was my perfect match. They told me we have so much in common. That we were almost exactly alike. Was I ever that meek? I can't help but muse as he scuttles out of the simulation room with his eyes staring at his feet.

Joel is sat in the foyer, waiting for me with an amused expression. It occurs to me Alec must have passed him on his way out. I wonder if either guessed who the other was. I never spoke much of either of them in the other's presence. When Joel smiles I'm not sure if I detect a slight twinkle in his eye. As awkward as it might have felt to recognise Alec as my Turtle Dove, perhaps he's hugely satisfied to know the experiment is over. I also notice Joel is smiling at a missing portrait of Cornelius Morgan in the foyer. It was taken down on Major Johannes Steyn's orders. When Hans comes to fetch us he walks between us both, out of HQ.

As I wait for Hans to unlock the truck I look back up at Iris. She continues to blink down on the city. They can't get rid of her. She's too iconic.

Hans glances at the sky and squints slightly. He was one of the first people I know to remove his WOLF lenses. Somehow he doesn't quite look the same as before. He opens the door pointedly for Joel and slams it shut behind him. It encases Joel in a box of metal and glass so Hans and I can have a moment alone again.

"I had one last look at Orbelle," I tell him quietly. "I saw the ranch and all the goats."

He says nothing and puts a hand on my shoulder. Perhaps once his eyes would have spoken for him, now only his touch speaks for his remorse.

"Did you see my father?" I ask.

"Aye. Right before I came here."

"And what did he say?"

Hans take a deep breath. "It's just as we feared it would be. All previous WOLF evidence has had to be abolished, thanks to Cornelius Morgan being sent down. Convicts like your father are to stand trial again. As of yet, we don't know when that's likely to be."

“I see,” I say. “And this time he’ll be doing it without his WOLF records to help him. He’ll be standing trial the same way Morgan was when faced with the Orbelle bombings and the treatment of Anna. Perhaps this will condemn him. And if it does, I’m partly to blame for that.”

“You have no idea how proud he is of you, Linn. Whatever the cost may be.”

Before I can speak, Hans hugs me tightly. That tells me more than any words or WOLF lenses could. I hop into the front seat and look at Joel in the rear-view mirror. I would wink, but I’m minus an eye. He looks a lot more uncertain than I do.

When Hans starts the ignition I’m happy to let him drive us to wherever my mother is waiting. Today that happens to be Doverhaven, where his aunt lives. Tomorrow, perhaps I’ll be driven somewhere else. It no longer matters if that place isn’t Orbelle. I’ve left that place behind now.

After several hours, Hans pulls up into his aunt’s driveway. There’s a welcome party of his relatives gathered in the doorway and they part to let my mother through. I’m so overwhelmed to see she’s unharmed and the same as ever. Except for her facial expression. She’s holding her white cane and I’m petrified it will strike me the moment she finds me.

"Linnea Hansen!" she exclaims "I'm never letting you out of my sight again!"

There is a pause as everyone takes in her outburst, and its lack of realism. Joel stops behind me in alarm and the moment gives way to laughter as I run forward to hug her. There aren't enough words for my apology. I promise her I'll never put her through such an ordeal again. No more self-mutilation and no more leaving her alone and confused. She holds me at arms' length and sighs.

"What on earth happened to you, Linn? I want to know everything."

Of course she does. It's high time she learned all that has happened to me over the last couple of months and why. I put my hand out behind me and pull Joel forward. His arm goes around my shoulder and we stand together, although completely unseen by her. I give Joel an encouraging look. My eye is hazel but he can sense the emerald green silently shining and nods back. I take a deep breath and smile.

"Mother, I want you to meet someone. This is Joel."

THE END

Naomi Wicks was born and raised in Devon, England. She has worked in various laboratories as a technician before devoting herself to her talent and becoming an artist. When she's not painting animal portraits she explores British history and writes fiction. She currently lives in Cornwall with her husband and their sons Jasper and Rupert. OPTIC FLOCK is her first completed novel.

Printed in Great Britain
by Amazon

50063266R00281